PRAISE FOR

Kissing Comfort

"The cast of likable, articulate characters—including the complicated, independent, and altogether impressive heroine—makes this an entertaining and sizzling offering for lovers of Gilded Age pageantry." —*Publishers Weekly*

"Jo Goodman's books are one of the main reasons why I love historical romance so much." —*The Romance Dish*

"Business, money, lies, betrayal, and love are a dynamic recipe . . . Jo Goodman is a master at historical romance. *Kissing Comfort* is charming, humorous, all-consuming, and a blast to read." —*Fresh Fiction*

"A wonderfully intense romance that entertained me from beginning to end . . . A captivating read." —*Romance Junkies*

"Jo Goodman is one of my favorite authors and is one of the few historical romance writers that still sets her books in America . . . I absolutely adored her latest book, *Kissing Comfort*, where she has spun a gripping tale that absorbed me to the very end." —*Night Owl Reviews*

"Goodman's longtime fans will recognize the author's signature style and new fans will enjoy this good, old-fashioned Western." —*RT Book Reviews*

"An exciting American romance starring two likable protagonists and an overall wonderful cast."

—*Genre Go Round Reviews*

continued . . .

PRAISE FOR THE NOVELS OF JO GOODMAN

"A perfect treat for readers who enjoy smart, sensual love stories à la Amanda Quick." —*Booklist*

"Goodman has a real flair for writing romantic tension and sexy love scenes . . . Fans of historical and western romances will also appreciate Goodman's witty dialogue, first-rate narrative prose, and clever plotting."

—*Publishers Weekly* (starred review)

"Exquisitely written. Rich in detail, the characters are passionately drawn . . . An excellent read." —*The Oakland Press*

"Jo Goodman is a master of her craft, and it's easy to see why she is a bestseller. She has the rare talent to put you in the hearts and minds of her characters . . . If you see her name on a book, it's a guaranteed good read!" —*Night Owl Reviews*

"For the pure joy of reading a romance, this book comes close to being some kind of perfection." —*Dear Author*

"Goodman's . . . prose is rich and luscious."

—*The Romance Reader*

"Delightful and exciting . . . Goodman holds the suspense as well as the surprises and never lets up on the passion."

—*RT Book Reviews*

"Goodman is a thoughtful and intelligent writer who can make her characters live and breathe on the page."

—*All About Romance*

Berkley Sensation titles by Jo Goodman

KISSING COMFORT
THE LAST RENEGADE

The Last Renegade

Jo Goodman

THE BERKLEY PUBLISHING GROUP
Published by the Penguin Group
Penguin Group (USA) Inc.
375 Hudson Street, New York, New York 10014, USA
Penguin Group (Canada), 90 Eglinton Avenue East, Suite 700, Toronto, Ontario M4P 2Y3, Canada (a division of Pearson Penguin Canada Inc.) • Penguin Books Ltd., 80 Strand, London WC2R 0RL, England • Penguin Group Ireland, 25 St. Stephen's Green, Dublin 2, Ireland (a division of Penguin Books Ltd.) • Penguin Group (Australia), 250 Camberwell Road, Camberwell, Victoria 3124, Australia (a division of Pearson Australia Group Pty. Ltd.) • Penguin Books India Pvt. Ltd., 11 Community Centre, Panchsheel Park, New Delhi—110 017, India • Penguin Group (NZ), 67 Apollo Drive, Rosedale, Auckland 0632, New Zealand (a division of Pearson New Zealand Ltd.) • Penguin Books (South Africa) (Pty.) Ltd., 24 Sturdee Avenue, Rosebank, Johannesburg 2196, South Africa

Penguin Books Ltd., Registered Offices: 80 Strand, London WC2R 0RL, England

THE LAST RENEGADE

A Berkley Sensation Book / published by arrangement with the author

PUBLISHING HISTORY
Berkley Sensation mass-market edition / September 2012

Cover photo by Claudio Marinesco.
Cover design by Rita Frangie.

For information, address: The Berkley Publishing Group,
a division of Penguin Group (USA) Inc.,
375 Hudson Street, New York, New York 10014.

ISBN: 978-0-425-25096-9

BERKLEY SENSATION®
Berkley Sensation Books are published by The Berkley Publishing Group,
a division of Penguin Group (USA) Inc.,
375 Hudson Street, New York, New York 10014.
BERKLEY SENSATION® is a registered trademark of Penguin Group (USA) Inc.
The "B" design is a trademark of Penguin Group (USA) Inc.

PRINTED IN THE UNITED STATES OF AMERICA

10 9 8 7 6 5 4 3 2 1

This one has to be for my terrific friends and colleagues at WVCCA. Remember, while I incorporate your names shamelessly, I haven't killed one of you off.

Yet.

Prologue

October 1888
Wyoming Territory

Kellen Coltrane looked up from his reading to acknowledge the stranger. The interruption annoyed him, but he did not permit himself to reveal it. It was impossible for him not to hear his mother's gentle admonishment at times like this, "There is no reason you cannot remove your nose from a book long enough to be civil." That's why a smile was tugging at the corners of his mouth when he met the eyes of the dead man.

Not that the stranger was dead yet. Just that he soon would be. The man's gaunt face was nearly drained of color, and in spite of the chill in the passenger coach, his skin had the damp sheen of a sickly sweat.

Then there was the blood. It was not immediately evident. The dying man was making some effort to hide his condition, perhaps even from himself, but his posture was listing now, the knees no longer locked to attention, and the hand he had pushed inside his coat to cover the wound was insufficient to staunch the flow of blood. A dark crimson bloom had begun to appear on his shirt above the button closures of his vest and coat.

Kellen looked around quickly and saw the man had attracted no particular notice. This passenger car hadn't been overcrowded since Omaha and was down to five other souls since the stop in Cheyenne. There were cars forward where passengers were still seated elbow to elbow. If there was a choice, most people opted to ride as close to the front of the train as possible, where they believed the cars swayed less. Smoke and cinders were inescapable wherever one sat, even in the Union Pacific's most expensive private coaches. For Kellen, his choice of seats hinged on how much conversation and company he wanted. He had moved several times to achieve exactly this much isolation.

Apparently, so had the dead man.

Kellen stood, placed a hand under the stranger's elbow, and slipped his dime novel under the man's coat. "Press this against your wound," he whispered. "Let me help you sit."

Summoning enough energy to glance at the book's colorful cover illustration, the man grasped it with bloodstained fingers. "Hate to see Nat Church put to such a use."

Kellen offered a thin smile. "If you believe the stories, he's seen worse."

"Oh, I believe. Believe 'em all."

There was a pause, and Kellen thought he was going to say more, but a weak cough and a spittle of blood on the man's lower lip were all that followed. Kellen eased the man down on the wooden bench and helped him slide into the corner beside the window, the same space Kellen had previously occupied.

Kellen bent low and spoke quietly into the man's ear. "I'm going to get help."

"No."

"The conductor passed through here a few minutes ago. He can't be far."

"No." This time the objection was more forceful, not easily ignored. The man turned his head and stared hard. His soft grunt revealed mild surprise and a measure of grudging respect when Kellen didn't blink or back away. "Guess I ain't in a position to argue."

"That's right." Kellen started to straighten and move away, but the dying man reached out and grabbed his wrist. His strength made Kellen hesitate even while it filled him with a greater sense of urgency. Perhaps he had mistaken the hopelessness of the stranger's condition. He looked down at the white-knuckled fingers gripping his wrist. "What is it?"

"My valise." He jerked his chin toward the narrow aisle. "Put it here. Beside me."

Kellen's own valise was stored under the bench. He didn't bother offering to put the stranger's bag there. He picked up the bag, discovered it was heavier than he'd anticipated, and hefted it onto the bench. He then went in search of the conductor.

He found Mr. Berg four cars forward. It had taken him more time than it should have because passengers two cars ahead had opened up their baskets and were sharing food across the aisle and between the benches. The atmosphere in that car was as festive as a summer picnic, and he was encouraged by every traveler of the female kind to sample a slice of this and a square of that. Exigency warred with civility. He was polite but firm, then coldly polite, and finally merely cold. No one offered him anything on his return passage.

The conductor, a smallish man with widely spaced eyes and spectacles that sat too narrowly on the bridge of his nose, had his hands full keeping two women from clawing each other—or him. Lying in the aisle between the would-be combatants was a flattened black velvet bonnet, artfully decorated with black-and-white glass beads and a large, black-tipped ostrich feather. Kellen assessed the situation as a standoff. While passengers on either side of the aisle called out their opinion and generally egged on the spitting and hissing females, Kellen slipped the toe of his boot under the bonnet's brim, gave a little kick, and sent the bonnet sailing toward the coach's ceiling. Both women leaped, and once they were airborne, Kellen reached between them, grabbed the conductor's arm, and yanked him free of the dispute.

Kellen couldn't be sure, but he thought he glimpsed a look of gratitude before the conductor began to make all the proper noises about not abandoning his post even as he was being dragged toward the rear of the car.

Between cars, Kellen explained the situation. He had precious few details to offer. No, he couldn't say who was responsible. No, he didn't know when the man was injured. Yes, he was certain it was a grievous wound. Yes, the man required a doctor's attention if one could be found.

The conductor, in Kellen's opinion, delayed their progress unnecessarily by insisting on proper introductions, and Kellen had the impression his name would find its way into an official report to the Union Pacific Railroad, or more concerning, to the local vigilance committee.

"There is a physician in the next car," Mr. Berg explained. "Go on ahead, while I'll ask him to attend us. I won't be but a minute or so behind you."

When Kellen arrived back at his car, he didn't immediately see the wounded stranger, and thought the impossible had happened and somehow the man had moved on. That wasn't the case. As Kellen moved closer to his seat, he saw the stranger was doubled over, bent so far forward as to be invisible from the front of the car. Far from being dead, the man was purposefully rooting through his valise. Kellen had a distinct memory of setting the bag on the seat beside the stranger. Had it fallen to the floor?

"What do you need?" asked Kellen. "Let me get it for you." The man removed his hand as quickly as a child caught in the act of swiping his finger through a freshly frosted cake. "Then let me get it out of the way." Kellen pushed it under the bench beside his own bag and sat down. "Conductor's bringing a doctor. Maybe you've got longer than you think." He helped the man straighten and situated him once more in the corner of the seat, allowing him to rest his shoulder against the side of the car. His head lolled against the window. Kellen removed his long leather coat, folded it, and placed it under the man's head and shoulder.

"You want to tell me what happened?" Kellen asked.

The stranger lifted one ginger eyebrow. "You interested?"

"I am."

"Didn't seem like you might be. Runnin' off the way you did."

Kellen had to lean close. The man's voice was weak, softer

than a whisper, and hard to hear over the steady clickety-clack of the train on the rails. He watched the stranger's lips and strained to hear.

"Thought you might be squeamish. Didn't think you were when I first noticed you, but you never know."

Kellen ignored that. "You're wasting your breath," he said. "Literally. Who are you?"

"Name's Nat Church. Heard of me?"

Arching an eyebrow, Kellen revealed his skepticism. "Nat Church." His wintry blue eyes dropped to where the stranger's hand disappeared under his coat. Somewhere beneath the heavy woolen overcoat, the man was still pressing a dime novel against his wound. "*Nat Church and the Ambush at Broken Bow. Nat Church and the Indian Maiden. That* Nat Church?"

"That's right."

"Huh."

"You don't believe me."

"Sure don't, but I don't think it matters." Kellen watched the man who called himself Nat Church shrug and immediately regret the small movement. A grimace twisted Mr. Church's mouth into a parody of a smile. Kellen looked away and in the direction of the passenger car's door. Help wasn't arriving as quickly as the conductor had promised. Perhaps the doctor was reluctant to offer assistance.

Several rows ahead of them, a father sitting with his young son glanced back. The father immediately turned away, apparently disinclined to become involved. When the boy started to swivel in his seat, the father clamped a firm hand on the back of his son's skull and made him keep his eyes forward.

Another quick survey of the car told Kellen all he needed to know about the likelihood that there would be help from another quarter. The passengers studiously avoided meeting his eyes. They all knew now that something unpleasant was happening within spitting distance of their seats, but their instinct was to maintain that distance lest some spittle attach itself.

Their reaction struck him as odd. They were behaving counter to his experience. In his travels, he'd found that people in the wide-open Western territories were more likely to step up and lend a hand than city folk or the denizens of small towns, where the yoke of lawlessness was still a heavy burden.

There was a possibility, however, that explained it. Kellen bent his head slightly and addressed Nat Church. "You told them to stay away."

Mr. Church did not pretend that he didn't understand. "Course I did."

Kellen had the impression that Nat Church was not only at peace with what he'd done, his fleeting smile seemed to indicate that he was satisfied that Kellen had figured it out. "All right," said Kellen. He concluded there was no point in challenging the dying man's assertion that he was Nat Church, in spite of the fact that he looked nothing at all like the hero described in all twenty-two of the wildly popular dime novels. The fictional Nat Church was in his twenties, easily half this stranger's age. Nat Church of the serialized adventures had hair as black as tar and eyes so impenetrable that light was neither emitted nor reflected. The man sitting beside Kellen had a face that was infinitely more expressive, eyes that were as gray as the wiry strands of hair at his temples, and a thin face with deep lines that were a map of life experience. The hero of *Nat Church and the Sleeping Detective* and *Nat Church and the Hanging at Harrisonville* had wide shoulders and wore a beaten, buttery-soft brown leather duster, not a woolen coat with the heavy collar turned up to hide a pencil-thin neck, and Church, the hero, sported scuffed brown boots with tarnished silver spurs, not ones that were polished to a military shine. "Are you going to let me see your wound?"

"Can't . . . lift the book . . . I'll bleed out."

"You were stabbed, is that right? Not shot."

"How you figure?"

Impatient with the man's need to hear an explanation, Kellen decided to humor him. He said, "You didn't board the train injured. It's my habit to watch people at the stops, see who's coming and going. I saw you walking the platform; saw you waiting to climb aboard. Hands at your sides. Patient to take your turn. Watchful but not worried. I saw enough to be confident that whatever happened, happened after you stepped on the train.

I didn't hear a gunshot. No one in this car reacted as if they'd heard one either. That leads me to conclude you were stabbed."

There was humor in Mr. Church's voice as he whispered, " 'Leads me to conclude.' You a lawyer?"

"No."

"Sound like a lawyer . . . maybe a politician."

"Neither."

Church nodded. "Can't abide either one. Thought maybe I lost my touch for takin' a man's measure."

Kellen was curious about what made this Nat Church choose him, but he didn't take the dangling bait. Maybe it was simply what he'd been reading at the time. He might have been passed over completely if he'd been holding *The Pickwick Papers.*

"Who did this to you?"

Again, the small smile. "Ain't it the way of life that most things is done *by* ourselves, *to* ourselves?"

"Philosopher? The Nat Church I read about is none of that."

"Even a good writer can't put all of me on the page."

"I see. So are you saying you stabbed yourself?"

"Hardly. Not such a fool as that. Just tryin' to say that I had some part in it."

Kellen watched the man take a short, steadying breath, drawing air through clenched teeth. In spite of the pain, it seemed to Kellen that Mr. Church wanted to take his time, tell his tale slowly in the fashion of Scheherazade, as though he might be granted a night's reprieve if he could spin the ending to another chapter.

Kellen put his next question bluntly. "Do you know the name of your murderer?" He gave Nat Church full marks for not flinching. Perhaps he had something in common with the man he purported to be after all.

"Never saw it coming . . . crowded in the aisle . . . people trying to get settled."

"One car back? That's where I thought you boarded."

Mr. Church tried to suppress a cough but couldn't. He pressed the ball of his free hand against his lips.

Kellen passed him a handkerchief.

"Thank you." He wiped his mouth and crumpled the

handkerchief in his fist. "Yes, one car to the rear. Did I say I never saw it comin'?"

"You did."

"Should have seen it. Half expectin' it since . . . since forever. Knew what I was up against. Wife would've tried to stop me." A short laugh had him raising the handkerchief to his mouth again. "Damn me if that don't hurt."

It had not occurred to Kellen until now that there might be someone to notify. "Who should I tell? How can I find your wife?"

"Can't. She's gone now. Same as me."

"There must be someone."

"Bitter Springs."

Not a person at all, but a place. Kellen's Western journeys had taken him past the town on several occasions. It existed on Wyoming's high flatland near the Medicine Bow Mountains, a survivor of the camps that sprang to life as the Union Pacific laid track from Omaha toward Utah. Instead of disappearing as so many of the camps did when the rails passed them by, Bitter Springs found commerce in cattle country and as a water way station for thirsty engines and their thirstier passengers.

Kellen had never seen anything from his train window that recommended Bitter Springs as a place of particular interest. Now he wondered what he might have missed by not spending a few days with the locals. "Is that your home? Bitter Springs? Were you going there?"

"Going there . . . not home."

"Expected?"

Mr. Church nodded. "Pennyroyal. Should find her . . . tell her . . . she's waiting."

"Penny Royal. All right. I'll be certain to—" He stopped, his attention caught by the coach door opening. Mr. Berg appeared on the threshold with a man on his heels that Kellen supposed was the doctor. The late arrival was explained by the doctor's condition. The man required the conductor's shoulder to keep him steady and upright. Kellen swore under his breath and got to his feet. "Right here," he said. He stepped into the aisle, backing up as he pointed to Mr. Church. He jerked his chin at the doctor but addressed his question to Mr. Berg. "You sure he can help? He looks as if he can hardly hold his bag any better than he can hold his liquor."

"Don't like the looks of you much either," the doctor said, answering for himself. He kept pace with the conductor and then switched places so he could sink onto the bench beside Mr. Church. He flipped the clasp on his medical bag and opened it, offering his credentials to Kellen as he withdrew a ball of tightly wound bandages. "Woodrow Hitchens. Late of St. Louis. Graduate of Philadelphia Medical College, class of 'sixty. Cut my teeth in the field hospitals at Manassas, Gettysburg, and Shiloh to name a few that you might have heard of, you still being a whelp and all. That suit you?"

Kellen accepted the rebuke, knowing it was deserved. The doctor hadn't slurred a syllable. Liquor didn't account for the man's unsteady gait or the slight tremble in his hands. Some sort of wasting disease did. "Suits me fine," Kellen said. "What can you do for him?"

Dr. Hitchens gave his patient his full attention while Mr. Berg inched closer for a better look until Kellen put an arm out to ease him back. "You're going to have to let me see your wound, Mr.—"

"Church. Nat Church."

"Well, that's something," the doctor said equably. "I've been known to enjoy your exploits. Especially liked *Nat Church and the Frisco Fancy*."

Kellen smiled wryly as Nat Church offered a modest thank-you. The man had no shame, perhaps another trait he shared with his fictional counterpart.

The doctor had some difficulty unbuttoning his patient's coat. Aside from the tremor in his hands, his fingers quickly became slick with blood. "Can't wait to read the new one. Have it on order."

"*Nat Church and the Chinese Box*," Church said as the doctor opened the coat at the site of the wound. "Got a copy for you right here."

The conductor blanched and sucked in a breath when he saw the bloody mess that was Mr. Church's midsection. Kellen took a step forward to block his view.

Kellen couldn't distinguish between book, blood, and bowel. The doctor tossed the latest Church adventure to the floor, shoved slithering intestine back inside the gaping wound, and held one hand against Church's bloody flesh while expertly unwinding the ball of bandages in the other. When he had a wad the size and thickness of his palm, he used his teeth to tear it off and replaced his hand with it. "Mother of God," he muttered, looking back at Kellen. "This man's been gutted. Who did this?"

"He says he doesn't know."

"Anything you can do, Doctor?"

"Put this away." Hitchens held out the unused portion of bandage to Kellen. "Take out the smallest syringe and give it to me."

Kellen followed the instructions, eventually taking the doctor's place beside Mr. Church and using his hand to keep the man's guts from spilling onto his lap. Hitchens wiped blood from his fingers and then filled the syringe from a vial of clear fluid that he extracted from the bottom of his bag.

Kellen saw both resignation and determination on the doctor's face. It wasn't so different from what he observed in the man who wanted to be Nat Church.

"Morphine?" asked Kellen.

The doctor didn't answer. Without a word of warning or apology, he plunged the point of the syringe into his patient's thigh.

There was only waiting after that. Nat Church eventually closed his eyes. He slept. He died. And none of those who stood as witness to his end had an explanation for it.

They agreed that the bloody tin star the doctor found pinned to Nat Church's vest might account for some part of the answer. Kellen Coltrane was left to wonder what accounted for the rest of it.

Chapter One

Bitter Springs, Wyoming Territory

Lorraine Berry wondered about the man arriving today. Allowing her thoughts to drift into the great unknown of possibilities and unforeseen consequences was as close to daydreaming as she ever got. The work facing her was considerable, and she was too practical to stray from it for long. Besides, she had deliberated at length, sometimes out loud, and she had done it for weeks before she began the correspondence with the gun for hire.

It had been a risk writing to him, but at the time it seemed that not writing was the greater risk. It troubled her that she no longer had the same firm sense that she'd made the better choice. Of course, it could be that if she'd done nothing, she would still be plagued by niggling doubt, and then she would have lost the opportunity to hire him. In spite of the fact that she answered *his* notice, Raine could not imagine that a man with his specialized talent was ever without work for long. In fact, Raine had supplied more information about her circumstances than he revealed about his own. Somehow this made her feel more comfortable about the arrangement, as though he were choosing her, not the other way around, and that he could be better trusted because of it.

It was not until his last letter that she learned who he was, and then because she requested it. He never signed his previous correspondence, so it showed a certain amount of confidence in her when he finally shared his name.

Best regards, Nat Church.

Raine looked up from arranging bottles behind the mahogany bar and caught her reflection in the gilt-framed mirror. Her wry smile was mocking, which was exactly as it should be. Nat Church? She might have ended their arrangement if he had penned that at the outset.

It wasn't that she believed it was his real name; it merely troubled her because it demonstrated a singular lack of imagination. Now if he had signed his name as Aaron Burr or John Wilkes Booth, that would have hinted at wit, however dark and ghoulish.

Raine's self-mocking smile deepened as she addressed her reflection. "You are most assuredly twisted, Raine Berry." She raised a hand to her hair. "Look at you. When exactly was it that the cat dragged you over the backyard fence?" One of her tortoiseshell combs had lost its moorings and was no longer serving the intended purpose of keeping her hair close to her head. When she was still a young girl and knew every sort of thing was possible, she held fast to the notion that her dreadful carroty curls could be tamed. As a woman full grown, she knew better and accepted as marginal consolation that sometime between four and twenty-four the color of her hair had darkened from carrot to copper.

Raine licked her fingers, smoothed back the strands trying to stand at attention, and anchored the comb so it was positioned on a symmetrical plane to its twin. In the event there was still more wrong in places she couldn't easily see, she felt for the coil near the crown of her head and rearranged a few pins to keep it in place. When she was satisfied that she had done the best she could with what she had, she nodded once at the mirror so her reflection could confirm it.

Raine turned away from straightening the bottles and picked up a broom before the mirror became a bigger distraction than the impending arrival of Nat Church. She swept behind the bar and was starting to make a pass under the tables when Walter Mangold walked in from the storeroom at the back. She was glad he didn't know how to tread lightly; otherwise his sudden appearance might have had her diving for cover.

Walt rested his large hands on his waist, his arms akimbo, and scolded Raine in a baritone so deep and dulcet that no sting could be attached to it. "Now, stop that, Mrs. Berry. Give me the broom. On no account should you be doing my work just because you can."

Raine didn't think about arguing. She held out the broom. Walt was her hardest worker, and what he lacked in quick-wittedness, he compensated for in size, strength, and steadiness. He was also loyal. While there was a certain amount of charm in his devotion to her, Raine also felt a responsibility to do right by him. There were plenty of people in town who looked out for Walt, but there were always a few who considered it a fine joke to make him the butt of one. Before she and Adam took over the Pennyroyal, Walt mostly worked for the Burdicks, and that family had a way of using a body that had nothing to do with useful. The passing recollection of the way they had treated Walt was enough to set Raine's teeth on edge.

"Goodness, but you got yourself riled up about something," Walt said. "There's color creeping up your neck."

Raine wished she still had the broom so she could make a playful jab at him with it. Instead, she immediately raised a hand to the hollow of her throat. She didn't know whether she really felt the heat or only imagined it, but she knew Walt was right about the color. She could school her fine features into an expressionless mask, but it usually served no purpose when her pale skin flushed pink with so little provocation.

"You think I'm riled now? Just stand there talking to me when you should be sweeping and I'll show you riled."

Walt grinned, flashing teeth almost as big as his fingernails, before he ducked his head and set to work.

Raine got out of his way. She started to pick up a rag to

polish the brass rail at the bar, thought better of it, and retreated from the saloon in favor of the hotel's dining room. Three overnight guests were already seated, the older married couple from Springfield at one table and the liquor salesman from Chicago at the other. Town regulars who enjoyed the company and coffee at the Pennyroyal occupied two more tables. Raine greeted everyone by name before she disappeared into the kitchen.

Mrs. Sterling promptly told her to get out.

"You're going to get underfoot," the cook said flatly. "You always do. And Emily will take her orders from you instead of me, and sure as God made little green apples, the next thing you know I'll be burning Mr. Wheeler's toast and scrambling Jack Clifton's eggs instead of turning them over real easy like." And in the event Raine had a conveniently forgetful memory, Mrs. Sterling reminded her, "It's happened before."

Raine stayed where she was just inside the door. To further placate her cook, she kept her palms flat against the raised oak panels. "I thought I might get my own breakfast," she said. "I haven't had anything to eat since yesterday's lunch."

Mrs. Sterling evinced no sympathy. She used one corner of her apron to swipe at the beads of perspiration outlining her widow's peak before she returned to flipping hotcakes on the griddle. "Whose fault is that? That's what I would like to know."

"It's mine," Raine said. She stepped aside to let Emily pass into the dining room with a pot of coffee and a platter of hotcakes. She tried to catch the girl's eye, but under Mrs. Sterling's more predatory one, Emily was having none of it. The fair-haired Emily slipped past Raine with otherworldly efficiency, like a wraith in a Gothic novel. Raine was left to inhale sharply as the cakes went by and hope the aroma clung to her nostrils until Mrs. Sterling invited her in.

"Did you say something, dear?" Mrs. Sterling asked. "Because I thought I heard you say something."

Raine knew the cook had heard her perfectly well, but she answered just the same. "I said it is my fault."

Mrs. Sterling nodded briskly. "Always good to have that out

of the way. Now, why don't you go up to your room, have a little bit of a lie-in, and I'll send Emily up with a plate of everything once I attend to the guests and the regulars?"

"The regulars are also our guests," Raine said.

"If you say so."

Raine smiled. "I always do." Mrs. Sterling had known Howard Wheeler and Jack Clifton since they worked beside her husband laying rails back in '67. She knew the other regulars just about as well. If they were visitors in her own home, which they hadn't been since Mr. Sterling was shot dead, then she would have called them guests. What she thought of them now, she'd told Raine, lacked Christian sentiment and did not bear repeating, so she was a better woman for just calling them regulars.

Raine watched Mrs. Sterling carefully tend to Mr. Clifton's eggs. Her smile deepened. In spite of the unchristian sentiments the cook insisted she harbored, she never broke one of Jack Clifton's eggs if she could help it and to Raine's knowledge she had never tried to poison anyone.

"Why do you think I should have a little bit of a lie-in?"

"Do I need to say it?"

"Apparently so."

Mrs. Sterling stopped what she was doing long enough to remove her spectacles from their perch above her forehead and place them on the rather pronounced bridge of her nose. It was all for effect because she stared at Raine over the top of the gold-plated rims. "Those bags under your eyes are so big that Rabbit and Finn would refuse to carry them, and you know those two would rather throw themselves in front of a moving train than admit there's something they can't do. Is that plain enough for you?"

Raine blinked. "Yes," she said when she found her voice. "It is."

"Well, you had to make me go and say it."

"Again, my fault. Perhaps the next time you'll simply tell me that I look tired."

"Mr. Sterling was always trying to put words in my mouth. It didn't work for him. I don't expect that it will work for you."

Sighing, Raine gingerly pressed her fingertips to the underside of her eyes. The skin didn't feel puffy, so the reference to bags was an exaggeration, but during her earlier conversation in front of the mirror, she'd glimpsed the same faint shadows that drew Mrs. Sterling's notice.

"I was late going to bed. The saloon was crowded last night."

"I've said it before, but it bears repeating. You're the owner, not the entertainment."

"I was behind the bar all evening."

"Pouring drinks with a smile and a kind word for everybody."

"I like to think it reminds them they're gentlemen, and it helps keep tables and chairs in place and the mirror in one piece."

Mrs. Sterling pushed her spectacles back above her salt-and-pepper widow's peak. She gave Raine a hard look, nothing feigned about it. "Were the Burdicks here?"

Raine shook her head. "No. No, they weren't."

The cook's shoulders had drawn together, tension pulling them taut. Now they relaxed. She began to plate eggs, steak, and fried potatoes. "You'd tell me, wouldn't you?"

"Of course I would."

"Hmm. That's because you know I'd hear about it."

"I'd tell you because you deserve to know. The same as I do. And there are others, you know, besides us."

Mrs. Sterling nodded. "I'm not afraid for myself. They did their worst by me already, taking my husband the way they did, but I can't help fearing for you and the others." She picked up Jack Clifton's plate and gave it a little shake. "I don't know what makes this man think he needs to stay around when he knows he could end up no better than my Benton." She raised the plate she'd made for Howard Wheeler and thrust it in Raine's direction. "And this man has about as much sense as a bag of hair or he would be on the next train to somewhere else."

"That didn't work for John Hood," Raine said quietly. "The Burdicks found him."

"I think it scares folks to say so out loud," said Mrs. Sterling. She returned both plates to the tray and looked past Raine to the door. Her voice crackled with her rising agitation. "Where's that girl gone to? Look in the dining room and see if she's wiping up something she spilled or flirting with Mr. Weyman."

Raine opened the door wide enough to catch Emily Ransom's eye when the girl stopped giggling at something the whiskey drummer from Chicago had said. She crooked her finger and gently closed the door, then moved out of the way until Emily pushed through. Mrs. Sterling gave over the tray and shooed the girl out again.

"I say it out loud," Raine said, picking up the thread of their conversation. "And Hank Thompson's been gone almost a year and no one in Bitter Springs has heard from him. He had friends. There should have been a letter by now. One to his mother, at least."

"That could mean anything. Maybe Agnes got one and isn't saying. She could be trying to protect him."

"You've known Agnes Thompson all your life. She can't keep a secret. No one's heard from him because he's dead."

Mrs. Sterling twisted her apron in her hands. "I don't like this talk."

"I know."

The cook hesitated. The question was drawn from her reluctantly. "You really think Hank's dead?"

Raine briefly closed her eyes. "I'm afraid so, yes."

"If it's true, it's not your fault."

"I appreciate you saying so, but I know differently."

"It's not your fault," Mrs. Sterling repeated. The steel was back in her voice. "I think I've proven I know how to assign blame when it's warranted. And it's not, not about this. I don't hold you responsible for my Benton's death. He knew what he was about, and he wanted to do the right thing. He was proud to stand up, and I was proud of him for doing it. Still am proud. You diminish his courage by thinking you pressed him to do something against his will."

Raine nodded, willing to be convinced for now because it

was important to Mrs. Sterling. "Maybe that's what Mr. Clifton and Mr. Wheeler are doing. Standing up."

"They did that. Now they're just standing around, and that's plain foolish. It's hard to be proud of fools."

Raine understood that Mrs. Sterling was determined to have the last word. It was wiser to change the subject and hope for the best. She yawned as if she meant it. "I suppose I'll have that bit of a lie-in after all."

"There's a girl." She added some water to the pitcher of hotcake batter and gave it a stir. "Give me a minute and you can take a couple of these with you."

Raine waited the requisite minute and a few additional ones so the cook could add an egg and a palm-sized serving of steak. Balancing her plate and a cup of hot coffee in one hand, she lifted her skirt with the other and took the stairs at the back of the hotel to reach her rooms on the third floor.

She had all the space she needed for herself on the uppermost floor of the Pennyroyal. Sometimes it was too much. She could find herself wandering from room to room, recalling that when Adam and Ellen were still with her, she had complained the apartment was too small for the three of them. It was a miserable memory, and she did her best to avoid tripping over it.

Raine used a forearm to clear a space for her breakfast on the writing table in her office. A couple of sheets of paper fluttered to the floor and she let them lie. Sitting down, she pulled out the fork she had squirreled away under her sleeve and cut into the hotcakes. Her stomach rumbled as she lifted two thick slices of molasses-soaked cakes. Just in time, she thought, and stuffed the double helping into her mouth.

She couldn't eat everything Mrs. Sterling gave her, but she had a taste of all of it, and when she pushed out her belly, her stays pushed back. She turned her chair away from the desk and inched it toward the window. The Pennyroyal was the tallest building in Bitter Springs, taller even than the spire on Grace Church, and the view from Raine's office took in the storefronts of half a dozen businesses on the opposite side of the street. Beyond that she could make out the rooftop of the parsonage, where Pastor Robbins and his family lived, Mrs.

Garvin's attic window, and if she tilted her head at just the right angle, she could see between the false fronts of the mercantile and the drugstore all the way to the privy in Mr. Webb's backyard. It always made her smile to think that a self-important man like Mr. Webb traipsed to an outhouse when her hotel had all the latest amenities including hot and cold running water and porcelain pots in every bathing room, which meant her guests did not have to visit the privy. After Adam had installed the water tank and boiler, the hotel was booked for eight weeks with townspeople who paid to spend a night just to open a faucet and wash their hands and face with hot water. Some even took a bath. Mr. Webb was not among the guests. The Burdicks surely would have insisted that the banker stay away. They controlled the bank; therefore, the banker.

Raine felt herself begin to nod off. She would have a crick in her neck for days if she slept in the chair. That prompted her to leave its relative comfort for her bed. She didn't disturb the coverlet but lay on top of it and plumped the pillows. When the coil at the back of her head pressed uncomfortably, she tore at the pins and unwound it. The combs followed.

There were so many things she still wanted to do before Nat Church arrived, and all of them would have to wait. She could have told Mrs. Sterling the truth: She didn't deserve to sleep, and the shadows under her eyes were there because she knew it.

It was one of the consequences of hiring a killer.

Curiosity gave Kellen the only excuse he needed to decide against going to Salt Lake City and get off the train at Bitter Springs. At least he preferred to think it was curiosity. The alternative explanation was that he had been moved by impulse, and that would have been worrisome. It was his experience that giving in to impulse meant the odds were better than even that he would be face-to-face with trouble at the end of the day, maybe before supper.

He set his valise at his feet and unclenched his fingers while he waited for the porters to bring his trunks. The bag was heavier than he recalled, and it occurred to him that he should have stowed it in the baggage car or accepted Mr. Berg's offer to carry it for him. It would have provided a moment's welcome comedy to watch the diminutive conductor strain to lift the bag, let alone haul it off the train. Every mile traveled since Nat Church surrendered his last breath had been fraught with more tension than the mile before, and Mr. Berg's desire to make sure no fault was attached to the railroad prompted him to take on the role of investigator, asking as many questions as came to him, and often asking them several different ways.

One thing Bitter Springs had to recommend it was that Mr. Berg wouldn't be there.

The station platform was only as long as the building that housed the ticket office, baggage area, and restaurant. Kellen walked the length of it several times just to shake off the confinement of travel. Passengers who'd left the train with Kellen had either already gone with their waiting party or were being herded back to their coaches after a frenzied meal in the station eatery. The stop at Bitter Springs, like so many others along the route, was not made for the convenience of hungry travelers. They merely benefited every fifty miles or so because the massive iron engines had requirements of their own. Passengers had exactly as much time to eat as it took the railroad tenders to load the coal and fill the water tanks, which usually necessitated a stop just on either side of twenty minutes. Kellen had participated more than a few times in the ensuing rush to order, pay, and consume a meal in the allotted time. The station restaurants made certain their waitresses could take an order quickly and collect the money even faster than they took the order, but getting the meal to the table, if it made it at all, took upwards of twelve minutes, leaving precious little time for consumption. On those occasions that his food arrived promptly, albeit somewhat less than hot, Kellen suspected he profited from a passenger on an earlier train who'd ordered, paid, and then had to leave before his meal arrived. He was philosophical about it, figuring that when he went hungry because the biscuit shooter took her sweet time bringing his meal, someone else would have the good fortune to receive the plate he hadn't.

Kellen's trunks arrived at the same time the last stragglers were boarding the train. Once the porters stepped back on board, Kellen was alone on the sheltered platform. He stood there for several minutes after the engine's sharp whistle signaled her intention to leave. Even as the great wheels began to slowly roll forward, he remained where he was, observing the passengers at the windows observing him. He recognized Dr. Hitchens, who acknowledged him with gravely set features and a nod, the travelers in his coach who all went to the platform side to get a last glimpse of him but would not meet his eyes, and finally, the woman who had emerged victorious in the bonnet war. She cast him a glance that seemed excessively triumphant given the fact that the hat she was wearing no longer sported the black-tipped ostrich feather.

Kellen touched the brim of his hat as she passed, his smile narrow and cool. It had the effect of turning her head, this time away from him and in a manner that was not complimentary.

It wasn't until the last car cleared the station that Kellen finally turned to face the station. There were no late departures from the train. It was what he wanted to know.

Kellen ignored the entrance to the restaurant and chose the door for tickets, schedules, and posting mail. The station agent was sitting on a stool behind the counter while he sorted letters from a mailbag that had been left in his possession. He didn't pause or look up from his work when Kellen walked into the office.

"Someone expecting you, son?" the agent asked. "Seemed like you were waiting for someone."

"Not waiting," said Kellen. "Saying good-bye."

"That so? Looked like you were waiting for someone."

Kellen looked over his shoulder to take in the same view the station agent had. The window afforded the agent an unrestricted view of the platform depending on how far he was willing to stray from his stool. Kellen had the impression the man strayed plenty. He wasn't aware of a station agent from Chicago to Sacramento who didn't divert himself by watching his passengers when they weren't looking.

Kellen turned back in time to catch the agent's eyes darting to the mail. Clearly the man was interested in him. "Is there something else you want to ask me . . ." He looked around, saw the nameplate affixed to the wall above the agent's head, and added, "Mr. Collins?" Kellen saw that the direct question gave Mr. Jefferson Collins all of a moment's hesitation, long enough for the agent's considerably sized Adam's apple to bob once in his throat.

"Wonderin' if you was witness to the murder, that's what I was fixin' to ask. Probably would have gotten around to it by and by. Never seen much sense in rushin' a conversation about dead folk."

"What do you know about it?"

Mr. Collins gave up the pretense of sorting mail, pushed it aside, and folded his arms across his chest. He regarded Kellen frankly. "Only what came in over the wire. Precious little, but then the railroad plays its cards close. Probably same as you."

"Me? What makes you think I play my cards close?"

"Nature of a gambler."

One corner of Kellen's mouth lifted slightly, the hallmark of a thin smile offered most grudgingly. "So it is." He watched Mr. Collins nod once, faintly, and concluded the agent was satisfied with his answer. "I suppose they told you the man's name."

"Sure. There was a thought that maybe he lived in these parts, but there aren't any Churches in town, nor any close outside of it. Strange that. Common enough name. You'd think we'd have one or two go by it. Got none."

"That does seem odd."

Mr. Collins nodded again. "Odd, too, that he'd be Nat Church. I guess just about everyone knows that name. Leastways I know it like it's my own. *Nat Church and the Best Gang*. That's a good one, maybe my favorite, though I sure did like *Nat Church and the Shooting Contest.* You read the novels?"

"I'm familiar."

"He's probably not the *real* Nat Church."

"No," Kellen said dryly. "Probably not."

The station agent scratched the underside of his bearded chin thoughtfully. "Good thing. Hate to think of the real Nat Church comin' to such an ignominious end. Doesn't set right with me."

"Ignominious?"

"Embarrassing. Means embarrassing."

"I'll be darned."

Mr. Collins stopped scratching and placed his hand flat on the countertop. "What can I do for you?"

"Recommend clean, comfortable lodgings."

"That's easy enough. You'll want to see the Widder Berry. She operates a fine hotel."

"I was wondering about private lodgings. A rooming house. I heard someone on the train mention Penny Royal. Does Mrs. Royal have rooms to let?"

Mr. Collins chuckled. "There's no Mrs. Royal. No Miss Royal for that matter. You misunderstood what you heard . . . or overheard. It's the Pennyroyal Saloon and Hotel. Widder Berry owns the place. You can't do better."

"I see. It's a hotel *and* saloon?"

"It is."

Kellen felt himself come under renewed scrutiny as the agent's stare narrowed and several deep creases appeared between his eyebrows when he drew them together. "All right," Kellen said. "That will be fine."

"Didn't think taking a room above a saloon would much trouble a gambling man."

"Would you like to live where you work, Mr. Collins?"

The agent surveyed the small office, his attention lingering on those parts that adjoined the front of the restaurant. The clatter and chatter from next door were hardly muted by the wooden walls. "Point taken. You can try the Sedgwick place. George and Amelia take on boarders, but they're partial to folks plannin' on staying a while. You aimin' to do that?"

Kellen ignored the question. "You said I couldn't do better than the Pennyroyal. I'll take you at your word. What about my trunks and bag?"

Mr. Collins used his index finger to motion Kellen aside,

and then he leaned a little to the right to look past him. "That's better. Could not recall if you had one bag or two."

"One bag. Two trunks."

"You must be travelin' for a spell."

"About my trunks," said Kellen.

"Oh, my grandsons will help you with those." Mr. Collins reached for a brass bell that had been pushed out of the way by the mailbag. He gave it a hearty shake, grinning widely enough to show a gold eyetooth when his visitor winced. "Once your ears stop ringing, you'll realize it was all for the best."

It took Kellen a moment to understand, but when he did, he had to agree with Mr. Collins. The bell's harsh resonance had the effect of quieting the clamor in the restaurant. The silence did not last long, but neither did the noise return to the level of a cacophony.

"It's worse when the passengers are in there. Next train's not due . . ." He consulted his timepiece. "Not due for another three hours. Mostly freight and the immigrant cars." He looked Kellen over again. "A man like you, well, you probably never rode with the immigrant cars."

Kellen had. Not merely *with* them, but *in* them. He'd done it to satisfy his need to know firsthand. And once done, it was not something he would forget or, given a choice, repeat. "A man like me, Mr. Collins?"

"Two trunks and a bag. There are entire families in those cars that make do with less than you stowed under your seat. They wear most of what they own on their backs and smell like they never been properly introduced to lye soap."

"Then you're correct. I have better than a passing acquaintance with soap." And one sharp memory of having his mouth washed out with it. Kellen let that memory slip away as his attention was drawn to the door by swift, multiple footsteps approaching. The door shuddered in response to the runners' barreling into it. There was a brief scuffle, an angry exchange of words, and then the brass bell brought it all to a halt.

Kellen was still grimacing and tugging on his right earlobe when the door finally opened, and Mr. Collins's errant grandsons simultaneously squeezed past the threshold. They all but spilled into the room and, far from making an apology for it, continued to jab each other with pointed elbows, each nudge a little harder than the last. The boys, both of them towheads with matching cowlicks, were far younger than Kellen had supposed them to be when the agent informed him they would be taking care of his baggage. The boys didn't appear to be twins, but that was only because one of them was half a head taller than the other. Except for the disparity in their stature, there was little enough difference to distinguish them.

"These are my grandsons," Collins said. It was almost a sigh. "Stand up straight, boys. Mind your manners. Stop jabbing."

Kellen watched the boys come to attention as if they'd heard a whip crack, but Collins hadn't raised his voice in the least. Kellen cast a glance back to see if the agent was threatening his grandsons with the brass bell, but no, he had already returned to the stool, his long expression more indicative of martyrdom than menace.

"Introduce yourselves, boys," Collins told them.

The taller of the pair, and in Kellen's estimation the elder by a year, maybe two, stepped forward first. "Cabot Theodore Collins. Folks call me Rabbit on account of me being fast as one."

Before Kellen could respond to this overture, the boy who was not Rabbit inched forward until he was sharp elbow to sharp elbow with his brother. "I'm Carpenter Addison Collins, but everyone but my granny calls me Finn on account of I like it better than Carpenter."

"Well, yes," Kellen said carefully, and wondered why he hadn't thought to choose a better name for himself when he was eight. "Finn. Of course."

Finn said, "*Carp*-enter. Fish have fins. See?"

"Yes, I do. Clever."

Jefferson Collins eyed his grandsons. "This gentleman wants to go to the Pennyroyal. You two think you can manage?"

The boys began to dance in place before Collins finished. "Is all that yours, mister?" Rabbit asked, jerking his thumb over his shoulder to indicate the trunks.

"It is."

Finn turned around to look where his brother was pointing. "Sure. We can put all that on the wagon. Won't be a bit of bother."

"Then get to it," Collins said, and the boys were out the door with significantly less commotion than when they entered. "They'll bring the buckboard around, back it up to the platform, and drag the trunks over to the bed. Won't take them but a few minutes. And in case you're wondering why they're so eager, it's because they like to visit with the widder."

"Good to know. I thought they sized me up as someone who would give them money for their trouble."

"Could be they did, but it won't hurt them to learn different." Collins picked up several envelopes and neatly squared them off, tapping one corner against the countertop. "You never did tell me your name," he said casually.

"You never did ask."

Collins chuckled. "You know what? I don't think I will. Nothing wrong with speculating on it until the boys get back from the hotel."

"You think they'll wheedle it out of me?"

The station agent spoke quite sincerely. "Wheedle? You count yourself fortunate if they don't set your hair on fire."

Bitter Springs had a wide main street typical of cattle towns that were serviced by the railroad. Corrals near the station accommodated the herd until the cows were driven single file onto the waiting cattle cars. Except for a half-dozen horses milling around close to the livery, the corrals were empty.

In contrast, the thoroughfare and the wooden walkways on either side of it were crowded. From his cushioned perch on the buckboard, Kellen observed that the station agent's grandsons knew everyone in town, or at least everyone that was out and about. In spite of a clear azure sky and a sun suspended overhead like a crystal ball, there was a chill in the air. It began to settle deeply in Kellen's bones almost as soon as he left the station. He sat between Rabbit and Finn with the collar of his leather duster turned up and the brim of his black Stetson turned down. For their part, the boys didn't seem to notice the sharp bite of the wind and frequently pulled down their scarves to call out an enthusiastic greeting to a passerby. Their cheeks were positively apple red with windburn and excitement, and Kellen thought the latter's influence might be the greater one.

Rabbit held the reins loosely, letting the dappled mare meander at a pace a three-legged mule could outrun, while Finn, often in the middle of his commentary about the town and its inhabitants, repeated his request to be allowed to have his turn.

Kellen turned his attention from the brotherly bickering by making mental notes as the buckboard passed one establishment after another. He learned that Mr. Ransom operated the livery and what he didn't know about horses wasn't worth knowing. Mr. and Mrs. Johnson owned the mercantile for dry goods and every kind of whatnot, including things Finn wasn't sure there was a use for. The land office was where Mr. Harry Sample and his cousin, Mr. Charles Sample, worked. Mrs. Garvin and her daughters, Millicent and Marianna, fashioned clothes and hats for the ladies and sometimes shirts for men as long as the shirts were for fancy occasions and not for range riding. The kind of clothes that a man needed for long days in the saddle and nights on the ground could be bought at Ted Rush's hardware along with tools for every particular job. Mr. Burnside was the town druggist, but his wife worked behind the soda fountain and made cherry phosphates for two pennies, or one if that's all you had and you asked her real nice.

There was a bathhouse and laundry owned by the Taylors, and a barbershop next door where you could get yourself nicked proper by Mr. Stillwell's apprentice if you didn't know enough to ask for Mr. Stillwell. Mr. Webb managed the Cattlemen's Trust Bank, although there was no sense to the name, Finn said, because his grandfather told him that cattlemen didn't really trust banks and spent their money as fast as they earned it on cards and dancing girls.

"There aren't any dancing girls in Bitter Springs," Finn said. "Leastways not the kind that kick their legs so high in the air you can see . . ." He leaned forward, looked around Kellen for his brother, and asked, "What do you call it?"

"France," Rabbit said. "They kick their legs so high you can see France."

Finn nodded. He looked up at Kellen. "You ever seen France?"

Kellen sighed feelingly. "Not in a long while."

"I almost saw it once," said Finn.

"You did not," said Rabbit. He shot Kellen a wise-beyond-his-years glance. "He did not."

"Did," Finn insisted. "*Nat Church and the Frisco Fancy.* Remember that?"

Surprised, Kellen interrupted. "You read that novel?"

Rabbit answered. "He didn't. Pap read it to us. Finn mostly stared at the dancing girl on the cover."

"So did you," said Finn. He puckered his lips and made kissing sounds. "You said you were going to marry her."

"Not her. Someone as pretty as her, though."

"Ain't no one as pretty as her." Finn nudged Kellen and offered a confidential aside. "If Pap held the book up just right, I could about see up her underskirts all the way to France."

Kellen nodded. "She did have a kick like a mule."

"That's what Nat Church said, too. I remember because Pap had a laugh about it. You know that story, mister?"

"I do."

"There's more of them, but Granny, well, she won't let Pap read them to us anymore. She says they're . . ." Frowning, he leaned forward again to look around Kellen and catch his brother's eye. "What is it that Granny says they are?"

"Unfit."

"She doesn't say that. What's the other word?"

Rabbit sighed. "Gruesome."

Finn sat back, satisfied. "Gruesome. I expect that's because there's blood and knife fights and shooting and such."

"I expect you're right," said Kellen.

"You shoot many people, mister?"

Rabbit's head jerked around and he glared at his brother. "We said we weren't going to ask him."

"You said. I didn't. I want to know. What about it, mister? How many people have you shot?"

Kellen could see the hotel on the right up ahead, but at the wagon's current speed, it might be as long as ten minutes before they reached it. They had just passed the marshal's office and jailhouse, and neither boy mentioned it as a point of interest, further proof their attention was solely focused on him. The station agent's grandsons were living up to their advance notice, and Kellen made the decision to surrender. "The name's Coltrane. Kellen Coltrane."

Rabbit took the reins in one fist and held out an open hand. "Good to meet you, Mr. Coltrane."

Finn asked, "You related to the Coltranes from Denver? Mister and Missus stay here when they're taking the train to Sacramento. They probably stop other places because Missus has the rheumatism, but they talk about here like it's the best. Mostly that's true. So, you kin to them?"

"I'm not, no."

"They're real nice. Don't think they ever shot anyone."

"How about that."

Finn's bright blue eyes narrowed on Kellen's profile. "You're not sayin', is that it?"

"I'm not sayin'."

"We saw the guns," Finn said.

Rabbit groaned at his brother's confession, but Kellen gave no sign that he'd heard anything at all.

Finn went on. "Are you figurin' on endin' trouble in Bitter Springs or causin' it? It could be that there's folks here that would hire you and your guns. Unless you already signed on with the Burdicks. That'd just be a shame. A real shame."

Rabbit flung an arm past Kellen's chest and shoved Finn's shoulder. "Will you shut up?"

"What? He doesn't shoot kids. You don't, do you?"

Kellen set his jaw and kept his eyes on the hotel. He spoke softly between clenched teeth. "I've never been tempted before."

"See?" Finn said to his brother. Then the full import of what Kellen said came home to roost, and he pressed his lips tightly together.

Rabbit felt compelled to explain. "It was an accident about the guns," he said. "The bag was heavier than I thought so Finn was helping out. We grabbed the opposite handles at the same time and the bag opened. The Colts were there, right on top. Guess you wanted it that way so you could get at them quick. I figure you for a detective with the railroad, but Granny says Finn's got a lurid imagination, and he figures you for a shootist."

It was an earnestly delivered explanation. Kellen nodded once, accepting it as close to the truth as he was likely to hear. "Your grandfather figures me for a gambling man."

Rabbit made a dismissive motion while holding the reins. The mare sidled to the left. "He doesn't know about the Colts. Besides, Pap thinks everyone's a gambler, but that's because our father is. That'd be Pap's son. On the road to ruin, Granny says."

"Your father doesn't live in Bitter Springs?"

"Used to. Now he rides the Union Pacific. And plays cards with men who have more money than sense."

Kellen supposed that Rabbit was repeating something he heard regularly from one or both of his grandparents.

"Maybe you met our pa," Finn said. "Thomas Jefferson Collins."

"No, I'm afraid not."

Finn's shoulders sagged. "Didn't think so."

"I don't play cards with professional gamblers. It's unlikely that our paths would cross."

"Oh." Kellen heard the boy's disappointment. He laid one hand on Finn's knee and placed the other over Rabbit's doubled-up fists. He tugged the reins to the right and gave Finn's knee a squeeze.

They traveled the last one hundred yards to the Pennyroyal in silence.

Walter Mangold leaned his broom against the porch rail the moment the buckboard stopped in front of the hotel.

The springy buckboards were sagging under the weight of

the trunks. "Both these trunks yours, sir?" he asked the stranger in the front.

Finn spoke up first. "And the bag. Better not forget the bag."

"Right," said Walt. "Why don't you and Rabbit take one end of a trunk while I take the other? Pass me the reins, Rabbit. I'll tether Ginny."

"I got it," Rabbit said, jumping down.

Once Finn was over the seat, Kellen stood. "I'll take my bag." He jumped lightly off the wagon and onto the porch steps at the same time Rabbit climbed up to help his brother. Kellen took the valise from the boys, making a fist around both handles to make certain it wouldn't open, and swung it against his thigh. He was prepared for the heaviness of the bag as he hadn't been when he carried it off the train. The extra weight of it was now explained.

Nat Church. Kellen remembered seeing Church bent over in his seat, riffling through his own valise. If he had gotten there a few moments earlier, he might have caught the older man in the act of transferring the guns. It made Kellen wonder what else Church had redistributed. There had been nothing in the former marshal's bag to identify him as a citizen of anywhere, and the single photograph of a handsome woman they all assumed was Church's dead wife was a standard studio portrait. The gold lettering in the right-hand corner that might have told them the name of the studio had faded to illegibility. When the doctor suggested that Mr. Church should carry the photograph to his grave, the conductor agreed. The rest of Church's belongings became the property of the railroad.

Except for those things Nat Church had not wanted the railroad to have.

While Walt, Rabbit, and Finn saw to the off-loading of his trunks, Kellen went inside.

He set the valise at his feet before he tapped the bell at the registration desk. He looked around while he waited for someone to appear. Above the walnut wainscoting, the walls were painted butter yellow. There was a bench just below the stairs for the weary traveler, and an area rug fashioned with the colors of every burnt shade of a high plains sunset covered most of the polished hardwood floor. Sunlight from the windows at his back dappled the walls and rug and . . .

And set the woman's hair on fire.

Blinking would have been too obvious. Instead, Kellen's wintry, blue-gray eyes narrowed a fraction as he took in the curling flames leaping and dancing away from the woman's scalp. Some might call that color copper, but Kellen Coltrane thought that understated the brilliance of the blaze and didn't explain why he had been struck dumb. It wasn't until she stepped from sunlight into relative shadow that he remembered why he was standing at the front desk of the Pennyroyal.

"I'm looking for the Widow Berry."

"Are you? About what?"

Kellen arched an eyebrow. He couldn't decide if she was being protective of the widow or if caution was in her nature. More than caution, he thought. Suspicion.

"About a room, for one thing," said Kellen. He spoke more firmly when he added, "And business."

She stepped closer, close enough for him to catch the fragrance of lavender. Her dress was plain, severely cut, and crisply pressed. He imagined her flicking lavender water over the dull green fabric before she set an iron to it and thinking herself daring for having done so.

"Mr. Church?"

Kellen watched her put out a hand, not to take his, but more tentatively than that, in the way a person does when there's a need to confirm that something is real. Her slender fingers hovered just above his elbow for several long moments then fell away. She didn't step back as he'd expected her to. Rather, she subjected his face to the kind of scrutiny that a wife was apt to employ when she expected to catch her husband in a lie. He stood for it because there was no harm in doing so, and just as important, it amused him.

The commotion at the entrance as the boys and Walt carried in the first trunk did not distract her from her study.

"Which room, Mrs. Berry?" Rabbit asked.

"Mr. Coltrane needs the biggest one you have," said Finn.

"Two trunks and a bag," Walt said. "Room six would probably be best."

"You're not Mr. Church," Raine said.

"You're the Widow Berry," said Kellen.

Finn nudged Rabbit when the three adults began talking at the same time. "When people get to talking like that, I'm always wishing I had Pap's bell."

Chapter Two

Kellen stopped unpacking to respond to the knock at his door. "Who is it?" There was a long pause, so long that Kellen began to think he'd only imagined the interruption.

"Sue Hage, Mr. Coltrane. The maid."

Kellen opened the door just enough for his frame to fill the space. The young woman in the hallway showed no interest in trying to see past him. On the contrary, not only did she keep her eyes averted, she took a rather sizable step backward. He thought she was probably not yet twenty, but certainly she was old enough to give a better accounting of herself. Her fingers twisted nervously in her apron, and she was biting down hard on one corner of her lower lip.

"Mrs.Berrysentmetoaskifyouraccommodationsare-satisfactory." She darted him a glance as she sucked in a breath. "Are they?"

Kellen had to mull the words over before he could seize their meaning. "I have need of a table and a chair," he said. "If that can be arranged, my accommodations will be entirely satisfactory."

The request appeared to flummox the maid. She fidgeted

with one of her long, straw-colored braids and shifted her slight weight from side to side.

Finally she said, "We do not serve meals to guests in their rooms."

"Then it's a good thing there are other uses for a table and a chair. You may tell Mrs. Berry that I intend to take my meals in the dining room."

"Yes, sir."

Kellen did not wait to hear if she had more to say. He shut the door.

Emily Ransom cornered her friend in the deserted dining room. "You spoke to him?" she whispered. "What is he like? Was he wearing his guns?"

Sue glanced around—the second check she'd made of her surroundings since Emily waylaid her. "You better let me pass, Emily Ransom. Mrs. Sterling is going to give you what for if she catches you lollygagging."

"I do not care about what for." Emily held her ground, giving Sue no opportunity to escape. "Just warn me if she's waggling her wooden spoon."

Sue grabbed the ends of her braids before Emily took to yanking on them like they were udders. "He shut the door in my face."

Emily's bright blue eyes widened a fraction. "He did not."

"There is no point in you asking me questions if you are not going to believe what I tell you."

"I believe you." She crossed her heart to add emphasis. "Did you speak to him at all?"

"Of course I did." Without releasing her braids, Sue recounted her conversation word for word. "And then he shut the door."

"Well, had you finished your piece?"

"Yes, but he did not know that."

"Perhaps he did."

"I should have known you would take his side, Emily

Ransom. You already have it in your mind that you can flirt with him."

Emily was not at all offended. "What I would like to know is why you don't have it in your mind. The man is as handsome as sin, and he's traveling alone."

"Maybe that's because no good woman will have him." Sue let go of her braids and set her hands on her hips. "And how do you know he is handsome as sin? You didn't see him."

"Ah-ha! He *is* handsome. I knew it. You only get yourself in a knot when they are prettier than dew on a rose."

Sue flushed. "Now you're speaking nonsense."

"I don't think so."

"Maybe he was wearing his guns. Did you think of that? Maybe that's why I'm tongue-tied."

"Was he?"

"No."

"Could you see them in the room?"

"No."

"Do you think Rabbit and Finn were lying about the guns?"

"Wouldn't surprise me if they were. They like to make themselves important."

Emily could not disagree with that. "Maybe I'll ask him about the guns."

Sue's mouth parted, snapped shut, and then parted again. "You wouldn't."

"I might." She showed Sue her saucy smile, the one that rarely failed to get noticed by male guests at the Pennyroyal. "I just might."

Sue pursed her lips in disapproval. She was one year Emily's junior, but in ways calculated by maturity and common sense, she was her senior by a decade.

"Oh, do not be such a prude," Emily said dismissively. "What color are his eyes?"

Sue hesitated.

"Did you even look at his eyes?"

"I looked," said Sue. "I'm thinking. It's not easy to describe that color that sits on the horizon in winter. You know, when the sun is still low in the sky, and the day is going to be nothing but cold. Bitter cold."

Emily blinked. "Why, Sue, you *did* look."

"I told you I did. Looked away, too. That's the kind of eyes he has. You want to look, but then you want to look away."

Emily was thoughtful. "Maybe the boys weren't telling tales. It sounds as if Mr. Coltrane has the eyes of a killer."

"I did not say that."

"Eyes like a wolf, I bet."

"I didn't say that either."

Emily ignored her. "Was he still wearing his hat?"

"No."

"What about his hair?"

"What about it? Do you think there is such a thing as hair of a killer?"

"I won't know until you tell me about it," Emily said practically.

"It's thick and unruly. Too longish for my tastes, riding on his collar the way it does. Maybe he'll want the barber. You could point him in Mr. Stillwell's direction. Better yet, tell him to ask for Dave Rogers."

"And see him scalped? I do not believe I will, no."

"Then perhaps you'll suggest a shave."

Emily lightly rubbed her cheek and pretended to think about it. "I suppose that depends on how much his stubble burns my tender skin."

Sue had had enough. She put her hands on Emily's shoulders and gave her a push. "Go. I know who you're sweet on even if you won't say. Just put Mr. Coltrane out of your mind. I have work to do, and I have to find Mrs. Berry."

"You found her," Raine said, entering the dining room from the lobby. Both girls flushed deeply, unsure how much she had heard. "Emily, I believe you have better work to occupy you."

"Yes, ma'am." She turned sharply on her boot heel and hurried toward the kitchen.

Raine watched Emily go before she set her sights on Sue.

Without preamble, she asked, "Mr. Coltrane?"

"He asked for a table and chair," said Sue. "He says if he has them, his accommodations will be entirely satisfactory."

"Entirely satisfactory. He said that?"

"His exact words, ma'am."

"You told him we don't serve meals in the room."

"I told him. He said they have other uses." When Raine did not immediately respond, the maid added in confidential tones, "I had a premonition that he was going to be bothersome."

Raine felt a smile tug at the corner of her mouth. It was a relief to know amusement was still possible. She was certain she had lost all appreciation for it upon making the acquaintance of Kellen Coltrane. "A premonition? Really? What do you suppose provoked it?"

Sue looked at Raine in surprise, as if the answer should be obvious. "You saw he has two trunks same as I did. A man hauling two trunks across the country must be persnickety about his person. I don't know anyone in Bitter Springs with enough clothes to fill two trunks."

"And a bag," Raine said, tempering her smile. "Do not forget he also has a valise."

"Well, yes, but we know there are guns in the bag."

"Rabbit and Finn say so. Did you see them?"

"No, ma'am, but then Mr. Coltrane kept the bag close. Carried it in himself and didn't hand it over for Walt to carry up to his rooms. I say that's a man who is persnickety about his belongings, and persnickety about every other thing. Mark my words; it's a table and a chair today and johnnycakes in his room tomorrow. Plain bothersome."

"Let us hope you are wrong, but remember, what cannot be changed must be endured, and Sue . . ."

"Yes, ma'am?"

"We will endeavor to endure in silence. Please keep your premonition to yourself. If you're correct, everyone will realize it soon enough." Raine waited to receive Sue's assurance that she would not breathe a word before she went on. "There's a small table and some chairs in the storage room. Help Walt clear the table and give it a polish, then tell him to deliver it and a chair to Mr. Coltrane."

Sue left in search of Walt, and Raine contemplated her next step. It was a certainty that she had to speak to Mr. Coltrane. Their brief exchange was wholly unsatisfactory, taking place as it did in front of an audience.

Kellen waited until the table and chair arrived before he began to unpack the valise.

Are you figurin' on endin' trouble in Bitter Springs or causin' it?

Finn had posed a good question, and Kellen had no answer for it. He was hoping the contents of the valise would provide a clue. Nat Church's intentions remained a mystery.

Should find her . . . tell her . . . she's waiting. That told him exactly . . . nothing. Nat Church's message did not seem cryptic when Kellen thought Pennyroyal referred to a person, not a place. Now that he knew differently, he had at least as many questions as Finn Collins and nowhere to direct them.

Kellen removed the guns and examined them one at a time. The lighter model was a .45 caliber centerfire Colt with a four-inch barrel and pearl grip. It was the preferred weapon of shopkeepers and sheriffs. Kellen was not surprised that Nat Church owned one. The second weapon was another in the Peacemaker line, a .44-40 caliber centerfire six-shooter with a seven-and-one-half-inch barrel and ivory grip. With a practiced hand, it was renowned for its accuracy at longer distances, the kind of weapon drawn by one man with the express intention of killing another.

The chambers of both guns were loaded. Kellen left them that way. Under his shaving kit, he found two boxes of ammunition, one for each of the Colts. He set them beside the weapons before he dug deeper into his valise. He removed two shirts, an extra pair of suspenders, a nightshirt, the brush and comb set, and his journals before he came to the books that filled the base of the bag. He removed the books and riffled the pages of each one.

He found one letter tucked between the pages of *Nat Church and the Watchers.* Two others had been secreted in *Nat Church and the Committee on Vigilance.* Kellen could only shake his head. The man who called himself Nat Church had a deeply ingrained sense of the absurd.

Kellen glanced toward the door when he heard footsteps approaching. He waited, sensing a hesitation in the footfalls as they neared his door, but the person in the hallway passed on. It wasn't until quiet returned that Kellen realized he had dropped the letters and that his right hand was hovering over the .44.

Kellen stretched his legs under the table and leaned back, then he examined the letters for their chronology and began to read.

July 22, 1888

I hope you will accept this letter as a proper introduction when there can be no other. A notice in the Chicago Times-Herald dated June 3 has recently come to my attention. It is by mere accident that I was in possession of the paper as it was left behind by a guest at the Pennyroyal Saloon and Hotel and was saved for the purpose of cleaning windows. I mention this because you might wonder at the delay in my correspondence and question my sincerity. Upon spying the notice, I rescued the Times-Herald from the bin. There was much to consider before setting my pen to paper, and for such delay as was caused by my cogitation, I accept responsibility. I want you to know this because I am now firm in my intentions, and this should be a consideration in my favor.

If I have understood the full meaning of your notice in the Times-Herald, and I believe I have, then I would like to invite you to travel to Bitter Springs and apply your talents on behalf of our town. I can promise you compensation commensurate to your skill and at least the equal of your most recent engagement. You might think I have consulted with others before making this offer of hire, but you would be wrong. I own this decision, and you would be working for me. If it is not clear to you already, I am a woman, and if working for a woman is a circumstance too grievous to contemplate, then you should not reply.

Having stated my aim to employ your services, I find that I am hesitant to lay the whole of the problem before you. If you are sufficiently interested and not otherwise engaged, I remain hopeful of your reply.

The letter was unsigned. Prudent, Kellen thought, given the nature of the correspondence. He turned the paper over, saw it contained no afterthoughts, and set it aside. Choosing the letter dated September 2, he began reading.

I am in receipt of your inquiry from August 13. While I am resolute in pursuing this action, I must remain guarded in my responses to your questions. It is understandable that you require more information, but I am also confident that if you journey to Bitter Springs and learn of our troubles, you will be persuaded by what you see and hear. You can be sure I will pay for reasonable expenses you incur on your journey and a ticket for your return trip if you elect to leave.

You asked me to be more exact in explaining my expectations. I expect that your involvement will save lives. I can be no more exact than that. It is my most fervent hope that your presence in Bitter Springs will put an end to bloodshed, not contribute to it. I want to be clear that it is protection I desire, but know that I have come to understand that protection in Bitter Springs requires more than the weight of law and judgment from the bench.

Mr. Benton Sterling, a fine husband, father, and grandfather, a man of principle and purpose, and the town marshal for five years, was ambushed and murdered twenty-two months ago. Mr. Moses T. Parker, a lawyer from Rawlins who stood for the people, also came to a bad end. Mr. John Hood, our mayor and a juryman, left town before Christmas and came back in a box at Easter. No one has heard from Mr. Hank Thompson, another juryman, and some of us, myself included, fear the worst. His mother suffers in his absence as his good humor was a source of comfort to her.

I am of the opinion that a Peacemaker will be required.

Perhaps you are not interested in our troubles and do not wish to involve yourself. If that is so, then I am much mistaken and give you yet another opportunity not to reply.

Most sincerely,
Mrs. Adam Berry

* * *

Kellen looked up from the letter to the pair of Colts. Nat Church had packed his Peacemakers. It was difficult to know if Mrs. Berry's reference was to the gun or a diplomat. She might very well have meant both. He set the letter with the other but did not pick up the third. Instead, he reached into the pocket of his vest and removed the badge he had taken from Nat Church, a six-pointed star with rounded tips, engraved by hand and bearing the words "U.S. Marshal."

He turned that badge over and examined the pin. It was bent halfway along its length. He didn't try to straighten it. Nat Church hadn't.

He had seen a great many badges, some of them on lawmen still living, too many of them on lawmen at death. They were a collectible curiosity in the East, where they could be purchased for a quarter. He knew women who wore them as brooches or as a garnish on their hats. Not all of them sold as genuine were in fact so, but he didn't believe that was the case here. This badge bore the faint evidence that it had been pounded and sawed from American or perhaps Spanish coin. The tarnish at the points and along the outline of the letters added to its authentic look. The act of pinning and unpinning it to different vests over the years added a layer of sweat and oils to the back that polishing could never quite erase.

Kellen returned the badge to his vest pocket and took up the last letter. This one indicated it was written September thirtieth, less than a month ago.

I am now in receipt of your correspondence from September 22. I am heartened that you are accepting the offer I made and look forward to your arrival in Bitter Springs on October 14. Do not distress yourself if your arrival is delayed by heavy snowfall. Winter can arrive early and unexpectedly in the Territories, but the railroad is prepared for adversity and has constructed snowsheds for the protection of the passengers but mostly the engines. If I may offer advice in the best interest of your comfort, it would be wise for you to pack such foodstuffs as can sustain you in the event you find yourself several days in a snowshed.

Kellen's mouth quirked. Here was the explanation for the sack of jerky, half a loaf of bread, and five apples they found when looking through Nat Church's valise for clues. As it happened, the food was unnecessary, but perhaps Mrs. Berry would be comforted that Mr. Church heeded her advice.

Whether or not there is snow, you should expect to find cold weather in Bitter Springs at this time of year. The locals will tell you the wind is breezy, but I am a relatively recent arrival in town and will tell you the truth. As winter approaches, the wind is a gale, and the good citizens turn their collars up to their ears or wear scarves that cover every portion of their face save for their eyes.

I have taken the liberty of arranging accommodations for you. Unless you express dissatisfaction with the arrangement, you will be staying at the Pennyroyal Hotel where I am the proprietress. I manage a clean establishment with such comforts as you might find in hotels in Chicago, St. Louis, or as I have been told by guests, New York City.

Kellen looked up from the letter and glanced around the room. The wide, iron-frame bed was smoothly turned out with a colorful quilt, two plump pillows, and a second quilt folded neatly at the foot. Small tables stood on either side of the bed at its head, each one a resting place for an oil lamp. The one on the left held a carafe and glass for water. The walnut armoire easily held his clothes and had a sufficient number of drawers on one side to store his incidentals. There was a stove in one corner and a bucket heaped with coal beside it. Neither the maid nor Walt had considered the temperature sufficiently cold to fire it up. Kellen was sorely tempted.

The bathing room was a revelation with its hot and cold running water and deep, claw-footed tub. He had a modest idea of the expense involved in making those amenities available in a hotel and wondered about the depth of Mrs. Berry's purse. Her first letter to Nat Church indicated she was prepared to pay generously for his services, and her second letter offered compensation for his journey whether or not he accepted her terms.

He did not think the Pennyroyal could account for all of her income. On the way to his rooms at the end of the hall, he counted only five other doors, and when he inquired about accommodations on the third floor, he was informed that the Widder Berry was in sole possession of those rooms.

After consideration, I have concluded it is better that our arrangement remains private, and others see our association merely as hotel guest and hotel owner. Therefore, I will not be meeting you at the station, but you can be assured that transportation and assistance with your belongings will be made available to you as they are to all of our guests. You only have to inquire after the Pennyroyal Hotel.

Finally, I have noted that you chose not to sign your previous letters. The situation in Bitter Springs is such that I must be able to identify you beyond any doubt. At the very least I require your name, and if you can suggest some additional manner in which I will know you, I would welcome it.

I will depend upon hearing from you once more before your arrival.

Sincerely,
Mrs. Adam Berry

Kellen did not recall tipping his chair back on its rear legs, nor did he think he was so engrossed with reading and reflection that he would not hear someone approaching his door, but at the first knock he nearly upended the chair and himself. Grabbing the edge of the table saved him from an ignominious fall.

His guess was that it was Widder Berry herself at the door.

He carefully folded the letters and returned them to the bottom of his valise. He packed several more items on top, closed the bag, and nudged it back under the bed with the toe of his boot. The only items remaining on the table when he invited his caller to enter were the Colts.

Raine closed the door behind her but did not step away from it. She nodded briefly. "Mr. Coltrane."

He appreciated her straightforward gaze. She could hardly miss the Colts, but she ignored them in favor of giving him her full attention. She had a husky, smoky voice that could not help undermining a good man's resolve whether or not that was her intent.

Kellen started to rise; she waved him back. "Mrs. Berry."

"I escorted Rabbit and Finn back to the station. I just returned from there."

Kellen nodded. That explained the deep pink color in her cheeks. Bitter Springs breezes. It had been tempting to flatter himself that he might be the cause.

A small crease appeared between Raine's eyebrows. "I spoke to Mr. Collins. He told me there was a murder on the last train that went through here."

"So I understand."

"You were on that train."

"I was."

"He offered the name of the murdered man." She pursed her lips. "You could have said something downstairs."

"I could have, but why would I?" Kellen shifted in his chair, drawing his legs from under the table and stretching them out in her direction. He set his forearms against his midriff, threaded his fingers, and lightly tapped the pads of his thumbs together. He regarded her with an absence of expression as she struggled to rein in her frustration.

"I should think that would be obvious. You heard me mistake you for Mr. Church."

"Yes, I did hear that." Kellen did not think her level gaze could cut more sharply, but it did. Her green eyes glittered brilliantly. He added, "And I was supposed to say . . . ?" He let the question hang for a long moment. When she did not respond, he said, "I regret to inform you, Mrs. Berry, but the man you've taken me for is dead. Would that have satisfied?"

Her nostrils flared slightly, and for the first time since entering the room, her gaze moved to the guns. It quickly returned to him. "Did the Burdicks hire you?"

Kellen didn't answer right away. He cast his thoughts back and tried to remember how he knew that name. The clear, youthful tones of Finn's voice came to him suddenly. *Unless you already signed on with the Burdicks. That'd be a shame.*

"What is it you really want to know?" he asked her.

"Did you murder Mr. Church?"

"I think you know the answer to that. I take you for a woman of reasonably good sense. I imagine you already put that question to Mr. Collins, and he told you I wasn't the killer. I had to satisfy the conductor of the train as to my innocence before I could leave the train at Bitter Springs. I would be surprised to learn if that wasn't communicated to Mr. Collins when he received word about the murder."

Raine's fingers curled into the stiff fabric of her gown. "Who *are* you?"

"Kellen Coltrane. I signed the registry."

"I know. I watched you."

"Then I am afraid I don't understand the question."

"I take you for a man of reasonably good sense," she said crisply. "Do not give me cause to regret it."

His lips quirked once and then he was sober. "All right, Mrs. Berry, but you must answer a question first."

"We'll see."

"Mr. Collins spoke of you as the Widow Berry."

"Widder," she corrected.

"Yes, you're right. That's exactly what he said."

"It's Finn's fault."

Kellen's chuckle stayed at the back of his throat. "I'm sure it is."

"It stuck."

Although she continued to keep her gaze leveled on him, he had a sense that she wanted to look away. He watched her draw a shallow breath and release it slowly. "Are you, in fact, Mrs. Adam Berry?"

"Is that your question, Mr. Coltrane? The one I must answer?"

"It is."

"Then, yes, I am Mrs. Adam Berry."

Kellen drew his legs back and stood, slowly unfolding out of the chair so as not to give the impression he meant to launch himself at her. He was impressed that she held her ground as he approached. He stopped when he was within arm's length and extended his hand.

"It is a pleasure to meet you, Mrs. Adam Berry. Nat Church sends his regards."

She did not put her hand in his. Her hands flew to her open mouth just in time to stifle a sob. Kellen reached for her when he saw her begin to buckle, but she caught herself without his help and stepped back so she could lean against the door. He waited to see if she would slide down the length of it. She didn't. She stayed pressed to the door, hands at her mouth, eyes closed, and Kellen had the impression she was praying or giving thanks for a prayer answered. In time, she straightened. Her hands fell back to her sides, and she returned to searching his face, unaware or uncaring that her stare had been made softer by the wash of unshed tears.

"Is it true?" she asked on a thread of sound. "He's really dead?"

"Yes, it's true."

"You were there?"

"I was. Not when the knife was slipped into him, but later. He sat with me."

"You knew him, then."

"Better than most, I suspect."

She nodded. "It's my fault that he's dead."

"I doubt that. He certainly didn't blame you. The truth is, he held himself responsible." Kellen turned slightly and indicated the chair he had vacated. "Won't you sit down?"

She hesitated. "I think I will, yes. Thank you."

He stepped aside to let her pass. Her skirt brushed him as she went by, and the fragrance of lavender lingered pleasantly. "I have a flask of whiskey. Would you share a drink with me?"

She shook her head.

Kellen went to one of the bedside tables and opened a drawer. He took out a silver flask and poured a small measure of whiskey into the glass beside the water carafe. He did not return the flask to the drawer but laid it on top of the table. He sat on one of his trunks in his guest's line of sight.

"You should have asked for two chairs," she said.

"I think Miss Hage was overwhelmed by the request for one."

A smile touched her lips. "I'm sure she was." The smile vanished as quickly as it came.

"And I don't make it a practice to entertain guests," said Kellen. "One chair discourages them."

"I am more of an intruder than guest, I think."

He didn't contradict her and commented instead on the worry that shadowed her expression. "You look as if you're wondering if you made a mistake."

"I don't know you," she said quietly. "Not at all. 'Nat Church sends his regards' is hardly a calling card. I think I might have assumed too much."

Kellen carefully set his glass beside him on the trunk lid. He reached into his vest pocket and took out the badge. Holding it between his thumb and forefinger, he held it out for her to see. "Better than a calling card, I think."

She sank her teeth in her bottom lip and nodded jerkily. Kellen kept the badge extended until she found her voice. "He said I would know him by the badge. He would show it to me, and I would know him. He described it in detail so there could be no mistaking it."

Kellen gave no indication of the relief he felt. When Mrs. Berry wrote that she would appreciate a manner of identifying the man she was hiring with something besides his name, Kellen wondered what Mr. Church might have proposed. He left the Colts on the table to see if they were Nat Church's other calling card, but the Peacemakers engaged more suspicion, not trust.

"Would you like to examine it?"

She leaned forward and put out her hand but couldn't quite reach it. Kellen stood and closed the distance. She thanked him. He remained standing while she looked it over, turning it onto its face almost immediately. She ran her forefinger lightly across the length of the bent pin.

"It's his," she said and gave it back.

Kellen returned the badge to his vest pocket before he sat. "I want you to be certain."

"I'm certain. He told me the pin was bent."

"Did he tell you how?" he asked. A smile edged his mouth, as if he might know something she didn't.

"As a matter of fact, yes. His wife bent it when she tried to tear it off his vest."

Kellen tried to recall what Nat Church had said about his wife. *Wife would've tried to stop me.* "She wanted him to be done with the life he'd chosen."

"That is not surprising. A woman chooses her man. Her man chooses their life. In her place, I might have stomped on the thing."

Kellen didn't doubt it. There was no vehemence in her voice, just the stiff backbone of resolve. "He was a widower. Did he tell you that?"

"Yes."

"You didn't tell him you were a widder."

Her smile was a trifle crooked. "No, I didn't tell him that." She absently brushed away a few fiery strands of hair that fluttered across her cheek. "I wrote that I was the owner of the Pennyroyal. I thought that would be enough."

Kellen was not prepared to reveal that the letters she wrote to Nat Church were the source of almost everything he knew.

Whatever Nat Church's intentions, Kellen had been charged with going to the Pennyroyal. *Should find her . . . tell her . . . she's waiting.* And now that he knew the content of the letters, it seemed clear that the *she* in wait was Mrs. Berry. Perhaps Nat Church had only ever wanted him to tell Mrs. Berry that he wouldn't be coming.

Except that it didn't settle right with him to leave it there. He still wanted to know why a man was dead and a woman was in so much pain she could wound you with a look.

"I wasn't sure you *were* the owner when we met," he said. "I knew we would figure it out eventually, and so we have. You can appreciate my caution. Nat Church is dead for lack of it."

She lowered her head and stared at her folded hands. "I didn't think I had to warn him. No one knew he was . . ." Her head snapped up; suspicion narrowed her eyes. "Tell me again how you know what you know."

"He wanted me to know. He made sure I did."

"Why?"

"I can't speak to his reasons. He wasn't one for explaining things like that. He trusted me."

"He never wrote that he was bringing anyone with him."

"Perhaps because he didn't want you to know that he thought better about doing the job alone."

"So he chose you?"

Kellen smiled again. "Looks that way, doesn't it?" The smile disappeared. He picked up his glass, emptied it, then leaned forward and rested his forearms on his knees. He rolled the glass between his palms. "You played your cards close."

"Not close enough. He's dead. Bringing you along didn't keep him safe."

"He didn't ask me along to keep him safe. The job, as I understand it, is to keep you safe."

She flushed. Her folded hands tightened. "I never asked for that."

"You asked for protection for the town. You're part of the town, aren't you?"

Her flush deepened, but she did not respond to the rhetorical question. "Someone found out that he was coming here and killed him."

"You have to consider the possibility his murder had nothing at all to do with the reasons he was coming here. He was a lawman."

"Retired."

Kellen had suspected as much.

"Retired, yes, but not without enemies. Not everyone hangs, you know. Not everyone is shot dead. Some go to prison, some of them get out, and some of them who get out go looking." He thought he saw her shiver. He stopped rolling the glass. "Should I start a fire in the stove?"

She shook her head. "No, not on my account."

He moved the glass to the table as he stood. "Then on mine."

"Where are you from?" Before he could answer, she said, "And please don't say you're not from around here. There is no point in being obtuse when that much is certain. I put your accent east of the Mississippi. Northeast?"

"I didn't realize it was still obvious. I haven't lived there for years." Kellen set about lighting the tinder and nursing the fire. "New England, generally. New Haven, specifically."

"New Haven. Isn't there a college there?"

"Yale," he said. "You're thinking of Yale."

"No, I was thinking of Harvard."

He chuckled. "I don't think anyone except students and graduates much cares if you confuse them."

"I think you might be a graduate of one of them."

"Well, I am." He closed the door on the stove and held out his hands to warm them. Glancing over his shoulder at her, he said, "Yale, if that's your next question. My father is a professor there. Humanities."

"Humanities," she repeated. "What does that mean?"

"He studies and lectures in disciplines that elevate humankind. Ancient languages. History. Philosophy. Religion. He enjoys literature above all the rest. Ancient Greek literature."

"I see."

He saw her eyes dart to the guns. "I don't share his interests. It's a disappointment to him." He briskly rubbed his hands together and returned to his seat on the trunk. "What about you? I seem to recall that you're a newcomer to Bitter Springs. Am I remembering that right?"

"I wrote to Mr. Church that I was."

"Then he might have told me. I still have Finn's voice rattling in my brain, so it's difficult to recall where I heard it."

"Yes, well, Finn knows something about everyone in town. Rabbit knows the rest."

"They take after their grandfather."

"Their grandmother. Heather Collins knows it all, and if you forget that, she'll remind you. I've spoken to the boys about the guns. They gave me their word that they won't tell anyone else what they saw in your bag."

Kellen was not confident he could trust the boys, but it was clear to him that she did. "Good to know."

"I came here from Sacramento."

"With your husband."

A brief hesitation, then, "After Adam, not with him. He wasn't my husband until I got here." Her glance swiveled to the empty glass on the table. "I think I will take that drink if you don't mind."

"Of course. Let me see if I can find another glass."

"There should be one in the bathing room."

He returned with it in short order, splashed it with a good measure of whiskey, and handed it to her. "How long ago did you arrive in Bitter Springs?"

"Six years ago. Adam won the Pennyroyal in a card game."

Kellen's eyebrows lifted. "I've heard of things like that. Never knew them to be true."

"This is true. He won it in a poker game that lasted three days. It came down to Adam and Mr. Israel Dunkirk of the Pacific Coast Railway. They had already cleaned the lint from the pockets of every other man at the table. The Pennyroyal was just one of the holdings he took away."

"The game was here?"

"No, Sacramento. Adam had no business being at that table, except that he parlayed a small stake into a bigger one and eventually bought himself a seat."

"He was a gambler?"

"Not as a rule."

"Lucky then."

She shrugged. "Not as a rule. I've always assumed he cheated."

Kellen laughed.

"I'm serious," she said.

"I know you are."

She laughed then, too, and sipped her drink. "This is good whiskey. Very smooth."

"Better than the stock in your saloon?"

"Buy a few drinks and decide for yourself."

"I might."

"I'll reimburse you. Room and board. Your drinks. Whatever you like."

"You're hiring me?"

"Yes."

"The same arrangement you offered Mr. Church?"

"I don't know your experience. Perhaps you aren't as practiced."

Kellen refrained from pointing out that he was alive while Nat Church was very much not. Standing, he picked up the Colt with the ivory grip, hefted it once, and then expertly spun it clockwise, then counter, and finally pretended to holster it at his side. After a pause, he set it back on the table.

"That's all well and good, Mr. Coltrane, but nimble fingers don't necessarily mean a steady hand. I want to know if you can shoot the eye out of a chicken hawk when he's circling the henhouse."

"Probably not. Did Nat Church say he could?"

"No. But it might be useful."

"If we were after chicken hawks. But we're not, are we? I was thinking you were after larger prey. The Burdicks, for instance."

"I'm not after anyone," she said.

"Protection," he said. "A peacemaker."

"Yes."

"There might be a price."

She closed her eyes briefly. "I am not naïve."

Kellen was not certain he agreed. "Someone else has to make the first move."

She nodded.

"I thought that had already occurred. Didn't you tell Church there were men already dead?"

"I did, but every circumstance is different, and except

for . . ." Her voice trailed away. She cleared her throat and finished. "The proof of fault has not been established."

"Except for?" he asked. "It's what you don't say, Mrs. Berry, that holds real meaning. Except for what?"

"Not what," she said. "Who. Except for Ellen Wilson. I know which Burdick murdered her."

The name was unfamiliar to him. He had to ask, "Who is Ellen Wilson?"

"My sister."

Chapter Three

"What will you have tonight, Charlie? A whiskey or a shot of the white lightning?" Raine held up a bottle in each hand and cocked an eyebrow at Charlie Patterson as the cowboy stepped up to the bar. "If you've been out no more than three days, I recommend the whiskey. Longer than that, the white lightning."

Charlie grinned. He had a wide smile and eyes about as large and brown as the calves he drove to their mamas. He was sweet on Sue Hage, but like Emily Ransom, he didn't know how not to flirt. He winked at Raine. "Give me the white lightning. I was out in the cold all day. It felt like four."

She laughed and poured. "Take it over to the table by the piano. I'm watching the door tonight, and even if I weren't, I think Walt talked Sue into playing."

The smile that wreathed his face settled in his eyes. "Glad to hear it, Mrs. Berry. Surely, now, I'm glad to hear it."

She chased him off and immediately engaged another customer in conversation. Kellen Coltrane had not made an appearance since he had returned to his room after dinner. In the dining room, he had remained apart, choosing to sit by himself in spite of overtures by the couple from Springfield and Emily Ransom's attempts to pair him with Mr. Weyman, the whiskey drummer, before Mrs. Garvin arrived with her two comely daughters in tow. Mr. Coltrane even managed to beat back Mrs. Garvin without using a stick. This was mostly open range country, but her shootist knew how to set up a fence as prickly as barbed wire.

She had spoken to him at dinner, just a few words in passing as she made her rounds. It annoyed her that she found even that brief exchange of words difficult.

Perhaps it was because she had spoken to him of Ellen earlier. He was a stranger, and even after so much time had passed, it still seemed wrong to speak of her sister to someone from the outside. Ellen would have been the first to laugh at the notion that anyone was an outsider. Her sister had welcomed everyone. She had been genuinely kind, friendly to a fault. She had taken it to heart that people should be treated as she wanted to be treated. It had been her idea to hire Walter Mangold, and Raine had never regretted listening to her.

But Ellen's sweet nature meant she did not always see the wickedness that was around her, and when she saw it, she made excuses for it and tried to be kinder, more generous, as though she could change character that had meanness bred in the bone.

Raine feared little for herself, but it had been her life's work to fear for Ellen. In spite of her vigilance, she had failed her sister. Ellen was dead.

Kellen Coltrane deserved an explanation. Raine had offered none. Once Ellen's name passed her lips, her throat closed. She had meant to be matter of fact, the way she was when she and Mrs. Sterling talked about the day Ellen died, but emotion overwhelmed and words failed her. She could not say one more word than she already had. Silence had been her refuge. It had also been painful.

It could only have been more humiliating if she had cried.

She wondered what had gone through Mr. Coltrane's mind as she sat mute. He didn't press her with questions, offer sympathy, or in any way indicate that he was uncomfortable. He simply sat there, and she had the sense that he was not waiting her out, but waiting with her. It was unexpected and oddly calming.

She had finished her drink, found her voice in the bottom of that glass, and promised that she would speak to him later. He didn't ask her to define what later meant. He stood the same time she did, took her glass, and walked her to the door. He opened it for her. It all seemed rather vague now, as though she had passed time in a dream, and she forgave herself for the passing fancy that she was being courted like a woman who deserved it.

Jem Davis, one of the ranch hand regulars, snapped his fingers in front of Raine's face. He had hands like small hams and fingers as thick as sausages. He liked to say that as appendages they represented the best parts of a pig.

Raine jerked her head back. "Take your hand out of my face, Jem Davis. What do you want?"

"Two beers and a whiskey for me and my brothers." He used his chin to indicate the two young men collecting cards at the table closest to the stairs.

"You're not playing poker with your brothers, are you? Someone always gets hurt."

"Someone always cheats. At least when we're the only ones at the table, no one ends up dead."

"True." She set him up with his order. "Try not to break anything tonight."

He laid his money down and picked up his drinks, calling out to his brothers. "Jessop. Jake. The Widder Berry says I'm not allowed to break anything but your heads."

Raine's smile was indulgent as the brothers whooped. Shaking her head, she began to gather up empty glasses and line up clean ones.

The hardware store owner sidled up to the bar. "Did you hear about the murder?" Ted Rush asked.

"If you mean the one on the train, I heard. Mr. Collins told me." She hoped that by invoking Mr. Collins's name, she would end the conversation. Ted was surely going to quote the same source. "What can I get you, Ted?"

"Stomach's been giving me the devil lately. You have any of that ginger beer you make?"

"Some. I'll get you a glass, but you know you should stop at the drugstore and ask Mr. Burnside for something."

"I like your ginger beer better."

Raine disappeared into the back room and returned with a bottle. She uncorked it and poured a glass for Ted Rush. She slipped the cork back into place and put the bottle under the bar. "There's more if you take to feeling poorly."

"It's the killing that did it to me."

Raine had almost made her escape, but she was still turned too far toward Ted to pretend she hadn't heard. She did not want to ask a question so she kept her features expressionless and began folding bar rags.

"That's right," Ted said. "I was on the train on my way back from Cheyenne. The murder happened in the coach ahead of mine. I came that close to seeing what happened. Who knows, maybe if I'd chosen a different seat, I could have stopped it. Maybe I could have caught the killer."

And maybe the earth would open up and swallow her whole, Raine thought. It could happen, it just didn't seem very likely. She tried not to allow any part of her skepticism to show. Except for his elaborations, Ted Rush was an honest man, and he ran a respectable business that delivered denim, flannel, and leather goods to the cowmen. Raine had never met Ted's wife. Mrs. Rush died years before Raine came to Bitter Springs. Now in his early fifties, Ted was still alone and it seemed to be by his own choice. She supposed that didn't mean he wasn't lonely from time to time. She tried to be patient with his patter.

"I had to answer questions before I could leave the train," he told her. "Seems the dead man was going to Bitter Springs. I got a glimpse of him, and I had to say I never saw him before. Of course that's the truth. I never did see him before, and it could be that we'll all sleep easier because he didn't get off the train."

"What makes you say that?"

"They say his name was Nat Church. That's trouble if ever I heard it. You know what he's like."

"Nat Church is a character in dime novels, Ted."

"That doesn't mean *Nat Church and the Watchers* ain't a true story. It doesn't mean Nat Church don't live outside a book."

"Did you read *Huckleberry Finn*?" she asked.

"Sure. Good story. Not as exciting as *Nat Church and the Sleeping Detective*, but good."

"And do you think Huck is a real person?"

"Well, hell, Mrs. Berry. Of course he ain't. No white boy is going to take up with a ni—"

"Mr. Rush," Raine said.

"Well, he ain't."

Raine sighed. Was there a line of reasoning anywhere that could make an impact? If so, she hadn't found it yet.

Ted moved to the left so another cowpoke could belly up to the bar. After Raine had served him and Richard Allen headed back to his table, Ted continued. "I heard there's a man staying here that saw it all."

"I don't know about that."

"Mr. Collins seemed to think your guest saw it all. I was thinking that I might want to talk to him, get his sense of what happened. Wouldn't hurt to compare stories."

Not inclined to encourage him, Raine shrugged. After Ted ambled off with his glass of ginger beer, she turned away, facing the mirror as she straightened the bottles beneath it, and was brought up short by the man reflected over her right shoulder.

She acknowledged this new arrival with a curt nod and turned around slowly. No one with a lick of sense kept their back to a Burdick if there was a choice. "What can I get you, Mr. Burdick?"

"Now you know Mr. Burdick is my father, Lorrainey. Haven't I asked you to call me Eli?"

"You told me to call you Eli, Mr. Burdick. It's not quite the same."

Eli Burdick had a helmet of thick, dark hair. He ran his fingers through it after he removed his hat. He set the Stetson on the bar but kept one hand on the pearl gray crown. "I notice you didn't tell me not to call you Lorrainey."

"Would it make a difference?"

"Probably not." He had a handsome smile, but it did not always touch his pale blue eyes. That was not the case now. His eyes fairly danced, but it was with the kind of amusement that rarely boded well.

It raised Raine's hackles. She repeated her first question, "What can I get for you?"

"Whiskey."

She set a glass in front of him. Before she could fill it, he took the bottle out of her hands, preferring that to the glass. "If that's your pleasure," she said, and wished immediately that she could call the words back.

"What do you think you know about my pleasure?"

Raine held her tongue this time.

"I thought so."

He spoke to her as though they were intimates and alone. She saw his eyes lift to the mirror and knew he was taking the measure of every man in the room. He didn't see a threat. She was not sure he would recognize one. It had been a long time since anyone outside of his own family had challenged him.

Raine remained attentive to Eli Burdick but did not fail to notice the man who came to stand beside him.

"Beer," Kellen Coltrane said. He slid a coin across the top of the bar. He set the toe of one boot on the brass rail and turned his head casually in Eli Burdick's direction. "Evening." He glanced at the bottle Eli was still holding. "The whiskey here that good that you don't want to give it up?"

Eli looked him over. "I don't know you."

"It would be strange if you did. I don't know you either." He held out a hand. "Coltrane. Kellen Coltrane."

Eli would have had to give up the bottle or release the crown of his hat. He did neither.

Kellen allowed his hand to remain suspended in the air for a few moments before he shrugged and withdrew it. He returned his attention to Raine.

"Is someone going to play that piano?" Kellen asked. "Seems a shame to let it sit idle."

Eli Burdick tilted the bottle to his lips and took a deep swallow. Then he used the sleeve of his coat to wipe his mouth. "You play the piano?"

"That depends who you ask. I've never had a teacher who thought so, but my mother says I have an angel's touch."

"An angel's touch?"

Kellen's shrug was sheepish this time. "She's my mother." He took the beer Raine passed to him. "Thank you, Mrs. Berry." He took a swallow, found it to his liking, and asked Eli, "What about you? Ever play?"

Eli's eyebrows took a hike toward his dark hairline. "Me? You don't know who I am, do you?"

"I thought we established that. I'm Kellen Coltrane and you are . . ."

The piercing pale blue eyes narrowed a fraction. "Eli Burdick," he said.

"Good to make your acquaintance." Kellen did not offer his hand a second time. "So what is it about being Eli Burdick that prevents you from playing the piano?"

Raine could barely draw enough breath to fill her lungs. She did not believe she had ever heard anyone try to engage Eli Burdick in a conversation about anything that did not have to do with cattle, cattle drives, cattle prices, and cattle rustling. Eli was known to talk about other things, mostly women and whiskey and sometimes cards, but those subjects were best left alone unless he brought them up. It was beyond absurd that he was being asked about the piano.

Every ear in the saloon was straining to hear how he would answer.

"Uriah Burdick," said Eli.

"Ah." Kellen nodded, understanding. "Your father? My pa didn't much care for it either."

Eli took another swig from the bottle. "My mother played."

Kellen raised his glass. "To mothers, then." He watched Eli's grip tighten. He was prepared to duck and feint if the bottle found the arc that would bring it crashing toward his head. That didn't happen. Eli tapped the bottom of his bottle to Kellen's glass.

"To mothers." He glanced at the piano. "Are you going to play something?"

"Perhaps later." He pointed to Sue Hage as she carefully wended her way toward the piano. "Looks like Miss Hage is going to entertain us." He didn't think it was possible for her to look more frightened than she had earlier standing in front of his door. She was proving him wrong. It occurred to him that she might faint before she reached the relative safety of the piano stool.

Raine saw it, too. Eli Burdick's presence always put Sue on edge. She called out to Charlie Patterson. "Hey, Charlie. Why don't you help Sue with her music?"

He jumped to his feet and almost turned the table over in his eagerness to lend assistance. He took the music Sue was carrying and set it on the piano. It was only then that he realized he had no idea what to do. He couldn't read a lick of music.

"Turn the pages when you see me nod," Sue said under her breath. "And pray Eli Burdick likes what I play." She set her hands on the keys and began playing the overture from *The Pirates of Penzance*.

"That's unexpected," Kellen said mildly.

"I like it," said Eli Burdick. He took another long swallow.

"Then I like it, too."

Raine was aware that customers were slowly turning back to their tables and once again speaking to their neighbors. The oppressive hush was lifting. Sue's playing was lively but did not overpower conversation. The Davis boys started trading cards and insults. Ted Rush cornered Richard Allen and launched into his near encounter with a killer. Charlie Patterson, sitting at the piano beside Sue, could not have been happier if someone called him a cat and dipped him in cream.

"If you don't play the piano, Mr. Burdick," said Kellen, "do you play cards?"

"I don't know anyone who doesn't play cards."

"What's your game?"

"There is only one." When Kellen only regarded him blankly, he said, "Poker."

"Oh, of course. I don't play it much myself. I prefer faro. Do you ever buck the tiger?"

Eli's strong features settled into thoughtfulness. His mouth tipped slightly to one side and his eyelids fell to half-mast. "There's no satisfaction bucking the tiger, but poker . . ."

Kellen held up one hand, palm out. "Not for me."

"One game," Eli said. "Small stakes."

Kellen considered that. "Not money. Something else."

Eli had been raising the bottle to his mouth. He stopped and regarded Kellen with suspicion. "Like what?"

"If I win, you try your hand at the piano."

"And if you don't?"

"Then I'll buy that bottle for you."

Eli glanced at the bottle. "This? I wasn't going to pay for it anyway."

Kellen pretended he didn't understand. "Well, now you can."

"You seem sure you're going to lose," said Eli.

"Not at all," Kellen said. "I'm just certain you're going to win."

Eli grinned appreciatively. "You're right." He looked up at the mirror, caught the eye of Jem Davis, and jerked his head to indicate Jem and his brothers should vacate their table. He expected them to move quickly, and they did not disappoint.

Kellen took his beer and followed Eli to the table. Cards lay scattered across the top. He gathered them up because Eli was still holding the bottle and his hat and didn't give either up until he was seated.

"Do you want to shuffle?" asked Kellen.

"No. You shuffle. I'll cut."

Kellen riffled the deck with his thumb, squared it off, and began to shuffle. He was slow and methodical, careful not to let the cards spill out of his hands. He felt Eli's eyes boring into him.

Eli clamped a large hand over Kellen's. "You foolin' with me?"

Kellen looked up from the cards. "Fooling with you?"

"I never saw a man trying so hard to mix the cards. Are you clumsy or just pretending to be?"

"Why would I pretend?"

"That's what I can't figure. Maybe you don't want me to know you're a card sharper."

"That would explain it, all right."

"So you *are* a sharper."

"No. But if I were, I don't think I would want you to know."

Still visibly distrustful, Eli removed his hand. It hovered for a moment before he snatched the cards from Kellen. "I think I will shuffle after all." He did so expertly and then slid the deck toward Kellen for the cut.

Kellen declined. He saw this had the effect of making Eli Burdick more suspicious, not less. There was nothing he could do about that. Eli Burdick was the sort of man used to taking others, not being taken. He waited for the deal and had to hope for the best, which meant he wanted the worst.

He fanned his cards. His soft groan was involuntary. Five hearts. He looked at Eli. The man was a stoic. Even so, it would be extraordinary for him to have a better hand than a flush. Kellen had watched him carefully as he shuffled and then dealt. There was no sleight of hand.

"How many cards?" Eli asked.

"I have to take three." He chose three hearts with the highest value and pushed them to the side.

Eli passed him three new cards before he examined his hand a second time. He plucked a card from the middle and set it facedown. "Dealer takes one."

Kellen closed his card fan. He had drawn a club, a spade, and another heart. He didn't even have a pair. He was feeling hopeful and he let it show. It couldn't hurt Eli Burdick to wonder and worry. Kellen saw the man's eyes dart to the piano.

Eli jerked his chin at Kellen. "What do you have?"

"Nothing." He turned over his cards and spread them out.

Eli leaned back in his chair and showed his hand. "Three lucky sevens."

Kellen thrust his fingers through his hair. "Well, then, it seems I'm buying your bottle this evening." He started to push his chair away from the table. "I'm going to settle up with Mrs. Berry."

Eli Burdick caught the sleeve of Kellen's jacket. He didn't pull but neither did he let go. "There's no hurry." He looked at Kellen's empty glass. "You want another beer?"

"I was going to get it at the bar."

"Lorrainey will bring it to you."

"Lorrainey?"

"The Widder Berry. Are you rooming at one of the boardinghouses or staying at the hotel?"

"The hotel."

"Well, it's her place. Lorraine." He looked past Kellen's shoulder and had no trouble catching Raine's eye. "She's been watching me," he told Kellen. "She always does." He raised an arm, then his voice. "Another beer, Lorrainey. And bring that glass I didn't want before." He lowered his arm and spoke in a tone that invited confidences. "Watch. She'll come fluttering. Moth to a flame."

That was not Kellen's observation. Mrs. Berry did not flutter. It was hard to imagine a behavior more at odds with her steady nerve. She did not hover, and she certainly did not flit. She set a fresh glass of beer in front of him, grazing his hand ever so lightly. He barely felt the paper packet she tucked under his palm. He made a fist around it as she placed a shot glass beside Eli Burdick's bottle.

"Is there anything else, Mr. Burdick?" Raine asked.

Eli patted his knee. "How about you sitting here?"

"Only if you were a pincushion and I was a pin."

He gave a shout of laughter. "That's a good one, Lorrainey. Go on." He waved her off and leaned toward Kellen when she was out of hearing. "Did you see? Butter won't melt in her mouth, but her eyes burn right through a man." He touched his chest with his forefinger. "*This* man."

Kellen thought that was true but not precisely in the way Eli Burdick wanted to believe it was. He offered a noncommittal nod and picked up his beer.

"What's your line of business?" Eli asked.

"I write for the *New York World*. Do you know it?"

Eli filled his shot glass and knocked it back. "Can't say that I do."

Kellen was amazed at Eli Burdick's capacity for drink. The man had yet to slur a word or show any indication that he was drunk. Under the table, Kellen scored the packet that Raine had passed to him and carefully began to tear it open. "Ever heard of Joseph Pulitzer?"

"I recollect I have. Doesn't he have a cattle spread over Dakota way?"

Kellen didn't blink. "He's the one."

"You writing about him?"

"I am writing about ranchers. About the life. People in the big cities are interested."

"That so?"

"It is. I got off the train at Bitter Springs because someone told me the Burdicks have the biggest spread in this part of Wyoming. I guess he was talking about you." He paused, frowning slightly. "Unless you're not one of *those* Burdicks."

"Only one family of Burdicks," Eli said. "Who was talking about us?"

"No one was talking about you. I was asking about cattlemen. Was the information incorrect?"

"No. My family has the biggest spread."

"Then I imagine you're well known."

"Sure."

"Then it doesn't matter who told me, does it?"

"Guess not."

"Good, because the newspaper discourages us from saying who we talked to if we didn't get permission."

"You'd tell me, though, if I put a gun in your crotch and said I'd shoot your balls off."

"Sure would. I'm partial to all my body parts."

"Good," Eli said, satisfied. "Just so I can depend on you when it's something important."

Kellen nodded. He lifted his glass and drank. Beer touched his upper lip, and he mimicked Eli and used the sleeve of his jacket to swipe at it. "How many Burdicks are there?" he asked.

Eli frowned deeply. "What the hell kind of question is that?"

"I was wondering how large a family it takes to manage the biggest spread in these parts."

Eli grunted. "There are four of us. My father, my brothers, and me."

"Ranch hands?"

"Fifteen give or take."

"Cattle?"

"One thousand seven hundred sixty-four head."

Kellen smiled. "Give or take."

Eli did not smile in return. "Cattle are serious business, Mr. Coltrane."

"I apologize. Call me Kellen."

"Maybe."

"Are your brothers around tonight? I wouldn't mind talking to them."

"I'd mind." He leaned forward and rested his forearms on the table. "But they didn't come to town with me so that's neither here nor there. Shouldn't you be writing down what I tell you?"

Kellen tapped his temple. "One thousand seven hundred sixty-four head." He shrugged. "I have a good memory. I'll write it down when I get back to my room." He went to reach for Eli's bottle but stopped short of touching it.

"May I?"

"I suppose that depends on what you mean to do with it."

"Pour another shot for you."

"Then be my guest."

Kellen picked up the bottle. "Who's that coming into the saloon from the hotel?" he asked. "Someone I should talk to for my story?" He waited until Eli turned halfway around in his chair before he poured. Granules of white powder fell into the slipstream of whiskey.

"That's Jack Clifton," Eli said. "I don't recollect that he's ever had much to say for himself."

Kellen wrapped his fingers around the shot glass, blocking Eli's drink until the last granule dissolved. He put the bottle to the side and slid the glass in front of Eli. "What should we drink to?"

Eli Burdick cast his eyes in Raine's direction. "To waking up beside a redheaded woman," he said, lifting his glass. When Kellen didn't join him, he offered a narrow, satisfied smile. "Good thinking, Coltrane. She's mine. Always has been."

Over the course of the next three days and nights, Raine saw nothing of Eli Burdick and very little of Kellen Coltrane. She was grateful for Eli's absence but found herself wondering from time to time at her hired gun's whereabouts and questioning the wisdom of their agreement. He was not in her thoughts, though, as she yawned wearily and slipped inside her rooms at the top of the house. Pressing the back of one hand to cover her mouth did nothing at all to stop the yawn short, but it did help to dampen the gasp that followed at the sight of the man sitting near her writing desk.

"Adam?" She blinked. It couldn't be Adam. Of course it couldn't. If she were not so tired, his name wouldn't have crossed her mind or her lips. It was only that the dim, yellow light from the oil lamp played a cruel trick, lending the man's hair the burnish of a polished chestnut. The narrow shape of his head, the strong jaw, the clearly defined bridge of his nose, were no longer single points of interest but the whole of a handsome face that was at once achingly familiar and frighteningly alien.

He had turned the chair away from her writing desk so that he faced the door. It was exactly what Adam had done when he wanted to speak to her. His forearms rested on the arms of the chair, and his long legs were stretched toward her, crossed at the ankles. Kellen Coltrane looked at his ease, which Adam rarely did when he had something to say. His posture was so relaxed he might have been boneless, a man comfortably contained by the skin he was in.

Raine's stare went from wide to narrow. She was squinting by the time she took her first step forward. She stamped her foot hard enough to send a vibration across the floorboards and under his chair.

Kellen's eyelids lifted.

Raine's husky voice took on a harsh edge. "Were you sleeping?"

"No. Just contemplating."

"Contemplating? Contemplating what?"

"Sleep."

His calm did not settle well with her. He was likely only six or so years her senior, yet he made her feel like a child. She was seized by an urge to kick him. The opportunity, not the urge, passed when Kellen shifted his legs.

Raine shrugged off her shawl and tossed it over the back of a chair. "What are you doing here?"

"Waiting for you. We haven't spoken much in days. I thought you might show up in my room again, but then I got to thinking that maybe you're avoiding me. Am I wrong?"

At her sides, her hands curled into loose fists.

Kellen observed this. "I make you want to throw things."

"At you," she said. "I want to throw them at you."

He was philosophical. "That was a given. You demonstrate more control than either of my sisters. Kitty especially."

Only one response came to Raine's mind. Her flat voice hinted at her skepticism. "You have sisters."

Her patent disbelief amused him. He held up two fingers. "Kitty. That's Kathleen. And Anne." He unfolded the remaining fingers and thumb, holding out his palm to forestall more questions. "Two brothers, also. Michael is older. Rob is younger. He and Anne are twins. I don't know how much you needed to know about Nat Church before you hired him, but I can tell you that Michael is a lawyer, Kitty and her husband run a private school for girls, and Rob and Anne are still at home. You already know my father is a professor of humanities at Yale. My mother, Katherine, is an advocate for temperance and women's rights."

Raine took all the information in. "I don't know if you can appreciate that none of that really eases my mind as to your presence in my rooms. Tell me, how would your family describe you?"

"Black sheep."

"Well," she said after a moment. "That puts it all into perspective, doesn't it?"

"Some have said so."

Raine sighed. She removed the combs from her hair, set them on one corner of the writing desk, and smoothed back the crown of her head with her palm. She would have taken the pins from the coil at her nape, but she had sense enough still to recognize it as an inherently intimate activity. Instead, she went to the stove in the corner of the room and added coals to the grate.

"What was your game the other night?" she asked, coming around to face him. "Did you give it any thought before you sidled up to Eli Burdick? He could kill you as soon as look at you."

"That occurred to me." Kellen opened his jacket and reached inside his vest. He held up a .51 caliber derringer with a burnished hardwood grip and laid it on the desk.

Raine looked at it, then at him. "You didn't have that the day we met."

"I didn't have it where you could see it," he corrected. "There is no point in strapping on one of the Colts when I'm in the saloon. That's telegraphing that I'm looking for trouble."

"How is striking up a conversation with Eli different from that? You stay holed up in your room most of the day, eschew company at dinner, and disappear again afterward, but when you finally decide to be sociable, you choose Eli Burdick as a boon companion? The first evening in town? Mr. Coltrane, I've been observing you, and I have to wonder at your strategy and at your ability to carry out the terms of our agreement without assistance from Nat Church."

Kellen gave her another moment in the event she found more words. When she did not, he calmly offered, "No one got shot, did they?"

Raine stared at him.

"I mean," he went on, "that is the point of the engagement, isn't it? You don't *want* people killed. You want the killing to stop. Or have I misunderstood?"

"I don't—"

He spoke as if she hadn't begun to. "Because I can assure you, it's a whole lot easier to kill people than it is to tiptoe around *not* killing them. Take Eli the other night, for instance. I could have put a bullet through the soft underside of his jaw anytime he tipped his head to knock back a drink. Calling you Lorrainey provoked me about as much as him drinking straight from the bottle. Now, even with two kinds of provocation, I wouldn't have shot him dead right then because I had no defense for it that a court would recognize. I don't have to consult my lawyer brother to know that what Mr. Burdick was doing is mostly considered an annoyance and not a good enough reason to kill him."

Raine found herself strangely fascinated. His voice was low and seductive, his argument absurdly diverting, and humor played about his mouth like a secret he meant to try to keep. Without being conscious of it at first, she moved closer. Her hands rested lightly on the shawl she had thrown over the back of a chair.

Kellen extended his feet again. "The dilemma, naturally enough, is how to encourage Mr. Burdick to reach for his gun."

"But not kill you," Raine said.

"I didn't think I needed to point that out," he said dryly, "but clarification never hurts."

Raine pressed her mouth flat to keep her lips from twitching. She vowed she would not say another word until he was finished.

"Mr. Burdick did not impress me as someone who required much in the way of encouragement to draw his gun. I could have insisted that he address you as Mrs. Berry, taken possession of his bottle without his permission, or beat him at cards. He would have taken out his gun, and he would be dead. It would have been self-defense, confirmed by every customer in your saloon."

Raine held her tongue, waiting. When he lifted an eyebrow, she recognized he was inviting her to applaud his brilliance. She braced her arms on the back of the chair and set her gaze level with his. "That is where you very much mistake the matter. You could count on my testimony to confirm what happened, but you should never depend on anyone else to come forward. Killing Eli Burdick is like poking a stick in a nest of vipers."

"The father and brothers, you mean."

She nodded. "Uriah, Clay, and Isaac. And every ranch hand employed at the Burdick spread."

"Fifteen, give or take."

"More like twenty."

"Eli told me fifteen."

"Eli cares about cattle, not men. He probably doesn't know the name of half of the hands that work for his father."

"So no one crosses them."

"Not any longer," she said. "Not since Isaac Burdick's trial."

Kellen reached for the lamp and turned up the wick. The flame flickered at first, then held steady. The circle of light widened and chased the shadows from Raine's finely wrought features. She faced his scrutiny head on. He said, "Walt hinted at something about a trial, but wouldn't elaborate."

"When were you talking to Walt?"

"I suppose you're not watching me as closely as you think. I've talked to Walt every night after dinner. I meet him on the porch when he's done with his chores. We sit outside and talk, watch people coming and going, mostly to and from the saloon."

"But it's been bitter cold out there."

He shrugged. "I dress for it. I go back to my room to get my coat." And the derringer, but Kellen chose not to mention it. "As for Walt, I am under the impression that he is impervious to the cold."

Raine nodded absently, vaguely troubled that she hadn't known what Kellen was doing. It didn't make sense, given the fact that he was hired for protection, yet she somehow felt obliged to offer it in return. She came around the chair and sat down. "Has Walter been helpful?"

He smiled, recalling how Walter's broad shoulders extended beyond the back of the rocker, and how the man had folded his arms to rest just below his chest because the arms of the rocker could not contain them.

"I admit I was surprised," Kellen said. "He doesn't seem the sort to offer conversational delicacies, does he? Turns out, he's very good at it."

Raine thought back to Kellen's conversation with Eli Burdick. "So that's how you knew you could talk to Eli about the piano. Did he mention that Eli's mother left his father for a railroad surveyor who regularly passed through the territory?"

"He didn't get to that, no."

"I didn't think so. I thought Eli was going to hammer your skull when you decided to toast mothers."

Kellen remembered thinking the same thing. "Do you like it when he calls you Lorrainey?"

Raine stiffened. "No," she said. "It makes my skin crawl."

"Then there is no understanding between you."

"He said there was an understanding? What did he say? What were his exact words?"

Kellen put out his hands. "Whoa."

"Whoa?" Raine looked at him sharply. "You said whoa to me?"

"I beg your pardon," Kellen said. He could have avoided Eli Burdick's bottle more easily than the Widder Berry's stare. Her green eyes had taken on a brilliance that gave them a razor's edge.

"I thought you said your mother advocated for women's rights."

"She does, and she taught me better," Kellen said. "In my defense, I believe I mentioned I was the black sheep."

"You must sorely try her patience," said Raine.

"It's been said, ma'am."

"Oh, for goodness' sakes," she said. "You may call me Mrs. Berry or Lorraine, but please cease calling me ma'am."

"Raine?" he asked softly.

It was what Adam and Ellen had called her. It was the name she gave to herself, the name of the woman reflected in her mirror. She wished she didn't like the sound of it quite so much on Kellen Coltrane's lips.

Mustering carelessness, she said, "If you like."

Kellen did. He figured she was probably already regretting it, but he wasn't giving her an opportunity to take it back. Raine. Her name lay cool and sweet on the tip of his tongue. It was a balm for the sting she could inflict with her eyes. He thought she looked uneasy, as though she was no longer certain of the ground she stood on. He gave her something to hold on to.

"But not Lorrainey," he said.

Raine flared. Heat rushed into her cheeks. "You wouldn't like the consequences."

Kellen decided she had recovered. "Probably not," he said, and meant it. He didn't need to know what the consequences were. "Now do you still want to know about Eli's understanding?"

"Yes."

"It's simple. He thinks you're his."

Raine rolled her eyes.

"And that you always have been."

She slowly shook her head from side to side. "I cannot explain it. There's no accounting for him being so single-minded. I have never encouraged him."

"Love."

"What?"

"Love accounts for it."

"No," she said firmly. "It doesn't."

"Then lust," he said. "Greed, because he wants all of you. And pride because you wound him."

"Wound him? His hide is as thick as a buffalo's."

His hide was at least that thick, Kellen thought, and his head was thicker. Still, he offered another explanation to Raine. "He has to pretend you don't hurt him, doesn't he? Otherwise he would look foolish to everyone within earshot."

"Are you suggesting I should stop prickling when he calls me Lorrainey and sit on his lap when he invites me?"

"No."

"Because I can tell you what would happen if I showed him a scrap of kindness."

"I understand."

"He'd have me right there. In the saloon."

"I understand," Kellen said again.

"On the bar."

"I know."

"With people watching."

Kellen put out a hand. "Whoa."

Raine stopped. She looked away and tucked her chin against her shoulder. "I'm sorry."

"So am I," said Kellen. "Did it sound as if I were trying to excuse him?"

"No." She raised her head, shook it almost imperceptibly. "It sounded as if you were trying to blame me."

A muscle worked in his cheek. He waited for her to look at him again. When she finally did, he said, "I am more sorry than I can properly express."

She smiled faintly. "Then you must be sorry indeed. I've been noticing that you know a whole lot of words."

He returned her smile because she seemed to expect it. She had forgiven him even if he had not forgiven himself.

He tipped his chair onto its rear legs. "What was it you gave me to put in Eli's drink? I'd like to know it's handy when he comes around again."

"Just a sleeping powder. Mr. Burnside, the druggist, makes it for me. Eli has a hollow leg. He never passes out. I usually slip it into his bottle myself, but he grabbed it too quickly. I was not confident you could manage him all evening. Did you have a plan?"

"Other than keeping him occupied?"

"Other than that."

"No. No plan."

"What did you think when his head hit the table?"

"That I finally bored someone to death."

Laughter bubbled to Raine's lips, leaving the imprint of a smile in its wake. "It was probably only a matter of time," she said.

He grinned. "Well, thank you. Eli slept it off in the back room?"

"Not entirely. I asked the Davis boys to throw him over his horse. They escorted him back to the ranch. That probably accounts for his absence these last couple of evenings."

Kellen dropped his chair onto all four of its legs. "I know what I needed to know. I should be going."

"Before you go," she said. "I want to tell you what happened to Ellen."

Chapter Four

Kellen fell into a troubled sleep. The images seared in his mind's eye could not easily be dismissed, and while each one passed eventually, it came around again like a dark, demonic horse on a carousel from hell.

At its barest bones, the story of what happened to Ellen Wilson could be stated in a single sentence. Isaac Burdick raped her, a pregnancy came of the violence, and she and the baby died in childbirth.

Raine had given him the bare bones first, and then she put flesh on them.

Through Raine's eyes, he saw Ellen at fifteen: a winsome dervish of a girl with strawberry blond hair, green eyes, an unfettered laugh, and little understanding of her own charm. He saw the eighteen-year-old Isaac Burdick, too. The boy was a pared-down version of his older brothers, slimmer, bonier, but with the same thick black hair, pale blue eyes, and squared-off jaw. When he was culled from the Burdick herd, he was less confident of his place. Arrogance faded, along with the sense of entitlement.

Left alone, he might never have gotten up the nerve to do

more than speak to Ellen in passing, but Eli and Clay, like Raine, saw where his affections lay. Raine feared that discouraging Isaac or cautioning Ellen would simply put the pair together more often. She watched instead and took every opportunity when Isaac was around to find something for Ellen to do that would keep her close. For their part, Eli and Clay were relentless in their ribbing. The first thing they did upon entering the saloon was to look around for Ellen and prod Isaac until he was moving in her direction. Raine eventually kept Ellen away from the saloon altogether.

Raine's maneuvering did not escape the notice of Eli and Clay, and she made the painful acknowledgment that it might have spurred them to concoct their plan. The motivation was to outwit her. Isaac was hardly more than a means to do so. Ellen was of no account.

It happened a little over four years ago in May. The saloon was crowded with men fresh from a cattle drive. Most of them worked for the Burdicks. Raine had Walt to help her at the bar and two girls who no longer worked at the saloon to take orders and fetch drinks at the tables. Because Clay Burdick had a fondness for poking at Walt, Raine didn't like to leave him alone for long. She already felt tied to the bar that evening and with heavier rope than usual because of the presence of Eli and Clay. She remembered feeling relieved when Clay finally stepped outside in search of fresh air. Eli stayed where he was, but he was less troublesome when he wasn't showing off for his younger brother.

Either one of them.

Raine remembered the fear as something so powerful it stopped her heart and stole her will. At the moment she realized that Isaac had never been with his brothers, and that Clay was gone, she couldn't breathe or move. The inability to act lasted mere seconds, but then, and every time she thought about it since, the time between comprehension and action yawned before her like a great chasm that she could neither jump nor bridge.

Raine took the backstairs two at a time to reach the third floor. Ellen was not in their apartments. Backtracking, Raine stopped on the guest floor, and saw Clay Burdick standing outside the door to the only room not let for the night. She charged ahead, her outcry mingling with the one she heard from inside the room. Clay braced himself for the impact of Raine's body. She was the one who lost her footing and staggered back. The second time she launched herself at him had as little effect.

She cried out for Ellen and heard her name come back to her in a strangled voice as desperate and frightened as her own. She threw her fists at Clay while she screamed at Isaac to stop. Neither brother responded.

Clay was mostly amused by her efforts until one of her wild punches caught him on the nose. Instantly Raine squeezed behind him. She was flush to the door when she managed to open it and practically fell into the room.

Ellen lying on the bed. Ellen with her skirt bunched at her hips, her thighs spread wide around Isaac Burdick's hips. Ellen's terrified eyes. Her clenched jaw. Blood on her lip. Isaac panting, rutting, his bony fingers digging into Ellen's pale buttocks. Apologies, too. He was sorry, so sorry, but he could not help himself. She wanted it. He knew it was the same for him. His brothers told him it would be like that.

Raine attacked, knocking Isaac sideways and shoving him to the floor. She pummeled his face until Clay got his arms under her shoulders and yanked her away. He held her back and told his brother he better finish what he started, better finish it, or he would. Raine howled as Isaac slowly got to his feet and stumbled back to the bed. Ellen hadn't moved or tried to cover herself. She was all but senseless and only whimpered when Isaac dragged her closer to the edge of the bed and lifted her hips. He was no longer aroused. The beating, Raine's presence, his brother's taunting, perhaps Ellen's pathetic cries, something had reached him. His cock was soft, a doughy lump between his thighs. He had to work to stir himself. Clay gave him direction. He was painfully slow in coming around but blessedly quick in coming.

Clay had no interest in Ellen but the violence and humiliation aroused him. Directing the scene was no longer enough.

He held a squirming, writhing woman in his hands, a woman who had broken his nose and bloodied his face, and in his mind, the Widder Berry was better sport than her virgin sister.

He told Isaac to get his whore out of the way, and then he half carried, half drove Raine to the bed and threw her on it. The force that he used to push her down stunned her, but she twisted onto her back and drew up her knees. When he would have fallen on her, she threw all of her strength into her legs and drove the air from his lungs with the soles of her boots. She rolled to the edge of the bed and went over the side, scrambling to her feet and using a chair to block Clay's advance.

Isaac was mute, backed into a corner by nothing but his guilt. Ellen lay curled on one side facing him. She did not react to her sister's fight, even when the bed was jostled and shoved. Raine never asked for help. She told her sister to get out, to run. Ellen did not move.

Eli came upon them before Clay wrestled Raine back to the bed. He put a forearm around Clay's throat and pulled him away. He held him in that stranglehold until Clay's knees sagged. When he let go, Clay dropped to his hands and knees and drew deep, gasping breaths. Eli kicked him in the ribs for good measure.

His gaze slid over Raine. "Clay's got no right to you. I told him that before." He cocked his head to where Ellen lay. "Isaac didn't mean anything by it. He's just a boy himself. Uriah offered to buy him a whore at Miss Selby's place, but he didn't want one. Problem is, the only cherry he ever had was on top of one of Mrs. Burnside's sundaes. Your sister was sweet on him. You know it, too. I reckon he was overcome the way young men are from time to time."

He bent, yanked Clay up by the collar—no mean feat since they were equal in size—and gave him a shove toward the door. "He won't be bothering you again, Lorrainey. Isaac, get out of here." He held up a hand and then used his forefinger to point to Isaac's open fly. "Sure, you're proud of it, but it ain't decent to wave it around once it's been used."

Raine believed the Burdicks did not expect Isaac to be arrested and, once arrested, did not expect he would stand trial.

She was certain they never took the trial seriously because even at that juncture they never considered that the outcome was in doubt. Isaac was the only one who looked scared from time to time, but a single glance from his father could put real fear into him and make the other fade away.

The town was dependent on Burdick cattle and Burdick money. Uriah Burdick owned the bank. He owned Miss Selby's whorehouse. He owned the corral where other ranchers sent their cattle for shipping. He owned several of the buildings along the main street including the government land office and Ted Rush's hardware and leather goods store. He had the largest ranch and hired the most hands. He spread his money around. He did not come into town often, but when he did, it stirred the merchants to display their finest goods and the citizens to find yet another reason to loiter on the sidewalks. Standing just over six feet, Uriah Burdick was still an imposing figure, not as handsome as his sons, but carrying himself with more distinction and dignity. And it was always counted as a good visit when he returned to the ranch with no bodies left behind.

There were many reasons for people to back down. Some of them did, but what surprised Raine was how many did not. Ellen was well liked. She was incapable of giving offense, and she spoke to everyone she passed in the course of a day. No one had an unkind word for her, and the blame for what happened did not attach to her.

Dr. Kent examined Ellen and confirmed the rape. Marshal Sterling took a deputy with him to the Burdick ranch and brought Isaac back. Mr. Collins sent a telegraph to the judge in Rawlins, explaining the situation. The marshal didn't hold out much hope for getting Isaac to trial outside of town, and the local magistrate, who would normally oversee the proceedings in a matter where there was no murder, lived in Uriah Burdick's pocket during trying times. The station agent was the first to admit his astonishment when Judge Abel Darlington agreed to sit for the trial. Moses T. Parker, also from Rawlins, was appointed prosecutor. The jury came together after that. Jack Clifton. Harry Sample. Terrence McCormick. They were the first to take their seats, the first of twelve good men. John

Hood was another, now dead, and then came Hank Thompson, chosen to be the jury foreman, now missing.

The trial lasted two days, but that was because Isaac Burdick's lawyer called upon every ranch hand on Uriah's payroll to give testimony that Ellen Wilson had seduced Isaac and then cried rape. Raine had never seen some of the men who were paraded in front of the jury, nor been aware of their number. It seemed to her that the ranks had swelled until there was a man for every cow. Judge Darlington eventually stopped the parade. The men and women who testified to Ellen's good character had their voices all but silenced by the sworn statements of Uriah Burdick's men.

Ellen took the stand and spoke without passion or inflection. Raine had expected that Ellen would look to her for strength during her testimony, but her sister carried that weight on her own. Ellen's eyes never left Isaac Burdick, and every member of the jury saw it was Isaac who ducked her gaze and looked away.

Raine also gave testimony. Mr. and Mrs. Johnson had cleared the floor of their mercantile to make space for the court. Every chair had someone sitting in it, and people squeezed in until they lined three walls shoulder to shoulder. Raine spoke clearly, only mincing those words Moses T. Parker judged as too crude or coarse for public airing. She was not allowed to say "cock," even in repeating Eli's words. There were things Clay said to his brother that the prosecutor also deemed unfit to be spoken by a woman. Even in Wyoming, where women enjoyed certain rights not shared by females outside the territory, plain speaking was not always one of them.

Raine was not hopeful at the end. The prosecutor had done well by Ellen, and the judge, who clearly could not show favor, seemed disposed to believe her story, but the verdict still rested with twelve men, any one of whom might have placed Uriah Burdick's interests above Ellen.

It was the gasp that woke Kellen now. He heard it clearly in his sleep, exactly as Raine had described it to him. It was the collective indrawn breath of every person in the courtroom at the moment Hank Thompson stood and delivered the will of the jury.

"Guilty."

Kellen pushed himself to sit up. He rubbed his eyes with the heels of his hands until he saw sparks and then leaned back against the iron rail head. He knew exactly where he was, but he could still hear the murmurs in the courtroom. It was as if he were holding a conch to his ear and listening to the sound of the ocean trapped inside.

He got up, added coal to the stove, and then padded to the bathing room to throw cold water on his face. Afterward, he braced his arms on the vanity and stared into the mirror. The light from the stove in the other room was too meager to push aside the shadows. He suspected they would be there if he held a lamp up to his face.

"Christ, Kellen. What have you gotten yourself into?" If his reflection had answered, he would have taken it in stride. More than that, he might actually have been relieved.

He rubbed his jaw. His stubble was rough against his palm, like sandpaper. He breathed out slowly and felt the tension resting in his neck and shoulders begin to ease. As tired as he was, returning to bed did not interest him. He left the bathing room and found his robe and socks. He put them on before lighting the oil lamp. From the trunk he never unpacked, he took paper, pen and ink, and a blotter and set them on the table beside the lamp. He looked it all over and pronounced himself satisfied.

He sat down and began to write.

The end of the trial was not the end. Isaac was sentenced to five years in the federal prison at Cheyenne. There was talk that he would not get that far, but not because there was any intention among the citizens of Bitter Springs to storm the jail and hang him. Rather, it was believed that the Burdicks would never allow the No. 3 train to reach the prison with Isaac on board.

Federal marshals joined Benton Sterling and his deputy to escort Isaac Burdick. The train came to a halt near Medicine Bow after midnight. A section of the tracks had been torn out and the timber made kindling for a bonfire the engineer could see in time to make the stop. The marshals were prepared to shoot to kill, starting with Isaac Burdick, but the masked raiders took passengers for hostages and Isaac was surrendered without a shot being fired. To rub salt in the wound, the raiders also broke into the mail car and made off with the strongbox.

No one doubted the Burdicks were responsible but proving it was another matter. Isaac was not at the Burdick ranch when the marshals rode out to get him, and the posse crossed tens of thousands of acres and never picked up a trail.

There was a shift in the mood of the town as time passed and Isaac could not be accounted for. Let sleeping dogs lie, some said, though never in Raine's hearing. She sensed it in their actions, in the way some of them could no longer meet her eye, and when it became apparent that Ellen was going to have Isaac's child, the blame that had never been her burden to carry was placed squarely on her shoulders.

It wasn't her fault that she was raped, but that she was pregnant, well, she must have wanted that. Couldn't she forgive Isaac? If he was found, did she truly want him to spend five years in prison? After all, he was the father of her child.

Everyone didn't hold to the same sort of thinking, but for Ellen it was as if the censorious voices were around her all of the time. Nothing Raine said made it different. Raine held out hope that the child would bring Ellen back to her and made herself believe she could love Isaac's baby if Ellen's own heart was healed. That dark irony never came to pass.

Ellen labored for two days to deliver a breech baby. Dr. Kent and the midwife did what they could to help her. In the end, they were only able to ease her pain. The baby, when it finally came, was stillborn, and Ellen died without holding it.

She was buried with her unnamed infant boy in the graveyard on the outskirts of town. Adam Berry's marker was beside hers. None of the Burdicks expressed condolences, but Raine learned they heard about Ellen's death from some of their drovers who came into the Pennyroyal. Raine was left to wonder if Uriah would have made a claim on the baby if he had lived. It pained her to admit that sometimes she thought it was a blessing that she never had to find out.

In Raine's mind, the Burdicks were responsible for Ellen's death. Isaac had murdered her. Clay and Eli had helped him. Uriah had raised his boys to believe they could take what they wanted, and mostly they had.

Thirteen months after Ellen was buried, Marshal Sterling went back out to the Burdick place because he heard rumblings that Isaac had shown up. He returned slumped in his saddle, shot once in the chest and once in the gut. Some said he was mistaken for a rustler, but no one came forward to admit being the one who made the mistake. Mrs. Sterling believed he was set up for it, first by the circulating rumors, then by his new deputy, who took sick and did not ride out with him.

Raine shared Mrs. Sterling's opinion.

Moses T. Parker, the prosecutor from Rawlins, hanged himself in his office three months later. John Hood, a juryman, read about the death and told everyone he was leaving Bitter Springs for Denver. Death found him in a fire in St. Louis and his charred remains were sent back to his family. Now the jury's foreman, Hank Thompson, hadn't been heard from.

Kellen placed a small question mark beside the man's name and put down his pen. Alive or dead? They might never know.

Rabbit and Finn sat on the bar eating smoked ham and mustard on a hard roll while Raine tallied the profits from the previous evening and worked on her liquor order. She looked up from her work when she heard heels tapping against the side of the bar. Finn caught himself but not soon enough.

"Sorry, Mrs. Berry."

The apology was garbled by a mouthful of food, but Raine judged it was sincerely meant. "You sound like a woodpecker."

"Yeth, ma'am."

"You boys have enough? Mrs. Sterling will make you more if you like."

Rabbit answered before Finn swallowed. "This is plenty of regular food, but if Mrs. Sterling has some brownies . . ."

Raine smiled. "I'm sure she does. Eat that first."

"Did you see where Mr. Coltrane went this morning?" Rabbit asked.

"I didn't," she said absently.

"Thought maybe he'd be back by now."

Finn said, "He's not, though."

Raine murmured something and continued to add figures.

"Do you think he's target shooting?" asked Rabbit.

"That'd be a fine thing to hear about," said Finn. "Leastways I would like to hear about it."

Raine set her pencil down and looked up again. "Why would Mr. Coltrane be target shooting?"

Rabbit and Finn exchanged glances. They were each using two hands to hold their ham rolls. They raised the sandwiches in unison and took deep bites.

Raine turned her chair away from the table and stared at them. They made a point of chewing thoroughly before swallowing. "Your granny would be so pleased." She held up one finger. "Not another bite. Tell me now. What's this about target shooting?"

Finn twisted his head to survey the saloon. He leaned so far backward over the bar to take a look that Rabbit had to grab him by the collar to keep him from going ass over teakettle.

"There's no one here," said Raine. "Walt's picking up supplies and Mrs. Sterling's in the kitchen. Tell me."

"He got a horse at the livery first thing this morning," Rabbit said. "We saw him from our bedroom window on account Finn had to piss and didn't want to use the privy."

"Rabbit was trying to shut the window on my—"

Raine's quelling look stopped Finn cold. "I understand. This was at sunup?"

"Not so you'd notice the sun yet," said Rabbit, "but you'd know it was coming soon. We saw him plenty clear."

"I see."

"Mr. Ransom gave him Cronus. I figure he must be a good rider."

"Or plum crazy," Finn said helpfully.

Rabbit rolled his eyes and went on. "We watched him for a

piece. We went up to the attic to get a better look. Saw him head out south and east. Figured he was goin' to follow the Medicine Bow a ways. Maybe where there's plenty of cover in the pines and boxelders. That's a good place to shoot."

"He wasn't heading to the Burdicks. That's for sure."

Raine shook her head. "You have guns on your mind. Both of you. Mr. Coltrane probably just wanted to see the country."

The boys were skeptical.

"You're used to walking outside with the plains and mountains as far as you can see. I don't think that's Mr. Coltrane's experience."

"Maybe not," said Finn. "But he was pretty smart to take his Colts just the same."

Raine frowned. "How do you know that?"

Rabbit shrugged and said, "Saw him pack them in his bag. He left the livery and didn't like the way things were settling on Cronus, or maybe Cronus was just being ornery, but he stopped, dismounted, and commenced to emptying his saddlebag. He strapped on one of the Peacemakers under his long coat and put the other back."

Raine forced a semblance of calm she did not feel and asked as if it were neither here nor there, "Have you mentioned this to your granny?"

"No. She doesn't want to hear about guns."

"Then your pap?"

Finn shook his head. "He thinks Mr. Coltrane is a gambler. Rabbit says we shouldn't try to change his ways. Makes him pained."

"That's probably wise." She picked up her pencil and tapped it lightly against the table.

"You sound like a woodpecker," Finn told her.

She managed a chuckle. "Why don't you take your rolls into the kitchen and see Mrs. Sterling about those brownies?" The boys jumped off the bar before she was finished. She watched them hightail it out of the saloon before she returned to her work. "What are you doing, Mr. Coltrane?" she asked under her breath. "What in God's name are you doing now?"

* * *

Kellen returned to the Pennyroyal a few hours before dinner was served. He used the backstairs to avoid the other guests and, he hoped, most of the staff. Sue Hage passed him in the hallway, but she kept her head down and hurried along. He bade her good afternoon, knowing she wouldn't take it as an invitation for conversation.

In his room, he immediately stowed the guns, holsters, and ammunition in the valise and pushed it back under the bed. He would require more ammunition and a gun belt for the .44. The other Colt felt too light in his hand and didn't have the range he wanted. It was a safe assumption that Nat Church did not strap on both weapons at the same time. The .45 with its shorter barrel was likely the last chance piece. Kellen decided that was the best use for it, tucked out of sight, perhaps at the small of his back, where it did not show under his duster.

He shrugged out of his coat and threw it on the bed, then went to the bathing room and ran hot water in the tub. He stripped, folding and stacking his clothes on a stool as he removed each piece. Too impatient for the water to reach his chest, he kept it running and slipped into the tub when it was only a few inches deep. He splashed water on the sides and back of the tub, then eased into a comfortable recline and closed his eyes.

Within moments he was asleep.

Mrs. Sterling had her hands full of dough and boys. She punched the dough hard enough to make a small dust cloud of flour rise from the breadboard. "Isn't your granny missing you about now?"

"Doubt it," said Finn.

"Don't you have chores?"

Rabbit rubbed his chin the way his pap did when he was thinking deeply. "No," he said finally. "I believe we got them all done. Pap asked us to bring the new feller here and that's what we did."

"Who is our new guest?"

"Mr. Jones. Mr. John Paul Jones. Just like the admiral."

Mrs. Sterling grunted softly as she folded the dough and put her fist into it again. "That's a lot of name to live up to."

Rabbit nodded. "He says he's no kin to the other. I asked. We had to explain it all to Finn since he didn't know who John Paul Jones was."

Finn took exception to this. "Sure, I knew. I watched him get off the express train same as you did."

"The *other* John Paul Jones. The naval hero."

"Oh," Finn said. "Well, there're no stories about him in my reader."

"That's because you're still in the primer." Rabbit could not have put more disdain in his voice. "When you get in the third reader, you'll learn all about him."

"Well, I know about him now, don't I? And I don't think he's as interesting as Mr. Coltrane."

Mrs. Sterling stopped what she was doing and cut the heel from a loaf of bread that was still warm from the oven. She spread a dollop of blackberry jam on it and handed each boy half. "I swear you two have a leg as hollow as Eli Burdick's."

"He eats you out of house and home?" asked Finn. "That's what the Widder Berry says we do. Except she has a hotel, so I don't think she's saying it right."

Rabbit jabbed his brother with an elbow. "Eli drinks. That's what Mrs. Sterling's saying. He drinks a *lot*." He looked at the cook for confirmation. "Isn't that right?"

"You did not hear it from me."

"I didn't. I heard it from my granny." He jabbed Finn again. "Stop that."

Finn looked up from the slice of jam bread. "What?"

"Stop sprinkling me."

Finn's look of bewilderment was sincere. "I don't—" A droplet of water splashed his jam bread. Studying it, his eyes crossed. "Hey! How did you do that?"

Mrs. Sterling looked up from her work to see what this fresh round of bickering was about. She was in time to see a water droplet hitting Rabbit's stubborn cowlick. Her eyes lifted to the ceiling. Another droplet was squeezing its way between the tin tiles. It hung for a moment, fell, and another one took its place.

"Oh, dear." She grabbed her apron to clean flour off her hands. "You boys run up to Mr. Coltrane's room and turn the water off. I'll find Lorraine."

Rabbit and Finn stared at her, hardly believing their good fortune.

"Go! Now!" She clapped her hands together to startle them to activity. "Hurry."

They jumped off their stools and tried to elbow each other out of the way as they ran out of the kitchen for the dining room and the main staircase.

"Should've gone the other way," Rabbit said as they charged up the stairs.

"Was goin' to," Finn said, "but you pushed me this way."

"Did not."

"Did."

Rabbit got the edge in the footrace when they rounded into the hallway and he had the inside curve. Finn grabbed the hem of Rabbit's jacket and hung on. They skidded to a halt outside of Mr. Coltrane's door with Rabbit slightly overshooting his mark.

Finn grabbed the glass knob and twisted it, but Rabbit got inside first. Neither of them bothered to shut the door but commenced to shouldering each other out of the way as soon as they were inside. They squeezed through the bathing room door together and lost their footing in the puddles on the floor. Finn thumped on his butt and bounced like a skipped stone before coming to a halt beside the tub. Rabbit had more forward momentum and went down face first, grabbing the stool as he fell and upending all the neatly folded clothes stacked on it.

The commotion roused Kellen from a deep sleep. He required a moment to make sense of where he was and then another moment to make sense of what he was seeing. He sat up, reached for the taps, and turned them off. He felt between his feet for the drain plug and gave it a tug. The water level started to dip almost immediately.

He looked over at the boys. They were frozen in place. Finn's head barely cleared the lip of the tub, and Rabbit was lying spread-eagle on the floor, clutching the stool but none of the clothes. "Don't you have chores to do at home?"

They shook their heads in unison.

"Huh." Kellen plugged the drain again and leaned back. He rested his arms on the rim of the tub. He was not abandoning a warm bath. "Did you bring a mop? Some rags?"

They shook their heads again. Rabbit offered, "Mrs. Sterling told us to shut the water off."

"Seems as though you should find something else to do since I took care of that job for you."

The boys frowned. There was some kind of hole in that logic, but they couldn't see their way through to it.

"There are extra towels in the bottom of the wardrobe. Put one by the stove where it will be warm for me and use the rest of them to wipe up. You might as well take my clothes and the towel I was going to use out of here. Wring them out at the sink first, then lay them over a chair in the other room and move the chair closer to the stove." A thought occurred to him. "And don't catch anything on fire."

"Yes, sir," said Rabbit. "Right away. We can do that."

Kellen nodded and closed his eyes. He listened to them scrambling to their feet and their under-the-breath jabs, but he did not comment. The boys thrived on an audience. It was no surprise that their grandparents set them loose on the town the moment they found themselves at sixes and sevens.

Rabbit and Finn marched back and forth between the two rooms in the completion of their new chore. Finn poked around a little in the bedroom, trying to see if he could find the guns, but Rabbit caught him and wouldn't let him out of his sight after that.

Finn was wringing out the last wet towel when the cavalry arrived. It was the Pennyroyal cavalry so Finn was not impressed that Walt was carrying a mop or that the Widder Berry had a bucket full of rags. He also thought it was strange that for all the fuss about a little water spilling into the kitchen, neither one of them rushed into the room. Walt let the Widder Berry go first, real gentlemanly-like.

"Well," Raine said, surveying the scene. "Rabbit. Finn. You have done an admirable job here. Leave the towel, Finn. I'll take care of it. You boys need to go. Tell Mrs. Sterling I said you could have a couple of brownies to take with you. She won't believe you, but you'll wheedle them out of her anyway." Behind her, she heard Walt chuckle quietly, and out of the corner of her eye, she saw Kellen's mouth twitch.

The boys thanked her and darted through the small space that separated her from Walt. When Raine heard the door slam behind them, she set her bucket on the floor. "I'll step into the other room, Walt. Mop up what the boys couldn't." To Kellen, she said, "We'll speak later."

Kellen took that to mean she would corner him at dinner or soon afterward. When he walked into the bedroom after Walt left, he found Raine was waiting for him. She was sitting on the bed since every other available surface had some article of clothing hanging from it. Her knees were drawn up and her heels hooked on the iron bed frame. Most surprising, she had thrown his beaten leather long coat around her shoulders and was huddled inside it. Kellen pushed aside the chair that was blocking the heat from the stove, but that was done primarily for his comfort. She had his coat. He had a towel.

Her concession to his modesty was to close her eyes.

"I think you're peeking," he said.

"No," she said. "I'm not. And don't flatter yourself that I'm lying." Which, of course, she was. Kellen Coltrane had broad shoulders and a torso that tapered to a vee. The towel hung loosely on slim hips. Droplets of water clung to the ends of his longish hair. Most of them fell when he rubbed the back of his neck. She followed the line of one particular drop all the way to the arrow of hair below his navel. She raised the collar of his coat and ducked her head to hide the flush in her cheeks.

He made a circling motion with his index finger, indicating she should turn around. When she didn't, he asked, "Do you mind?"

"No, I don't. I really don't."

Perhaps she wasn't looking, he thought, and then wondered why she wasn't. If there was ever an opportunity to reverse their positions, *he* would be looking. He wouldn't make her guess. His eyes would be wide open.

"I need to get my clothes," he said. When she didn't respond, he just shook his head and went to the wardrobe to take out what he needed. He threw it all over one arm and carried it into the bathing room and closed the door.

"I visited Ellen's grave this morning," he called out.

The oddness of that struck Raine dumb.

"I wanted to pay my respects."

She found her voice. "That was kind of you."

"I saw your husband's marker just where you said it would be. How did he die? You've never said."

"Didn't I? I suppose not. Uriah Burdick shot him dead."

Kellen opened the door and came out as he was putting on a silver-threaded vest. He was wearing black woolen trousers and a shirt with suspenders. "Uriah Burdick? Did I hear you right?"

Raine raised her head above the coat collar like a turtle coming out of its shell. "Yes. Adam was playing cards with the Burdicks. Uriah accused him of cheating, which he was, and killed him for it. Adam had a death wish, Mr. Coltrane. He had a cancer inside him. He knew it before we came out here, and Dr. Kent was treating him, but neither of them held out any hope. Adam did well for a while, did most of the work here on his good days, but then the pain set in permanently and there was no help for it. He wanted to die, and I wouldn't let him. That's why he invited himself to play poker with the Burdicks and why he allowed himself to be caught. He was no clumsy card sharper. No one had ever called him out before. He knew what he was doing."

"I'm sorry."

"So am I, Mr. Coltrane."

"Did it happen here at the Pennyroyal?"

She nodded. "In the saloon. At the same table you were sitting at last night. I wasn't there; neither was Ellen. Adam spared us that. Howard Wheeler came upstairs to find me. Witnesses to the shooting swore the cards were on Adam's person. They also found a Remington derringer in his boot, and the Burdicks claimed he went for it. I didn't challenge anyone because it did not matter. Knowing Adam as I did, I am confident he arranged his own death."

Kellen picked up his boots from where they rested beside the stove and carried them to one of the trunks. He pushed aside the damp towels spread out across the lid and sat. "Did you think of returning to California?"

"No. Not for a moment. This is home." She hesitated, looked away toward the window. The view from where she was sitting was an endless expanse of sky. "I think about going places," she said quietly. "St. Louis maybe. Chicago. I think I would like to see New York." She pulled her gaze away and returned to Kellen. "But I know that no other place will hold me forever. This place will always call me home."

Kellen wondered how much of that call came from the graveyard. Adam and Ellen were buried in the shade of a young cottonwood. All the graves were neatly tended, even the ones outside the cemetery proper marked with crude wood stakes that labeled the deceased as scoundrels and no-accounts. It was a serene setting, where the contemplation of life was more in keeping with the purpose than ruminating about death.

"Where else did you go this morning, Mr. Coltrane?"

Kellen finished pulling on the first boot before he answered. "Kellen. I got a horse from Mr. Ransom, who must be your waitress Emily's father. I thought I might get the lay of the land. I followed the river for a while. Went into the hills."

"That's what the boys thought you probably did. Finn and Rabbit saw you at first light. They can see the livery from their bedroom window."

"They're observant."

"They're nosy. I'm sure they almost killed each other trying to get to the attic window. That's how they followed your progress." She waited, but when he didn't say anything, she added, "They told me you had your guns. Were you target shooting?"

He nodded. "I thought I was far enough away to fire some rounds without being heard."

"You were. At least no one who's come in here today

mentioned it. The boys figured that's what you were going to do. They have it in their minds that you're a shootist. It was part of my arrangement with Mr. Church that discretion would be observed, and now there are two young boys who can barely contain their excitement that there is a shootist in our midst." Raine let the coat fall off her shoulders, but she still kept it close. It smelled faintly of horse, saddle soap, and the man . . . Kellen. "I just can't help but think Mr. Church would be handling this more discreetly."

"Mr. Church is dead."

Raine's head jerked back. "Forgive me. I forget that he was your friend."

Kellen's voice was flat. His wintry blue-gray eyes bore into her. "He wasn't my friend. He chose me to help him. We weren't friends."

"But he—"

"I'm going to learn who killed him, Raine. Our arrangement doesn't much matter to me. You can end it anytime, but it doesn't mean I'm leaving. I'm not giving up my room to the next man you hire. I'm staying put and seeing this through." He jammed his foot into the second boot and stamped the floor hard. His heel slipped solidly into place. "What do you want to do?"

"The Burdicks killed Nat Church."

"Prove it."

She couldn't. She didn't say anything.

"What do you want to do?" he asked again.

"I want you to help me."

"Very well," he said, getting to his feet. He tilted his head toward the door. "You need to go. I can handle the boys. I'm not so sure about you. Discretion is not precisely your strong suit. Your staff is going to wonder what's become of you."

Raine pursed her lips at this rebuke. The effect was prim righteousness. She shed the coat as she stood. "If my staff think anything at all about me being in your room, they're thinking I'm still haranguing you for flooding my floor and almost causing Mrs. Sterling to have a conniption."

"So you're here putting me in my place and assessing damages."

"Yes," she said. She started to cross the room but stopped abruptly in front of him. "What do you mean that you can handle the boys, but you're not so sure about me? What have I done to make you think I require handling?"

"Not what you've done," he said. "What you will do."

"Oh? And what is that?"

"This."

Raine blinked, but it was her only reaction as his right arm struck with the speed of a bullsnake. It wrapped itself around her waist and hauled her in. Once he had her, his grip didn't ease. Like the predator, he held her fast, surrounding her as though he might crush her.

He took the breath from her instead.

He gave her time, a long moment to think about it as he slowly lowered his head. It was important to him that she knew she had a choice. It would be important to her.

His mouth touched hers, lightly at first, so lightly that the touch could be imagined more clearly than it could be felt. He cupped the back of her head in one hand, held it still, and pressed his mouth against hers with more purpose.

With more passion.

She moaned softly. It tickled his lips. He drew back a fraction, waited. Her mouth parted, and she closed the distance. Their mouths found a different slant. They kissed and parted, kissed again. He felt her try to raise herself on tiptoe. He loosened the arm around her waist. She stayed flush to his body as though she might climb it. Her heels lifted. Her mouth caught the corner of his. She pushed herself hard against him. He turned his head. The kiss deepened.

His fingers pressed against her scalp. Pins fell from her hair. The coil at her nape unwound so that when he moved his fingers, her hair cascaded over the back of his hand. He wound it around his fist. It was as soft and liquid as her name.

Raine. He whispered it against her mouth. The tip of his tongue touched her upper lip. He felt her knees give way. He pulled her up, held her there, and took her mouth for the delicacy it was. The scent. The heat. The damp.

Her mouth was honey. Her mouth was a drug.

Kellen lifted his head before he died of wanting it.

Raine wanted to put her hand to her mouth, seal the stamp of his lips on hers. Her heart thrummed against her breastbone and blood still roared in her ears. She couldn't hear the sound of her own breathing, couldn't feel the intake of air.

A shiver seized her. She gasped.

Kellen smiled and tipped his head. He rested his forehead against hers. "Well," he said softly, "that was—"

"Unexpected?" she whispered.

His chuckle was deep, resonating from the back of his throat. "The opposite," he told her. "Everything it's supposed to be."

"You should let me go."

"I should." His arm did not relax. The hand at the back of her head stayed where it was. He lifted his head a second time and searched her face. "I will." His hold on her eased, and she came down off tiptoes. Up or down, she still fit neatly against him.

"You knew this about me?" she asked.

"I knew it about you and me."

"Oh." The word was merely an expulsion of air.

Kellen's hands fell to his sides. When she did not step back, he did. A faint smile lifted the corners of his mouth. "You should go."

"I should." She closed the distance between them, clutched his vest, and pressed a kiss to his mouth. "I will." She danced away before he could catch her. At the door, she said, "Look suitably abashed when you come to the dining room. You *did* cause a mess, you know."

He nodded, and then she disappeared into the hallway, closing the door gently behind her.

Raine hurried to the end of the hall and secreted herself in the stairwell that led to the kitchen. Her hands shook. She raised them to her mouth and kept them there until the trembling passed.

Ridiculous. It went through her mind that she was being ridiculous, silly actually. No kiss deserved so much excitement attached to it. Her breasts were swollen, the nipples tender. She hesitated then passed her palms over them, more as an exploration than a caress. Still, it should have been his hands touching her. She was damp between her thighs. Uncomfortably warm. She pressed her legs together and waited for the sensation to pass. She felt herself contract. The shiver that had seized her when she was in his arms seized her again, this time from the inside. She leaned against the wall and sank her teeth into her lower lip. It was enough to silence the moan that rose at the back of her throat.

From downstairs she heard raised voices in the kitchen. A moment, she thought, just a moment longer. A door opened. Closed. Footsteps pounded across the floor and another door opened, this one to the outside. She heard Mrs. Sterling yell for Walt.

Raine Berry did what she didn't think she could. She pushed every thought of Kellen Coltrane from her mind and started down the stairs.

Chapter Five

Raine saw Kellen at dinner. He sat alone again, which meant that the newcomer, Mr. John Paul Jones, sat with the couple from Springfield on their last night in Bitter Springs. Mr. Benjamin Petit of Virginia, a naturalist and photographer of stereographs, and Mr. Alexander Reasoner, late of London and touring the American West, shared a table with the whiskey drummer. Emily Ransom hovered at the tables like a hummingbird, flitting this way and that, flying off when she sensed the nectar was sweeter somewhere else. Raine let her go. It was necessary to keep peace in the kitchen. Mrs. Sterling was thoroughly out of sorts because her piecrusts had been a casualty of what she was now calling the great flood. Her reaction was out of all proportion to the actual event, but there was no consoling her when she spiraled downward into one of her dark moods. Even good-natured, hardworking Walt had been on the receiving end of the cook's sharp tongue.

Raine took it upon herself to work beside Mrs. Sterling and spare everyone else. She did, however, save one slice of the burned apple pie before the cook threw it away. It gave her a certain perverse pleasure to carry it into the dining room and place it in front of Kellen Coltrane.

She did not see him again until he arrived in the saloon. He came in through the front doors, not from the hotel side, which meant he had been out again, not in his room as she supposed him to have been. Since Walt was helping her at the bar, she assumed Kellen had been on his own. Her fist closed tightly around the bar rag she was holding when Eli and Clay Burdick followed his trail.

Kellen came up to the bar while Eli and Clay took their usual table close to the stairs. Tonight, no one had to vacate the table to give the Burdicks what they wanted, so there was none of the tense silence that could occur on those occasions.

Kellen found a place at the bar between Howard Wheeler and Jack Clifton. He knew from talking to Walt that the two friends regularly ate breakfast at the hotel and frequented the saloon three or four evenings a week. The pair had been at a table a few nights earlier and looked as if they might have been on the verge of leaving when Eli came in and took a seat. Now Kellen understood that remaining behind had been purposeful. They were two members of the jury that had convicted Isaac Burdick.

"What will you have, Mr. Coltrane?" asked Walt.

"Three beers."

Walt glanced past him to where the Burdicks were sitting. He looked doubtful. "Eli and Clay usually take a bottle of whiskey."

"I know, but I have some questions for them. Beer to begin."

"Right away."

Kellen caught Raine's eye. "Excellent pie this evening." He was careful not to grin when she pretended she didn't hear him and turned and walked away.

Jack Clifton said, "I thought you must be Coltrane."

Kellen turned his head. Clifton had a lean, leathered face and dark eyes. He wore his Boss of the Plains Stetson tilted back on his head and sported a mustache that hid all of his upper lip.

"I am. You are . . ."

"Jack Clifton."

They exchanged nods, not hands. "Good to meet you, Mr. Clifton." Kellen reached across the bar to take the first beer Walt put out for him.

Howard Wheeler inserted himself into the conversation. He was broader and sturdier than his wiry friend, and he had a nose with a hook large enough to hang his hat on. "Couldn't help overhearing what you said about asking the Burdicks questions."

Kellen pulled the second beer toward him. "I'm writing a story for my paper," he said. "The *New York World*."

Howard frowned. "I recollect reading that's Mr. Pulitzer's paper."

"Just an expression, gentlemen. It's not *my* paper, but I work for it."

"So what's your business with the Burdicks?"

"My business," Kellen said, scooping up the third beer, "is none of yours."

He turned and left the bar, heading for Eli and Clay's table. Before he had set the beers on the table, he could see Clifton and Wheeler putting their heads together in one corner of the saloon.

Clay Burdick pulled a beer toward him.

Kellen passed a beer to Eli. The brothers sat close enough at the round table to prevent a third person coming between them. On a clock they would have been at five and seven. The arrangement suited Kellen. He nudged his chair to twelve o'clock and sat.

Clay took a deep drink and wiped the damp from his mustache on his sleeve. "Eli says you're some kind of newspaperman."

"That's what I told him," said Kellen. Clay's mustache was not as aggressively large as Jack Clifton's, but it was definitely a source of pride. At a glance it was the feature that differentiated him from his older brother. Beneath their Stetsons, Kellen imagined they parted their hair on the same side. They dressed similarly, but not so different from anyone else. Their vests were cut from more expensive cloth, but it was the same cloth, a blue and green stripe with gold-colored thread separating the stripes and holding the buttons in place.

"Uriah says he never heard of a rancher in Dakota named Pulitzer," Clay said. "But he did know that Pulitzer owns the *New York World*."

"That's right," said Kellen.

Eli gave him a narrow look. "You told me he owned a big spread."

"No," Kellen said easily. "You told me. I asked you if you knew Pulitzer, you mentioned a rancher, and I figured you knew something I didn't, you being more familiar with the territory than I am. It was vain of me, but I did not want to show my ignorance. I never said I wrote a story about him."

"That's true," Eli told Clay. "He never said that."

Clay snorted. "You had a three-pony escort home that night. I don't think you know what was said."

"You did drop like a stone, Mr. Burdick," Kellen said to Eli.

Eli merely sighed. "Sure did." He picked up his beer and drank deeply. "I still got the head to prove it."

"You're not a whiskey man," Clay said. "Stay with beer."

Eli glowered at his brother. "I don't need a nursemaid."

"Uriah doesn't agree."

"You might want to ask yourself who's watching who tonight. When's the last time you rode into town without an escort?"

"When's the last time you rode out without one?"

Except for the weapons, it was like being with Rabbit and Finn, Kellen thought. He moved his beer to one side and reached into his jacket. The brothers rounded on him at once, their wrangling stopped by what they perceived as an outside threat. Kellen held up one hand, palm out, and slowly withdrew the other from under his jacket. He showed them a notepad and pencil.

"Tools of my trade," he said. "I thought we could begin the interview."

Raine left the saloon after Kellen pulled out the notepad. In the moment immediately preceding it, she thought the Burdicks were going to draw on him. How she managed not to shout a warning, she would never know, but in the aftermath, she recognized the danger her interference would have put him in. For now at least it seemed that Kellen was safer if she left him to manage on his own.

She told Walt to take over the bar and passed Charlie Patterson a few dollars to help him. Charlie would have done it for free because Sue was going to play again, but Raine insisted he take the money to ensure he stayed behind the bar.

She went to her rooms and read for a time. She purposely avoided the new Nat Church mystery in favor of Felicity Ravenwood's romantic adventures, but even dear Felicity, who often startled her friends with her acerbic wit and extraordinary hats, could not hold her attention.

Raine gathered her coat, gloves, and green woolen scarf and headed out of doors. The sky was clear, with only the brilliance of the stars to distract her from her course. The air was crisp, but the wind had quieted, and the cold was tolerable because it did not go deeply into the bone.

Raine wore her scarf over her hair and wound the rest around her neck. She walked briskly, avoiding the unevenly planked sidewalks in favor of the street. A fingernail moon provided little light, but then she needed very little. She could have found the graveyard with her eyes closed.

The ground was too cold for sitting, so Raine leaned against the pale, ridged trunk of the cottonwood and faced Adam's and Ellen's graves. She hugged herself. Although no living person was around to hear her, and no dead person could, she spoke anyway, quietly and with feeling.

"I did not expect him, you know," she said. "Not a man like him. I think I would not have continued a correspondence if he had been the one to answer. Nat Church, the man I hired, impressed me as steady and cautious. And older. This man is reckless and an irritant, a pebble in my shoe. He pointed out, correctly I must tell you, that Nat Church is dead, so perhaps I set too much store by steadiness and caution. And age."

She smiled wistfully. "You would say it if you could. There's no getting around it. The oddest thing is that he's more like

Nat Church than Nat Church. Do you understand? I don't. Not really. Nat Church, the character, not the man, is reckless. Do you recall in the *Committee of Vigilance* how he nettled Mr. Billy Bragg into making a confession? It is the same with Mr. Coltrane. He nettles. I've said things, many things I didn't think I would tell him, but somehow they spilled out of me like barleycorn from a split sack. That's what he does, just niggles and nettles and you know he's doing it, but he's funny about it. Amusing, I mean. But real subtle about it. Cagey. Like I said, he's the pebble in my shoe, but sometimes he makes me forget I can take my shoes off."

She shifted to find a more comfortable ridge in the bark. She went on in a firmer tone. "And he is too confident for my tastes. That is an aspect of character that does not translate so well off the page. It suited Nat Church in the *Frisco Fancy*, but it is an annoyance when Mr. Coltrane thinks he knows so much. Even when he's just sitting there, saying nothing at all, you can tell he's amusing himself. You can tell he knows something you don't."

Raine fell quiet. She considered what else she might tell them, what else she might confess. After a time she closed her eyes. "He kisses very well. I never thought about how Nat Church might kiss, but I think it would also be very well. Before he left the *Indian Maiden*, it seemed he might kiss Miss Lansdale. He never did, though, so I can't say whether she would have welcomed it." Her voice was barely audible now. "I did."

She opened her eyes and stared at the pale whitewashed wooden markers. "It is not the worst thing to be alone, but it's terrible to be lonely."

Raine swiped at her eyes with gloved fingertips and offered a watery smile up to the darkness. "You see what I have become? Mawkish. I am everything I despise. Maudlin and self-pitying. You know I am not vain, but this looks truly unattractive on me." She imagined Adam and Ellen were agreeing with her. She swiped impatiently at another tear and then sucked in a deep breath to hold back the tide of those that threatened to follow.

She stayed a little longer, drinking in the night and embracing the calm. Settled, she pushed away from the cottonwood and quietly bade Adam and Ellen good night.

Raine passed under the wrought iron archway that marked the graveyard entrance and slowly walked in the direction of town. She was halfway between the cemetery and the Pennyroyal when she realized she was no longer traveling the narrow road alone. She stopped and cocked her head, straining to hear whether the footsteps were coming from behind or ahead of her. It was more concerning when she didn't hear them at all.

"Who's there?" she asked. "I know someone's there." She raised one hand to her brow, flattening it like a visor to block the light from houses in town and help her accustom her eyes to the dark. Squinting, she looked for a shape out of place among the cottonwoods and prairie grass.

The figure, though, appeared on the side of the road. It rose up from the ground without warning and remained motionless. Raine understood that what she had mistaken for a boulder was actually a man huddling close to the ground.

"Who are you?" she asked again.

"Is that you, Mrs. Berry?"

She did not recognize the voice, which relieved her in some ways and alarmed her in others. "Tell me who you are."

A match was struck and the man's face was briefly illuminated in the orange light. "Mr. Jones," he said. He shook the match, extinguishing the fire, and tossed it aside. "We met this afternoon, Mrs. Berry. I am a guest in your hotel."

John Paul Jones. The man Rabbit and Finn had brought from the station that afternoon.

Raine's heart was slow to stop hammering. "I'm sorry, Mr. Jones. I didn't recognize you. Why didn't you answer me?"

"I didn't? I thought I did."

"Not the first time I called out."

"I apologize, then. I did not hear you."

Still wary, Raine started forward but not at the same pace she'd set earlier. "What were you doing crouching in the road?"

"Nursing a twisted ankle, I'm afraid." He took a halting step in her direction and winced audibly.

"Stay where you are, Mr. Jones. Let me examine it."

She drew closer but stopped with an arm's length still separating them. "I could look at it more thoroughly if you would sit."

"I don't think that's necessary. If you would lend me your shoulder . . ."

Concern warred with caution. Caution won. "Just give me a moment. I'll find something for you to sit on." Raine stepped off the road and into the knee-high grass. She asked him questions while she searched. "What are you doing out here?"

"I suspect the same thing you are. I find an evening walk clears my mind."

Raine found a fallen log by stubbing her toe on it. Swearing softly, she picked up the log and carried it over. "I promise you it will be better than the ground, and you won't harm your clothes. They look very fine." Raine waited as he gingerly put weight on the twisted ankle. She thought he sat awkwardly for a man in his thirties with such a slight injury. She was used to men shrugging off wounds that were infinitely more grievous in nature.

Apparently Mr. John Paul Jones did not have the constitution of his admiral namesake, who was alleged to have said, when the battle seemed lost, "I have not yet begun to fight."

Raine did not mention this. Mr. Jones was a slim, fit man, narrow of face and shoulders, and had a rather delicate way of turning his hands when he spoke. He had a long nose and a carefully groomed mustache below it. His beard was neatly trimmed and the same sandy color as his hair. His height was imposing. His lanky arms and legs, the long torso, put Raine in mind of a locust, and his countenance for that brief moment it was illuminated by the match had been as unpleasantly humorless as one.

Once he was seated, Raine asked him to stretch his leg toward her. Only then did she hunker down. She placed her hands on either side of his ankle. "Can you rotate it?"

He did as she asked, wincing.

"I do not want to remove your boot," she said. "Your ankle might swell. It doesn't seem as if you've broken it."

"There's a mercy."

"Some people say a sprain hurts more and takes longer to heal."

"Well, that is not good news. I need to travel."

Raine felt around the boot again, this time manipulating the foot. She heard him suck in his breath. "Truly, Mr. Jones, I think you will be able to continue your journey. You indicated that you would be staying at the Pennyroyal for upwards of a month. That is sufficient for your recuperation. You will experience little difficulty after that."

"My new journey begins here, Mrs. Berry. I'm a surveyor for the government."

"A surveyor. Well, that puts your injury in a different light." She released his foot.

Mr. Jones held his knee and carefully rotated his left foot on his own.

"Hey, Mrs. Berry!"

Raine peered toward the sound of Finn's voice. Finn and Rabbit were coming up the road from the direction of town. They had but a single silhouette because they were walking so closely together.

"I can't begin to imagine what you boys are doing here," she said. "You should be in bed."

They stopped a few feet in front of her. "Hey, Mr. Jones," Finn said.

"What happened?" asked Rabbit. "You get something stuck in your boot?"

They were not even subtle about ignoring her, Raine thought. She had an urge to knock their towheads together. "Boys?"

"Granny sent us to get Pap," Rabbit told Raine. "He's at the saloon. There was a package that came for Uriah today that never got claimed. Pap thought he might come across Eli or Clay at the Pennyroyal and pass it along."

Finn nodded. "He didn't want to ride out to the Burdick place if he could help it."

Rabbit said, "But he hasn't come back, so she sent us to get him."

"So what are you doing out here?" She pointed toward town. "The Pennyroyal is that way. I don't see your pap with you."

"He wasn't ready to leave," said Finn. "Told us to go home and tell Granny he was staying put for a piece."

Rabbit heaved a sigh as long in suffering as any that had ever come from his pap. "But Granny told us not to come back without him, so you see we are ridin' the longhorns of a pretty big dilemma."

"That's a steer that's gone loco," Finn said helpfully. "I didn't know what it meant until Rabbit explained."

Raine pressed a fist to her lips and cleared her throat. "Thank you, Finn. I hadn't realized." When she was certain the bubble of laughter was thoroughly suppressed, she said, "That does not quite explain what you're doing out here."

"On our way to the graveyard," said Rabbit.

"He's says I'm too scared to go," said Finn, "but I'm not. I've been there before."

"Not at night," Rabbit said.

Raine saw where this was headed. She clapped her hands together. "Boys. We have an injured man here. Mr. Jones twisted his ankle. I was going to assist him, but I think the two of you will make a pair of excellent crutches." She turned to Mr. Jones. "Are you ready to get up?"

"Eager," he said, his tone as dry as dust. As soon as he started to push up on the log, the boys jumped in to assist. They quickly inserted themselves under his arms and heaved. He hopped on his right foot until he was able to steady himself using the boys' shoulders.

Their progress was slow but steady. When they reached the Pennyroyal, Raine went into the saloon by herself and asked Jem and Jessop Davis to assist Mr. Jones to his room. She directed everyone to use the hotel's entrance, and told Rabbit and Finn they could lead the way. They dashed ahead in their usual fashion while the Davis brothers and Mr. Jones set a less frantic pace. Raine stayed behind.

Walt stopped filling a glass from the tapped keg when he saw Raine's reflection in the mirror. She was approaching the bar and had not yet tried to catch his eye. He finished what he was doing, set out the beer for Jefferson Collins, and waited for her to wind her way through the maze of tables.

"Something wrong?" he asked. "Thought you were going to take a night off. Charlie and me are doing pretty well on our own."

"I'm sure you are, but I need your help with something else. Let me come around the bar." She eyed Mr. Collins and his drink before she went. "You stay right there," she told him.

He grinned. "I have no other plans."

"We'll talk about that." She rounded the long bar and waved Walt over to where she was standing. She unwound the scarf from her head and removed her gloves. "Will you take a box of salts to Mr. Jones? He injured his ankle and will appreciate soothing it in a salt bath."

"Sure. That won't take but a couple of minutes."

She laid a hand on his forearm. "Take a basin, too. Jem and Jessop helped him up to his room."

"So that's where they went. I never saw you talking to them. You should have taken Jake, too. He hardly knows what to do with himself."

Raine smiled, understanding. She unbuttoned her coat and gave it to Walt to put in the back room along with her gloves and scarf. "His brothers will be back any minute. Thank you, Walt. I'll wait here and help Charlie until you return. Oh, and send Rabbit and Finn down right away."

"Rabbit and Finn?" Walt's eyebrows climbed toward his receding hairline. "Never mind. I don't want to know."

Raine stepped aside to let him pass and then went straight to Jeff Collins. She waited until he set his beer down before she took it away. She held up a finger to stall his protest. "I could have taken it right out of your hand," she said. "I probably should have. Mrs. Collins sent the boys to fetch you and you sent them back. That's the kind of cross-purposes that would make boys with a lick of good sense scratch their heads. We both know that Rabbit and Finn don't have half a lick between them."

The station agent peered at Raine over the rim of his

spectacles. "How deep is the hole they dug for themselves this time?"

"Oh, they're fine," she said, waving aside that concern. "There's no hole. In fact, they were helpful and they could not have arrived at a more opportune moment, but they came upon me on the road leading out to the graveyard."

"What were you doing there?"

"Mr. Collins, what I was doing there is hardly your concern. That Rabbit and Finn were there is the point."

He shrugged. "Boys go to a graveyard when they want to scare themselves stupid."

"Mr. Collins."

He sighed. "I come here for a few moments' respite, Mrs. Berry. And the beer is good, too. May I please have my glass back?"

She slid it in front of him. "You are a fraud. Rabbit and Finn are you through and through."

"Where are the boys now?"

"Upstairs at the moment. Walt is sending them down before they bedevil Mr. Jones." She told him what happened and her story conveniently ended at the same time he finished his beer. The boys appeared a few moments after that, and Mr. Collins was persuaded he had to make the best of it. Raine watched him go to his grandsons. It struck her that he didn't take them by the collar to lead them out. Instead, he took them under his wing.

Kellen followed the direction of Raine's gaze and understood the reason for her smile. "They're something, aren't they?"

She nodded absently before she came back to herself. Her head swiveled around. "You're still here?"

He raised a single eyebrow.

"Of course you are. It was a ridiculous question."

"I'm heartily glad to learn you know it."

She gave him a narrow look, darts at the ready. "What I meant," she said, carefully enunciating each word, "is that you were not here when I came in and elicited the help of two of the Davis brothers."

"Perhaps it's only that you didn't see me."

"You weren't here."

"Well, I won't flatter myself that you noticed my absence."

"Good for you."

His slim smile was like a warning shot. "I went back to my room for a few minutes. There was a commotion in the hallway. When I heard Rabbit and Finn, I decided to stay where I was until it passed."

"Probably wise."

"I thought so." He leaned an elbow against the bar. "Could I get a beer?"

She nodded and poured him one. Jessop Davis appeared at the bar, and she gave him a beer and two more for his brothers. "Compliments of the house," she told him.

"Thank you, Mrs. Berry, but Jake didn't do anything."

"He waited for you and Jem. That certainly was a hardship for him."

Jessop grinned, swept three beers off the bar, and went back to the table where his brothers were waiting.

"They were part of the commotion?" asked Kellen when Jessop was gone.

"Since you have to ask, I imagine they were the quiet part."

"What happened?"

Raine shook her head. Charlie was coming toward her from behind the bar, and Dick Faber was approaching the front of it. "Can we speak later?" she asked under her breath.

He nodded. "Just so you know, Eli and Clay left when Mr. Collins brought the crate. Apparently Uriah's been talking about it. They decided he would want to have it right away."

"All right."

Kellen thought she looked relieved. Satisfied with that, he took his beer and left.

Kellen expected to hear about the previous night's commotion at breakfast. When a shadow crossed Kellen's newspaper, he looked up in anticipation of seeing Raine. He masked his annoyance when he saw it was one of the Pennyroyal's new guests.

"Mr. Coltrane, is it?" Mr. Jones asked.

"Yes. You're Jones?"

"John Paul Jones."

"I saw you at dinner yesterday."

"My first evening here. May I join you?"

Kellen wondered why Jones did not respond to any of the things that he was doing that kept others away. The paper was not a deterrent. Neither was the fact that Kellen avoided the pleasantries that everyone else offered when Mr. Jones entered the room. Kellen had actually shifted in his chair to give the newcomer a better view of his shoulder than his profile. Most telling, he had deliberately shown no curiosity when others remarked on Mr. Jones's limp.

Yet here the man was, standing at his table, holding on to the edge for balance and support with the tips of his precisely clipped fingernails.

"Please," said Kellen. He folded the paper and laid it beside his plate. "Sit. Do you need help?"

"No. I can manage." He pulled out a chair and eased himself into it. "A minor inconvenience."

Kellen did not inquire. He raised his hand and got Emily Ransom's attention. She came close to scalding Howard Wheeler when she missed his cup as she hurried over. "Not an emergency, Miss Ransom," said Kellen. "I want the hotcakes and more coffee."

"No eggs for you?" she asked, carefully filling his cup. "Mrs. Sterling will make them any way you like."

"Just the hotcakes."

"Bacon?"

"The hotcakes."

"Fried potatoes?"

"Hotcakes."

Emily sighed. She could not hope to extend their exchange by suggesting toast and jam. "You, Mr. Jones?"

"All of that," he said. "Scramble the eggs, and ask the cook to keep them on the wet side. I do not care for dry eggs. Also, I would like toast. Two slices. And blackberry preserves, if you have them."

"Certainly, Mr. Jones." Emily poured a cup of coffee for him, and then hovered just long enough that Kellen gave her a nudge in the direction of the kitchen.

"What a silly girl," Mr. Jones said, watching her go. "I don't suppose she can help it."

"She enjoys herself. There's no harm."

Mr. Jones added cream to his coffee. "You don't find all that fluttering wearing on the nerves?"

Kellen did, but he was also feeling perverse. "No. It's easy enough to overlook." He picked up his coffee and sipped. "What brings you to the Pennyroyal, Mr. Jones?"

"John Paul," he said. "Please."

"Kellen."

Jones nodded. "I am working for the U.S. Geological Survey. I have been assigned the eastern half of the Wyoming Territory and the southwestern portion of the Dakota Territory."

"Isn't that a lot of ground for one man to cover?"

"I'm here in advance of the team that will follow. I can hire locals to help with some preliminary work. The government's interest is water and mineral resources."

"This would be the Department of the Interior."

"Correct." He nursed his coffee. "What about you, Kellen?"

"Working on a story."

"Is that right?"

Kellen nodded. "About the ranches. Ranchers. There is still a lot of interest about that life in the East."

"There is certainly a lot of interest in it in Washington."

Kellen merely arched a brow.

"Well," Jones said, lowering his cup. "You know, of course, that the drought of eighty-six put considerable stress on the water sources all over the West, and then winter arrived with one blizzard after another. Add the ranchers and the farmers fighting over water rights and the land that's fit for irrigation, if we don't get a good survey of the region and identify sites for reservoirs and hydraulic works, there will be blood on the prairie."

"You think the cattlemen and the farmers will do to each other what the Cheyenne and the Sioux couldn't?"

"I think that is precisely what they will do. So does Washington. Congress just authorized this survey. Here I am."

"Are you staying here long?"

"A month at least. This will be my base for a while."

Kellen sat back when Emily appeared with a plate of hotcakes in one hand and a platter of everything else in the other. She dipped in front of Mr. Jones and slid the platter into place in front of him, then laid the hotcakes at Kellen's setting. She pointed to the white pitcher that held the syrup. "Do you want more coffee?" When they both said yes, she went to get it.

Raine caught Emily with the coffeepot before the girl left the kitchen. "I'll take it in," she said.

"But—"

"I'll take it in," Raine said again, brooking no argument. "Help Mrs. Sterling with the turnovers."

"I need her help with the dishes," Mrs. Sterling said.

"Do whatever she wants," Raine told her. "No fighting." She took the coffeepot and ducked out of the kitchen before there was an exchange of words. She visited all of the tables, purposely leaving Kellen and Mr. Jones for last. All the while she was pouring and chatting, she had an ear trained to the conversation at their table. Most of what she overhead she believed she was hearing incorrectly. They could not be discussing reservoirs and dams.

"Coffee, gentlemen?" she asked.

Mr. Jones held up his cup. "Please. Thank you for sending the bath salts up to my room. Your man told me it was your idea."

"Were they helpful, Mr. Jones?"

"Very much so."

"Good." She raised the pot for Kellen. "Mr. Coltrane?"

"I didn't get any bath salts."

Raine's mouth flattened. "Coffee?"

"Yes." He did not lift his cup, nor did he say please. He thought she might pour coffee in his lap, but if the thought was there, she restrained herself. He thanked her.

"Won't you sit with us a spell, Mrs. Berry?" Jones asked.

"It's a kind and tempting offer," she said, smiling. "I don't know if I—" Raine looked around the dining room. Everyone was settled and entertained. She set the coffeepot on the table. "Do you know? I think I will. Thank you."

Mr. Jones got up and held out the chair on his left for her. It put her directly across from Kellen. He had politely risen halfway as she was seated. Now he dropped back in his seat and gave all of his attention to his hotcakes.

"You are doing well today, Mr. Jones?" she asked.

"Tolerably well. I believe I will soak my foot again after breakfast."

"That's probably wise. I suppose you will not be taking your regular walk this evening."

"No, and I will miss it."

Raine directed her next comment at Kellen in spite of the fact that he only had eyes for his plate. "Mr. Jones takes a daily constitutional," she told him. "He is completely dedicated to it."

Kellen's fork was heavy with three triangles of hotcakes wet with molasses. He used it to make a gesture of salute in Mr. Jones's direction and then managed to get it all in his mouth without spilling a crumb or a drop.

"That's commendable," he said around a mouthful of food.

Raine was tempted to kick him under the table, but she doubted he would let it pass. She decided to ignore him instead. "Please, Mr. Jones, you must eat. Your food will grow cold." When he made some vague noises that were a polite protest, she insisted. "I will leave if you don't eat."

"Very well." He smoothed the napkin in his lap before he picked up his knife and fork. "Did those young ruffians get home safely?"

"They did. Mr. Collins escorted them home."

"Ah, yes. Their pap, I believe they called him. The station agent."

"That's right. It was fortunate, really, that they were out last night. I don't know that I could have managed on my own."

"You seem very capable, Mrs. Berry. I believe I was in good hands even before there were so many of them." He speared some eggs. "The boys? Do they come here often? They seem overly familiar."

"They are frequent visitors, yes." She tilted her head to one side and regarded him with interest. "I believe you are not fond of children, Mr. Jones. Is that right?"

"Guilty," he said without apology. He pressed his napkin to his mouth, and then laid it across his lap again, smoothing it just so. He picked up his coffee cup. "They have so few redeeming qualities, don't they?"

Raine chuckled. "And yet we all passed that way."

Kellen glanced at Jones. Every gesture the government man made was precise, perhaps even practiced. He held himself correctly, though not stiffly, and while he had a tendency to mannered behavior, he was not fussy, at least not annoyingly so. The exact part in his hair, the well-groomed mustache and beard, and the way he liked to press the napkin over his lap, all made Kellen wonder how well the Department of the Interior had chosen their leader.

He finally put his finger on what was rubbing him the wrong way. Mr. John Paul Jones had all the markings of an academic.

"Maybe John Paul spent less time as a child than the rest of us," he said. "Did you?"

Jones laughed politely. "I am quite certain I did not. I had as few redeeming qualities as the ruffians, although I do not think I flatter myself when I say my grammar was better."

Raine saw Kellen had something to say about that, and she spoke quickly to cut him off. "I promise that Rabbit and Finn will not pester you, Mr. Jones, but I cannot promise that you won't see them around. They are charged with bringing trunks and bags to the hotel from the station, and I find they are useful here. I will not bar them from coming or toss them out on your account."

Kellen waited to see what the reaction would be. He observed that Mr. Jones was properly appalled.

"I would be unhappy if you did, Mrs. Berry. It is one thing to operate an establishment with the comfort of your guests in mind, quite another to operate it according to their whims."

"I'm glad you understand."

Mr. Jones continued to apply himself to his meal while Kellen pushed his empty plate away and reached for his coffee.

"I was thinking I would go for a ride this morning," Kellen said. "Can you suggest a direction, Mrs. Berry?"

Raine assumed he meant to do more target shooting. "I believe you will find it pleasant to follow the river south and east."

"The road that winds past the graveyard looked as if it might be promising," Jones said.

"Perhaps tomorrow," said Kellen. "Is that an area of interest that you mean to survey?"

"I mean to survey everything, but yes, that's an area of particular interest."

"You will want to speak to the Burdicks," Raine said. "They own most of the land heading out that way."

Jones grew thoughtful. He used a thumb and forefinger to smooth his mustache and let his napkin lay where it was. "I don't need their permission to make a survey for the government."

"That may be true," said Raine, "but I do not believe the Burdicks will care."

Kellen reached for the coffeepot and topped off his cup. "I would give Mrs. Berry's words some heed, John Paul. I haven't been here much longer than you, but I've already heard the story of how Uriah Burdick's wife eloped with a railroad surveyor. I don't get the sense Mr. Burdick will take kindly to you carrying your equipment onto his property."

Jones blinked as widely and slowly as a barn owl. He turned those eyes on Raine.

She nodded. "There was also a man shot dead because someone thought he was a rustler," she said. "He happened to be our marshal."

Kellen spoke before Jones could. "I'll be damned," he said. "No one told me that."

To Raine's ears, he sounded convincing. It was gratifying to know that being an accomplished liar was one of his talents. "It happened several years ago."

Jones folded his napkin and laid it over his plate. "Still, I would be foolish to ignore it. How do I arrange to speak to Mr. Burdick if visitors are discouraged?"

"You could speak to one of his sons," said Raine. "Mr. Coltrane has had drinks with them. They come in the saloon several times a week this time of year."

Jones turned to Kellen. "You would arrange an introduction?"

"If you like." Kellen shrugged. "But I have to tell you, there's no getting around the fact that you're a surveyor. I have a feeling that won't set right with them."

"I cannot lie about it," Jones said.

"No, I don't suppose you can. You have to do your job." He finished his coffee and returned the cup to its saucer. "I don't pretend to know Eli and Clay well. In fact, I'm not claiming that I know them better than anyone I've shared a couple of drinks with, but I think if you offered something of value to the Burdicks, showed them how the geological survey could be to their advantage, they might not kill you where you sit."

Jones pushed his lower lip forward and exhaled through his mouth. The hairs of his mustache stirred. "I should probably apply to Washington for some guidance in this matter," he said at last.

"If you think that's best," Raine said. "Mr. Collins will telegraph your message."

"I'm wondering if I shouldn't write. This is not a situation that can be adequately explained in a telegram." He indicated his ankle. "And I have some time. There is only so much I can do while I am recuperating."

"Probably wise," said Kellen. He nodded in turn to Raine and Jones and pushed back his chair. "If you'll excuse me, I need to return to my room before I head out. Good meeting you, John Paul." He stood. "Good day, Mrs. Berry."

Jones waited until Kellen left the dining room before he spoke. "He is somewhat abrupt in his manner, isn't he?"

"Forgive me, Mr. Jones, but I make it a practice not to discuss one guest with another."

"I understand. I should not have looked to you for

confirmation. I could see very well that he is. He spoke little of himself, which I suppose is an excellent quality in a newspaper writer. More listening. Less talking. The seeds of a story are sown in the listening, I imagine."

"Is that what he is?" she asked. "A newspaper writer?"

Jones chuckled. "See? That's how little he says. Yes, I managed to get that much from him. He's doing a story on cattlemen. It's occurred to me that he would be an excellent addition to my survey group."

"You want to hire him?"

"I think he might be just the man to approach the Burdicks."

Chapter Six

After the odd exchange at breakfast, Raine thought she might see more of Mr. John Paul Jones. Instead, he asked for an exception to the Pennyroyal's policy of not serving meals in the rooms and requested that luncheon and dinner be brought to him. Although Raine might have encouraged another guest to make the effort to come to the dining room, she did not ask it of this particular guest. Instead, she sent Emily with a tray and decided that would be his punishment. She could not make herself believe the sprain he sustained was worthy of confinement.

Kellen did not return until after lunch had been served. The dining room was empty, the dishes cleaned and put away, and Mrs. Sterling was taking a few minutes with her feet up while she contemplated what she would prepare for dinner. Raine was in her office when he arrived, so she wasn't witness to what transpired, but she had it all from Sue, and then Emily, and they reported that Mrs. Sterling fell all over herself making Mr. Coltrane a special meal of sausages and baked apples. She also gave him both heels from a loaf of freshly baked bread when he asked prettily for them.

Raine did not know what was more difficult to believe, that Mrs. Sterling would give away both heels or that Kellen Coltrane was capable of asking prettily for anything.

According to Sue, and verified by Emily, Kellen retired to his room after that. No one saw him again until dinner.

At eight o'clock, when the Burdicks had not shown themselves at the saloon, Raine was satisfied they were not coming. She handed management of the saloon over to Walt and told Charlie Patterson in passing to keep an eye on him and Sue.

Raine paused at the entrance to the second floor on her way to the third. She did not linger long. All the rooms were filled now, and she did not want to be seen coming and going from Kellen's, at least not without an armful of towels. She wondered what he was doing and where he had been.

Raine entered her apartments and removed her shawl. It was an afterthought that made her lock the door. She tossed the key in an empty vase on the entry table and laid her shawl over the chair at her desk. She lit one lamp in the office and another in the sitting room as she passed through. The final lamp she lit was at her bedside, and this one she carried into the bathing room while she turned on the taps.

She returned to her bedroom and began undressing, loosening the front lacings of the bodice first, then removing the brooch from her jabot and setting it aside. After she eased out of the bodice and hung it in the wardrobe, she took off the jabot, checked it for stains, and finding none, folded it and placed it in a drawer. The red dotted sateen skirt was next. She untied the ribbons at the back, fussed with the panniers and straw bustle, and finally was able to step out of all of it. The white muslin underskirt came next. She sat on the edge of the bed while she removed her red kid slippers and carefully rolled her white stockings over each knee and calf until they were balanced like small puffs of pastry on the tips of her toes. She kicked each one into the air and caught it before she tucked them both inside her shoes.

The front-laced bodice required that she wear a corset with laces at the back. She had managed to get it on that morning with a minimum of trouble, but she discovered now that the laces were hopelessly knotted. She tried to shimmy out of the corset, and for all the reasons that steel stays worked so well, the undergarment remained precisely where it was. Her attempt to twist it was unsuccessful. She began to wriggle again.

"Would you like help?" Kellen asked.

Raine spun around so fast she lost her balance and fell back on the bed, barely catching herself before she sprawled across the top of it. "Mother of God." The hand that she pressed to her heart had nothing at all to do with preserving her modesty. She tried to put Kellen in his place with a sharp stare while her breathing settled.

"I suppose you think I meant to do that," he said.

"Try to scare me to death? Why would I think that? You already assured me you don't work for the Burdicks."

Kellen leaned a shoulder against the jamb in the open doorway. He folded his arms against his chest. She was recovering her sass, which was a good sign, and she wasn't reaching for anything to throw at him, which was a better one.

"So," he asked after a moment. "Would you like help?"

"How did you get in? I know I locked the door."

"I was already in," he said.

"But where? I didn't—"

"You didn't go in all the rooms. I was sitting in the bedroom with the pink roses on the wall. I thought it was yours."

"Ellen's," she said.

"I realize that now."

"You should have told me right away that you were here. Better yet, you shouldn't have come here without an invitation."

"I'm sure you're right about all of that."

"That's not an apology."

"No, it's not."

Raine set her jaw but not so hard that it would become a source of amusement to him.

"When I heard the water running," he said, "I was going to let myself out, but I couldn't find the key."

"I doubt you would have found it much of a challenge to turn the lock without one."

"Perhaps not, but I did not need another challenge."

"Another?"

"I was eluding Mr. Jones when I came up here. I caught sight of him standing outside my door and made a hasty retreat up the stairs."

If it was a lie, Raine thought, it was a good one. She decided she would believe it. "The key is in the vase by the door."

"I didn't look there."

"Evidently." When Kellen did not move, she raised an eyebrow.

Kellen lifted his forefinger and pointed to the bathing room door. His cocked eyebrow mirrored Raine's.

"The tub!" Raine leaped forward and charged for the bathing room. Kellen followed but at a slower pace. He was still in time to see her rush the tub and seize the spindle of each faucet in her hands. She turned them hard.

Raine sat on the rim, catching her breath. The corset did not help. "Thank you," she said. "I forgot about it."

"It was the least I could do."

"The very least," she said dryly.

Kellen made himself comfortable in this new doorway, setting his shoulder against the frame.

Raine waved him out. Her gesture had no effect. "You can't stay there."

"I can," he said. "I doubt that I will, but I don't doubt that I can."

Shaking her head, Raine stood. She retrieved two towels from the cupboard beside the sink, aware all the while that his eyes were following her. "If you truly want to be useful," she said, "you could stoke the fire in the stove. Add coals if you think it needs more."

"All right."

He moved out of the doorway and bent to open the grate. Raine immediately ran to the door and pulled it shut.

"I knew you were going to do that." He grinned when he heard her laugh. She had a husky laugh made more intriguing by its edge of wicked amusement. "What about your corset?"

"I will manage."

His grin deepened when she responded with a certain amount of prickly in her voice. When they were young, his sister Kitty would have answered in just that fashion, and then tattled to their mother that he was teasing her again. "You stay confident," he called through the door. "I will remain hopeful."

He heard her swear softly, and he didn't stray far. Two minutes did not pass before she opened the door and presented her back to him.

Kellen did not say a word. He applied himself to the Gordian knot she had made of her laces.

Raine tried not to show her impatience, but she could feel his fingers at the small of her back and it was frankly unsettling. "You're taking an extraordinarily long time."

"I assume you don't want me to use scissors."

"No."

"Or my teeth."

Raine craned her neck to try to see over her shoulder. "No!"

He stopped what he was doing to gently push her head back. "Then you will have to be patient."

She faced forward and pressed her lips together.

"Almost . . ." He managed to snag one of the laces with a fingernail and loosen it enough to pull. "There. Just a moment." He quickly finished separating the laces.

Raine heaved a sigh, not only because he was finally finished but because she could finally breathe. Her thin muslin shift still clung to her skin. She held the corset in front of her as she turned to thank Kellen. "I need to get my robe. I left it in here."

He stepped out of the way and watched her pass. If she had turned then and caught him staring, he would have acknowledged guilt but no remorse. His hands had spent enough time at the small of her back to come by an itch to be there again.

Raine retrieved her robe and went back to the bathing room. Kellen let her go unmolested. In truth, she did not know how she felt about that. She didn't think she would have turned him away, but neither was she sure she would have welcomed him. She found her confusion disturbing, a state of being that made her head feel thick and her stomach knot as tightly as her laces.

Raine poured lavender-scented salts into her bathwater before she sank deeply into the tub. Hot water lapped the rim. She rearranged her hair so that it was loosely secured closer to the crown of her head. That allowed her to lean back comfortably and rest her head against the tub. Sighing softly, she closed her eyes.

When the door opened a few minutes later, Raine did not stir.

Kellen stayed in the doorway. Ribbons of fragrant steam rose above the tub and curled the copper halo of hair around Raine's face. Her splendidly realized features were composed, even serene, and shone golden in the lamplight. She looked otherworldly, the stuff of fairy stories and legend. She might have been the Lady of the Lake holding her magical secrets as closely as she held the sword Excalibur, or one of the sirens who trapped Ulysses with her beauty and her song. Kellen caught the drift of his thoughts and reined them in, but not before he had to clear the wry chuckle that lodged itself deep in his throat.

Raine opened one eye and looked askance at him. "Will you not even allow me the luxury of pretending you aren't there?"

"I am profoundly sorry."

He did not sound contrite in the least, but Raine let it pass. She closed her eye and slipped a fraction lower into the water. "You will keep your distance, won't you?"

"Reluctantly."

That had the ring of truth, she thought. "Why are you still here? I told you where the key is."

"I am confounded by the problem of what to do with the key after I unlock the door. If I leave it behind, then I'm leaving you alone, in your bath, I might add, with no way to immediately lock the door after me. If I lock the door after I exit, not only am I in possession of your key, but you have no simple way to get out. You see my quandary."

"What I see is that you are riding on the longhorns of a pretty big dilemma."

Kellen's brow furrowed. "I am doing what?"

"Something Rabbit said. At least I think it was Rabbit. It might have been Finn."

It was all the explanation Kellen required. "I see."

"They did not endear themselves to Mr. Jones," Raine said. "He made that clear."

"Several times," said Kellen. "What were you doing out while I believed you were safely tucked in for the night? You understand, don't you, that I can't provide protection when you're eluding it."

"I understand, but the Burdicks were with you. I didn't expect a confrontation."

"Perhaps not, and that's a serious miscalculation." His tone was devoid of humor. "You know, or you should know, that the direct threat is not the Burdicks. It is the men the Burdicks hire. Stay close, Raine. I mean it."

She felt vaguely threatened and thought it was his intention to make her feel that way. "There are other people you have to consider," she said. "I explained that to you. I cannot be your sole concern."

"Nine of the twelve men who sat on the jury were in your saloon last evening. Did you know that?"

Her frown gave her away. She hadn't known. "Nine? You're sure?"

He ticked them off. "Sample. Rogers. Allen. McCormick. Faber. Pennway. Reston. Jack Clifton and Howard Wheeler went to their own corner as soon as the Burdicks arrived. Considering that John Hood is dead and that Hank Thompson is missing, the only person unaccounted for was Matthew Sharp."

"Matthew is a Mormon," she said quietly.

"Pardon?"

She opened her eyes and carefully sat up, drawing her knees close to her chest. She looked over at Kellen. "He's a Mormon. He doesn't drink. That's why you haven't seen him around, and why Walt never gave you that tidbit. Matt lives on land annexed to the town. He and his wife and children mostly keep to themselves."

"Wife? Only one?"

She nodded. "Beatrice. Bea. She works the farm side by

side with Matthew. If he decides he wants another wife, they'll leave. No single man in Bitter Springs is going to let him have two."

"No, I don't suppose they would. That was his farm I saw when I rode south yesterday? The one with all the chicken coops?"

"Yes. Bea and Matthew have the best chickens and the best eggs. That's where we buy ours."

Kellen did not care about that. He cared more that the Sharps were isolated, and that Matthew Sharp had a good reason for not joining his fellow jurymen at the Pennyroyal. "Are you aware of any threats made expressly to Mr. Sharp or his family?"

"No. But I don't know that they would say anything if there were."

"I'll speak to them."

"Speak to them? How—" She stopped, remembering what Mr. Jones told her. "Are you telling people you are writing a story?"

"I have to tell them something, don't I? I told Eli I was researching a story for the *New York World*."

"Well, that explains the little notebook I saw you take out. Were you actually making notes?"

He nodded. "I think they would have noticed if I drew pictures."

She blew out a breath. A puff of air stirred the copper fringe of hair at her forehead. "But the *New York World*? A newspaper everyone knows? What made you choose that?"

"A moment's inspiration."

"That's what I was afraid of."

She reached for the soap that was sitting on a metal tray between the faucets. The water was cooling rapidly, and she needed to wash and get out. She searched around for the sponge and found it beside her feet.

"I wish you had told me what you were saying to people," she said. "I didn't like learning it from Mr. Jones."

"You were talking about me?"

"*He* was talking about you. I told him I don't discuss my guests with other guests."

"Wise. What did he say?"

She made a prim line of her mouth while she lathered her shoulders. "I don't discuss my guests with other guests."

He gave her a wry smile. "Amusing."

Raine rubbed the back of her neck with the sponge. "He is thinking about hiring you for his survey group."

"Hiring me? To do what?"

"To beard the lion in his den. In this case, the lion is—"

"Uriah Burdick."

"That's right. I imagine he's thinking that you can go in first, offer some reasoning that will make Uriah agreeable to the survey, and if he doesn't run you off or kill you, then Mr. John Paul Jones has his foot in the door."

"And his equipment and men all over the Burdick ranch."

"Yes. It's a clever idea."

"You're saying that because he's not trying to throw you to the wolves."

"Lions."

Kellen's dismissive grunt remained at the back of his throat. He fell silent, thinking.

Raine tipped her head back and squeezed the sponge so soapy water ran down her chin and into the hollow of her throat. She continued washing, first one arm, then the other. She ran the sponge along the length of each leg, outside and inside, keeping them under the water the entire time. She only raised her feet long enough to attend to her toes.

When Kellen's silence lasted an inordinately long time, Raine looked over at him. She thought she might find him watching her, but all of her discreetly performed ablutions appeared to have been unnecessary. He was staring at the floor, and whatever was occupying his mind had cut grim lines on either side of his mouth.

"Please tell me you are not considering his offer," she said.

Kellen was slow to meet her eyes. Her voice came to him as though from a great distance. "Did you say something?"

"Mother of God," she said, sighing. "You *are* considering it."

He did not understand her reaction. "Of course. That's why you told me about it, isn't it?"

"No. I told you so that you could prepare an excellent reason for turning Mr. Jones down."

"That part of your plan does not seem to have worked."

She threw the sponge at him. It was heavy with water, but she pitched it with enough force to carry it all the way to the door. Her aim was true. She had only neglected to account for his reflexes. He dodged it easily, and it fell harmlessly to the floor with a loud *thwack*.

Kellen studied it for a long moment, contemplating his retaliatory strike before he bent and picked it up. He hefted it once in his palm, judging its weight and potential to harm, and when he decided there would be no injury, he launched it at Raine, choosing a line that made it sail above her head.

She responded predictably, throwing her arms up in the air and rising to her knees to catch it. She was gleeful as she brought it back to her chest until she realized that he'd been the victor in the encounter. He hadn't wanted to hit her with the sponge at all. He'd wanted to see her breasts.

The water felt even colder after Raine's deep flush suffused her skin with heat. She watched water slosh over the edge of the tub as she dropped back. The sponge and her folded arms preserved her modesty after the fact.

"Do you want me to apologize?" he asked.

"No. If you're sorry, it's only because you didn't throw it higher."

Laughter rose from deep in his chest, and it required some effort to keep it moderately restrained. "Where are your other towels?" he asked. "I'll wipe up the floor."

"You don't have—" She didn't finish because the look in his darkening blue-gray eyes said he did. "In the cupboard over there," she told him, using a finger to point to the sink. "Would you allow me a few minutes to finish?"

His answer was to back away from the sink and disappear into the bedroom.

Raine completed her bath quickly, not confident that he wouldn't reappear, and even less confident that she did not want him to. She dried off without much attention for it, and reentered her bedroom still slightly damp.

Kellen barely looked at her as he passed. He took the towel she held out to him and carried it into the bathing room. As soon as Raine's hands were free, she undid the belt on her robe, shook out her shift to keep it from sticking to her skin, and then settled more comfortably into her robe and secured the belt. She could hear Kellen moving around and let him be.

Raine put on slippers, picked up her brush, and went to the sitting room. Kellen joined her before she had finished unwinding her hair. She invited him to sit.

"We will have to speak quietly," she said. "Voices sometimes carry to and from this room."

He nodded, taking the armchair opposite the small sofa where Raine sat. She was curled in one corner, her legs drawn up to the side, most of their impressive length hidden by the claret-colored robe.

"Would you like a drink?" she asked. "I have whiskey, of course, but I can put a pot of water on one of the stoves and make coffee or tea."

"Nothing, thank you."

"All right."

He looked around the sitting room. In addition to the furniture he and Raine were occupying, there were two more chairs, one of them wide and overstuffed, the other a delicate cabriole with an embroidered seat. A small, round table was situated between the sofa and unused chair. Another table, large enough to use for dining, was positioned near the window. The walls were painted white.

There were touches in the room that made it homey but not personal. There were several plaster figurines on the end table, the kind that were mass-produced by the thousands and available by mail order. A tall, heavy vase made of cut glass was at the center of the larger, gate-legged table. Like the vase on the entry table, it held no flowers. Yarns in a rainbow of hues, embroidery hoops, needles, and threads filled a basket that rested at the foot of the sofa. Several books, all of them dime novels, lay on the floor beside the basket, but built around the window on the far wall were shelves that were crowded with more books, some of them expensively bound. He could not read the titles from where he sat, but he spied the thin, colorful spines that were characteristic of the Nat Church adventures.

He could only shake his head.

Raine caught the movement. "What is it?" she asked, following the direction of his gaze.

"I thought I saw some of the Nat Church novels over there."

She smiled faintly, nodded. "Adam liked them. I think there are twenty, maybe twenty-one, in the series. He read the first five or six before he died. Ellen read them, too."

"You?"

"Yes."

"What did you think when you realized you'd made your arrangement with Nat Church?"

Her mouth screwed up at one corner. "I thought about ending it. You knew him. Even if he wasn't your friend, you knew him better than I did. Was Nat Church truly his name?"

"It was the only name he ever told me."

Nodding thoughtfully, Raine slowly pulled the brush through her hair. "Do you know there are people in Bitter Springs who think Nat Church is a real person?"

"I was confronted with that view of Nat Church when I met your station agent. Mr. Collins is one of the believers."

Raine sighed. "It's no wonder Rabbit and Finn have the imaginations they do."

"Don't the boys go to school? There's a schoolhouse. I saw it."

"We haven't had a regular teacher for a while. Hank Thompson was the schoolmaster."

"Oh."

"Precisely. We have several people willing to teach until we can find someone, but they all have other responsibilities as well. There's no one regularly there. When someone can give a morning or afternoon or both, Pastor Robbins rings the church bell and the children who can, go."

"Are you one of the volunteers?"

"No," she said regretfully. "I simply have too many things to do here. Sometimes I help Rabbit and Finn with reading and sums. Their granny doesn't have the patience for it, and they are able to distract Mr. Collins too easily."

"Imagine that."

She chuckled softly. "It's too bad you told the Burdicks you wrote for the *New York World*. You might have done admirably as a teacher."

"Oh, no. This apple does not fall anywhere close to that tree."

"You never wanted to follow in your father's footsteps?"

"Never." He pointed to himself. "Black sheep, remember?"

She regarded him, making her own assessment. "I wonder if that's true."

"My family will provide you with references."

Raine gave him a mocking smile and continued brushing.

Kellen watched, finding her movements hypnotic and calming. He was struck by how easy it was to be with her. That was rarely his experience with the women of his acquaintance. Those who shared the society and the interests of his mother and sisters wanted him to be, if not something different than he was, then something *more*. There were other women, those who had little in common with the females he knew well, but they could not hold his attention outside of a bed, let alone a bedroom.

Raine stood outside his experience. She was strong-minded, unafraid to challenge him. She was also willing to listen and allow that she could be wrong. She had a soft heart for rascals and a hard one for people who wronged her. He knew from her letters that her decision to hire a protector was not the judgment of a moment. She carefully considered most of the things she had to confront. She was thoughtful in ways that demonstrated different meanings of the word. She did not shy away from thinking through a problem, and she was clever.

Kellen thought that perhaps her most impulsive act in the short time he had known her had been when she came out of the water to catch the sponge, and he certainly had provoked her.

Venus rising.

The image was seared in his mind like a brand.

Raine put her brush aside and drew her hair over one

shoulder. She threaded her fingers through it to make three distinct ropes and began to loosely plait it. It was impossible not to be aware of Kellen's eyes on her hands. The intensity with which he watched made her normally deft fingers clumsy. She had to draw his attention away from what she was doing or risk having to braid her hair all over again.

"Why do you suppose the jury is congregating in my saloon?" she asked. "That was your point earlier, wasn't it?"

Kellen dragged his eyes away from Raine's fine hands. "I can't say with certainty why they're all there, but I imagine if you think back, you will recognize that it's been occurring for a while. I noticed there are two other saloons in Bitter Springs, so it's not as if the men who frequent the Pennyroyal don't have choices. Walt tells me that you have the only piano, but somehow I don't think that's the draw. I think the men are coming here as much for their own protection as yours. I don't know how organized they are—I suspect they came together more by accident than design—but it seems likely they've come to recognize the intelligence of staying together."

"I wonder if they have a plan."

"Other than to stay alive?"

Her mouth flattened briefly. "Other than that."

"I doubt it."

Kellen shifted, stretched his legs. He set his hands on the arms of the chair. "You still haven't told me why you were out last night by yourself."

Raine had been dreading the moment when he would come around to this again. "Is it important?"

"I think so, but you can lie if you like."

"I walked to the graveyard." She *was* perverse, she thought, and too easily goaded. "I often go there when I need to think."

He nodded. It was easy for him to imagine that she probably thought aloud, but he didn't press for that information. "It would be better if you did not go alone."

"That rather defeats the purpose."

"I understand." Kellen ventured a compromise. "Will you tell me when you're going out?"

"So you can follow me?"

"You won't know I'm there."

She heaved a sigh so heavy with resignation that the tip of her braid fluttered. "I will find some other place to be alone," she said finally. "The root cellar comes to mind."

He couldn't tell how serious she was, and he did not want to press her any more than he already had. Instead, he gave her back her privacy. "I won't come here again except at your invitation."

"Even if you are about to be cornered by Mr. Jones?"

"Even if."

"Then, thank you."

He nodded. "I *am* sorry I scared you this evening."

"I believe you." She waited to hear if he would apologize for anything else . . . such as for tossing the sponge over her head. He didn't. Which, oddly, pleased her.

"Good night, Raine," he said, drawing his legs back and moving to the edge of the chair.

She stood when he did, folding her arms in front of her and slipping her hands into the wide sleeves of her robe. "I'll get the key."

He let her lead the way to the door and waited while she reached in the empty vase to retrieve the key. He noticed that her hand was not entirely steady, but he didn't comment. She might have been cold, or she might have been . . .

He let the thought slide away before it became fixed in his mind.

Raine slipped the key into the lock, but she didn't turn it. She hesitated, her hand hovering, and then she was the one turning.

He was there, so close, not waiting because he expected her to face him, but because he hoped she would. She made a place for herself in his arms before they were fully open, and when his embrace circled her, she made it tighter by clutching his shoulders and pressing herself flat against his chest. He pushed her against the door.

Raine grew still; only her eyes moved as she searched his face. Her breath quickened. Her eyes grew darker. She breathed in the scent of him and felt her body respond in unfamiliar ways. Her nostrils flared. Her skin tightened. Her breasts swelled. Between her thighs there was a sense of weight, of heaviness, a contraction that felt like throbbing, and most disturbing of all, an emptiness.

A muscle jumped in his cheek. She wanted to put her mouth there. She wanted to put her mouth everywhere. Her lips parted. Her tongue cleaved to the roof of her mouth. It did not matter. There was nothing she wanted to say to him. There were things she wanted to do.

He watched her closely. His eyes grazed her face, and there was such intensity that she felt it like a touch. He kept her pinned to the door, but there were movements she could make, couldn't help making, and every one of them carried a charge.

One of his hands lifted from the small of her back. His palm slid upward along the length of her spine. He found the tail of her braid, wrapped his fist around it, and pulled.

What he did didn't hurt, yet she heard a small sound of distress and realized belatedly that it had come from herself. She had no time to wonder at it. He was lowering his head until only a hairsbreadth separated his mouth from hers, and then there was not even that.

His mouth closed over hers. There was nothing delicate or precise about the kiss. It was hard and hungry, frankly devouring, unapologetic in its need.

Her need matched his, and she did not shy away from showing it. She kept her fingers tightly curled in the sleeves of his jacket and held on so he couldn't set her away. Her tongue speared his mouth. He made a rough sound at the back of his throat that made her more aware of the urgency she felt.

She ran her tongue along the ridge of his teeth, touched the underside of his upper lip. He pushed back, tasting her. She thought she must be delicious. She certainly was desired.

He tugged on her braid a second time. The movement broke the kiss, turning her face slightly to one side. When his mouth touched her again, it was at the hollow just below her ear. He pressed his lips to the curve of her jaw, her neck. She held her breath as he left a damp trail on her skin with the edge of his tongue. She sipped air again when his mouth was at the base of her throat.

She felt as if she were risking everything when she released his shoulders. Relief mingled with satisfaction when he didn't move away. She placed her palms on either side of his face and lifted his head. A moment later, she lifted her own.

She kissed him. Her mouth brushed his lips. On the next pass her lips lingered. She nibbled. Bit. Her fingers drifted away from his face and slipped into his hair. They threaded together behind his head. She parted her lips wider and slanted her mouth hard across his.

She kissed him deeply. Slowly. Her tongue moved languorously against his. It was not that she no longer felt a sense of urgency, but that she understood how it could be harnessed and tamed. The expression of it would be at her will.

Or his.

She opened her eyes, startled when her feet left the floor. Her hands were still clasped behind his head, but now they were there out of necessity, holding him because he was steady and she was not. He did not carry her to the bedroom. He took her back to the small sofa and set her down in the corner she had recently abandoned. He followed her, turning on one hip so that he hemmed her in but didn't cover her.

She had only a passing notion of being trapped. The abiding thought was that she was being protected. Why, and from whom, was not a consideration. She accepted it and took it to heart.

He drew her braid over her shoulder and slowly unraveled it with his fingertips. She watched him. She could not dismiss the fancy that he was undressing her. He worked carefully, deliberately. She remembered how his hands had felt at her back untangling the knotted laces of her corset. Then his knuckles had brushed the curve of her bottom. Now they brushed the curve of her breast.

She pressed her teeth into her bottom lip. She thought she was quiet, but something must have given her away because he looked up and surprised her into meeting his eyes. His pupils were so wide and dark they all but eclipsed the blue-gray iris.

His eyelids were heavy but not slumberous. He was watchful, alert, the way a predator was aware of its prey.

The feeling that he was protecting her vanished, and what was left in its passing made her heart trip over itself.

The hand that had unwound her braid moved to the belt of her robe. He unfastened it and parted the material. He laid his palm against her shift in the soft curve under her ribs. He raised it slowly until his hand rested between her breasts. Still watching her, he extended his thumb and brushed her nipple.

Her entire body came to attention. She sucked in a breath and held it while she waited to learn what he would do.

What he did was smile. It was his maddening, slowly revealed smile, the one that lifted the curves of his mouth so carefully that it seemed he must be guarding a secret.

She wanted to know that smile. She wanted to know the secret.

As if he knew the bent of her mind, he lowered his head and pressed his lips to the pulse in her throat. Her blood thrummed. She closed her eyes. She felt his lips move upward along the sensitive cord in her neck until they rested at her ear. His breath was warm and humid, and when he spoke, his voice never registered above a whisper.

"There's so much more."

The words had impact. She shivered and grasped the wrist that lay between her breasts in both hands. He lifted his head and met her eyes.

"Show me," she said.

She had a second glimpse of the secretive smile just before it touched her lips.

Kellen twisted his wrist. Her fingers opened like a blossoming flower, releasing him from her grasp. Her hands fell away while his hand moved to her breast. She filled the cup of his palm. The thin muslin kept him from touching her skin but was no barrier to feeling all of her heat.

She returned his kiss and arched with feline grace under him. He heard her whimper softly when he removed his hand from her breast. She moved restlessly under him, seeking, and quieted the moment his fingers began to manipulate the small buttons that closed the neckline of her shift.

When the opening at her throat was wide enough, he grazed her skin from neck to breastbone with his fingertips and then followed the same trail again, this time with his mouth.

Raine's head fell back against the sofa, exposing the long line of her throat. His lips moved slowly, deliberately. Sometimes he stopped to sip her skin. When he reached her breasts, he nudged the shift to one side. There was no hesitation on his part, no time for her to think about it. He took the puckered nipple into his mouth, laved it with his tongue, and made it tender and responsive with his lips.

She thought she should do something with her hands. They lay as still and heavy as anvils at her sides, and the picture of that made her laugh abruptly. She was sorry for it because the sound made him rear back suddenly and stare at her. He did not look like a man who was suffering from a loss of confidence, merely one who could not let his curiosity go unsatisfied. At least that was how she interpreted the arch of his eyebrows.

"I cannot possibly explain it," she whispered.

His voice sounded vaguely hoarse to his own ears. "Then you're not ticklish."

"No. Well, yes." She darted a quick glance at her breast. "But not there. That is, I don't think . . ." Apparently it was all he needed to know because he lowered his head and took her between his lips again. The humid suck of his mouth made her gasp. "No," she said when she could speak. "Not there."

With such exquisite attention given to her breast, it was only a matter of moments before she could not think clearly. Her hands, though, no longer seemed to require direction, and they found his shoulders and moved to the back of his head. Her fingertips ruffled the softly curling hair at the nape of his neck. Her nails lightly scraped his scalp. A small shudder rippled the muscles of his back.

He parted the lower half of her robe and laid his palm over her knee. While his mouth moved to the curve of her throat and then to her lips, his fingers scrabbled and raised the hem of her shift.

Her hands fisted in his hair when he slid his palm over the outside of her thigh, and when he moved to the inside, she was aware that her skin no longer fit as well as it used to. She felt tight, not uncomfortably so, but there was no escaping the urge to move, to shrug it off. She was restless and unsettled.

He was neither.

When he raised his head, she touched his cheek with her fingertips. He did not turn away, and for a moment, she did not move. Touching him steadied her. She let her fingers drift along the line of his jaw. His stubble lightly abraded her fingertips. She dragged her thumb across his mouth. On the second pass she felt the damp, darting edge of his tongue.

He let her take her time. One palm rested warmly on her inner thigh. The other sat on the curve of her shoulder. His eyes were dark mirrors, reflecting her desire. She was suddenly less certain they reflected his.

"Are you always so patient?" she asked.

"You think I'm patient?"

"You don't rush your fences."

"It's a matter of strategy."

"I didn't realize."

A wry smile changed the curve of his mouth. "I know."

Raine heard a hint of regret underscoring his husky voice. She looked past him to the door to her bedroom. "You're not going to take me in there, are you?"

"No," he said. "I'm not." A small crease appeared between her eyebrows, and he spoke to the question she had not yet asked. "I'm not, and you don't want me to."

"I think I do."

He simply held her gaze.

"Do you want to?" she asked.

"Yes."

She believed him. It didn't help her understand. "Is it because of our arrangement?"

"No."

Raine closed her shift over her breast. She thought she heard him sigh, but when she glanced at him, she saw resignation, not regret. He removed his palm from her thigh before she could do it for him. She pushed her shift over her knees and closed her robe.

Kellen straightened but didn't move away. Raine sat up, her back stiff. He was tempted to take her hand and lay it against his groin. He knew something about stiff. He was no longer confident that she did.

Raine looked away. She fixed her stare on the oil lamp. "Why did you begin if you didn't mean to finish?"

"I'm not sure that I did begin it," he said. "But I know that I meant to finish it."

Her head came around. "Then why—" She stopped because he was looking at her with eyes that gave no quarter.

"Tell me about Adam," he said.

Chapter Seven

Raine pushed herself out of the corner of the sofa, and he did not try to stop her. She stood, tightening the belt on her robe.

"I am putting the kettle on for tea," she said. "Will you want any?"

"No. But I'll take that whiskey now."

She busied herself with the preparations for tea before she poured Kellen a whiskey. After she gave him his glass, she retreated to the warmth of the stove.

"Why do you want to know about Adam?" she asked.

There was a slight hesitation as Kellen raised his glass to his mouth. "You know why."

Raine did, but a twenty-mule team wasn't strong enough to pull the words out of her mouth. She set her lips firmly together.

Kellen rested his glass on his knee and turned it slowly as he considered what he wanted to say.

"Widow Berry," he said quietly. "Mrs. Adam Berry. There are generally some assumptions that can be made about the person known by those names. But I wonder if those assumptions would be inaccurate in this case."

Raine flushed deeply, but she did not look away. "What did I do wrong?"

Kellen shook his head. "Not a damn thing. There is no right or wrong, and if your experience were the equal of your eagerness, you would know that."

"I don't understand."

He sighed. "I know."

The kettle rattled a little on the stove, drawing Raine's attention. She used part of the sleeve of her robe as a mitt to grasp the hot handle. The sleeve also hid the trembling in her hand when she poured water into the teapot. She stood at the table while the tea steeped, collecting herself while she had a reason to be partially turned away from Kellen. After she poured a cup and carefully measured out half a teaspoon of sugar to add to it, she returned to the sitting area and took up the chair he'd previously occupied.

"Your own experience must be considerable," she said evenly.

Kellen merely lifted an eyebrow.

"With women," she clarified, raising her cup to her lips. "In the bedroom."

His mouth quirked. "Yes."

"Are you married?" She realized she was coming to the question rather late, but it had not occurred to her before to inquire.

"No. And I never have been." He sipped his whiskey. "It's been my experience that women don't always want to know."

"I asked because I'm curious."

"You asked because it *matters*."

Her chin lifted. "Maybe it doesn't."

"Then there's no point in hurrying things along until both of us are sure." He rolled his glass between his palms. "I figure Adam was already very sick when you married him."

Although they had been circling the topic of her marriage and Adam for a while, Raine still required a moment to get her feet under her. She tried to recall what she had told Kellen about Adam. She had no idea what Walt or any other of the hotel staff might have said.

"Yes," she said finally. "He knew about the cancer when he came here. Ellen and I arrived a few weeks later. We could see that he was considerably worse than when he left us in Sacramento."

"You married him here?"

"He made his proposal here. I accepted." It was too difficult to look at him now. "We were never together as husband and wife, and we did not share a bed before that. I nursed him, cared for him, but never slept with him. I loved him. We were brother as to sister, not husband as to wife."

Raine held her teacup like a bowl, warming her hands. She took a small swallow before her eyes darted back to Kellen. "I loved him," she said again, and left no room for doubt that she meant it.

Kellen nodded, finished his whiskey, then set the glass on the table. He stood. "I'd better be going. About that invitation I extended, I think it would be better if you didn't take me up on it."

"All right. Whatever you like."

"It isn't what I like," he said. "But it's what's best."

That did not do anything to lessen her humiliation. She bit back a childish response.

"Raine."

She turned away, stared at her cup.

She waited until she heard his footfalls on the stairs before she moved to lock the door.

Mrs. Sterling was beside herself by the time Raine entered the kitchen. Emily had failed to show up, and the cook had steak, eggs, and fried potatoes all ready to go to the dining room by the time she wound down her complaints.

"Did you ask Walt to go to the Ransom home to see if Emily was there?" Raine gathered each plate as soon as Mrs. Sterling slapped food on it.

"Course, I did. You don't see him here, do you?"

"He'll walk in with her any moment," Raine said. "And I have two hands to help you in the meantime."

"Sure, and you'll need them to carry the bags under your eyes."

Raine sighed. Emily's absence had only delayed the inevitable. "Give me that last plate," she said, extending her hand so her forearm could serve as a tray.

"Be careful," Mrs. Sterling said. "That's for the four at Howard Wheeler's table."

Raine pushed her way into the dining room, pasting a smile on her face. She quickly noted everyone present as she served Howard, Jack Clifton, Ted Rush, and Charlie Patterson their first course. Taking the coffeepot from the sideboard, she went around the tables, pouring coffee.

When she returned to the kitchen, there were four more plates ready for her, this time on a tray. "Did you see the whiskey drummer out there?" Mrs. Sterling asked.

"No, no Mr. Weyman." She ticked off the diners on her fingers. "Mr. Jones. Mr. and Mrs. Stanley. Mr. Petit."

"Who's Mr. Petit?"

"Our guest in room four," Raine reminded her. "The man from Virginia with all the camera equipment."

"Oh, of course. . . . What about that fellow from London?"

"I forgot. Mr. Reasoner's there. He asked for tea."

"Is every Englishman as particular about it as he is? Because there is no pleasure in making it for him when he turns up his nose while he's drinking it. I can't say that I'll be sad to see him go, and I won't miss his accent either. How much longer is he staying?"

"He's decided to stay for at least another month," Raine said. "Blame Mr. Petit. They've become friends." She laughed at Mrs. Sterling's long face. "It's not that terrible. They're gone as often as they're here. Mr. Petit takes his photographs for stereographs and geographic periodicals, and Mr. Reasoner assists him with the equipment in exchange for Mr. Petit acting as a guide. You only have to make tea a few times a week."

The cook was hardly placated. She harrumphed softly and

thrust the tray at Raine. "Take this. I'll make tea in the special pot for Mr. Reasoner."

Raine swept back into the dining room, passed plates to another group of diners, and took a few minutes to chat with the Stanleys, who were leaving later in the day. Kellen Coltrane still had not arrived. It was probably just as well. Every table had at least three people seated and several had four. If he showed up, he would have to tolerate company. It might press him to draw his guns.

Mr. Jones looked up as she passed. He said nothing, but there was most definitely an invitation in his eyes.

Raine pointed to the kitchen and smiled regretfully. "I'm afraid I don't have a minute to call my own this morning. Emily's not here."

"And we are all poorer for it."

"Indeed." She smiled again, more brightly this time, and hurried off. When she reached the kitchen, Walt was there. Emily was not. Her absence had required filling, and two more girls, Renee Harrison and Cecilia Ross, had been sent for to help with the service. The cousins generally worked well together, finishing each other's sentences and anticipating what the other needed before it was requested, but now they were bumping into each other in their haste to do Mrs. Sterling's bidding.

"Is Emily sick this morning?" Raine asked Walt.

"Can't say. She's not at home. Her ma's frantic. She didn't know Emily wasn't here until I came around looking for her. I walked to the livery with Mrs. Ransom 'cause I figured you wouldn't want me to leave her when she was so upset. I suppose she was hopin' Emily would be there or that Mr. Ransom would know something. T'ain't neither that was true. Now Mr. Ransom's got to runnin' around like a chicken without a head. He don't rightly know what he wants to do. When she shows herself, I think he's goin' to hug her once and whup her twice."

Mrs. Sterling said, "That girl doesn't have enough sense to make change for a nickel. I've seen her with Mr. Weyman, and I know what thoughts she's been putting in his mind. The drummer's got a sideways glance for her, too."

"Anyone else?" Raine asked.

"Anyone? There's everyone."

"Mrs. Sterling." Raine quelled her with a look. "That's not helpful. Emily is a flirt. But she's not free with her favors."

"That's only because we watch out for her." She looked to Walt for confirmation. "Don't you watch out for Emily, Walt?"

"I do," he said gravely.

"Did you walk her home last night?" asked Mrs. Sterling.

"I did. Sue, too. Well, Sue and Charlie walked together. I stayed back with Emily. Saw her straight to her door. Said good evening to her pa and he thanked me."

"See?" said Mrs. Sterling. "Now, what happens when we're not around is speculation, but I can speculate plenty."

Raine sighed. "I'm sure you can. Walt, go help Sue with the rooms. I'll be in the saloon. Mrs. Sterling, come and get me if she shows up. I do want to talk to her."

In the saloon, Raine used her talent for figures and figuring to try to push thoughts of Kellen Coltrane and worries about Emily Ransom out of her mind. She found herself tallying some of the columns several times before she was confident of her answers.

"Mrs. Sterling said I could find you here."

It was the town's deputy.

Raine closed the ledger in front of her and set her pencil down. She managed to school her look of annoyance, but only just.

Dan Sugar hooked his boot around a chair and dragged it from the table. He spun the seat toward him and straddled it. Deputy Sugar had a cherub's cheerfully rounded features and the disposition of a man with a chronic toothache. He was short of stature and temperament and disliked having to leave his office except to take a whiskey in the saloon across the street. He had been Benton Sterling's deputy for only a few months before Benton was killed. There was talk of making him marshal since no one else came forward to take the job, but the appointment was never made. Uriah Burdick made it known the position should go to Deputy Sugar, but he did not try to push it through. Dan Sugar's title was of little consequence. He was the law, and he did what the Burdicks wanted.

"Mr. Ransom wants to know what happened to Emily,"

Sugar said. He lifted his hat, wiped his broad brow, and set it back on his head. "I aim to find out."

"Good. I would like to know as well."

"What time was she supposed to be here this morning?"

"Six. The same as always."

"No one saw her around?"

"I didn't. I think that's also true for Mrs. Sterling and Walt, but you should ask them."

"I have. They said the same as you." He leaned back, pulled out his pocket watch, and checked the time. "It's almost eleven thirty."

Raine had no idea it was already so late. "What do her parents think?"

"You know them. Sarah's sure she's dead. Ed's sure she's run off with a man."

"They don't have any thoughts that are less calamitous?"

"Do you?"

"Perhaps she went for a walk and injured herself. Or maybe she's visiting someone. Have you started a search? Begun to go door to door?"

"I'm here now, aren't I? You have a door. Several, in fact."

"She's not here. It was Walt who went looking for her. He and Mrs. Sterling are the ones who missed her."

"You sent Walt to see the Ransoms."

"Yes. Naturally."

"Did you send him upstairs here at the hotel?"

"I did later so he could help Sue." She frowned. "What are you suggesting, Deputy?"

He shrugged broad, lumpy shoulders. "I understand Sue and Walt clean the rooms while the guests are at breakfast."

"That's right."

"But if a guest doesn't go to breakfast?"

"Then they tidy it later."

"And if the guest doesn't leave his room?"

"Sue would probably knock and ask if the guest required anything."

"If there was no answer?"

Impatient now, Raine tapped the point of her pencil against the ledger. "Have you asked Sue?"

"As a matter of fact, I did. She says that she did not go into Mr. Weyman's room."

"That's understandable."

"She also did not speak to Mr. Coltrane."

"He makes Sue nervous," she said and immediately wished she could call the words back. Dan Sugar was looking at her as if she'd just spit a ruby into his lap. "Sue is easily flustered."

"Is she? I hadn't noticed."

That was a damn lie, Raine knew, but she let it go unchallenged. "What do you want from me?"

"Permission to go into the rooms that Sue and Walt didn't. I don't need it, of course, but I thought it was only polite to ask."

"I'll go with you," said Raine. "I just need to get the spare keys."

"I'd rather take the keys and go alone, if you don't mind."

"But I do. Mind, that is. This will only take a minute."

After retrieving the keys from behind the registry desk, Raine led Deputy Sugar to the second floor. George Weyman's door was the first one they came to. She knocked politely and asked to be allowed to enter.

There was no response.

"I'll use my key," she said and inserted it into the lock. It turned easily. She pushed the door open a few inches and called again before letting it swing wide.

They both saw at a glance that Mr. Weyman was not in the bedroom. The bedclothes were rumpled. One pillow lay at the foot of the bed, the other lay on the floor. Raine crossed to the wardrobe while the deputy looked in the bathing room.

"He's not in here," said Sugar.

"His clothes are gone." Raine looked around and noticed what she hadn't before. "His drummer's suitcase is missing."

"The whiskey samples?"

"Whiskey. Bourbon. Scotch. Rye. It's all gone."

"So he left town."

"He was supposed to leave next week. He was waiting for

a telegram from his company. They were mapping out a new route for him. Expanding his territory."

"Maybe he got word early. I'll check with Jeff Collins."

Raine nodded.

"You think Emily Ransom ran some?"

Raine did not think Deputy Sugar was as clever as he thought he was. "I hope you will not repeat that again."

"I might. Some folks around here have a funny bone." When she said nothing, he told her he was finished with the drummer's room and waved her out. He followed behind, closed the door, and waited for her to lock it. "I still want to talk to your other guest that Sue didn't see this morning. Mr. Coltrane, is it?"

"Yes." She led him down the hall to the last room. Deputy Sugar rapped his knuckles hard against the door before she had the opportunity, but she called out for Kellen first and announced the presence of the deputy immediately afterward.

There was no answer. Sugar prompted Raine to insert the key. She had it pointed at the lock when the door began to move away.

Kellen's body filled the opening. He looked from Raine to the man standing just to the rear of her shoulder. "Yes?"

"This is Deputy Sugar, Mr. Coltrane," Raine said. "He would like to have a word with you."

"Deputy," Kellen said, nodding briefly. "What can I do for you?"

"Invite me in, for one thing."

"Is your business with me or my room?"

Raine was standing close enough to Dan Sugar to feel the deputy stiffen. "Emily Ransom did not come to work this morning. She's not at home. No one knows what's happened to her."

Kellen stood aside and let them in. "She's certainly not here, but you're welcome to look around."

Deputy Sugar looked at Raine. "You can go, Mrs. Berry. No reason for you to be here while I ask Mr. Coltrane a few questions."

"I don't mind if she stays," said Kellen. "She would probably like to have her mind set at ease."

"Suit yourself," Sugar said carelessly. He went to the bathing room first and stood on the threshold, glancing around. Shrugging, he went to the large wardrobe and opened the doors slowly.

Kellen observed how the deputy braced himself as if he expected Miss Ransom to leap out at him. Kellen studiously avoided looking at Raine. "You'll want to look under the bed."

Sugar did eventually, but to demonstrate that he did not appreciate the suggestion, he pointed to the two trunks and asked to see inside.

It was an absurd request because neither trunk was big enough to hide Emily Ransom. Rabbit could have squeezed into one, his brother into the other, but both wiry little boys could not have managed to make a home in one of them at the same time.

At Kellen's nod, Sugar lifted the lid on the trunk at the foot of the bed. It was empty. The other trunk was positioned near the table and chair in such a way that it was obvious Kellen had been using it as a footrest. Sugar looked inside.

From where she stood, Raine had a glimpse of one of the hotel's colorful quilts. It was an extra one—probably one he requested and that Sue or Walt had given to him from the linen closet.

Sugar brushed off his hands as he stood after examining under the bed. "She's not here."

"I'm glad to hear it," Kellen said gravely.

"Couldn't take you at your word," Sugar told him. "Not when I don't know you from Adam." He glanced at Raine. "That's just an expression, Mrs. Berry. I wasn't talking about your Adam."

"I understood that."

"Good." Sugar turned his attention to the writing utensils and paper on the table. Most of the paper appeared to be blank, but several sheets had been scrawled upon. He reached for one.

"That's private," Kellen said before Sugar's fingers had closed over it. "My work."

"I heard you were some kind of reporter for a New York paper."

Raine spoke up. "The *New York World*."

Sugar's thick fingertips grazed the table as he drew his hand back to his side. "I suppose you want me to buy the paper before I read your story."

"That's right," said Kellen.

"Fair enough. You've been here all day?"

"Yes. Working."

"Did you hear anything down the hall?"

"Nothing that I haven't heard every other morning."

"Would you know Emily's voice?"

"I would know her giggle."

Raine said, "George Weyman is gone."

"Weyman," Kellen repeated. "The whiskey drummer?"

"That's right. He's cleaned out his room."

"Do you think Emily's eloped with him?"

The deputy shoved his hands into the pockets of his coat and rocked forward on the balls of his feet. "That's a possibility. Trouble is, Mrs. Ransom says that Emily didn't take anything with her except the clothes on her back. Can't see that anything's missing. No note either. Strange that she wouldn't leave some kind of explanation behind. Keep her ma and pa from worrying."

Raine's stomach clenched, and she hugged herself. "Perhaps she was afraid the note would be found while she could still be stopped."

Dan Sugar continued to rock on his feet. "Could be. I guess the same might explain why she didn't take any clothes with her."

Kellen asked, "If she's gone with Weyman, how did they go?"

"Train most likely," said Sugar. "I have to talk to Collins."

Kellen considered that. He was not holding out for a happy ending. "Are you looking for help to start a search?"

"Could be. You volunteering?"

"Yes."

Dan Sugar's eyes narrowed to the point he was only squinting out of them. "Now that wouldn't be because you want to write a story about it for your paper, would it? That doesn't set right with me. Won't set right with other folks."

"I understand. No reporting."

"All right. You'll need a horse. Men will be gathering at the livery. After I talk to Collins, I'll see you there."

Raine was grateful that her knees waited for the deputy's departure before they began to wobble. She took the few steps necessary to reach the trunk at the foot of the bed and sat down hard.

"Are you going to be all right?" asked Kellen.

She nodded. "I just need a . . ." She did not finish the sentence. She didn't know what she needed. "Emily and my sister were close. Things that Ellen couldn't or wouldn't tell me, she told Emily. They were confidants and good for each other. Ellen could be so serious, and Emily . . . well, even on short acquaintance, you know that Emily was not."

Kellen hunkered in front of Raine. He almost took her hands in his and then thought better of it. "Look at me," he said. She did. "Do you think Emily's disappearance has something to do with Ellen and the trial? Or as distressing as this is, is this just about Emily?"

"I don't know. I can't know that until we find her."

"Tell me about Daniel Sugar. Do you trust him? Can I?"

"Not if this has anything to do with the Burdicks. He's their man. You have to remember that. He'll do right by Emily as long as he doesn't get a whiff of the Burdicks. If that happens, he'll point in any direction except theirs."

"That's good to know." He started to rise.

Raine reached out impulsively and caught his fingers. "Be careful."

By the time Deputy Sugar arrived at the livery, Kellen and the other search volunteers had chosen and saddled their mounts and were waiting for their instructions. They listened attentively to Sugar as he reported on his conversation with Mr. Collins. The station agent had confirmed that neither Emily nor Mr. Weyman could have left town by rail. As all the horses, wagons, and surreys were accounted for, it seemed possible there might be a foot trail, and therein lay the hope of catching up with the missing pair. Sugar was still deliberating the best way to use his volunteers when Matthew Sharp rode into town to report that rustlers had made off with two of his mares. Sugar grasped it was a lead worth following and quickly divided the men into two search parties that would fan out from the Sharp farm.

Kellen elected to stay with the deputy. The search party rode out to the Sharp place and followed the trail until the signs disappeared. At that point, they spilt into four groups, agreed on shot signals in the event they found something, and moved out.

The route that Kellen, the deputy, Walt, and Jem Davis followed took them along the river and into the hills. Kellen had taken a similar path his first day out, but this one was less rugged and therefore more likely to be used by two people who had only partially lost their minds.

Kellen was more concerned they had lost their lives.

Raine sat at a table in the dining room with Mrs. Sterling and Sue. The only hotel guest in residence at the moment was John Paul Jones, and Raine had offered to serve the surveyor dinner in his room because she could not bear an outsider in the dining room this evening. Mr. and Mrs. Stanley had boarded the No. 348 train early in the afternoon. Mr. Petit and Mr. Reasoner had left with Mr. Petit's photographic equipment soon after they spoke to Deputy Sugar and still had not returned. None of the regulars showed up for dinner. Most of them were taking part in the search, and those who weren't probably had as little appetite as Raine.

She pushed her spoon through Mrs. Sterling's meaty stew but didn't lift a bite to her mouth. The cornbread on her side plate was still untouched. From time to time, she sipped her coffee.

Sue Hage ignored her bowl of stew in favor of chewing on the end of one of her long, yellow braids. Periodically, Mrs.

Sterling would pull it away from Sue's mouth, but it always found its way back, usually within minutes.

"I don't understand why we don't know anything yet," Mrs. Sterling said. It was not the first time she had said it, and when no one answered, she let it go. "Do you think I should take some stew down to the Ransoms? Sarah might like to have something extra on hand."

Sue stared at her bowl. "Do you think the Ransoms will be any hungrier than we are?"

Mrs. Sterling sighed. "No, but I have to do something. Waiting is always the worst. I told Benton that, and he said he understood, but he didn't. Not really. Men don't. The only time they wait on a woman is when she's in labor, and as soon as it's over, they puff up, pat her and the baby on the head, and disappear. Then she's waiting again."

"I don't think I want to get married," Sue said glumly. "I like Charlie well enough, I suppose, but what if it's not love? There has to be powerful love there if I'm going to do all that waiting."

"Charlie's not a lawman," Raine said. "He's a ranch hand."

Sue took the braid from between her lips without being asked. "That's a good point. I bet he wouldn't keep me waiting long."

Raine and Mrs. Sterling exchanged amused glances before they were reminded of the gravity of the situation. Their eyes fell away and they continued to spoon through their food.

Sue slouched in her chair. "I didn't think Emily was all that sweet on Mr. Weyman."

Raine's eyes darted in Sue's direction. "What do you mean?"

"Oh, she was real nice to him because he was a regular guest, and sometimes he gave her some coin for just being a pleasure to talk to, but she told me he was a practice piece."

"A practice piece?" asked Raine.

Sue nodded. "I played them to get better at the piano. I suppose you could say that Emily played men like that. Like she was practicing for her special man."

Mrs. Sterling whistled softly. "Well, that's something I never heard before."

Raine laid her hand on Sue's forearm. "So you don't really think she's run away with Mr. Weyman?"

Uncomfortable, Sue released a long breath and shook her head slowly. "No, ma'am. Now if Mr. Coltrane had shown some interest in her, I think she would have saddled the horse and yelled giddyup."

Raine and Mrs. Sterling stared at her.

Sue Hage dropped her braid and promptly burst into tears.

It took some hand-holding, soft entreaties, and the better part of a quarter of an hour before Raine and Mrs. Sterling were able to bring Sue back from great, wrenching sobs to tiny, hiccupping ones. Raine offered to escort Sue home, but she wanted to stay, certain she'd know more quickly what happened than if she waited with her family.

"My mother is going to fret about me working here," Sue said, wiping her reddened nose with a handkerchief. "Father will want to forbid it, but we need the money so he won't. And please don't say anything about us needing money. My parents would be ashamed that I told."

"We won't speak of it," Raine assured her.

"Not a word," said Mrs. Sterling. "Your parents are fine folk on hard times. It was Mother Nature that did them in. The drought. The blizzard. It's a wonder you all survived when the cattle didn't."

"My father doesn't like putting up fence for the Burdicks, but there's no other work."

Raine nodded. "I know. He made a hard choice for his family. It's all right. We all understand how that is."

Mrs. Sterling's chair scraped the floor as she pushed back from the table. "I'm going to make a pot of tea just the way Mr. Reasoner likes it. He sets store by it like it has some kind of healing powers. Why don't we just see if there's some—"

Mrs. Sterling was halfway to her feet when she stopped. Her head jerked up, and she cocked an ear toward the windows. The other two women were immediately alert.

"What is it?" Raine whispered. "What do you hear?"

"They're coming." She stood and went straight to the windows. "Benton led enough search parties when he was marshal that I know the sound of one coming back." Raine and Sue crowded around her. "Do you hear?"

They all strained to find the same sound that Mrs. Sterling heard. Raine felt it as a vibration first, running through the floorboards of the Pennyroyal. Sue caught the deep bass notes of faraway voices.

They hurried to the front porch and stood three across on the lip of the uppermost step. A cold wind fluttered their gowns and raised gooseflesh on their arms and legs, but it did not budge them.

The search party that turned the corner onto the main thoroughfare was eighteen strong. They rode as a disciplined unit, six across, three deep. The troop moved slowly, no one breaking rank, making it impossible for the women to see the lone horse trailing behind until the men were within twenty yards of the hotel.

Raine saw it first. She found Mrs. Sterling's hand and clutched it. Mrs. Sterling put her free arm around Sue's shoulders.

The horse was not without a rider, but the rider was slung over the saddle, not sitting up in it. A blanket wrapped the body. It was large enough to cover everything but the wind-whipped double row of white lace flouncing attached to a deep purple flannel hem.

The women held each other up. None of them spoke. None of them could. The party approached and stopped in front of the Pennyroyal.

Deputy Sugar lifted his hat a fraction and gave them a nod. "Could use your help before we take her to her ma."

Raine stared at him. Her worst fears realized, she couldn't draw a breath. Beside her, she felt Mrs. Sterling begin to tremble. Sue could not stifle a deep, wrenching sob. Raine was surprised to hear herself say, "Of course. Bring her in through the saloon. We'll wash and dress her properly."

At Sugar's signal, Jem and Jake Davis dismounted and went to the rear to lead the mare carrying Emily's body forward. They unstrapped her from the saddle and eased her off. Jem carried her in his arms. He was dry-eyed now, but Raine saw evidence in clustered upper lashes and red-rimmed lower ones that he had been weeping.

Raine knew she spoke, but it was as if she were standing outside herself, disconnected from her own voice, confronting this horror as a distant observer. "Put her on a table close to the bar, then go. We'll take care of her."

Dan Sugar disbanded the search party, but no one left. Some of the men dismounted and stretched their legs. They didn't allow their horses to break formation. Before Raine slipped into the saloon, she noticed that Mr. Petit and Mr. Reasoner had somehow become members of the party.

She stopped Jem on his way out and asked him about it.

"They're the ones that found her, Mrs. Berry." Jem looked over Raine's head to where Mrs. Sterling and Sue were unwrapping Emily's body. "Came across her while they were on their way up to Apple Pie Ridge. Mr. Petit, he took photographs so Sugar would know how they found her. She's been cut up real bad." He added, "It's not because she fell. What happened to her ain't natural."

Raine steeled herself when she heard Mrs. Sterling gasp and Sue make a retching sound. It seemed they had just discovered what Jem was talking about.

"They found a horse tethered close by. It was one of the mares that was taken from Matt Sharp's place. If it hadn't been tied up, it would have been long gone. Petit and Reasoner took care of Emily the best they could and headed back to town. My group came across them about five miles northeast of the old Hage homestead."

"Thank you, Jem. Wait outside. We won't be long. Her mother's waiting."

Chapter Eight

Emily Ransom was laid out in her home where her family could stay with her throughout the night. Friends came and went, brought food and sympathy, and left shaking their heads and whispering, *How could this happen to one of our own?*

Sarah Ransom had the appearance of a stoic, grim determination in the face of this tragedy. She had buried three other children, all boys, all before they reached the age of two. They were terrible losses, and she had grieved deeply, but they were deaths she could comprehend. Illness struck randomly, without warning, and it dealt most harshly with the young. Sarah accepted that and found comfort that her girls possessed more robust constitutions. But what was a healthy constitution in the face of murder? How did one accept a random strike, or even a deliberate one, when the hand was not God's, but man's?

While Ed Ransom sometimes wept openly, Sarah remained dry-eyed. Ed had difficulty speaking, even to accept condolences. Sarah always found the right words but none of the emotion. No visitor to the Ransom home mistook Sarah's steadiness for strength. To a person, they recognized her fragile state and wondered privately at her breaking point. It would have caused little comment if she had thrown herself onto Emily's box when it was lowered into the ground.

She did not, and no one was relieved by her restraint.

Emily Ransom was three days buried and the townspeople grieved collectively and alone. In the Pennyroyal Saloon some men drank too much whiskey; others had no taste for it. Civil conversation was often listless, while disagreements excited tempers to flare. Sometimes the saloon was just quiet. Laughter felt wrong and out of place. Speculation, mostly about the murder and the weather, was a presence at every table. Among the speculators, the disappearance of Mr. Weyman pointed to him as Emily's murderer, and the harsh, bitter wind that carried snowflakes over her grave pointed to another hard winter.

Raine wiped down the bar, erasing the wet stains of whiskey and beer. She poured a drink for Richard Allen and discouraged him from standing at the bar by pointing out that the Davis brothers were looking for a few more players at their table.

Walt sidled over to her. She had given him the evening off since business was slow, but there was nowhere else he wanted to be. "I finished stacking the cases in the back," he told her.

"Thank you, Walt. You deserve to sit down, put your feet up."

"Maybe I will. Not just now." He took the rag from her hand and began polishing the bar. "I don't see our new guests."

"I don't think we will, not this evening." The rooms recently vacated by the Stanleys and Mr. Weyman had already been filled, but the couple with two young children had no use for the saloon, and the gambler, after learning about the town's recent tragedy, likely had sense enough to know his play would not be welcome.

"Some folks should be as smart," said Walt, lifting his chin toward the entrance to the saloon from the hotel. "Looks like Mr. Coltrane left his little notebook behind."

Raine thought Kellen Coltrane would be treated with less suspicion if he walked into the saloon carrying a gun. Since Emily's murder, his notebook made people nervous. As much heartache and fear as the town experienced at the hands of the

Burdicks, it was made relatively tolerable by its secrecy. To have Coltrane expose Bitter Springs as a town as violent and lawless as Deadwood and the Pennyroyal Saloon as no better than a bucket of blood felt to some like a betrayal. They were guarded now, treating him with wary respect and no warmth.

For his part, Kellen seemed to be oblivious. Or perhaps, Raine thought, it was exactly what he wanted.

Kellen approached the bar and asked for a whiskey. Raine poured it for him. They did not exchange a word. He pushed a bill across the counter. Frowning slightly, Raine looked at it and then slipped it under her sleeve. Kellen nodded once, satisfied, and took a seat at a table. Alone.

"Would you mind taking over for me, Walt?" she asked. "This was supposed to be your free night, but if you're going to be here anyway, I wouldn't mind having some time to myself."

"Sure. I'll take care of everything."

She laid her hand on his forearm and nodded. "I know you will. Don't let Renee and Cecilia bully you into taking over. Their job is at the tables, not at the bar. I'll be upstairs if you need me."

Kellen kept his eyes on his drink as Raine left the saloon. He did not need to watch her to be aware of where she was in a room. She caught his attention because she tried so hard not to. She smothered her laughter, quieted her voice, and remained polite to a fault. Her manner was even more correct than her carriage, and she already held herself as though a steel rod had replaced her spine. Kellen was intrigued. And concerned.

He took his time finishing his drink, and no one came by to ask if he wanted another. He stayed to hear Sue play one Stephen Foster tune and placed a quarter on top of the piano for her before he left.

Raine was sitting in the dark in his room, waiting. When the key turned, she held her breath and released it slowly only after he was inside. The light from the lamps in the hallway had briefly illuminated his figure, but she would have known him regardless. He had a fluid, nearly soundless way of moving that made him seem easy in his skin. He never wasted a gesture.

She knew no one else so deliberate or set so full of quiet purpose.

"Good," he said after closing the door. "You're here."

Raine thought she'd made herself invisible by standing in the deepest shadows. She stepped forward. "You summoned me." She slipped two fingers under her right sleeve and came away with the dollar bill that Kellen had passed to her across the bar. "Now I'm waiting."

"Move away from the window," he said.

"What?"

"You're in line of sight from the alley. As soon as I light one of the lamps, you'll be visible to anyone standing outside."

She could tell he did not like having to explain himself. "Don't you think that's a—"

"Humor me."

Raine's eyes had adjusted to the dark while she waited, and she found the lip of the table and eased herself around it so she could sit on the edge of the bed. "Better?"

"Yes. Stay there."

Kellen went straight to the table and struck a match. He was expecting the brilliant flare and knew to look away. Raine was momentarily blinded by it. She closed her eyes and rubbed them. When she opened them, Kellen was fitting the glass globe back into place. He moved the chair so he could face her with his back to the window. He took off his jacket and laid it over the back of the chair before he sat. He carefully rolled up his shirtsleeves until they were just below the elbow. From inside his vest, he removed the derringer and placed it on the table.

Raine looked from him to the gun and back again. "Are you going to shoot me?"

"Are you going to provoke me?"

"Not intentionally."

"And I won't shoot you . . . intentionally."

Raine's mouth flattened and she regarded him with disapproval. It proved to be an ineffective method of upbraiding him because he simply gave her back the wry edge of his smile.

"I came because I thought you had something important to

tell me," she said, starting to rise. "But if your message was for your own amusement, I believe I'll see myself out."

"Sit down."

To demonstrate that she was not his subject to command, Raine waited two full seconds before she put herself back on the bed. She held out her hand. "Your note."

Kellen took it, folded it, and slipped it into his vest pocket. "I have something I want you to see. You will find it disturbing." Because she looked as if she wanted to argue the point, he added, "*I* find it disturbing." He riffled through the stack of writing paper on the table. From somewhere in the middle, he produced a photograph. He held it in such a way that she could not see the image. "Do you know what this is?"

"I think so," she said on a thread of sound. Whispering did not disguise the dread in her voice. "Jem told me Mr. Petit took photographs of Emily after he and Mr. Reasoner found her."

"That's right. I was asking Dan Sugar if he'd made any progress toward finding Mr. Weyman when Mr. Petit came by and delivered two photographs. He claimed they were all he had. The deputy believed him. I didn't. I took this from his room. I don't know if he'll miss it, but I'm fairly confident he won't mention it. He has a dozen similar ones, different angles and exposures, but essentially the same."

"Why would he keep them? Do you think he means to sell them?"

Kellen shrugged. When he saw Raine's mulish look, he said, "I really can't tell you what he intends to do with them. Perhaps there is a market for them, or he is a man with peculiar tastes."

Raine frowned. It was a common practice to take photographs of the dead in their final, restful pose, but only criminals were photographed with all the indignities of their violent death exposed. Had Mr. Petit subjected Emily to the same ignominy? Raine had begun to prepare herself to see Emily lying at the foot of a pine under a canopy of boughs; she envisioned a glen with a trickling stream and tall grasses and Emily settled peacefully, her eyes closed and her hands crossed and resting comfortably at her breast.

Raine had cared for Emily's battered body, cleansed and

closed the worst of the wounds, washed beads of blood from the young woman's throat, and bathed her face as gently as she would a baby's. She knew the worst of what had happened to her sister's friend, and she had been tender in her ministrations. She did it for Emily and Emily's family. She did it for herself.

What had Mr. Petit's camera seen when it stared at Emily Ransom from its cold, indifferent lens?

Raine took a deep breath and released it slowly. She held out one hand. "Show me."

Kellen gave it to her facedown and watched as she turned it over. Whatever preparation she had made wasn't enough. She still sucked in a sharp breath. Her stricken expression stopped his heart.

Emily's body was sprawled on the rocky bank of Elk Creek. She lay on her back, her slender frame contorted by the bed of rocks. Her eyes were open but void of lively light and sparkle. Her head was tilted slightly to one side so that she seemed to be staring directly at the camera. Her coat was open; her scarf was attached to one wrist. It looked as if she'd been bound at one time and struggled free. The sudden vision she had of Emily fighting off her assailant had the power to squeeze Raine's heart.

Emily's dress had been the color of dark, ripe plums. In the photograph it appeared to be black. Raine could not make out the tears in the fabric where Emily's murderer had plunged his knife, nor could she see the spread of blood that she knew was there.

The skirt of Emily's dress was bunched around her thighs. The ruffled hem of her petticoat lay skewed across her legs just above the knees. Her drawers were torn, split at the thigh. Here the blood was evident. The cut had been shallow but long. Blood stained the rocks between her legs.

Raine averted her eyes. Her skin prickled as blood ran cold in her veins. She squeezed her damp palms into fists and took measured breaths. Bile rose in her throat, but when she felt Kellen begin to pull the photograph away, she shook her head. Emily had borne this, was all she could think. She could bear it, too. For Emily's sake, she could bear it.

Raine's attention was drawn back to Emily's sightless eyes and the angle of her head. "It's as if she's looking directly into Mr. Petit's camera."

Kellen nodded. "I thought so, too."

Raine sensed a slight hesitation. "What is it?"

"I told you Mr. Petit has a dozen or so similar photographs."

"Yes?"

"Those photographs are similar to this one, but the two he gave Deputy Sugar are different."

She frowned. "You mean he moved the camera around."

"No, I don't mean that."

"Then what—" Raine stopped. "He moved *Emily*?"

"Yes. In the photographs that Petit gave Sugar, Emily is lying on her side. She's facing the creek so the camera's view is largely of her back. Petit would have needed to set his tripod in the water to get another perspective, and for whatever reason, he didn't do it. Also, even though Emily's gown is much as it is in this picture, she is less exposed. Her legs, her arms, are drawn closer to her body, and it's not possible to see whether her scarf is tied to her wrists as it is in this photograph."

Raine could not look at the photograph any longer. She turned it over but held on to it. "Which set of photographs represents how Mr. Petit and Mr. Reasoner found Emily?"

"I don't know. If there is some way to determine that, I don't know what it is. I saw the photographs Sugar was given, but I didn't ask if I could study them. There could be a slight difference in the slant of shadows, but Petit took the photographs in a relatively short period of time, and you can see in this picture that the pine boughs scatter sunlight."

"And Deputy Sugar knows nothing about this photograph or the others like it?"

"No."

"Perhaps Mr. Petit found Emily in this fashion but couldn't bring himself to deny her the dignity of a less provocative pose."

Kellen arched an eyebrow. "If that's the case, he was slow

coming to that conclusion. And if he found her lying on her side, why take the other photographs at all?"

"What about Mr. Reasoner?" Raine asked. "He was there when Emily's body was found."

"Yes, he was."

"What do you suppose his role was in this?"

"That's not clear."

Raine shook the photograph in her hand. "Do you think one of them murdered Emily?"

"I don't know."

His admission made her hesitate. "But the common belief is that Mr. Weyman is responsible."

"Among some people. For now."

"You don't believe it."

"Neither do you. He never boarded at any station between Rawlins and Cheyenne. I don't think he ever left the territory. His body just hasn't been found. Sugar thinks he's holed up somewhere north of here, but there's no trail to follow. I suspect the deputy is going to change his mind about Mr. Weyman very soon."

"What does that mean?"

He spoke without inflection, his expression revealing nothing. "It means I'm going to need an alibi."

Raine could only stare at him.

Kellen pointed to the photograph she still held. "Turn it over and look at the rocks at Emily's feet."

She turned it over slowly, reluctantly, and studied the photograph.

The object lay in a shallow crevice between two rocks. It was round, about the size of her thumbnail, and visible only because it was brighter than its rocky cradle. The rocks absorbed the dappling sunlight. This object reflected it.

"What is it?" she asked, looking up. "A charm? A locket? I don't recognize it as something of Emily's."

Kellen did not answer her. Instead, he got to his feet and went to the wardrobe. He opened one of the drawers, searched briefly, and palmed the item he wanted. When he returned to Raine's side, he took the photograph and dropped what he was carrying in his fist into her open hand. He did not sit. He hitched a hip on the table, folded his arms in front of him, and waited.

"It's a cuff link."

"It is."

She turned it over so the link lay against her fingers and the beautifully engraved disks lay flat in her hand. The elaborate flourishes of the initials wound like ivy around the circumference of each gold plate face. The letters should have disappeared in the ornate scrolling, but to Raine they were so immediately clear that she ran a fingertip across the surface to convince herself they were not raised.

KMC

"What's your middle name?" The absurdity of the question did not strike her until after she'd asked it. Color rushed into her cheeks, and she quickly shook her head to communicate that she did not expect him to answer.

"Maxwell."

"Oh."

His faint smile was wry. "I'd assumed you would have something else to say."

"I'm sure I will. Eventually."

"Yes, well, it's an unexpected turn." He held out his hand for the cuff link and pocketed it when she gave it to him. "I am confident you realize that I used to have two. One of the pair is missing. That's what you saw in the photograph. Do you want to ask me if I lost it when I murdered Emily?"

"No. I don't want to ask you anything like that. I want to know if it's visible in the photographs that Dan Sugar has."

"I have to assume it is. I didn't notice it, but I told you that I didn't ask to study those photographs. I thought showing too much interest would raise suspicion."

"If it's in the other photographs, what do you think Deputy Sugar will do?"

"He won't be able to identify what it is from the pictures alone, but if he's curious about it, and in his place I would be, then he should visit the site where her body was found. He's been there once, the morning after Petit and Reasoner came across Emily. He took a couple of men with him, and they used that location as a starting point to look for Mr. Weyman. None of them saw the cuff link or I would have already been questioned about it. It could have fallen between the rocks when Petit and Reasoner were tramping around. They did wrap Emily in a blanket and lift her onto the saddle. The horse also could have trampled it."

"Are you going to try to get it back before it's found?"

"I wish I could, but the chance that I'd cross paths with Sugar is almost a certainty. He's already watching me."

"He is?" She glanced toward the window. *"Now?"*

"Probably not at this moment, but it doesn't hurt to be cautious. He has the Davis boys helping him."

"How do you know that?"

"Because I saw him talking to Jem at the Ransom house, and Jem couldn't stop himself from looking my way. He and his brothers have been looking my way ever since Emily was laid to rest. They don't know how to be subtle."

Raine agreed. The Davis boys did not have a cunning bone in their bodies. "Do you think Emily took the cuff link from your room?"

"I've thought of that. It's very tempting to make the case that she took it. That explanation presents fewer problems for me because it follows that I wasn't necessarily with her at the time she was murdered, but I can't accuse her of theft to save myself."

"I've never had a complaint from a guest about Emily. She was a good girl."

"Which is why I don't believe she stole it."

Raine was relieved that he thought so, and it showed in a softening of her expression. "And yet someone did take it, and apparently left it by Emily's body to throw suspicion on you. Is there one person you suspect more than another?"

"No. Not yet, but I doubt it was Mr. Weyman. His disappearance is not coincidental. He's being offered up as a scapegoat as well."

"Why would the murderer point fingers in two different directions?"

"Perhaps he didn't. Weyman is only a suspect in Emily's murder until his body is found. I believe that will happen soon enough. My cuff link at the site makes me a suspect in both murders."

She nodded. "What do you need me to do?"

"I haven't worked that out yet."

"I think you have," she said. "I think you don't want to ask me."

His narrow smile confirmed it. "Something like that."

"I do have an idea."

"I'm listening."

Nodding, Raine began to lay it out before him.

Uriah Burdick tossed a log on the fire, gave it a nudge with an iron poker, and once he was satisfied that it hadn't smothered the flames, he turned around to face Eli and Clay. He saw he already had their attention, but out of habit, he tapped the tip of the poker against the fireplace's stone apron. His boys took their height from him, which was why he preferred to address them when they were sitting. They would show him deference regardless, but he believed in looking over them when he could.

"You'll have to talk to him," he said without preamble. He rolled his broad shoulders, easing the tension across his back. "Tell him he doesn't want to see me. Right now, I'd shoot him dead as soon as look at him. You can tell him I said that, too."

Uriah's flat blue stare shifted from one son to the other. They shared a glance between them and then nodded. There was never any question in his mind that they would do exactly what he told them, but they always did it a little better when there was a sense of competition between them. That was what the silent exchange had been about. It had been that way since they were boys, and while Uriah fostered the contest they made of everything, he had come to understand that what he did, he did out of necessity. Looking at his boys, there was no denying they were his sons, but in their ability to think and act decisively on their own they were as different from him as salt was from sugar.

Uriah put the poker away and picked up his tumbler of whiskey from the mantel. His hands were large, and when he closed his fingers around the glass, it disappeared. "Remind him of what he was hired to do. If he steps sideways again, I'm finished with him. More to the point, he's finished."

Eli plowed his fingers through his dark hair. "He might say we got it wrong, Pa. He might say he didn't do it."

"Are you likely to believe that?"

"No, sir."

"Good. Because if he says something like that, he's a god-damn liar." Uriah squeezed his glass as though he meant to crush it. His knuckles whitened. It felt right, and he held the glass that way for a long moment. It was only after he relaxed his grip that he took a drink. "Still, if he swears he's innocent, tell him he needs to show us who's guilty."

Clay drummed his fingers against the flat, wooden arm of his chair. "Don't forget, there's suspicion that it was the man she ran off with that did it. The whiskey salesman. Weymouth. Weymar."

"Weyman," said Eli.

"Weyman," Clay repeated. "He's going to tell us it was Weyman."

"And what will you say to him in return?" asked Uriah.

Clay stopped drumming. "I reckon I'll tell him that suspicion isn't proof."

Uriah nodded. "Good." He looked at Eli. "Does that sound about right to you?"

"Yes, sir."

Uriah finished his drink and returned the tumbler to the mantel. "You boys need to be mindful of how you approach him. He likes it in close so keep a respectful distance." They nodded in unison. "Flank him. Best if you stay public but not so anyone can overhear your conversation. Don't let him see you're afraid."

Eli and Clay exchanged glances again. Eli spoke for both of them. "We're not afraid."

It was what Uriah expected to hear. "You damn well should be. You know what he is. I didn't hire him because he's not dangerous. I hired him because he is. Now he might be smart enough not to bite the hand that feeds him, but it's hard to know in the face of the poor judgment he showed with Emily Ransom. Don't trust him. Don't let yourself be at ease with him. Remind him he's paid up through Nat Church." He paused. "You did put the money in his account, didn't you?" When they nodded, he went on. "So we're square. He can take it and go, or he can go on. He knows the list. Emily Ransom sure as hell wasn't on it."

Clay shook his head. "She sure as hell wasn't. Even a sassy little bit of up-to-no-good like her deserved better."

"I suppose you think that you're the better she deserved," said Eli. "Emily would cross the street before she would bring you a drink. She was always trying to stay out of your way."

"That's on account of all the lies Ellen Wilson told her. And I never saw the Widder Berry give you a smile that wouldn't freeze the balls off a man who had a pair."

Uriah thrust out a hand when Eli started to get to his feet. "Enough. That discussion's for outside. Always has been." He waited for Eli to settle. "Good. Now as to the other matter we've talked about. I've decided I would like to speak to the reporter. From what I'm seeing already, I'm not sure this winter's going to be any better than last, and Washington needs to pay attention to its territories. We're providing beef to a nation. I think there's something to be gained by having our story told in the *New York World*."

"You want us to invite him here?" asked Eli.

"Better if he sees the spread for himself, don't you think?"

Eli nodded. "That's what he wants."

"Well, then, I'm feeling downright generous. Let's give the man what he wants. What's his name again?"

"Kellen Coltrane," Clay said before Eli could. "I have to tell you, Pa, he's not much for cards or drinking."

"Not every man is," Uriah said. "And I count that as a real shame. Still, I won't take advantage of a weakness. Neither should you." His eyes swiveled to Eli, and he fixed his stare. "Or you."

Eli did not try to defend himself. He simply nodded. "How

about we bring him back after we take care of the other matter?"

Uriah shook his head. "Invite him, but tell him to come the following morning. Riding out alone will be a test of his mettle, and he can spend the day. You can escort him around some of the spread. He can't see it all in an afternoon, but he'll get an idea of the length and breadth of it. Do you know if he's talked to any of the other ranchers?"

"Didn't seem like he had," said Eli. "I'm not sure he's planning to. He was interested in our ranch."

"My ranch," Uriah said. Although he said it without rancor, the distinction was important to him. It kept the competing interests of his children at the forefront of their minds. It also kept his youngest son at the forefront of his. "Either one of you seen Isaac lately?"

It was Clay who answered. "He's still working with Sol, putting up fence in the Cross Creek parcel."

"That isn't what I asked. Have you seen him?"

"No, sir."

"You, Eli?"

"No. It's been two weeks since I laid eyes on him."

"One of you will have to go out there and make sure he knows not to show himself when the reporter's here. That's a story we don't need."

"I'll go," said Clay. "First thing in the morning."

"I'll go tonight," said Eli.

Uriah took in both of his boys at once and smiled.

Emily Ransom had been cold in the ground for ten days when Dan Sugar strode into the Pennyroyal Hotel with one hand hovering near his gun. The Davis brothers accompanied him, Jem on the right, Jessop and Jake just behind his left shoulder.

All activity in the dining room ceased, but as the diners had all left, it was only Renee and Cecilia who were shocked into stillness. As this was an unnatural state for them, only a few seconds passed before the cousins dropped the plates and utensils they were holding and threw up their hands.

The crash and clatter brought Raine from the kitchen. She took in the tableau in a single glance, the frightened expressions of the girls, the fierce ones of the men, and forced down the wild fluttering of her own heart. It was happening. She wasn't ready, she thought. She had merely wanted to believe she would be, and now she knew the truth.

"Are you arresting them, Deputy?" she asked with credible calm.

Sugar let his hand fall to his side. "Of course not. Put your arms down, girls."

Renee and Cecilia obeyed, but slowly. They looked uneasily at each other, then over their shoulders at Raine.

"Go wait with Mrs. Sterling in the kitchen," she told them. "You can clean up this mess later." They didn't wait to hear if there were counterinstructions from the deputy. The girls hurried past Raine and disappeared into the kitchen, closing the door solidly behind them. Raine's accusing stare encompassed the deputy and the Davis brothers. "I hope you're ashamed for scaring them the way you have. If you're not, you should be. I imagine it's by accident rather than design that you are here after my diners are gone."

She noticed that the Davis boys were all glancing away, looking distinctly uncomfortable. She didn't blame them. They were taking Sugar's lead, and whatever they were doing following him, it was because they thought they were doing it for Emily. Deputy Sugar, though, stared right back at her. She thought his chest puffed a little, but she was willing to put it down to her imagination.

"What is it that you want, Deputy?"

"We're here for Mr. Coltrane."

"Why?"

"That's not your concern."

"I think it is."

"You run this establishment, Mrs. Berry. You don't run the town. Now I'll let you escort us to his room just so you know we're not doing your place any harm, but then I'll be asking you to leave. If you don't like those terms, then we'll go up on our own. I remember the way."

Raine's mouth flattened briefly. "I'll take you." She removed her apron, tossed it on the back of a chair, and without a second look in Sugar's direction, she headed for the lobby. The deputy stayed on her heels up the stairs. She could tell from the leaden footsteps following him that Jem and his brothers were keeping a more respectful distance. It was probably better that Sugar had men with him, and the Davis boys were as good as she could have hoped for. As far as she knew, she had more credibility with them than the deputy. They would be inclined to give her every benefit of the doubt, and they could prove to be valuable as witnesses.

Raine knocked lightly on Kellen's door. She counted to three in her head and then rapped on it twice more. Her hand was still raised when Kellen opened up. He looked past her to the men standing behind her.

"Deputy," he said. "Boys. What can I do for you?"

"Not a social call," Sugar said. "You can leave now, Mrs. Berry."

She didn't step aside. He would have to shoulder her out of the way if he wanted entry to Kellen's room. She didn't think he would do that, not with Jem, Jessop, and Jake hovering. "I'd like to stay." She watched him turn the consequences over in his mind but was still surprised when he did not argue.

"Suit yourself."

Kellen opened the door wider and let them file in. He rested his back against the door once it was closed. "Not a social call? I guess that means it's business. How can I help you?"

Sugar reached into the pocket of his black wool coat. When he withdrew his hand, it was a fist. "Found something that I think probably belongs to you. I was hoping you could tell me if I'm right."

"Sure."

The deputy's fingers unfolded. In the heart of his broad palm lay a gold-plated cuff link.

"I'll be darned," Kellen said, approaching. "May I?" When Sugar nodded, Kellen took the cuff link out of his hand and examined it. KMC. "It's mine." He extended his hand toward Raine. "This is the one I told you about, Mrs. Berry."

Raine took it and subjected it to the same study Kellen had. "It matches the other perfectly." She handed it back to Kellen but looked at the deputy. "He came to me five, no, six days ago and told me it was missing from his wardrobe drawer. I've asked my staff. We've all been looking for it. Walt even took out all the drawers to see if it had fallen behind them."

"Where did you find it?" asked Kellen.

It was Jem who answered. "Back where Petit and Reasoner found Emily."

Kellen frowned deeply. "What? How is that possible?"

Jem straightened, threw his shoulders back, and took a rigid stance. "Don't you dare accuse Emily of taking it. She wouldn't. I've known her all my life. She's not a thief."

"I have no intention of accusing anyone of anything. I've always assumed I misplaced or lost it."

"I'm still thinking you did," said Sugar.

Kellen's eyes narrowed. "What are you trying to say?"

"Didn't think I was trying to say anything. Thought I was saying it. You're not denying the cuff link is yours, and we're telling you where we found it. Most people would see how the two connect right away."

"Most *guilty* people would see how the two connect. I'm not guilty, so bear with me. I've never been to the site where Emily was found. I was with you when we came across Petit and Reasoner. You didn't want to go on, remember? We brought Emily back, and I haven't been away from town since. You didn't ask me to join you when you continued the search for Mr. Weyman."

"But you've been out that way."

"There's a lot of way out that way," said Kellen. "I did some exploring after I got here. I wanted to get my bearings, add some color to my writing. I can't say if I ever got close to where Emily was found, since I don't know where that was. What I can tell you, though, is that I wasn't wearing my dress shirt and cuff links when I went."

Raine watched Deputy Sugar rock slowly back on his heels. She recognized it as something he did when he was unsure of himself. If the Burdicks had been with him, he would have let one of them take the lead and shown off his badge as support. His footing was unsteady when he was the one in charge.

"How do you think it got there?" Sugar asked, rolling forward on his toes.

Kellen refused to accept what was essentially a challenge. "I don't know. I will leave it in your capable hands to sort out." He tossed the cuff link into the air, caught it, and then carried it to the wardrobe. He opened the left-hand door, then the uppermost drawer. Before he dropped the cuff link inside, he lifted its mate out and held it up for the deputy's inspection.

"I appreciate you returning it," he said. "A gift from my parents on my eighteenth birthday."

The deputy shook his head and held out his hand. "I'm not returning it," he said. "Not yet."

"Why not? I've proven it's mine."

"It's evidence."

"Of what?"

Dan Sugar set his jaw hard. The pained look that often shadowed his expression returned. "I'll tell you when I decide." He kept his hand extended.

Shrugging, Kellen scooped it back out of the drawer and dropped it in the deputy's palm.

Sugar pocketed it. "If you weren't with Emily the night she was murdered, where were you?"

"Here," said Kellen. There was a perceptible hesitation and a glance in Raine's direction. "In the hotel."

Sugar missed neither the pause nor the glance. He reckoned someone thought he could be led around by the nose. "Which is it? Here in this room? Or here in the hotel?"

Kellen hesitated for a second time.

"Think before you answer, Coltrane."

"Here," he said. "In my—"

Raine stepped into the breach, cutting him off before he could finish. "Don't, Kellen. Don't do it on my account. It's not right. We can tell them together." Her chin came up as she addressed the deputy. "What he does not want to say is that he was with me the night Emily was murdered. In *my* rooms.

Specifically, in my bed. All night. Have I thoroughly answered your question?"

Sugar shifted his weight from foot to foot. He said nothing.

"You look surprised, Deputy. Have I surprised you?" Raine wondered if her cheeks were flaming. They did not feel warm, but sometimes she couldn't tell. Her hands, though, were cold. She refrained from making fists or plunging her fingers into the folds of her skirt.

"I think you have, Mrs. Berry. Never heard that you took up with your guests. A thing like that usually gets around."

"Be careful, Deputy," said Kellen.

Raine knew that Kellen never moved, yet it seemed as if he was closing the distance that separated him from the deputy. Out of the corner of her eye, she saw Jessop and Jake inch backward. They must have sensed the same thing she had.

"I'm making no judgment," Sugar said.

It was exactly what he was doing, but Raine managed to keep from saying it aloud.

"Have you considered what will happen when Eli Burdick finds out?"

"And how would he do that?" asked Raine. She looked at each of the Davis brothers in turn, repeating the question, only this time with her eyes. When she gave her attention back to Sugar, there was a certain satisfaction in her expression. "I believe they have no intention of telling anyone. Are you prepared to say the same for yourself?"

"I won't have to say a thing, and the Burdicks will learn about it just the same. They always do."

"I think what he means," Kellen said, "is that it will be in his report. Is that right, Deputy? You'll make a report?"

"I will. Murder demands it. I have to have something should it come to an arrest and trial."

Kellen nodded, and his gaze slid past Sugar to take in Raine's ashen face. "It's your decision, Raine. Tell him or not."

"He shouldn't be the first to know," she said.

"Tell me what?" asked Sugar.

Raine ignored him. "I haven't told Mrs. Sterling. My God, she'll never forgive me. And Sue? She'll be so hurt."

Dan Sugar came close to stamping his foot. "Tell me what?"

Raine stood at the center of everyone's attention. She chewed on her lower lip and stared at the floor. It *was* her decision. Kellen had left it in her hands. She could back away from her own plan, and he would not hold it against her. She had only ever had his reluctant agreement in the first place. He was not convinced that Dan Sugar would prove himself so mean-spirited. She never had any doubt.

"People will need to stop calling me the Widder Berry. I'm Mrs. Coltrane now."

There was a long silence, then Jake Davis said, "Well, ain't that somethin'?" He tipped his hat to Raine and clapped Kellen on the back. "When did you two jump the broom? It seems you ain't been here but a minute, Mr. Coltrane."

Raine spoke so Kellen didn't. "The arrangements were made before Kellen came to Bitter Springs."

Jessop Davis lifted his hat to scratch his head. "What does that mean exactly? Are you some kind of mail-order bride, Mrs. Berry?"

Jake elbowed him and whispered out of the side of his mouth. "Coltrane. She's Coltrane now."

"Right. How about it, Mrs. Coltrane? Is that what you are?"

"Not precisely," she said. She could feel herself faltering, wondering what words she should use to explain their situation.

"I'm the mail-order bride," Kellen said. His expression was as flat as his inflection when their heads all whipped around to stare at him. At least the attention was off Raine for a moment. He couldn't be sure that she wasn't already regretting her revelation, but she had to realize there was no retreating from here. "Now you know."

Jem Davis whistled softly. His brothers followed suit. There was nothing musical about the overlapping tones.

Dan Sugar was not similarly impressed. "Why keep it a secret?" he asked Raine.

"It wasn't a secret. I just wasn't ready to tell everyone."

"You mean you're not ready for Eli to know."

"No, I'm not. It will cause trouble. I'd like to avoid that."

"You should have thought of that before you signed the certificate. Eli's going to take this real personal."

Jem thrust his hands in his pockets. "We still don't have to say anything. Eli can find out when everyone else does, when they're ready to tell folks. You understand what I'm sayin', Sugar? That cuff link got us all barkin' up a flagpole thinkin' it's a tree. Sure, we found it there where Emily was, but we've got Mrs. Ber—I mean, Mrs. Coltrane's word that it couldn't have been her husband that left it behind. And I know sure as I'm standing here that it wasn't Emily who took it. That makes me want to look at things differently. It would probably be good if you did the same."

Sugar set his jaw again. His expression turned sour. "I'm keeping the cuff link." He started to leave, got as far as the door, and turned. He looked from Kellen to Raine and back again. "If you're thinking about a wedding trip, my advice is that you leave before Eli hears about it."

Chapter Nine

"You can have one of the bedrooms at the front," Raine said. She thrust an armful of fresh linens against Kellen's chest, forcing him to accept them.

"What's wrong with your bedroom?"

"I'll be in it." She gave him a nudge in the direction she wanted him to go. He didn't move. Raine set her hands on her hips. "Are you purposely being difficult?"

"I don't think so."

"Then what is the problem? The other bedrooms are in *that* direction."

"Does this mean you don't intend to honor our vows?"

Raine extended an arm, hand, and index finger toward the bedrooms that he could occupy. "Go."

Kellen went.

Raine thought he might have been smiling as he turned. A glimpse of it usually made her heart stutter, but just now it made her want to throw something at his head. "I'm not a violent person," she called after him.

He kept on walking. "Good to know."

Raine waited to see which room he would choose and was

marginally relieved when he did not choose the one that had been Ellen's. It was when he lit the lamp on the bedside table that she turned toward her own bedroom.

She had it in her mind that she would undress, wash her face, take the combs from her hair, and tumble into bed. What she did was sit on the edge of the bed fully clothed and fall backward. She lay there unmoving, staring at the ceiling, and wondering yet again about the consequences she couldn't anticipate. It was like gazing at the sky at midday and trying to find the stars. You knew they were there, but knowing that never allowed you to see more than one. She was blinded by the sun or, in this case, Kellen Coltrane.

Raine closed her eyes and rested a forearm across them. She swore softly under her breath. The second exhalation was only a sigh, but it was a long one.

The Davis boys had filed out of Kellen's room soon after Dan Sugar left. They accepted her explanation without question, and as certain as they had been about Kellen's guilt when they arrived, they were equally certain of his innocence when they left. She wondered what it was like to see things so clearly in terms of black and white. That had never been her view. There was always nuance. Always gray.

She believed she knew what Dan Sugar would do, and not because she thought of him as a bad man, merely as one with a faulty compass. Occasionally he could find true north, but it was wiser not to depend on it. Since Marshal Sterling's death, Deputy Sugar's compass generally pointed in the direction of the Burdick ranch.

He was going to tell Eli Burdick about her marriage, and it would happen sooner rather than later, perhaps on Eli's very next visit to town. Eli was due. The last time the Burdicks rode in was to pay their respects to the Ransom family at Emily's graveside. They spoke to almost no one else. Raine knew because she'd watched them, looking for signs that would hint at their involvement in Emily's death. She saw none. Eli and Clay took their demeanor from their father, and Uriah had embraced the very essence of solemnity for the occasion.

Eli Burdick had no claim on her. She could not think of an instance where she had encouraged him to think he did. Her marriage to Adam was motivated in part by Eli's first overture just after she arrived in Bitter Springs. There was no rebuffing him gently because his attentions were overbearing from the beginning. Adam had been right that marriage would protect her, and for as long as Adam was alive, Eli had at least been tolerable. After Adam's death, it became clear to Raine that Eli had only ever been biding his time. He made a proposal the day after she buried Adam, and this time what he proposed was marriage.

She remembered that he had seemed genuinely surprised when she turned him down, just as he had seemed every time since then. It had been several months since he'd mentioned marriage, but she never assumed he would not bring it up again. Anticipation of another proposal put her on edge when he was around.

Raine wondered what part of what she had done had been about trying to save Kellen Coltrane and what part had been about saving herself.

She pressed her forearm harder against her eyes as tears threatened to undo her completely.

There was no reason for her to know that Kellen was standing in the doorway, yet she had a clear sense of him being there. Had she heard him approaching but not registered it consciously? Or was it that she had always known that they weren't finished for the night?

Without lifting her arm from her eyes, she spoke. "What do you want?"

"Permission to use the bathing room."

"Of course."

Now that she was listening for him, she heard him pad softly across the floor. Somehow he had possessed the wherewithal to remove his shoes and socks. Raine was jealous. Her shoes were squeezing her toes, and the garters that held her stockings above her knees seemed to have stopped blood flow. She imagined Kellen was already stripped down to his shirt and trousers, suspenders hanging loosely at his sides. He might have unbuttoned his shirt at the throat. He might have unbuttoned his trousers at the waist.

She sighed again and smiled unevenly as she recognized that the tenor of this sigh was significantly different than her earlier one.

Raine listened to the water running. With her eyes closed she could make herself believe she was anywhere but where she was. The freedom was heady, and she saw herself standing at the edge of the great Niagara, the roar of the falls filling her ears and the mist shrouding her in mystery. She barely had time to take it in before she was lying on a white Pacific beach, frothy waves tickling her toes. A moment later, she was sitting curled on a window seat, an unopened book in her lap. She was watching rain splash on the cobblestones and widen puddles that carriages spattered as their drivers raced for cover. She couldn't read the signs above the shops but she recognized the street from an old postcard. *Le boulevard des Capucines*. Ah, yes, she was in Paris.

Lovely.

Kellen turned off the water. Bracing his arms on the sink, he stared at himself in the mirror. He was not feeling introspective, so he didn't stand there long going over all the same arguments he had made earlier to Raine. She hadn't wanted to hear them then; he did not want to hear them now.

He toweled his damp hair and dried his face. His lip curled as he regarded his reflection, but he could not quite raise a scowl. Shaking his head, he left the towel hanging over the sink basin and returned to the bedroom.

"I'm wondering about that old adage," he said, pausing beside Raine's wardrobe. "The one that says if you make your bed, you have to lie in it."

"Hmm?"

"I'm noticing that we made the same bed but you are the only one in it." He waited and was rewarded for his patience with an abrupt little snore. Kellen's eyebrows lifted. "You didn't tell me about that," he said softly. "And, damn me, I didn't ask."

He hunkered at her feet and unlaced her boots. She didn't stir as he eased them off, but he thought he heard her hum her pleasure. He massaged the balls of her feet and the soft arches. Her toes wriggled several times and then remained still.

Reaching under her skirt, he rolled the garter and stocking on one leg over her knee and down her calf. When he took it off her foot, he separated the garter from the stocking and slipped the first on his arm and neatly folded the second and placed it in her boot. He repeated this for her other leg, doing it all as carefully as before but perhaps a bit more slowly.

Kellen stood and nudged Raine's boots under the bed with his foot. He stared down at her. There was probably a distinction to be made between assisting her and taking advantage. He was a little fuzzy on that distinction at present. "Two reasons," he whispered, picking up her legs at the ankles. "I'm tired. You're tempting." He swiveled her so that she lay lengthwise on the bed instead of across it. Her forearm still rested over her eyes, and he left it there.

Kellen attended to her skirt, loosening the ribbons that held it in place and gently tugging it down. He freed her from the bustle next, and when he pulled it out from under her, it seemed that the whole of her slender frame went limp. Her arm was finally dislodged from its resting place, but her eyes remained closed. Kellen rolled Raine on her side long enough to unfasten her bodice and corset. Neither was easy to remove without her help. He persevered because it was what he did, not because he expected that she would thank him for it. What he expected was the very opposite of that.

She was on her back when he left to hang her clothes in the wardrobe and curled on her side when he made his way back to the bed. He did not try to get her under the covers. Instead, he pulled up the quilt from the foot of the bed and drew it over her shoulders. He tucked some of it under her knees. He saw her eyelashes flutter. A sleepy smile curved her lips.

Kellen had never pretended that he was made of stone. He bent and kissed her on the mouth. Her lips were warm and soft, and there was a moment when he knew she kissed him back. He touched his mouth to her forehead. "Good night, Raine."

* * *

Raine was used to waking early and, at this time of year, when it was dark. Still, she knew as soon as she opened her eyes that it was nowhere near a reasonable hour for getting out of bed. She stretched, realized she was on top of the bedcovers and under a quilt, and struggled to set that right with a lot of tugging and yanking. She eventually surrendered, deciding that the effort was hardly worth the result.

She lay quietly for a time. There was a gap in the curtains where moonlight shone through. She studied the long slant of pale, silver-blue light on the floor. It looked as if it would be cool to the touch.

Her eyes became accustomed to the dark. She did not remember turning back the lamp on her bedside table or the one in the sitting room. She supposed that Kellen had done it. There was meager light coming from the stove, but it merely drew attention to the stove, not to anything around it.

Raine had no idea whether she had been asleep for one hour or four, but she felt rested, so much so that she did not think she would easily fall back to sleep. She pushed herself up in bed, dragging the quilt with her, and leaned against the headboard. She couldn't recall undressing, but one glance under the quilt assured her that she was wearing only her shift. Kellen again.

When she thought back, she had no clear memory of anything after he asked if he could use the bathing room, although there was something in her mind about Paris.

She wondered if he was awake, and if he wasn't, whether or not she would have the nerve to wake him. She wished she hadn't fallen asleep before they'd talked. She was even regretting that she had pointed him to another bed.

Raine threw back the quilt and swung her legs over the side of the bed, then pulled the quilt around her as a substitute for retrieving her robe. The quilt swept the floor behind her as she headed to find Kellen. The door to his room was closed, but there was a seam of light coming out from under it.

Raine rapped gently. There was only a short pause before

he answered. She wondered if he had been expecting her. If he had, it was further evidence that he knew things about her that she hardly knew about herself.

He was sitting up in bed much as she had been. The difference was that he had a book propped on his knees and was reading it. He didn't look up as she slipped into the room, or when she wrestled with the quilt to bring it in behind her. He was still reading when she sat down hard at the foot of the bed, and he seemed to take the jostling in stride.

She determined right then that she would wait until he finished the book if she had to. Perhaps he suspected as much, because it was a mere two minutes later that he closed his book and set it aside.

"I wanted to finish the chapter," he said.

She tried to see the title of the book, but he had set it upside down with the spine facing away from her. "What is it?"

"Something I found on your shelves. *Treasure Island*."

"A favorite of Adam's. You've never read it?"

"Once. When it was first published here. I had forgotten how much I enjoyed it."

She folded her hands together in her lap to keep from twisting them. "Have you slept at all?"

"A little. I couldn't seem to stay asleep."

"What time is it?"

Kellen reached for the pocket watch that he had placed next to the lamp. "Twenty minutes after three."

She remembered leaving the saloon shortly after ten. Kellen had been invited to play poker with Jem and his brothers, and in the interest of showing that there were no hard feelings, the prudent thing to do seemed to be to accept the offer. After his lucky streak ended, he went to his room, took a few things that he thought he would need for the night, and then joined her in the apartment. It had been close to eleven by then.

"I slept very well," she said. "Until I didn't."

He smiled. "That's the way it happens sometimes."

Raine took a breath and released it slowly. "Do you think Dan Sugar is going to ask to see our certificate of marriage?"

"I never know what you're going to say." He pushed a hand

through his hair. "I think it's possible, but we planned for that. Are you worried that it won't arrive soon enough?"

"It takes six days to go from New York to Sacramento by rail. That's if nothing goes wrong. It could be longer. If it occurs to Sugar to ask, he'll do it before then. Perhaps as soon as tomorrow morning."

"Raine, it will arrive in time." Kellen didn't know it for a fact, but there was no point in alarming her with his uncertainty. The morning after he had agreed to Raine's scheme, Kellen went to the station agent's office and sent a telegram to his attorney brother in New Haven. This could have been accomplished in a straightforward manner if Kellen had trusted Jeff Collins with his life, but there were few people Kellen put so much faith in, and he did not count the station agent among them.

He did, however, trust the wily charms of Rabbit and Finn to cause a distraction that would pull their grandfather from behind his desk in the station house long enough for Kellen to send the telegram himself. Kellen only asked for a reply in the event Michael declined to help. He did not expect his brother to refuse the request. Michael never had before, and this was hardly the most peculiar favor he had ever asked. There would be a lecture, a variation on one he could expect from his father, and Michael would deliver it with conviction in his best courtroom voice. A small price to pay. Kellen's profession meant that he required the services of a good lawyer, and Michael Coltrane was a very good lawyer.

"You can't be sure that your brother received the telegram," Raine said.

"I trust the science. He received it."

"And you're confident that he will arrange everything?"

"Yes. I'm confident that it's already done and that he sent the papers by express mail days ago. Bitter Springs isn't Sacramento. Everything will be here in the morning or the day after. I'll meet the mail train myself. There's no point in taking the risk that Mr. Collins will open it before I do."

"I know you think that he could be the one who read the correspondence between me and Nat Church, but I'll never believe it."

"Someone read at least some of it."

"I know, but it wasn't Mr. Collins."

Kellen saw no point in arguing. Raine did not want to believe a friend might have betrayed her. Kellen believed that until he knew the truth, it was foolish to believe anything else.

"Is this why you couldn't go back to sleep? Because you were worried about our certificate?"

Raine shook her head. "I'm more worried about our marriage."

Kellen cocked his head so he had a better view of her expression. In profile, she gave nothing away. "Raine?"

She turned her head and looked at him.

"You know we won't really be married."

"Of course I know."

Kellen raised his hands, partly as an apology, partly to ward off an impending attack.

Raine snorted and focused her attention on the quilt, tugging on it impatiently while she drew her legs up and folded them tailor fashion.

Kellen gave her another moment to settle. "Are you regretting telling them about our counterfeit marriage?" When she did not answer, Kellen interpreted her silence. "You are."

"No, I am simply confused. I thought I would be able to defend you by telling them you were with me all night, but when Dan Sugar turned malicious and the Davis boys looked at me as if I were a disappointment, the rest of the explanation tumbled out. I suppose I care more for my reputation than I'd imagined."

"We discussed it," he reminded her. "We planned for it. You have to live in this town. It's better this way. Frankly, I was concerned for a while that you *wouldn't* say it."

"Is that why you pressed me?"

"Did I do that?"

"Yes."

Kellen shrugged. "There was my own reputation to consider."

"You don't have a reputation here."

"I would if everyone thought I had ruined the virtuous Widder Berry."

Raine's mouth quirked. "Debaucher."

"Something like that."

"You *are* the black sheep, aren't you?"

"In my family. In every other circle, I'm quite ordinary."

She looked him over. "I doubt that."

"Flattery?"

"It was not a comment on your appearance, although I'm sure you know you look well enough."

"Definitely not flattery."

"I meant that if Nat Church chose you to accompany him, he must have had confidence in your skills. Those skills don't make you ordinary."

"Unless I'm sitting at a table with Wyatt Earp, Tom Horn, and the Dalton brothers."

"Oh." She frowned a little. "Have you ever sat at a table with them?"

"Not together."

"Well, even separately, it's extraordinary company."

"I'll give you that."

She nodded faintly, turned away to face the far wall, and fell silent.

Kellen studied her profile. She looked pensive. She raised one hand to her throat and lightly stroked it while she thought. His fingers twitched once. They had their own memory of curling around her slim, warm neck and supporting it when it seemed that she could not. Kellen glanced at his hand when it twitched again. He flattened his hand over his knee to keep from reaching for her.

Raine idly fingered her neckline. "Do you know where Nat Church is buried?"

Kellen was glad he had not spent a moment trying to divine what she was thinking. He had made better use of the time staring at her neck. "They took his body off the train at Westerville. I understand the town has an undertaker."

"Do you know if the railroad paid the expenses?"

"Who else would have?"

Raine looked at him sharply. "That's not an answer, is it? Yes or no would be an answer. It seems to me that you tiptoe past a lot of doors you don't want to open."

"I've never tiptoed in my life."

"Did you pay for Mr. Church's burial?"

"Why would you think that?"

Raine's blue eyes were at once brilliant and cold. She dared him to avoid her again.

"Yes," he said. "I paid the fees to make sure he had a good box and decent service. Why is that important to you?"

"I'd like to reimburse you. If the U.P. had paid, I'd want to do the same."

"I don't want your money. Not for that."

"All right. Maybe I can arrange for a headstone. Unless you specified differently, he probably only has a marker."

"Why do you want Church to have a headstone?"

"Because he's alone. He had a wife once, and it's likely that he had a different name, but he was put in the ground separated from both. It seems as if he should have something more permanent to show for his life."

Kellen felt his throat thicken. It surprised him, this sudden surge of emotion for a man he hadn't known at all and for a woman he wanted to know better. He didn't speak. Couldn't speak. He invited her to sit beside him, first by patting the space at his right, then by holding her gaze with eyes that slowly darkened.

Raine's uncertainty kept her motionless while her heart beat hard against her chest. She pressed her lips together, nodded faintly, and then released the quilt so she could untangle herself.

Kellen threw back the covers to give her an opening. She scooted across the bed until she was beside him, and then he drew the sheet and blankets over both of them. She took the extra pillow and pushed it behind her back. She wriggled into place, drawing her knees close to her chest once she was comfortable. She thought that she and Kellen looked like a pair of slightly mismatched bookends.

"Are you warm enough?" he asked.

"Yes." There were points of heat where they touched. Shoulder to shoulder. Arm to arm. She felt as if she had brushed up against the stove. "Why did you call me virtuous?"

"Hmm?"

"You called me the virtuous Widder Berry earlier."

"Oh, that. Well, aren't you?"

"I value honor and honesty, but I don't hold myself out as a model of those virtues. I told more lies this evening than I can properly count, but they're hardly the first ones I've ever told. You cannot ruin me in that regard."

"Perhaps there's another regard."

"That would lead to my ruination?" She smiled wryly. "I don't think so. I thought I made my bargain with the devil. Imagine my astonishment when I realized that I made it with a decent man."

"You're talking about Nat Church."

His voice lacked inflection. Raine truly could not tell if he was pretending to be obtuse or sincerely believed what he said. "I'm talking about *you*."

"I'm not decent."

"And I'm not virtuous."

Kellen said nothing for a moment, then a soft, husky chuckle rose from the back of his throat. "Decent. Virtuous. They are not precisely stains on a person's character, are they?"

Raine's quiet laughter mingled with his. Her head dropped to his shoulder and rested there. Her smile lingered for a long time after her laughter trailed away. "It's a considerable burden to be so damn upright."

"Puts a crick in my neck."

She sat up. "Show me."

Kellen leaned forward and placed one hand at the base of his neck. "Right here."

Raine brushed his fingers aside and replaced them with her own. "Here?"

"Mmm."

She massaged the spot with her fingertips. "Most people don't appreciate that being so decent can put your muscles in a bunch."

He rolled his shoulders.

"There, too?" she asked.

Kellen nodded. "All across my back."

Raine nudged him forward then she got up on her knees and moved behind him. She laid her hands on his shoulders and pressed her thumbs into the taut muscles of his back. She made circles with her thumbs, kneading coils of tension. She pushed, but there was very little give. She curled her hands into fists and used her knuckles to glide up and down on either side of his spine. He arched a little, but not in a way that suggested he wanted to escape. If she had any doubt about it, his soft groan was proof that he was grateful.

Neither of them spoke while she worked. Raine's approach was methodical. What relief she gave him on the right, she also gave him on the left. He began to anticipate where her fingers would alight, and sometimes he sighed when her hands were only hovering.

Raine tugged on his nightshirt. He shifted his weight so she could pull the tail free. He felt her gather it in bunches and raise it to his shoulders. He ducked his head and she pushed the shirt over and off. She released it and let him decide what he wanted to do with it. What he did was pitch it to the foot of the bed.

Raine laid her palms flat against his back. A shiver somersaulted down his spine. Her thumbnails followed that trail until they came to rest at the small of his back. She pressed to keep him leaning forward and massaged the area all around the twin dimples near the base of his spine. She slowly worked her way up his back until she reached his neck.

Kellen expected to feel her fingers slide into the curve of his neck and shoulders. What he felt, though, was her mouth, and he thought he might slip into liquid at the pleasure of it.

With her hands still warm on his back, Raine pressed kisses across his nape. Her lips followed the line of his shoulder. His skin was warm, and in spite of that, she felt him shiver again. It was a proud, powerful thought that she was the cause of it.

No, she was not virtuous.

Lowering her head, she whispered that truth in his ear.

Kellen gave her no time to reconsider her confession. He twisted, pulled her around, and put her flat on her back before she finished drawing her next breath. She stared up at him but not in a way that reflected surprise. No, Raine's steady regard held more than a hint of humor, and what remained after that was all heady satisfaction.

"And I'm not decent."

"Thank God," she whispered.

He kissed her hard. In any other circumstance it might have been a punishment, but now it was about need. His and hers. Desire was a flame that flickered, licked, and then burned steadily between them, hot and bright. He caught her wrists, pinned them to the bed, and ravaged her mouth. She offered no resistance, but then he had not captured her to win concessions. He held her because he could not imagine letting her go.

He was naked. She was not. He flanked her and threw one leg over both of hers, careful that he claimed without crushing. His open mouth worked over hers. They shared a breath. He caught her full lower lip between his teeth and nibbled. His tongue swept the sensitive underside. She challenged him, pushing at him with her tongue, spearing him. They battled for a while, fiercely at first, then more slowly, altering the deep rhythm of the kiss to something that vibrated through them with the heavy resonance of kettledrums. Their hearts pounded. Blood roared in their ears.

Raine's hips bucked. She felt his groin hard and hot against her. As thin as the fabric of her shift was, it was still an irritant and a barrier. Her fingers curled. She wriggled, trying to work the shift up her thighs. He chuckled against her mouth, maddening her at first, and then calming her with a kiss that eased into sweetness.

He released her wrists, and she stretched her arms as wide as a pagan sacrifice before lifting her hands to the back of his neck. She stroked his nape, wound her fingers around the curling ends of his hair, scored his skin lightly with her nails.

Kellen's hands fisted around her shift and began to tug. He had to lift himself away from her to pull the shift above her knees and over her thighs. Raine lifted her bottom and felt the whisper of soft muslin sliding past her hips. He let go when it bunched around her waist, and she took over, brushing his hands out of the way. She shimmied out from under him, sat up, and pulled the shift over her head. He made a grab for it as it sailed over the edge the bed, but his fingers only clutched air.

"I'm not crawling out of bed to get that for you later," he said as Raine scrambled under the covers.

"If you keep me warm, I won't need it."

Beckoned by Raine's husky voice, Kellen joined her. In moments his body was flush to hers. He hovered over her, supporting himself on his forearms. "Warm? That would satisfy you?" He kissed her before she could answer, and as long as the kiss went on, and as thorough as it was, he left her wanting something more. One of his eyebrows kicked up as he looked down at her.

"I could stand warmer," she said.

He lowered his head as if he meant to kiss her again, but at the last moment, he ducked under the covers and found her breast with his mouth.

Raine did not recognize the strangled sound that lodged in the back of her throat. She closed her eyes, dug her heels into the mattress. Her fingers curled like talons into the sheets. When his tongue darted across her nipple, her skin ignited.

Kellen poked his head out long enough to reveal a wickedly amused smile. When he disappeared, it was to give equal time and attention to her other breast.

Raine released the sheet and made deep furrows in Kellen's thick hair instead. He laved her aureole, drew her nipple between his lips. Even the slightest tug made her womb throb.

She ground against him, lifting, pressing, circling. There was no consciousness behind it. Need guided her. When he left her breast a second time, she expected him to come back to her mouth. What he did was go lower. The damp edge of his tongue made a trail down the center of her abdomen. He dropped kisses like breadcrumbs along the way. Her skin retracted under his touch. Sometimes he made her breathing catch. Sometimes he made her lips part and breath left her as quietly as a departing thief.

She raised the covers when his mouth drifted even lower. "What are you—" But then he *was*, and the point of asking the question seemed absurd. She was on the cusp of whimpering and pressed her lips together to silence it. She inhaled sharply. He pushed her knees up and apart, making a tent of the blankets. She released them and looked for purchase by pressing her palms flat against the headboard.

It banged the wall, startling her and making the bed shudder.

The next time she started and shuddered, it was because of what Kellen did to her. His darting tongue was like a dancing, licking flame. His breath fanned the fire. A rosy flush stole across her skin, climbing up her chest and throat and coloring her cheeks. Her arms and legs prickled with sensation and grew taut. She arched her neck, closed her eyes, and felt every muscle grow taut.

Pleasure hovered, teasing her. It was always within her grasp yet eluded every attempt she made to embrace it. This, too, was Kellen's doing. He maddened her with his mouth, the change in rhythm, the deep caress, the exploration that was so intimate that she would have called it a violation before it was done to her.

Her breathing quickened, and sounds that she meant to swallow would no longer be contained. She cried out softly. She lifted. Stretched. Pleasure alighted briefly, skipping across her body like a hot spark. She felt it at her breasts, at the hollow of her arm, skimming over her belly, and then suddenly, finally, settling with certainty in the nub of flesh that Kellen's dedicated attention had made slick and swollen and sensitive.

Pleasure spread from the center like a prairie fire. She was not meant to escape it, rather to embrace it. She did, absorbing the shiver that rolled through her instead of shaking it off. She wanted the memory of so much pleasure to go deep into sinew and marrow, to be there for recall when she was alone and comfort was a hug that she had to give herself.

In spite of her wish for it to be otherwise, pleasure passed. Her body quieted, her breathing slowed. When Kellen raised his head and shrugged off the blankets, she had a weak, crooked smile for him but no words to accompany it.

"We're not done," he told her.

"Mmm."

He took that as agreement and settled himself between her thighs. He lifted her hips and tilted his own. He told himself that he would be careful, not gentle perhaps, but careful, but it was only a fleeting thought, not a plan, and when Raine's hand found his cock and circled it with her fingers, there was no thought at all, not even a fleeting one.

She was ready for him or believed she was. Certainly she wanted him. When her fingers closed over him, the hot pulse and hardness made her hesitate. She stared at him. His face was already taut with pleasure denied. A muscle jumped in his cheek. His eyes were dark and focused and naked in their need. He wanted *her.*

His hips jerked. She gave herself over to instinct. They found their way together.

Kellen's first thrust met resistance. Raine bit down hard on her lip and made no sound that might cause a decent man to reconsider. She breathed again when he was deep inside her. Her hands cupped his buttocks, held him close. Her ability to accommodate him was a revelation. Without quite releasing her lip, she managed a tentative, wary smile and nodded faintly.

Kellen had had women who offered more encouraging signs, but none that were more sincerely given. He lifted his hips, withdrawing just enough for Raine to sense the loss before he rocked forward again.

There were initial moments of awkwardness when Raine tried too hard to help, but he was patient, watchful, and he knew the exact moment that she stopped thinking about what she was doing and gave herself over to it. Her trust was absolute, in herself certainly, but also in him.

It only took time to find the rhythm that suited them, and Kellen would not be hurried. Their movements were easy at first, carefully measured, but eventually they were more deliberately accented until the cadence beat a steady tattoo, and offered Kellen no choice but to surrender to it. His body demanded that he give in. Raine demanded it as well. She held him so tightly, so warmly, that being inside her was deeply satisfying while leaving her made him ride the sharp edge of a pleasure so intense it was almost painful.

He wanted both to last, and he fought the quickening, but his thrusts came sharp and shallow in spite of his efforts, and tension seized the muscles of his neck, his back, and his thighs. The contraction held him immobile for long seconds before the trigger was pulled. The kick and shudder rocked him, and when the vibration left him, it went into her.

Raine absorbed all of his fierce energy, locking her legs around his hips and not allowing him to pull away when he would have done so. From the beginning, perhaps from the first kiss, she knew that accepting this experience meant accepting all of him.

He caught himself before he collapsed on her, rolling slightly to one side and anchoring her with one of his legs. Or maybe, he thought, he was anchoring himself. He'd always believed he traveled with purpose, but what if he had merely been drifting?

His breathing slowed. He watched the rise and fall of her chest as hers did the same. She caught the slant of his gaze and reached for the blankets. He laid a hand over hers and shook his head.

"You're lovely." He smiled then because she blushed. She couldn't seem to help herself. For all the straightforward, give-no-quarter staring that she turned on him to pin his ears back, Kellen liked knowing that he could rattle her with a sideways glance. "Are you all right?"

She nodded.

"You never slept with your husband."

"No. I never did. I told you that. Not the way . . ." She hesitated. "We didn't. Couldn't. I'd rather not . . ."

"You don't have to say anything." He slid his leg away from her, searched for his nightshirt with his toes, and flipped it toward him with a sharp jerk of his foot. He caught it neatly in one hand, shook it out as he sat up, and pulled it over his head and arms. He levered himself over her and climbed out of bed. "I'll only be a few minutes."

He thought Raine might ask him where he was going, but

she either wasn't interested or she knew. His absence presented her with an opportunity to make a grab for the covers, and she was cocooned before he reached the door.

Chuckling too softly for her to hear, Kellen made for the bathing room. He ran the hot water but ended up washing while it was still only tepid. He collected a basin of warmer water for Raine, tossed in a sponge, and threw a towel over his shoulder. He wasn't sure that she knew that she needed all of it, and she might very well flee to the bathing room on her own, but he could not think of a more delicate way to broach the subject.

Holding the basin carefully in front of him, Kellen headed back. He hadn't reached the door to Raine's bedroom when he heard her coming at a run. He stepped aside, gave her plenty of space to charge past him, and simply shook his head as he watched her go. He could hardly fail to notice that she was clutching an armful of bed sheets against her chest. This particular embarrassment had not put color in her face. She was as pale as the shift she was wearing.

Kellen changed direction and followed at a slower pace. She kicked the door closed just before he got there. He stared at it at close quarters for several moments until discomfort with his own indecision forced him to action. Balancing the heavy basin with one hand, he rapped on the door with the other.

"Go away."

Kellen recognized that this was a command, not a suggestion. He ignored it anyway. "At least take this bowl of water. You'll probably want the sponge, and I have a towel."

"Go. Away."

He didn't move. He heard her turn on the taps in the tub, and he had to speak over the sound of running water. "Some women bleed more than others the first time."

There was a pause then her voice came to him from directly on the other side of the door. "Stop. Talking. Go. Away."

He nodded. "I'll wait over by the bed." He didn't know if she heard him because she didn't answer. He forgot himself and shrugged. The movement caused water to slosh over the rim of the basin and puddle around his feet. He expelled a soft curse because the moment seemed to call for it, and he felt marginally better afterward. The curse wasn't directed at himself anyway. Neither was it meant for Raine. Lately, all of his curses were variations on a theme.

Damn it, Nat Church. Christ, Nat Church. Hell and Jehoshaphat, Nat Church.

Kellen wondered if Nat Church ever suspected he'd be cursed roundly and regularly, and if he'd suspected, would it have made a difference?

Kellen moved aside some items on the night table and set the bowl down. He used the towel to swipe at the water on the floor. Raine would shoot him where he stood if she slipped on her way out. She deserved a dignified exit.

He tossed some coals into the stove, warmed himself in front of it for a while, then sat down on the bed and hooked his heels on the frame. It was tempting to go after her, tempting to believe she did not know what she wanted, but being raised by a mother whose equal rights rallying cry was that women *did* know what was good for them, Kellen thought he should honor Raine and his mother by staying put.

Goddamn it, Nat Church.

Kellen could feel himself beginning to nod off. If she meant for him to fall asleep while he waited for her and thus avoid a confrontation, it was a respectable plan, even a diabolical one. He determined he could wait her out.

Raine approached the bed quietly when she saw he was sleeping. She took a woolen blanket from the chest at the foot of the bed and drew it over him. She was just tucking it around his shoulders when his hand slipped out from under it and caught her by the wrist. She gave a slight tug, not enough to pull away from him, but enough to see whether or not he would let her go. He didn't.

"You were sleeping," she said.

"And now I'm not."

She thought he looked unnaturally alert for someone who had been breathing so deeply moments earlier. He didn't even yawn. "I'm sorry I woke you. You can sleep here. I'll stay in Ellen's room. I'm not going to put fresh linens on your bed tonight."

"That's fine except for the part about you going to Ellen's room. Stay here. With me."

Raine spared a rather longing glance at the bed and did not refuse him out of hand. "I don't know if that is a good idea."

"I'm sure it's not. But it's what I want, and if you're being honest, so do you."

"You're not much for sweet talk."

"No."

"It's probably just as well. I'd be suspicious."

"That was my thinking."

She nodded and looked back over her shoulder. "I need to tend the lamps."

"Leave them."

"Move over."

Still holding her wrist, he inched backward. Raine peeled back the covers and slid between cold sheets. She left it to him to decide if he was going to stay on top or join her under them. By the time she settled in, he was ready with his decision. As soon as he released her, Raine held up the blankets so he could slip under. She warmed her bare feet by rubbing them against his legs.

"Better?" he asked when she was finally still.

"Yes." She turned on her side and faced him. Their knees bumped. It felt comfortable rather than awkward. "I don't know what you thought earlier, but I wasn't without some understanding of what might happen . . . you know, afterward." Her voice dropped to a whisper, and she could not quite meet his eyes. "Of what *did* happen."

"Afterward."

"Yes."

"Because you ran through here like your hair was on fire." His fingers sifted through the heavy lock of coppery hair that had fallen forward. "But then, your hair always looks as if it's about to spontaneously combust."

Self-conscious now, Raine swept her hair behind her. She thought he would leave it there, but he reached over her shoulder and drew it back. He wound part of it around his finger. "You know that belongs to me," she said.

"Only because it's still attached to your head. I have it in my mind to cut it free, press it between the pages of a book, and keep it with me always."

"And people say you're not much for sweet talk." His secretive, sensual smile made her heartbeat falter. It also raised her suspicions. Her eyes narrowed. "What book?"

"*Nat Church and the Raine of Fire*."

"There's no such book." Her eyes narrowed to slits. "Wait. Is that 'reign' as in the Reign of Terror, 'rein' as in a leather ribbon, 'rain' as in water falling out of the sky, or 'Raine' as in Lorraine?"

He shrugged.

"Then you admit there's no such book."

"Maybe it's being written right now."

"I'm sure that's it," she said dryly. "Perhaps you should consider relating your plan to Max McCartney since he figures so prominently in it."

Kellen absently wound more of her hair around his finger. "Max McCartney?"

"The author."

"Oh, *that* Max McCartney. No one ever mentions him."

She chuckled. "Did Rabbit and Finn finally convince you that Nat Church is flesh-and-blood real?"

"Something like that."

She took his hand to stop him winding in one direction and gently nudged him to circle the other way. "You were coming back to the bedroom to take care of me, weren't you?"

"If I say I was, are you going to level that accusation of decency at me again?"

"No, I won't do that."

"All right. I was. It seemed the decent thing to do."

Smiling, Raine gave him a little poke in the chest. "Did you always suspect that I'd never been with a man?"

"I suspected that your experience was not the equal of your enthusiasm."

"I see."

"You had . . . have . . . a great deal of enthusiasm."

"It would be better if you stopped talking now."

He changed the subject instead. "Why didn't you sleep with your husband, Raine?"

Her eyes slid away from his as she considered what she might say and whether or not she wanted to say it.

"Was it really because of his illness?"

She contemplated the easy lie and did not like the taste of it on her tongue. "No," she said at last. She met his gaze squarely. "I didn't sleep with him because he wasn't my husband. Adam Berry was my brother."

Chapter Ten

Kellen wished he could see her face more clearly. "Your brother," he repeated. "And Ellen?"

"She's my sister," she said. "And Adam's. Our half-sister. Her father is Andrew Wilson. Ours was James Berry."

"I know that name," he said. "Andrew Wilson, not James Berry."

"I thought you might."

He waited for her to help him out with a prompt, but she made him arrive at it on his own. "Coastal Railroad. San Francisco to Seattle. Paper mills and the timber route."

"That's right. He's a robber baron. One of the lesser ones, to be sure, but rich is merely relative when you're seated in the company of Leland Stanford and James J. Hill."

"What you told me about how you acquired the Pennyroyal, was it true?"

"Most of it. Adam did win it in a card game, but the stake that I told you that Adam used to get into the game wasn't parlayed from earlier winnings. He stole it from our stepfather. He used Andrew's money to win this place and a good deal more besides."

"Your stepfather didn't suspect?"

"Not until Adam disappeared. Then he became more . . ." She stopped, considered her words carefully before she continued. "Difficult. Unpredictable. Dark moods, Mama used to call them. When we were growing up, she was always sensitive to the signs that one of those dark moods was coming on. She put herself front and center to protect us."

"He hit her?"

"When he could. When he couldn't get to Adam. Or me. My father was a drunk, Kellen. Mama knew something about ducking a fist. Adam and I learned the same. When James Berry walked out, Mama thought that life was behind us, and when she met and then married Andrew Wilson, she was certain she had secured peace for all of us. She didn't understand that dark moods lived in places other than the bottom of a bottle. In Andrew's case, I've always thought that mood slithered out from under a rock. Once Adam left, it was impossible to know when Andrew would strike. Even Ellen, whom he adored and we protected, saw through to the threatening side of his nature."

"You were just a child when your mother remarried. You were only five years older than Ellen. How did you know so much?"

"Don't children always know? Look at Rabbit and Finn. Adam had six years on me and ten on Ellen. Cautious, quiet Adam. He never caused a stir, and he always paid attention. I was eight when he promised that he would take me out of that house, and I was eighteen when he made good on it."

"You took Ellen with you."

"Of course. There was an outbreak of influenza not long after Adam left. It would have killed him if he hadn't gone when he did. I would have joined him sooner—that was the plan—but I stayed to nurse Mama. She died. It was her wish that Ellen go with me. She didn't know where Adam was, and it was better that way, so she died without knowing where we were going and without being able to tell her husband."

"Wilson never found you?"

"I'm not sure he ever cared enough to look."

"Your brother stole from him. And the daughter you said he adored left him. I'd think that pride would make him want to do something."

"Well, if he found us, he knows by now that I'm the only one left. I don't matter."

"To him. You don't matter to him." It seemed important that he make that distinction. "Why did you and Adam agree on the pretense of marriage?"

"Several reasons. We had talked about it before he left. He knew he was dying, and he wanted to be sure I could inherit. The laws in Wyoming supported it, but it seemed there would be no question if we were married. People made assumptions that we never corrected. It became fact because folks believed it was fact, not because we told them it was. The first time I introduced myself as Mrs. Berry was when I met Eli Burdick. He hadn't been to town since my arrival, so he didn't immediately connect me to Adam. He thought I was a guest in the hotel, and he put himself directly in my path. It did not take me long to realize that my marriage to Adam was a fraud I needed to sustain."

"And that was enough to keep Eli at bay?"

"Often, yes. He said things, of course, but never when he could be overheard. It's a pretty big sin in these parts to take another man's wife. I told you that his mother ran off. Eli's oddly honorable about some things."

Kellen stopped twisting Raine's hair and watched it curl on its own when he released it. "What about after Adam was killed? What did Eli do then?"

"You saw him. Heard him. It's always the same."

"Has he ever asked you to marry him?"

She nodded. "The first time was just after I buried Adam. He asks me from time to time even now, but I can't imagine what he would do if I ever said yes. Uriah would never approve. Eli knows that. Isaac. The trial. No, Uriah would not permit it."

"I'm going to tell Eli that you're my wife the next time I see him." He put out a hand to keep Raine from bolting out of bed. She started so sharply that she kicked him. He grunted in surprise.

"I'm sorry. No. I'm not." She kicked him again.

Kellen got his hands under the covers and caught her just below the knees. He managed to keep her from striking him a third time. "I'm not your enemy."

"No, you're the man I hired to help us. You can't do it if Eli shoots you first."

"He's not going to shoot me. He's probably not going to draw on me unless it's for show."

"What do you mean, unless it's for show?"

"I mean that Eli might not be as smitten with you as everyone—including you—thinks he is."

"But he—" Her brow furrowed. "Why do you think that?"

"Because I think he's smitten with me."

Raine's eyes widened as her eyebrows lifted.

Kellen let go of her legs. Except for an occasional blink, she wasn't moving. "You know about men like that?" he asked.

"Adam told me," she whispered. "I thought he was making it up."

"He wasn't. Did it come up during a conversation about Eli?"

"I don't remember. It was so long ago. Maybe even before we came here."

"It's not important. I wondered if Adam might have suspected."

"He certainly never hinted at it. It really doesn't make any sense. Why would Eli propose?"

"Why wouldn't he? It's what is expected. He's a man. Men propose."

"What about the things he says to me? Why would he make so many indecent remarks and behave so crudely?"

"Perhaps so you *will* keep him at arm's length. Has he ever paid as much attention to anyone else?"

"I'm not sure. Not since I've been here, but before I came, there must have been someone. I seem to recall Mrs. Sterling saying something about one of Mrs. Garvin's daughters. I remember wishing that Eli would make time for her again." Her lower lip thrust forward as she blew out a breath. Strands of hair fluttered against her forehead. "If you're right, what does it mean? Is Eli going to gun me down for stealing you away?"

Kellen liked that he couldn't always tell how serious she was. "I don't think it will come to that, but if it will help, you can carry my derringer."

"No, thank you." Raine plumped the pillow under her head and rolled onto her back. "Maybe he won't be coming into town anytime soon."

"That probably doesn't matter. I've agreed to go out to the ranch on John Paul Jones's behalf."

"About the government survey?"

"Yes, and there's also the matter of my story for the *World*."

She sighed. "That story again. You're very dedicated to a job you don't have."

"It's part of being dedicated to the job I do have."

"Are you?" she asked. "Dedicated to it, I mean. I can never tell what you're doing."

"Good. It's not supposed to be obvious."

"But shouldn't I know something?"

"You know that Eli Burdick likes me more than he likes you. That's something, and I learned it in a fairly short time. You've been here six years."

"You only *think* it's true that he's sweet on you. You don't know that it is."

Kellen remained confident of his answer. "I know," he said. "And it's probably better if you don't believe me. I don't want you to do anything that would draw his attention to your suspicions. *That's* when he would be dangerous. This is a secret he needs to keep."

"Then I should allow him to treat me as disrespectfully as he always has?"

"No. You should answer him just as you do now. Snap at him. Show your displeasure. It's what he wants." Kellen watched Raine. She fell silent, thinking it over. He hoped he would not regret telling her. He kept his head propped on his elbow, waiting her out.

"Why did Eli take part in taunting Isaac to the point of

practically daring him to rape Ellen?" she asked. "Why did he save me from Clay?"

"I'm not saying I understand it myself, but I imagine Eli's always trying to figure what's expected of him. Sometimes he falls in with Clay to keep the peace and protect himself from scrutiny, and sometimes, as when he interfered to get you away from Clay, he's able to act as if he has some sense. Remember, even when he moved to protect you, he made a claim on you. He established again that you're his woman."

"I remember." She tilted her head to the side and looked at him. "You have to admit it's confusing."

"Certainly."

She nodded and returned to staring at the ceiling. "This is a little confusing as well."

"This?"

"Being with you after *being* with you. Sharing my bed."

"Do you want me to go back to the other room? Tell me where I can find another set of sheets, and I'll make up the bed."

"No, I want you to stay." She added quickly, "Unless you'd rather leave."

"I'd rather stay." He found her hand under the covers and threaded his fingers through hers. "What's confusing?"

"Well, you still work for me for one thing."

"You could fire me."

"And give up even the illusion of control? No, I don't think I want to do that."

Kellen chuckled deeply. "What is another thing?"

"You are so at ease with the arrangement."

"And you're not?"

"I feel as if I'm lying on a bed of nails."

"Confusing *and* uncomfortable. Anything else?"

"This is my second marriage without an exchange of vows."

"I don't suppose that having a certificate this time is sufficient consolation."

"I don't have a certificate yet. And no, it won't be."

"Is there a particular promise you'd like me to make?"

"I'm not sure I know them."

"To have and to hold, from this day forward, for better, for worse, for richer, for poorer, in sickness or in health, to love and to cherish till death do us part. And hereto I pledge thee my troth."

Raine stared at him, open-mouthed. A few seconds passed before she regained the power of speech.

" 'Peculiar' doesn't begin to do you justice."

"My grandfather is a Lutheran pastor. My mother's father. My grandfather on my father's side was an academic like my father."

"I'm not sure the pedigree explains it." She simply shook her head when he offered a helpless shrug. "About the vows, I think if you promise that you'll be here for better or for worse, that will do."

"That more or less describes the terms of my employment."

"I know."

"Not richer or poorer?"

"I'm richer. You're poorer. If you just promise the other, that will be enough."

"All right. I promise."

"That's all you're going to say?"

"I promise that I'll be at your side for better, for worse, for at least as long as I think you need me."

She frowned slightly. "Not for as long as *I* think I need you?"

"No. I don't trust you."

"Are you trying to be insulting or is it an unfortunate consequence of your overwhelming arrogance? Don't answer that. I'll work it out on my own. Are you concerned that I'll lie and say I need you just to keep you around?"

"The opposite."

"You think I'll send you packing too soon?"

"You might try."

"If I do, it's because you've provoked me past reason."

"I could do that. I've been told I can provoke a saint to sin."

"Your mother said that?"

"And my father. Usually just before sending me outside to fetch a willow switch."

She sighed heavily, and the sigh became a yawn. "You wear me out." She pressed the back of her hand to her mouth and partially stifled the next one.

Kellen moved closer. "For warmth," he said. He slipped an arm around Raine's waist, but he didn't pull her toward him. She found that cradle herself, turning on her side and fitting her back against his chest, her bottom against his groin. "Sleep well," he whispered.

In moments she did.

Heavy footfalls on the stairs woke Kellen. Raine stirred beside him but didn't open her eyes. He eased an arm out from under her, clenched and unclenched his tingling fingers, and carefully moved to the other side of the bed. He reached the door quickly but not in time to stop a fist from beating hard against it.

He unlocked the door, yanked it open, and squared off on the threshold.

Walt took a startled step backward, his fist still raised.

"Close your jaw, Walt," Kellen said. "You'll catch flies in that trap."

"What're you doin' here, Mr. Coltrane? Is it Mrs. Berry? Is she all right?"

"She's fine. What are *you* doing here? Is there a problem in the hotel?"

"No, sir. Except for the boiler, the Pennyroyal's quiet. I come for Mrs. Berry. She'll want to hear this right away."

"Can't it wait until morning?"

Walt shook his head. "Don't think so."

"Very well." Kellen stepped aside and ushered Walt in. "I'll get her. Wait here. Adjust the wick on that lamp, will you? It's too dark in here."

Raine was already up and moving by the time Kellen reached her. "I'll wait here," he said. "You go on."

Nodding, Raine finished pulling on her robe as she approached Walt. She looked him over from head to toe. One side of his broad face still had the imprint of his pillow, and his hair was a thatch of spikes.

"What is it, Walt?"

"Thought you'd want to know right away. Scott Pennway's dead."

"Dead?" A chill swept through her. She hugged herself. Scott Pennway was a husband, father of three, the town's blacksmith and well digger, and the seventh juror picked for Isaac Burdick's trial. Raine gripped the back of the chair she was standing behind. "How?"

"What I heard is that he was feeling poorly. Left his bed to go out to the privy and never came back. Annie got worried after a bit and went looking for him. She found him lying at the foot of the porch steps. Neck broke."

Even though she had not moved, Raine felt a need to catch her breath. "How do you know this, Walt? Who told you?"

"Howard Wheeler came to get me. You know, he is neighbor to the Pennways." At her nod, he continued. "I guess Annie raised such a ruckus that she woke Howard. All of her children, too. Howard needed help getting Mr. Pennway into the house, so he sent one of the boys to get me . . . You going to be all right? You look a tad peaked, if you don't mind me sayin'."

"I'm sure it's more than a tad, but I'll be fine." She tried to smile and then wished she had not made the effort. She felt her lips trembling.

"Maybe you should sit down."

"In a moment." Her fingertips whitened on the back of the chair. "Did Howard try to move Scott before you got there?"

"I don't think so. He was lyin' all twisted up. Mr. Pennway, I mean. It wasn't natural the way his head was turned. Anyone could see his neck was broke."

"Did you see a reason for his fall? A loose step? Something he might have tripped over? He was in the saloon this evening. One of the last to leave, as I recall. I did not notice that he was feeling out of sorts. Did you?"

"No, ma'am. He played cards with some of the guests, listened to Ted Rush at the bar for a while, and played the harmonica while Sue was at the piano. Not a hint that he was feelin' poorly."

Walt's recollection was better than Raine's, but then, she reminded herself, she'd had other things on her mind following Dan Sugar's visit. "Did he drink a lot? I think I served him once."

"He had a couple of beers while he was playing cards. Mr. Reasoner was buying, but Mr. Pennway didn't take advantage. He was walking the straight and narrow when he left here."

"And what about the porch where you found him?"

"I wasn't really lookin' around much. Truth is, it was hard to look anywhere but at Mr. Pennway. Annie had a lantern with her so it wasn't too dark. There was a broken lamp, some spilled oil, but Annie's the one who dropped that when she found him. She was bringing out the lantern when I got there. I think Howard asked her to get it to give her something to do. We had a little bit of a time getting Mr. Pennway up the steps. I remember that. They were slick."

"Because of the lamp oil?"

Walt frowned. "No. Annie dropped the lamp on the porch. There wasn't enough oil for it to spread to the steps."

"Then what made them slippery?"

"Could have been ice. It's cold enough."

"But they would have had to have been wet first."

"Can't say one way or the other about that."

Before Raine gave full expression to her frustration, Kellen emerged from the bedroom. He was dressed to leave. "Where are you going?"

"To get my hat and coat, and that's all you need to know."

Raine opened her mouth and closed it again. Out of the corner of her eye, she saw that even Walt looked surprised.

"Walt. I could use you. C'mon."

Walter looked to Raine for permission. "Is that all right with you, Mrs. Berry?"

Kellen had reached the door to the stairwell. "She's Mrs. Coltrane now, Walt. Keep it to yourself for the time being, but you should know that I'm looking out for her the same as you."

Walt gaped at Raine. She ignored him in favor of glaring at Kellen. His smug expression remained unchanged.

"Go," she said. "Both of you. Just go."

"Lock the door," Kellen said.

She wanted to tell him to go to hell, but the point of having common sense was to use it. Raine held her tongue, locked the door, and put the kettle on for tea. There was no percentage in pretending she was going back to sleep.

The first thing that Kellen did when he and Walt reached the Pennway house was take note of the occupants through the parlor window. Annie Pennway was being consoled by one of her friends. Howard Wheeler was still there. Kellen couldn't see the children. He and Walt moved quietly to the backyard so Kellen could study the porch steps. Walt was right about the lamp oil not reaching the lip of the small porch. It was still pooled around the glass shards that no one had swept up. Most of it had either been absorbed by the wood planks or slipped through the cracks between them.

Kellen removed the glove on his right hand and ran his palm over the edge of the porch and both steps. "The wood is not slippery now." But it was damp. "Did Howard Wheeler comment on the condition of the steps?"

"I was the first one up. He saw me slide. I almost dropped Mr. Pennway's feet. Howard told me to mind myself."

"What about Mrs. Pennway? Did she ever step off the porch? Was she with her husband when you got here?"

Walt shook his head. "She was standing just where she dropped the lamp. Like I said, she had a lantern by then, but she didn't go any farther than she had before."

"The children?"

"One of them is just a young'un. She was hanging on her mother, cryin'. The younger boy hovered in the doorway. The other fella was the one that Howard sent for me. He helped as best he could with his pa."

Kellen knelt beside the steps and reached behind them. He patted the ground. It didn't take him long to find where the ground was wet. A thin film of ice still covered one shallow depression. He sat back on his haunches and pulled his glove back on.

"Where was the body?"

Walt looked critically at the steps and then at the ground. He took up a position a little more than three feet away from the lowest step. "Right here."

"Head?" When Walt regarded him blankly, Kellen said, "Show me how he was lying when you got here."

"You want me to show you exactly?"

"That would be helpful." Walt was stretched out on the hard, cold ground before Kellen could stop him. "All right. That's exact."

Walt's head was closer to the steps than the rest of his body and twisted to the right in a position that probably wasn't as awkward as Scott Pennway's had been. His left arm was flung in the direction of the outhouse. The right, partially folded under his body. One leg was bent at a right angle under the other.

Kellen thought the sprawl looked convincing. It was the distance that did not seem right. "You can get up." He held out a hand and helped Walt to his feet. Clapping him on the back, he brushed him off. "Stay there."

"Here?"

"Yes." Kellen took measured steps back to the porch and then he climbed up and turned. Standing on the edge of the porch, he tried to imagine how far he would fly if his feet slid out from under him. He did the same on the next step and the next. He stood on solid ground and imagined it again. "I can't get there from here," he said.

"How is that again, sir?"

"Talking to myself, Walt. How far does Dr. Kent live from here?"

"Just a piece. It's the land office, the milliner's, and then Dr. Kent."

Kellen got his bearings. "I know the house. Go on back to the hotel, Walt. There's something I need to do. It's better if I go alone. You might want to tell Raine that I won't be long. I doubt if she went back to sleep."

Walt kicked at the ground and hunched his shoulders.

"About that, Mr. Coltrane. Is it true what you said back there? She's really your wife?"

"It's true. We're not ready to tell everyone. You understand?"

"Real good of you to tell me."

"Anyone can see you're important to her."

Walt's chest puffed out. "She does right by me. Always has."

Kellen waved Walt forward. "Let's go before someone sees us and wonders what we're up to."

"I've been wondering the same thing myself," Walt confessed.

Rosy ribbons of light were unfolding across the horizon by the time Kellen made it back to the Pennyroyal. He went straight to the kitchen and found Raine turning hotcakes on the griddle while Mrs. Sterling separated strips of bacon for the frying pan.

Mrs. Sterling waggled her knife at him. "Mr. Coltrane, you don't belong here. Take yourself off to the dining room."

Raine gave him a helpless shrug. She couldn't leave the hotcakes.

Kellen noticed Raine's pinched features. "Can I get a couple of hotcakes and a cup of coffee?"

"You can," said Mrs. Sterling. "In the dining room."

Kellen backed out of the kitchen.

"Empty-handed, I see," John Paul Jones observed as Kellen passed his table.

Kellen shrugged and strode to the table by the window before Jones could invite him to sit down and angled his chair so he had a wider view of the street than the dining room. Mr. Petit and Mr. Reasoner came in together and took a table. Several of the regulars came in soon afterward, including Howard Wheeler. It was clear from the expressions of his companions that he'd already told them about Scott Pennway. Jack Clifton's face was not merely lean, it was gaunt, and his dark eyes looked hollow. Richard Allen looked as if he was nursing a hangover. The shadows under his eyes were like bruises.

Kellen paid attention to the conversation going on around him, but he didn't participate.

Mr. Reasoner added sugar to his tea. "It's inconceivable to me that he's dead. I played cards with the gentleman last night. Nice chap. Friendly."

Petit's brow furrowed. "You say it was a fall? Can that be right?"

Howard Wheeler confirmed it. "Off his back porch. Looked like his feet went right out from under him."

"Unfortunate," said Jones. "Truly unfortunate."

"There are three children," said Richard Allen. "It's a shame, is what it is. A damn shame."

Jack Clifton held out his coffee cup to Raine as she came up on their table. "I don't like it." He held Raine's eyes while she filled his cup. "I don't like it at all."

Nodding faintly, Raine moved on. She put a plate of hotcakes in front of Kellen. With her back to the others, she asked him, "Can we talk upstairs?"

"Later. I have to go to the station. Meet the first train in."

She closed her eyes for a moment. Of course. Their certificate. She had forgotten all about it. "Yes. Later." More loudly, she said, "The molasses." She pushed the small pitcher toward him and moved on.

Mr. Jones took more coffee. "Are you well, Mrs. Berry?"

"I am, Mr. Jones. Naturally, I am distressed by what's happened to Mr. Pennway."

"Naturally. He frequented your saloon, didn't he?"

"Yes. He was also a good friend. His wife is a kind, dear woman, and my heart aches for her and the children."

"I understand."

She almost took issue with him. He *didn't* understand. He couldn't. Raine took his order instead, committing it to memory before she returned to the kitchen. She rattled it off to Mrs. Sterling as she went to Sue's side. The young woman was sitting on the stool by the table, chewing on the end of one straw-colored braid. Her eyelids were swollen, and her cheeks were mottled with unflattering shades of red and rose. Raine put her arm around Sue's shoulders.

"Do you want to leave?" asked Raine.

Sue shook her head. "I helped Annie when her baby took ill. It was a hard time for her. I know this is harder." She looked up at Raine helplessly. "How does a man fall off his porch and break his neck?"

Raine had the same question. "Are you going to be able to help this morning, or should I send Walt to fetch Renee and Cecilia?"

A small shudder gripped Sue when she swallowed a sob. She spoke when it passed. Her throat was clogged with tears, but her voice was steady. "I can do this." She shrugged off Raine's arm and stood. She took the tray that Mrs. Sterling held out to her and sucked in a deep breath, and then she made her solemn way back to the dining room.

"The girl's as fragile as an eggshell," Mrs. Sterling said. To prove her point, she tapped an egg against the rim of a glass bowl and expertly cracked it open. "You knew about this when you came down this morning, didn't you?" She did not wait for Raine to answer. "I shouldn't have to learn about it from Sue; she didn't need to hear it from Howard or Jack or anyone else. You should have said something right away."

Raine accepted the dressing-down as deserved. "Walt told me shortly after it happened." She explained Walt's involvement but nothing about Kellen's. "I suppose I didn't want to believe it. Telling you and Sue would have meant that I had to."

Mrs. Sterling turned back to the stove. She made clucking, sympathetic noises while she pushed bacon around the frying pan. "Do you think it was an accident?"

"Walt seemed to think it was."

"I didn't ask after Walt's thoughts. I want yours."

Raine sighed. "I just don't know. I really don't."

"Seems strange."

"Yes, it does."

Rabbit and Finn spied Kellen from their bedroom window when he was still fifty yards from the station. They ran downstairs, called out to their grandmother as they flew past her in the kitchen, and tumbled out the back door in their usual dervish manner. They were out of breath when they intercepted Kellen.

"Hey, Mr. Coltrane," said Rabbit.

"Hey, Mr. Coltrane," said Finn.

Kellen stopped short of striding over them. He put a hand on the shoulder of each boy and separated them so he could keep walking. "Good morning, boys. No school again today?"

"Nope," Rabbit said cheerfully. "Granny's going to make Finn do sums and take-aways later, but I only have to show her I know all the times eights and then I'll be done."

Kellen thought he shouldn't ask, but somehow he always did. "Times eights?"

"One times eight is eight. Two times eight is sixteen. Three times . . ." Rabbit stopped when Kellen squeezed his shoulder. "You know them?"

"I do. All the way up to the times twelves." He observed that Rabbit was suitably impressed. Finn, on the other hand, was looking downright sorrowful about sums and take-aways. "Maybe your granny will let you go up to the hotel so Mrs. Berry can help you."

The suggestion dramatically brightened Finn's face. He grinned widely. "Are you going to be there?"

"I think so. Why?"

Finn shrugged. "Could be you might show us your guns."

"Don't hold your breath."

"I can, though. For forty seconds." He took a big gulp of air, puffed out his cheeks, and proceeded to demonstrate.

Kellen marveled at Finn's ability to change direction so quickly. The boy's thoughts had no orderly progression. They ricocheted. Kellen glanced down at Finn's ballooning cheeks. "That's a real talent you have there, Finn."

"Keeps him quiet, too," said Rabbit.

"And that's what makes it a gift." Kellen climbed the steps to the station platform.

"You come here to wait for the train?" Rabbit asked.

"That's right."

"Expectin' someone?"

"No."

Finn's cheeks deflated as he pushed all the air out of his lungs in a long, loud whoosh. "Forty-five seconds. Best ever."

Kellen managed to look suitably impressed. He saw that Rabbit didn't even try. The boy poked him with his elbow and whispered that his brother always counted too fast. Kellen knew where this was going to go. He slipped into the station as soon as the boys began exchanging barbs.

Jeff Collins waved him in. "No need to stand way over there."

"I'm holding the door closed."

"The boys out there?"

Kellen nodded. "They followed me."

"Well, they do seem to have taken to you. When you think about it, you'll realize you only have yourself to blame. Most likely you encouraged them." The station agent returned his pen to the inkstand and pushed aside the paper he was writing on. "What can I do for you, Mr. Coltrane?"

"I came down to take delivery of a package."

Collins consulted his pocket watch. "The No. 5 won't be here for another twenty minutes, give or take. You think you can hold back the heathens that long?"

"Probably not."

"I'll see that you get it right away."

"I'll wait."

"Suit yourself."

"I have something I want to send out. When does the next eastbound train come through here?"

"If you're looking to send it by regular freight, that'd be No. 437. She'll stop this evening between five and six. I never set my clock by the 437 because it seems there's always something that pushes her off schedule. Now if you wait a day and send it with the express mail car on No. 448, it will probably get there faster. Wherever *there* is."

"New York."

"Something for the *New York World*? I didn't figure you went out to the Burdick place yet. That's what everyone says you're writing about."

"Word does get around, doesn't it?"

"You probably noticed right off that we don't have a paper. I suppose no one sees the need any longer for reading about what goes on right under our noses. Talkin' is good enough for that."

"It seems to work for Bitter Springs."

Collins removed his spectacles and rubbed the lenses on his shirtsleeve. "So. Have you been out to the Burdick spread?"

"Not yet. Soon, I hope."

"Then what kind of story are you sending to the *World*?"

Kellen was starting to wish he hadn't been so quick to shut out the boys. He could still hear them bickering on the other side of the door. It was tempting to let them in. "I never said I was sending anything to the paper. You did."

The station agent stopped cleaning his glasses, grunted softly, and then resumed the activity. "So I did. I suppose I'm a mite prickly these days. It seems like you might be pokin' around, stirrin' the pot. I'm not sure I like it. Maybe it's because you were with Nat Church on the train, and he's dead, and the U.P. still doesn't know what happened, and while no one else was gutted after you got off, we're staring at three people dead since you stepped on my platform."

"Three?" asked Kellen.

"Emily Ransom. Mr. Weyman. And Scott Pennway last night."

"Dan Sugar hasn't found Mr. Weyman's body, so it's premature to pronounce him dead." But not wrong, Kellen thought. "Most folks think he murdered Emily." The station agent made a noise at the back of his throat that Kellen thought hinted at skepticism. "I heard about Mr. Pennway this morning, and what I heard is that it was an accident. Did you hear something different?"

Collins returned his spectacles to his nose and regarded Kellen over the rims. "No. I heard exactly the same as you."

"Then what are you saying?"

"I'm not saying anything. Just making an observation."

The pending arrival of the No. 5 train ended their conversation. The shrill whistle blew, signaling the engine's approach.

Rabbit and Finn twisted the doorknob at the same time, and when that didn't gain them entry, they pounded on the door. Kellen let them in, and they breathlessly announced what the adults already knew.

Collins shooed them back outside as he came around the counter. "You can carry the mailbag," he told them. "But stay off the train." He allowed Kellen to go ahead of him. "You might as well take your package now."

Kellen stopped him. "Do Rabbit and Finn know about Mr. Pennway?"

Collins shook his head. "No. I haven't said anything to them yet, but I can't put it off forever. Scott's boy is a friend of Rabbit's. They have to be told."

"If they want to come up to the hotel later, I don't mind."

"I don't know what they'll want to do, but I suspect you mean it as a kindness." He faced Kellen squarely. "I know you're not responsible for any of the things I mentioned earlier. I'm not a bad judge of character, but Rabbit and Finn are better. Still, I can't shake the notion that you're not quite what you seem."

"Do you still think I'm a gambler?"

"Oh, I haven't really changed my mind about that, Mr. Coltrane." He smiled faintly. "It goes to the very core of who you are."

Kellen watched the station agent turn and catch up to his grandsons. It wasn't often that he was left without a reply, but then it wasn't often that someone hammered him with such a deft touch.

Rabbit and Finn held out their hands for the mailbag and pretended to collapse under the weight of it when the clerk tossed it at them. They stumbled backward against their grandfather's legs. He steadied and restrained them at the same time.

"You have anything else for us?" Collins asked. "Mr. Coltrane is expecting a package."

The clerk nodded. "Got it right here. I'd call it a crate, not a package. It's about the size and how it's bundled. This is a crate."

Kellen watched the clerk push the wooden box forward until

it rested at the edge of the mail car's floor. It was about the size of a carpetbag, not so big that the clerk couldn't have lifted it, but heavy enough that he didn't want to.

"I'll take it," said Kellen.

"Not so fast." The clerk hunkered down and squinted at the stamp on the top of the crate. "Are you Mr. Kellen Coltrane? The Kellen Coltrane that's staying at the Pennyroyal Hotel?"

"Yes. Yes to both."

The clerk glanced at Collins. "You vouching for him?"

Kellen waited for the station agent to confirm his identity, but instead, Collins's attention was pulled to the right. Turning to follow the man's gaze, Kellen saw Raine approaching. It was immediately apparent that she'd overheard the clerk's question. "I'm vouching for him, Mr. Spall." She pulled down her scarf so the mail clerk could clearly see her face. "Mr. Coltrane's a guest at my hotel."

"That's all I need to know. You can take what's yours, Mr. Coltrane."

Kellen stepped forward and hefted the crate off the train. He could see Raine's brow puckering as she stared at what he held in his hands. The crate was not at all congruent with what she was expecting. It served her right. She wasn't supposed to be here.

"Anything else for us?" Collins asked.

"That's it." The clerk stood, gave the boys a salute, and pulled the sliding doors closed.

They all stepped back as the train pulled away.

"Let's go, boys," Collins said. "You have my work in your hands." They bounded off, juggling the mailbag between them. "Good to see you, Mrs. Berry. I would have vouched for Mr. Coltrane, though, so I hope you didn't come on account of that."

"No," Raine said. "Not at all. A mere coincidence. I went to pay my respects to Annie, and afterward, well . . ." Shrugging, she looked away.

"I understand. Sometimes we all just need to be somewhere else. Do you want to come in for a spell? I have coffee, and the boys will lighten your heart."

Raine hesitated and avoided looking at Kellen.

"You, too, Mr. Coltrane," Collins said. "I have a crowbar inside that will help you open that if you like."

"I'd appreciate it. Thank you."

Once they were inside, Kellen set the crate on the counter, and Collins sent Rabbit after the crowbar. The station agent confided that sending both boys after it was sure to get one of them clobbered. No one disagreed, not even Finn.

Raine stood by the stove to keep warm while Collins poured coffee. She accepted the tin mug and held it between her gloved hands. She would have been the first to admit that her chill had nothing at all to do with the weather.

Kellen picked up Finn and put him on the counter beside the crate. Finn entertained them by trying to guess what was inside until Rabbit returned with the crowbar. Finn was fairly certain now that it was a telephone because he had seen a picture of one and knew it would fit in the box. He was detailing his plan to speak to President Cleveland about the government surveyor he didn't much care for when Rabbit appeared hoisting the crowbar.

"I'll take that," Kellen said, smoothly lifting it out of Rabbit's hands.

"Do you really want to open that here?" asked Raine.

"There's no reason not to. There is something for Mr. Collins inside. You, too, if you want one."

Finn's shoulders sagged. "It's not a telephone?"

Kellen chuckled. "No, it's not a telephone. Write to Mr. Cleveland. It's what the rest of us have to do." He slipped the wedged working end of the crowbar under the crate's slatted top and pried it up. He repeated this along the other three sides until the lid gave way. Then he handed the crowbar to Mr. Collins and set the lid beside Finn. He brushed aside the excelsior and grinned.

He was staring at the cover of *Nat Church and the Chinese Box*. There were two stacks of the dime novels packed closely together. He thumbed through the first few stacks to make certain they were all the same. There was no point in giving people a gift of something they already had. He took out the novel on top and held it out to Mr. Collins.

"The newest Nat Church adventure."

The station agent blinked. "This is the one I've been trying to get." He dropped the crowbar and seized the book, gripping it in two hands. "I was told it would be two months before I could get a copy. Maybe longer. How did you—" He stopped, his eyes drawn back to the cover where Nat Church was holding a black enameled box under one arm and a fetching yellow-haired damsel under the other. The caption under Nat Church's feet read, *A True Story of White Slavery.*

"This is really for me?" asked Collins.

Kellen nodded. "You said you enjoyed the Nat Church adventures, and I've heard the same from others. I thought you might like it." He looked at the cover again. "You might not want to read this one to the boys."

"But how did you get them?"

"A friend sent them to me."

Finn peered into the box, his eyes widening as he looked over the cover. "You *know* Nat Church?"

"No," Kellen said firmly. He returned the lid to the crate. "My friend knows the author."

Mr. Collins jabbed at the caption on the book with his forefinger. "Here. Right here. It says a true story. That proves what I've been saying all along. Nat Church is as real as you are."

Chapter Eleven

Kellen carried the crate on his shoulder all the way up to the apartment. Raine cleared a space on the table in the sitting room. As soon as he set it down, she walked away.

"Raine?"

She put up a hand, declining to talk, and continued in the direction of her bedroom.

Kellen observed that Raine's back went up the moment he revealed the contents of the crate. She returned with him to the hotel, but she only exchanged a few curt words to him along the way. In contrast, she was determinedly polite to passersby.

"All right. You're angry." He took a step in her direction, but she crossed the threshold to the bedroom and firmly closed the door. "You probably think I know why. I don't. I rarely do." She didn't answer or crack the door. Was she listening on the other side? How loud did he have to talk to be heard without being overheard? He approached the door, grasped the knob, and twisted it. It opened without any resistance.

Raine sat on the edge of the bed, her hands folded neatly in her lap. She stared straight ahead. "There's no lock," she said. "I never needed one. Most people respect a closed door."

"I usually do. It seemed as though I should make an exception. Did you hear me say I don't know why you're angry?"

"I heard you."

He waited. "You have to say something," he said finally. "There are rules." That prompted her to look at him, although her green glance was crackling. If his back hadn't been to the wall, he thought he might have retreated a few steps.

"I don't know what kind of fight we're having," he said. "It feels, if you'll pardon the expression, *married*. At the risk of patronizing you, I am obliged to point out again that we are not married. If your dissatisfaction is with me as your hired gun, I encourage you to find another way of expressing it because walking away does not support my confidence in you." Kellen pushed away from the wall and turned to go.

"Wait. You're right. Don't leave."

He came around slowly and shed his duster, hat, and gloves. He held on to them until Raine pointed to the chest at the foot of the bed where she had thrown her things. He considered sitting, but she had advantages she didn't know she had, and he decided he would do better to keep his feet under him.

"Why didn't you tell me about the books?" she asked.

"This is what you're upset about? They were a surprise."

"What about the proof of our marriage? What about that? You told me we would have something to show for all the lying I've done, and what I have to show for it is a crate of dime novels. I don't care about Nat Church or the white slavers or what's in the Chinese box. I don't want Dan Sugar to demand proof we don't have."

"I should be more concerned about that than you, don't you think? I'm the one who needs the alibi. Dan Sugar doesn't suspect you of murder."

"Not until he finds your body."

"Amusing."

"You wouldn't think so if you knew how well I've planned it." Raine impatiently tucked a stray strand of hair behind her ear. "What do we do now? Scott Pennway's dead. What if Dan Sugar looks to you for the cause of it?"

"Walt knows I was with you last night."

"Walt knows you were with me when he got here. He doesn't know how long you were with me before that. Walt's thinking is straightforward."

Kellen put up a hand. "Forget about Walt for the moment. No one is saying that Pennway's death was anything but an accident. Deputy Sugar did not hear about it until this morning, just like most everyone else."

"Walt told me you asked for directions to Dr. Kent's. Did you go there?"

"Yes. What happened to Pennway forced my hand. I had to know beyond any doubt that it wasn't the fall that killed him. I asked Dr. Kent to go over to the Pennway home, judge for himself."

Raine frowned deeply. "What possible reason did you give him for your involvement?"

"You." When that didn't ease Raine's frown, he went on. "I explained that Walt told you what happened to Scott Pennway and that you needed to know more. He understood why you asked someone other than Walt to carry the information back. He figured you chose me because he heard I was a reporter and more likely to keep the facts in order. Keep in mind that Dr. Kent has good reason to learn the truth for himself. He's as likely to be a target of the Burdicks' vigilante justice as any of the jury. He stood up for Ellen the same as that lawyer from Rawlins. In his place I'd be hoping that being the only doctor around would give me more time than the lawyer."

Raine closed her eyes while she briefly rubbed the bridge of her nose. Her sigh was long and heartfelt. "He shrugs off worry when I ask him about it, but I know he thinks there's something to worry about. He won't leave town, and after John Hood arrived home in a box and no one's heard from Hank Thompson, it's hard to fault him or anyone else for not wanting to pull up roots."

"If it helps, he thanked me for alerting him. I waited at Kent's house until he returned. He confirmed your suspicions and mine. It wasn't the fall that broke Pennway's neck. There was no evidence that Pennway ever hit his head. No lumps. No bruising. The ground was hard, but we both believe it would have required a longer fall to snap Pennway's neck." Kellen described his observations of the porch and backyard and repeated the information Walt had given him. "Mrs. Pennway doesn't know any of this. Neither does Howard Wheeler or Mrs. Stillwell. They were both with Mrs. Pennway when Kent arrived. He quieted Mrs. Pennway with some laudanum so Mrs. Stillwell could help her to bed. When they went upstairs, he and Wheeler took care of the body."

"Do you think Howard knew that Dr. Kent was doing an examination?"

"I asked Kent the same thing. He said Wheeler never asked any questions."

"Perhaps because he doesn't want to know the answers."

"Or perhaps because he already does. You knew from the first that it wasn't an accident."

She blew out a small breath. "What now?"

He held up an index finger. "Give me a moment."

Kellen went out to the sitting room to retrieve the crate. He set it on the floor in front of her.

She stared into the open box. "I am not opposed to giving my customers a copy of that book, and perhaps I'll read it myself sometime, but on the other hand, I'd just as soon set them all on fire." She pointed to the stove to indicate that she had the means to do so close at hand.

Kellen knelt and began to unpack the books, shaking off the curled wood shavings that clung to the covers before he dropped them on the floor. He took out two dozen copies before he sat back, grinning.

"Go ahead," he told her, pointing to the crate. "You take it out."

Raine's eyes narrowed with suspicion. "Is it alive?"

"No."

"Is it a telephone?"

He chuckled. "No telephone. Go on. Reach inside and take it."

She leaned forward for a better view. A large folder covered most of the remaining books. Her heart thudded, and she abandoned the bed. She pretended that she couldn't see Kellen's amusement as she lifted the folder. The excelsior scattered everywhere as she opened it.

The certificate of marriage lay inside. All the information was there, including the name of the judge who married them in absentia. The only requirement remaining was for them to sign it. "How well do you know this judge?"

Kellen tipped the folder so he could see the certificate. He recognized the bold hand. "Macaulay Packard? I don't know him at all. That's my brother's writing. The M is familiar. He cannot resist the flourishing detail. He would have preferred to have been born John Hancock."

"It's impressive."

"I'll tell him you thought so."

Raine ran her fingertips over the certificate. "There's something under it." She lifted the document and saw the envelope with Kellen's name scrawled on top. She handed it to him.

Kellen opened it and smiled wryly as he read. When his brother was not writing a closing argument, he was a man of few words.

"May I know what he's written?" she asked.

"He says there better be a good story to answer for this." He handed it to her.

Raine looked it over. "Does your family think you're a reporter?"

"No. They know what I do."

"Is it difficult for them to accept?"

He shrugged. "Some more than others, my father most of all."

"I don't suppose any father hopes his son will grow up to be a gunslinger."

"At least not a bad one."

Raine returned the letter so he could put it away. "How long has it been since you've seen your family?"

"Six months."

"Are you welcomed?"

"Like the prodigal son. That lasts until we have our first Sunday dinner together. I can't stay long after that."

"Do they know you're a good man?"

He smiled a little. "I think so. My parents simply want me to be a better one."

Raine nodded slowly. There was an ache behind her eyes that she recognized as the press of tears. She did not want to think about why it was there. She closed the folder. "I'll put this in the hotel safe, if you don't object."

She slid the folder under the nightstand to put it out of the way and picked up one of the Nat Church novels. She thumbed the pages. "Did you know there were books in the crate before you opened it?"

"No. I kept my request simple. I didn't have much time. This was his idea, and a good one as it happens. Even if Dan Sugar shows any curiosity about our certificate—which I doubt—there'll be nothing to suggest that we only took delivery of it this morning. An envelope might have got him thinking. But Nat Church novels?"

"You could have told me about it once we left the station."

"I thought you understood. I was trying to figure out what the burr was under your bustle. I didn't understand until you asked about the proof of marriage."

"And you still didn't tell me."

"I don't remember you giving me a lot of room for explanation, but even if you had, it's possible I was feeling a touch bristly by then and took some satisfaction in keeping it to myself."

It was his honesty that undid her, and that he offered it a shade grudgingly made the admission that much sweeter. Raine did not want her heart to turn over. She did not want it to jump. It tumbled and fluttered anyway.

She had never been in love, had given little thought to it in any serious way, and she wasn't ready to claim that what she felt now was that emotion. She was confident it was a new experience, identifiable as kin to the love she had for Adam and Ellen, for her mother, yet distinguishable from it as well. This feeling was more acute, intense in a way that was both splendid and uncomfortable. Once her heart stopped its frantic beat, she felt her skin flush hot and her breath lodge in her throat, but when she could breathe again, she merely felt warm all over.

"Are you all right?"

Raine realized she was the subject of Kellen's scrutiny. Not liking it, she scowled at him.

He smirked.

Her eyes were drawn to his beautiful mouth. The smirk did not detract from it at all. Still worse from her perspective, there was a tiny crescent of a dimple at the left corner of his lips. She had never noticed it before. She was not particularly happy about noticing it now, but she was aroused.

Raine pushed the crate out of the way as she came up on her knees. Slipping her hands around his neck, she kissed him full on the mouth, erasing the smirk, the dimple, and all hint of amusement. It was not a long kiss, but it was a heady one, and when she drew back, she was satisfied to see that his darkening eyes were vaguely unfocused.

She couldn't help herself. She smirked.

Raine didn't think about fending him off. She let him topple her back on the floor, let him stretch out beside her and pin her down with one of his legs. His face hovered over hers. She did not turn away from his study. The movement of his eyes across her face was like the graze of his fingertips against her skin. He touched her cheeks, her temples, the bridge of her nose. His eyes lingered on her chin, then her bottom lip, and when her lips parted, they lingered on the space between them. It was as if he willed her tongue to appear because she couldn't think of any reason why she chose that moment to wet her lips, but she heard the sharp intake of his breath when she did.

"You're going to kiss me, aren't you?" The huskiness of her voice made it almost unrecognizable to her. "I want you to."

"Something we agree on. But first . . ." He fiddled with the pins and combs in her hair and ignored her when she batted at his hands. "There's nothing I'm doing that can't be repaired. And this . . ." He lifted her head just enough to loosen the coil.

He separated her hair with his fingertips, carefully combing through the strands. "It's like wading through a pool of fire."

"It is?"

He nodded. "Liquid to the touch. Brilliant to the eyes."

She stared up at him, said nothing.

"I think I better kiss you now."

Raine pressed her lips together, but she nodded. If he didn't, she would burst into flame. She might do exactly that anyway. When his mouth covered hers, Raine's body lifted, arched. His touch was electric, and the current made her limbs seize, not painfully, but wonderfully. If she had been standing, she would have been in his arms, her breasts flush to his chest, and her heels would have been raised off the floor. She might have even sparkled.

The fancy struck her, and she smiled into the kiss and wondered if he could feel the shape of it on her lips. She knew everything about the shape of his mouth now. She knew that the wry twist thinned the right side and that the smirk lifted the left. She knew the exact distance he thrust out his lower lip when he released a long-held breath. She had intimate knowledge of his mouth against the hollow beneath her ear and at her throat. She had watched it sip her skin, her nipples, and make a damp trail across her collarbone. When he kissed her, she felt as if he was teasing her with the secrets he guarded. Eventually she would know them all.

Raine felt herself being taken from want to need. Her mouth clung to his. She matched the slant of his kiss, the hunger that drove it harder. Her fingers fumbled with the buttons on his vest and pulled at his shirt. She slipped her hands under his trousers and unfastened the overlap of his drawers. She pushed. He tugged. Her skirt rode up her legs. His knee urged it higher. She guided him to the crushed, uncomfortable bustle at her back. He pushed her hands out of the way to get at the ribbons, and when she was finally free of the damnable contraption, they both shoved it hard under the bed. Laughing, she lifted her bottom when his fingers scrabbled under her petticoats to remove her cotton drawers. She stopped laughing when he spread her legs and jerked her close.

She watched him steadily. Waited for him. And knew before he did when he would come to her.

"Ah!" Her sharp cry made her press her knuckles against her mouth. She did not want him to draw back, to ask if he was hurting her. She was tender, but her body remembered him, welcomed him, and the warm pleasure of being joined to him made the tenderness insignificant.

He didn't ask, but she felt the cadence change from the frenzy of the first thrusts to something slow and deep and powerful. Sometimes he held himself back to kiss her, and the kiss was exactly the same, slow and deep and powerful.

Her hands slid under his shirt. She rubbed his back, ran her palms across the muscles bunching in his shoulders. His skin was warm, and she had a memory of it being warmer still when she slept in the cradle of his body.

She found the dimples at the base of his spine. Her fingers spread out from there, clutching his taut buttocks, leaving the imprint of her nails like a brand. She raised her face, brushed her mouth against his when he dipped his head.

In the late morning light, she could see his face as she had not been able to the night before. Without the soft glow of the oil lamp, the edges of his features seemed sharper, less likely to yield. His eyebrows were dark slashes, his nose, a blade. His jaw had the hard line of a granite block, and the wintry blue-gray color of his eyes lent him the watchful, perceptive gaze of a predator.

"Mmm." The sound did not part her lips, but it was perfectly audible. She started to cover her mouth again. He nudged her hand out of the way, and the next thing she said was his name. "Kellen."

"Yes," he said. "Raine."

Somehow he made her name sound raw, primal. It moved her. Pleasure had already wound her as tight as the string on a child's top, and when he said her name like that, it was as if he'd pulled the cord.

She spun and spun, and as dizzy as he made her, she never lost sight of him. She flung her arms wide. Her hands balled into fists. She gave herself up to pleasure and to him and then made certain he could do the same.

She matched him measure for measure, letting him use her body as a cradle this time, and when she felt him still, she contracted all around him, his shoulders, his back, his thighs, his cock, making surrender his only choice. The sharp, shallow thrusts that he couldn't restrain spilled his seed into her.

He landed on considerably softer ground than she did.

Raine nudged Kellen's shoulders. She didn't mind his weight as much as she minded the steel cage of her corset. "A little breathing room," she whispered.

Nodding, he eased out of her and rolled onto his back. He trapped Raine's arm under his neck. "Sorry." He lifted his head, and she freed her arm. While she began to straighten her clothes, he looked longingly at the bed. "How did we not get that far?"

Raine glanced at him, saw the direction of his gaze, and realized what he was asking. She chose to believe the question was rhetorical and therefore better left alone.

Kellen tugged and tucked his drawers, trousers, and shirt before he sat up to button his vest. He ran his hand through his hair, making furrows where she had ruffled it. Raine was still lying down, her eyes closed, the corners of her mouth turned up a mere fraction of a degree.

"You look indecently pleased with yourself."

"Not so virtuous, am I?" When Raine didn't hear Kellen chuckle, she opened her eyes. "You're working up to saying something I don't want to hear. I can tell."

"I won't say anything if you don't want me to."

"I don't want you to."

"All right."

Raine closed her eyes again, but the smile that was hardly there disappeared entirely. "I know you'll be moving on," she said when the silence became unbearable. "You'll realize that I don't need you, and you'll go. That's the promise you made to me, and I take you for a man of your word. If you weren't more decent than you like to let on, you wouldn't be thinking about whether or not I'm getting all twisted up with feelings for you. You'd just be gone one day. That's what you usually do, isn't it?"

"Do you want me to talk now?"

She hesitated, then nodded.

"Yes. It's what I usually do. I haven't had to answer to anyone for a long time."

"You don't have to answer to me." She stole a glance at him. "I don't want the responsibility."

"A child might change your mind."

Raine blew out a frustrated breath as she sat up. "You said it."

"That's what you didn't want to hear?"

She started to rise, but Kellen caught her wrist and pulled her back down. "What?"

"I don't have any bastards, Raine."

"I don't know what I'm supposed to say to that."

"I *don't* have any bastards," he repeated. "It's not because I'm decent; it's because I'm careful. Or I was. Until now."

"I won't expect anything from you."

"Christ, Raine, you don't understand at all. I expect something from myself."

Raine jerked her wrist out of his hand. "I am not trying to make this hard for you. I am trying to make it easy."

"Stop trying. I'm not interested in what you think I want to hear. I'm interested in what you think." He began collecting the scattered copies of *Nat Church and the Chinese Box* and returning them to the crate. Raine handed him one that was under her skirt. He took it, grumbled a thank-you, and tossed it with the others.

Raine got to her feet. This time Kellen did not stop her. She carefully stepped over the novels and around him and went to the bathing room, where she shut the door. When she came out, he was gone.

Because of Scott Pennway's death, the saloon was crowded, but the crowd was subdued. Raine had all three of her girls working the floor while she tended bar. Walt came and went, restocking the liquor, sweeping up outside, tapping a new keg. He kept himself busy with small tasks because it was just what he did. It seemed to Raine that it was especially important tonight that each one of them do just what they always did. Routine was a comfort. Veering outside of it was not.

There was talk at the bar about Scott's death, some discussion about whether Annie and the children would stay in Bitter Springs or go to Denver, where she had family. Raine did not contribute to the conversation. She caught Ted Rush telling Jessop Davis that he'd gone head over bucket down his own steps one night on the way to the necessary. When he got to the part of how it could have been him sprawled in the backyard with his neck broke, Raine moved as far away as she could. It wasn't long before she observed Jessop doing the same.

What was missing from all the exchanges she heard or overheard was speculation that what happened to Scott Pennway wasn't an accident. Ever since she had been made aware that the jury from Ellen's trial came together in her saloon, Raine had taken to making a mental note of their presence. With the exception of Matthew Sharp, who stayed away for religious reasons, everyone else was part of the assembly. It made the absence of John Hood, Hank Thompson, and now Scott Pennway more pronounced. She imagined that the others had taken notice of it as well. Perhaps none of them saw the point of debating accident versus murder when their numbers were dwindling and a killer might be buying them their next drink.

Someone asked Sue to play, and Raine nodded her approval. She hoped the girl chose something counter to the mood of the room. These men craved a lively tune, not a dirge. So did she. Raine held her breath, waiting to hear what Sue would play, and when the first nimble notes of an old English melody were struck, she finally smiled.

"Good to see," Walt said as he approached carrying a case of ginger beer. He put the case under the bar and left without explaining himself.

It wasn't until he was gone that Raine realized he had been commenting on her smile. She supposed it was the first genuine smile she had indulged in all evening.

With the introduction of music, the talk was livelier, the laughter more vigorous, and the occasional argument showed real spirit. The noise had just reached the barely tolerable level when Eli and Clay Burdick walked into the Pennyroyal.

It was not that anyone ceased what he was doing. Charlie Patterson kept on singing, though his voice veered off-key and there was noticeably less gusto when he got to the refrain. Sue played, but her fingers were not as deft as they had been a few measures earlier. Ted Rush continued telling his story to Richard Allen, but no longer so loud that it could be heard by men on the other side of him. The Davis brothers kept on arguing but used more gestures and finger-pointing than words. Even Mr. Petit and Mr. Reasoner, who had little contact with the Burdicks, took their cue from everyone else and changed the tenor of their laughter to something less ribald and more restrained. The men who had gathered to hear their stories did the same. Mr. Jones held court at one table where there was considerable interest in water rights and irrigation, but he let everyone else do the talking when Eli and Clay passed by.

Raine watched Kellen to see what he would do. There had been the occasional companion at his table. Dr. Kent had wandered in and sat with him for a time. They mostly sat in silence, exchanging only a few words, and when the doctor finished his drink, he left. Ted Rush occupied a seat at Kellen's side long enough to relate his own close encounter with the grim reaper on account of a fall. As soon as he left, Kellen caught the attention of Cecilia and asked for a whiskey.

Now he was alone, and Raine believed it was purposeful. She saw him raise his hand and wave the Burdicks over. The man did not know how to wait for trouble. He invited it.

Eli slid into the chair beside Kellen. He shooed Renee and Cecilia as the girls closed in on him.

"Hey," said Clay, watching the girls go. "I want a drink."

"Lorrainey will bring it," Eli told him. "Lorrainey! Two whiskeys." He looked at Kellen's empty glass. "You want another?"

"I could use one."

Eli added another finger to the two he had up. "Three whiskeys. Bring them yourself."

"Why do you do that?" Kellen asked.

"Do what?"

He pointed to Raine. "Pull her away from the bar to serve you when there are girls who could do it just as well."

Eli grinned. "I like to watch her walk. You ever notice how she walks?"

"As a matter of fact, I have."

Clay's lip curled. "Like the ground ain't good enough for her feet."

"He means she kinda floats," Eli said.

"That's what you say. I say the Widder Berry walks like she thinks she's better than everyone else."

"Maybe she is," Kellen said mildly.

Clay's expression turned dark, but Eli laughed. "Damn, but you could be right about that." He jerked his thumb at Clay. "My brother's not real partial to Lorrainey after the trouble she caused us, but I never figured there was sense in holdin' on to a grudge like it was a bronco you were trying to bust."

Clay shoved his chair back and stood. He grabbed one of the whiskey glasses from Raine's hand before she could set them down. "I'm goin' to talk to the photographer fellow that's been nosin' around the spread and takin' his fool pictures." He jabbed a finger in Mr. Petit's direction. "That's him, ain't it, Lorraine?"

"He's a photographer, yes. I don't know whether or not he's been on your property."

"Now why don't I believe you?" With that parting shot, he turned his back on all of them.

Eli watched him go. "Miserable cuss. Always has been." He smiled at Raine, but it was more leering grin than greeting. "Doesn't share my disposition or my affections."

"Here's your drink." She set it down hard in front of him. "And here's yours." She was only a little less deliberate with Kellen's glass than she had been with Eli's. "Let me know if you want the bottle." She gave them her back the same as Clay.

"She's not so sweet on you tonight," Eli told Kellen.

"We're arguing."

Eli's blue eyes narrowed a fraction. His jaw swung a little to the side. "Is that so?"

"Sure is."

"Never heard that the Widder Berry argued with her guests. Reputation is that she's accommodatin'."

"She argues with me, and she's accommodating."

"What do you mean by that? Exactly."

"I'll tell you, but I'd rather see both your hands on the table before I do."

Eli already had one hand wrapped around his whiskey glass. Frowning, he brought up the other slowly. "You got them where you want them."

"We're arguing about you, actually. I want to tell you. She doesn't. She thinks you'll start trouble. I think she's never understood that you're in love with her and that because you are, and probably have been since you first watched her walking toward you, what you really want is to see her happy. I know a little about the trouble you say she's caused you, and I—"

Eli interrupted him, "Does she say different?"

"No. Not at all. She knows what she's done. She also knows that because of it, she can never accept a proposal from you. Raine told me that she was the cause of your father being separated from one of his sons, and she couldn't do that again. She believes your father would not take her in. It's her opinion that he would send you away."

"She told you all that?"

"In her letters," Kellen said, nodding. "She explained all of it in her letters. It's probably the reason she went looking for someone like me, because she couldn't have someone like you."

"Jesus, Mary, and Joseph," he said under his breath. He glanced over at the bar. "She's watching us."

Kellen kept his eyes on Eli, especially on Eli's hands. "Does she look worried?"

"Not so much. I'd say she's got her dander up."

"You know her better than I do. You're probably right."

Eli's attention swiveled back to Kellen. "So when you say she went looking for someone like you . . ."

"Mail order," said Kellen. "Courting by correspondence."

"And how has that turned out?"

Kellen watched Eli's fingers loosen around his glass. They

slid to the edge of the table and began to drop below it. "This is where I really need to be able to see your hands, Eli."

"You think I'm going to draw on you?"

"I'm thinking that if I were sitting where you are, I might be tempted. Do you know what a dog in a manger is?"

"Sure. I know Aesop. I'm not cattle smart and book stupid. The dog grudges the ox what he can't enjoy for himself. I guess you figure me for the dog."

"Are you?"

"I don't like it, Coltrane, you bein' with her. I don't like it at all. But she's right about Uriah, and I don't suppose she'd believe me if I said I've contemplated leavin' now and again."

"She might believe you," said Kellen. "But she couldn't accept being the reason for it."

"I probably should have told her about that." He raised his glass for another whiskey. "You haven't touched yours."

"Still waiting to learn where you stand."

"Hands are on the table, aren't they? You goin' to marry her?"

"Already did."

Eli looked Kellen over. He whistled softly. "So it really was mail order, just like you were a sewing machine or a thresher from Montgomery Ward."

Nodding faintly, Kellen offered a slim, vaguely embarrassed smile. It drew Eli's focus to his mouth. Kellen held steady and pretended not to notice. "She's coming with the bottle."

Still looking at Kellen's mouth, Eli said, "You don't mind if I watch her walk this way? It's kind of a habit."

Kellen turned his hand over in a gesture that granted permission. "It's worth admiring, isn't it?"

Eli stared at Kellen's profile as he turned his head. "It sure is."

Clay Burdick was eventually able to corner his man when everyone else sitting nearby scattered. He crooked a finger at Renee, asked for a beer for himself and one for his companion.

"I prefer whiskey," the man said when Renee sashayed away.

"But I'm buying beer." Clay directed the man's notice across the saloon to where Eli was sitting with Kellen. "Can't figure him out."

"Your brother? Or Coltrane?"

"Either of them, I guess. They don't seem a likely pair. Uriah's going to let that Coltrane fellow write a story about the ranch. He decided to invite him to come out, if you can believe that. I suppose that's what Eli's talking to him about. They have about as much in common as a snake and a stick. You might mistake one for the other, but only one of them will kill you."

"Your brother? Or Coltrane?"

"See? Now you're just pissin' down my leg. Uriah's not real pleased with you, but I guess you know that."

"You know about Pennway?"

"Eli and I heard about it outside. Walt told us."

"Walt? Oh, the man Mrs. Berry keeps around for odd jobs. The slow-wit."

"That's the one. Eli and I figured since it was Scott Pennway, and Walt was saying how it was an accident, it probably all comes around to you. Is that right?"

"You know my work. Tell Uriah he owes me."

"My pa is thinking how it's you that owes him." Clay waited until Renee put their glasses down and swept away the others. When she was gone, he said, "That business with the girl wasn't part of the contract."

He shrugged.

"Make sure it doesn't happen again. Uriah had no quarrel with the girl and none with her parents. He says he'll shoot you himself if you do something like that again."

"I bet he'd try."

"He means it," said Clay. "Take it elsewhere if that's your pleasure."

"Elsewhere?"

"Rawlins. Cheyenne. Denver, if you like. Keep it out of Bitter Springs. Uriah says if you step sideways again, he's finished with you. More to the point, you'll be finished."

"You said she was a whore."

"A sweet one. Helpful, too. All sass and ass, that's what I

thought. Uriah, though, says differently, and he's the one putting money in your account." Clay took a swallow of beer, wiped his mouth with the back of his hand. "What did you do with the whiskey drummer that went missing when she did?"

"I find it interesting that you're asking me."

"Who should I be asking?"

The man shrugged. "Is Uriah worried about him?"

"About him being found."

"I don't think that's likely, Clay, do you?"

"Christ, you make me want to shoot you myself."

"You can try."

Clay didn't accept the challenge. "Who's next?"

"I haven't decided. There's opportunity and circumstance to be considered. You see how they all congregate like flies on pie. Dr. Kent was here earlier. That doesn't happen too often."

Clay looked around. He quickly spotted Richard Allen, Harry Sample, and David Rogers at a table with the Davis boys. Clifton and Wheeler were together at the bar. McCormick, Dick Faber, and Paul Reston were scattered.

"Matt Sharp isn't here. He's out by himself on his farm. That's an opportunity."

"There's a reason that your father hired me." He stopped, left the rest unsaid.

"You think I'm wrong?" asked Clay, pressing.

"Sharp isn't alone. His family is with him. His farm is isolated, difficult to approach without being seen, and an unlikely site for an accident."

"So? Shoot him."

The man sighed, sipped his beer. "I'll think about it. I'm not as intemperate as you."

Clay's dark eyebrows lifted. "Then how do you explain Emily?"

"I don't have to. You do." He pushed his untouched beer at Clay and left the table without a backward glance.

Raine dropped the key to the apartment door in the empty vase. Closing her eyes, she pressed her fists to her temples and massaged them. She could hear Kellen moving around the bedroom, *her* bedroom, and the headache that had been nagging at her all day, chipping away at her calm, finally rolled through her skull like thunder.

Her headache powder was in a cabinet in the bathing room, which meant that she could not avoid Kellen. It was her hope, then, to avoid a confrontation, and failing that, to avoid a loud one.

His trunks were in her bedroom, and the wardrobe that had been in the other room was now on the opposite wall from hers. He had almost finished unpacking his clothes. He stopped when she entered, looked her over, and then resumed what he was doing.

Raine hurried into the bathing room. She turned on the tap, found the packet of powder that the druggist recommended, and mixed it with water using her index finger as a spoon. She drank it down and chased away the bitter aftertaste with a second glass of water. Bracing her arms on the edge of the sink, she waited for the wave of light-headedness to pass before she removed all the pins and combs from her hair. The combs fell in the sink, but the pins scattered on the floor. She left them there. A second wave of dizziness caught her unprepared as she turned away from the mirror. She would have stumbled, probably fallen, if Kellen hadn't suddenly appeared at her elbow to steady her.

"When did you last eat?" he asked.

She frowned, trying to recall.

"If you can't remember, then it was too long ago." He had one hand firmly under her elbow, the other at the small of her back, and was prepared to guide her to bed, but when her feet didn't move when he nudged her, he picked her up and carried her. The fact that the only sound she made was all surprise and no protest told him that she was in a bad way.

Kellen set her down gently. "Is it a headache?"

She nodded, winced.

"Don't move. Was that medicine I saw you drinking?"

"Yes."

"All right. Just lie still. Close your eyes. Let me help you." He made short work of her shoes, stockings, skirt, and the tailored cuirass bodice. He removed her bustle for the second time that day and then freed her from the corset. He could see the imprint of the steel stays in the cotton camisole and did not have to see the soft flesh of her abdomen to know there would be similar markings.

When she was down to her camisole and drawers, Kellen helped Raine get under the blankets. She murmured something he couldn't make out when he tucked her in. "I'm going to the kitchen and find you some food. You don't have to eat anything now, but you might want it later. Do you understand? I'm going to leave you alone."

"S'fine."

Kellen stoked the fire in the stove before he left. His foray to the hotel's kitchen was brief. He found a couple of rolls in the bread box and took an apple from the bulky sack leaning against a table leg. He found an open jar of blackberry preserves and tucked it under his arm. Carefully balancing the foodstuffs, a knife, and his lamp, he returned to the third floor.

As quick as he had been, Raine was already sleeping when he returned. Kellen cleared space on the nightstand on Raine's side of the bed and laid out the rather meager feast. He turned back the lamp, undressed in the semidarkness, and then extinguished the lamp altogether. He felt his way back to the other side of the bed and crawled in.

Raine stirred but didn't wake. Kellen put the back of his hand to her forehead. She wasn't fevered, merely exhausted. He edged closer but kept a clear space between them. He thought she'd probably have something to say about the sleeping arrangement when she woke. Kellen was less sure that he'd be around to hear it. There hadn't been any time to tell her that he was riding out to the Burdick ranch in the morning.

It was still dark when Raine woke. The time did not matter to her. She felt surprisingly rested and alert. The headache had vanished, and when she tentatively tested the waters by turning her head first one way, then the other, there was no pain, no rolling thunder, and most important, no dizziness.

She was aware of Kellen sleeping beside her. She'd have something to say about that when he awoke, but she was too hungry to dwell on the particulars of that conversation. It was tempting to delay getting something to eat, especially when the bed was comfortably warm and any movement outside of it was bound to be cold and unpleasant, but the emptiness in her stomach was a real ache and required her attention.

She eased out of bed, attended to the fire, and then found her robe and slippers and put them on. It wasn't until she was in the kitchen, elbow deep in the bread box, that the vague memory of Kellen offering to get her something to eat tugged at her consciousness. She wondered how much she could rely on such a foggy memory and decided that she couldn't. True, she voted with her stomach. Its rumbling really could not be ignored.

Raine cut a thick slice of oat bread and drizzled it with honey. She bit into it while she pushed the stool closer to the table and sat down. The oil lamp bobbled when she bumped the table with her knee, and the pool of light around it quivered. Raine watched it until it stilled, and then she stilled as she heard the back door open. Footsteps marched in place as the person shook off the cold and the dirt from his shoes. It lasted only a few moments, and then there was silence in the stairwell.

She held her breath, waiting to see if the intruder would enter through the kitchen or climb the stairs to the guest rooms. Would the lamplight draw him to the kitchen to investigate or turn him away? Her hand slid across the table toward the knife block. Raine knew better than to suppose it was Walt on the other side of the kitchen door, and it certainly wasn't Mrs. Sterling come to get an early start on her bread. Neither one of them would have hesitated as this person was doing.

She decided she would rather know than always wonder, and if the intruder fled when she called out, then that was all right, too.

Raine set her oat bread on the table and turned a little toward the door. Her fingers hovered over the handle of the carving knife. "Who's there?"

The kitchen door opened, and Mr. Jones stepped in.

As casually as she could, Raine let her hand fall back to the table. Her fingertips grazed the knife block. "Mr. Jones. What on earth—"

"I couldn't sleep," he said. "Sciatica." He limped toward her. "Aggravated by the sprain, I suspect. I spoke to the druggist about it, and he gave me something that smells like licorice but tastes like tar."

"Mr. Burnside is a great believer in the worse it tastes, the better it is for you." Raine noted his pinched features, particularly the tightness around his mouth. "It doesn't seem to be working in your case."

Jones shrugged. "I'll try it for a few more days. Walking helps. Standing is tolerable. It's lying down that is so painful." He leaned against the table. "Is it true that you and Mr. Coltrane are married?"

Raine blinked. "Who told you that?"

"I had it a little while ago from Mr. Eli Burdick himself."

Chapter Twelve

Kellen was sitting on the edge of the bed, rubbing his eyes, when he heard Raine come through the door. He swiveled around so he could see her when she came into the bedroom. As soft as the light was from the oil lamp, it still forced him to squint to make her out. Oddly, the first thing he noticed was the plate of food in her hand.

He pointed to the nightstand. “I brought you something to eat earlier.”

“I was already in the kitchen when I thought I remembered you talking about it.” She placed her plate on the chest and returned the lamp to the nightstand. “Why are you up?”

“I was going to look for you, but since you’re here . . .” He lay back down and turned on his side, dragging the covers up to his shoulders as he made a nest for himself. He closed his eyes.

Raine kicked off her slippers and shrugged out of her robe. She compared the food that he brought her against what she’d made herself. The blackberry preserves decided her. She left her plate on the chest and climbed into bed beside him.

“What are you doing?” he asked.

"Spreading preserves on a roll. There are two of them. Do you want one?"

He didn't open his eyes, and his voice was partially muffled by his pillow. "What time is it?"

"I'm not sure. I never looked. Somewhere between three and four, I imagine." His soft groan spoke eloquently of his distress. "It's just as well that I went downstairs when I did. I was witness to Mr. Jones returning from a very late night walk. He came in the back door, which I found peculiar because it's so dark behind the hotel. I told him from now on that he should come in at the front, that's if his sciatica doesn't improve and he has to venture out again to take his mind off the pain."

"Is your headache gone?"

Raine supposed that it was telling Kellen about Mr. Jones's pain that prompted his question. "Yes." She put down the knife and bit into her roll. The blackberry preserves were sweet on her tongue. She savored the bite and then spoke around it. "You heard what I said about Mr. Jones, didn't you?"

"Every word. Swallow."

She gave him a sour look that he couldn't appreciate because he remained steadfast in his determination to keep his eyes closed. She swallowed. "Did you tell Eli that we're married?"

"Yes. I said I would."

"I saw that you talked to him for a long time, but he never said anything to me before he left. Neither did you. Mr. Jones asked me about it. He said he heard it from Eli."

"I didn't see Eli with Jones this evening. Jones and Clay were together for a spell. Maybe he meant Clay."

"Clay sat with a lot of people tonight, mostly I think he didn't want to sit with you, but then he never spent time with Eli again either." She took another bite of her roll. "Anyway, Mr. Jones heard it from Eli on the street, not in the bar, and definitely not from Clay. Eli and Clay must have gone down to Whistler's Saloon when I started closing up. I thought they were leaving town, but I guess not, because Mr. Jones heard Eli telling Clay all about our marriage as they were leaving

Whistler's. The explanation involved something about a sewing machine and a thresher."

"Mail order. That's what he meant."

"Oh." She finished the roll, dusted off her hands, and cut into the apple. Her mouth watered. "How did Eli take it?"

"Well, he didn't shoot me."

"Do you want a slice of this apple? It's crisp." She took his groan as refusal. "So how did you explain it to him?"

Kellen punched his pillow once and rolled onto his back. He opened his eyes, which was a mistake because he saw the apple. He put out his hand, palm up. "Eve."

She glanced at him sideways. "Did you say 'Eve'?"

"Please. I said please."

Raine dropped a slice into his hand. "It sounded like you said 'Eve.' "

"Huh." He ate the apple slice, and then related everything he'd told Eli.

Raine took it all in, and skepticism slowly gave way to astonishment. "He believed you? He actually believed I turned down his proposals because I couldn't bear to see him estranged from his father?"

"He certainly seemed to." Kellen offered a modest shrug. "But then I was convincing. I almost believed it myself."

She gave him another slice of apple. "Lies come easy to you, don't they?"

"Well, I suppose it depends on your perspective. Lying is difficult, but telling a story? That comes naturally."

Raine chuckled. "Not to Ted Rush it doesn't. I think he must have told everyone tonight how it could have been his neck that was broken because he has a porch and steps and sometimes even walks on them."

Kellen finished his apple wedge and shook his head when she offered him another. "Ted's mistake is that he's always at the center of the story. He'd do better if he observed more and took himself out of it. Like Walt. He tells a good tale because he watches people, pays attention to the details."

"Not many folks listen to Walt."

"Their loss."

Raine nodded. She put the apple core and the knife on the table then lay down next to Kellen, turning on her side as she stretched. She slipped one arm under her pillow to elevate her head and studied his profile. Strands of his rumpled, chestnut hair looked burnished in the lamplight. She itched to push back the unruly spikes that fringed his forehead, but let them be because they made him seem a little disreputable, and it was better for her when she thought of him that way.

He blinked, drawing her eyes to his thick, dark lashes. "It's a shame God gave you those eyelashes."

"So my sisters tell me."

"They don't make you look pretty, though."

"I'm glad to hear it."

"The way they shade your eyes sometimes . . . when you're looking around but not so that anyone can be sure . . . I think they make you look dangerous."

"I'm glad to hear that, too."

"You want to look dangerous?"

"Sometimes." He turned his head just enough to let her see the pointed lift of his eyebrow. "Sometimes I only want to be left alone."

"I'm thinking you should have slept somewhere else."

"It's occurred to me." He returned to staring at the ceiling.

"When did you move all your things here? I assume these are all your things."

"Walt did it for me while I was in the saloon. Most of the hotel guests were there, so it seemed like a good time."

"He never said a word."

"Not all of us chatter like we're freezing."

"I'm not going to dignify that with a response."

"I think you just did."

Raine sighed. "There's just one other thing."

Kellen didn't respond. He waited to hear it.

"Mr. Jones asked me to ask you if you would mention the survey when you go out to the Burdick place tomorrow."

"Well, that explains why you're still wide awake and pushing me in that direction."

"So he's right. You *are* going out there tomorrow."

"Today, now. I want to leave as soon as I can after there's light."

"When were you going to tell me?"

"In the morning, if you were awake. If you weren't, I would have left a note. And yes, before you ask, I harbored some small hope that you'd be sleeping."

"Coward."

"And yet I am not offended."

"Don't pretend you're more afraid of me than the Burdicks."

"But I'm not afraid of the Burdicks. You, on the other hand, terrify me."

She pushed up on her elbow so she could see his face more clearly. "You don't mean that."

He shrugged.

"You *do* mean that?"

"You'll have to decide. I said it. I'm not going to explain it."

"Could I stop you from going out to the Burdick ranch?"

"Don't ask. You're not going to try. We have an agreement, and this is part of seeing it through."

Raine gave him a faint, reluctant nod. "Do you know when I can expect you back?"

"Late. Very late, I think. It could be the following morning, depending on whether I'm invited to spend the night. Eli didn't mention that, but he did say I would be joining them for dinner. They intend to take me on a tour of the ranch."

"That could require more than one day. It's a big spread."

"I don't need to see it all to write about it. I explained that to Eli. He also knows that I want to interview Uriah. His father apparently is looking forward to talking to me."

"If he is, it's because he thinks he can use you."

"I'm certain of it. Perhaps he has a grievance that he wants to make public. The *New York World* is a very public stage."

"You know you don't actually work for Pulitzer."

"I do realize that." He remembered saying something very like it to her, but the subject had been their marriage. "Your point is nicely made."

"Thank you."

"Are we finished now?"

"Yes. You can go back to sleep."

Kellen turned, pulled her into his arms. "I'm not as interested in sleeping as I used to be."

The eight-mile ride out to the Burdick homestead was uneventful. Kellen knew from Raine and Walt that he was on Burdick land at mile five. Marshal Sterling had been shot somewhere between miles six and seven. Kellen did not think he was riding into a trap; nevertheless, the hair stood up at the back of his neck and he remained watchful.

He was met by a couple of ranch hands when he got in sight of the house. He declined their escort. They went with him anyway, not because they were expecting trouble, but because it was what they were told to do when they saw strangers close to the house. Kellen approved of their ask-questions-first policy.

Eli and Clay came out on the porch of the log home just as he was dismounting. His escorts took Cronus off to the corral to care for him. Kellen rolled his shoulders to relieve some of the tension still pulling his muscles taut. Wind buffeted his duster around his legs. He reached into the pocket of his long coat and removed a notebook and pencil. When he looked up, Clay's hand was hovering near his gun.

Kellen held up the notebook. "I'd like to sketch the house, if you don't think your father will mind. I don't take photographs myself, and after what you said last night, I didn't want to presume that I could invite Mr. Petit to come with me."

"Good thinking," Clay said.

Eli gave approval for the sketch, and Kellen roughed it out quickly. It was a large house but low to the ground and so wide that it looked as if it squatted on the land. It was solidly built and generally in good repair, with curtains at every glass window and a fine oak door. The features that had been added for Mrs. Burdick's pleasure, such as the window boxes and the porch swing, were still present but had been allowed to weather and now appeared fragile. Walt had warned him to tread carefully around any mention of Uriah's runaway wife, and looking at the shabby state of the empty window boxes and the listing porch swing, Kellen knew it was good advice.

When Kellen finished the sketch, he approached the porch and held it up for Eli and Clay to critique. Eli said it wasn't bad. Clay offered a grunt.

"You want coffee, something to drink?" asked Eli.

"Nothing."

Eli nodded. "Uriah's inside. He wants us to show you around first. He says there's no sense talking to you before you know anything, and he figures a feller from back East needs more than a little education."

"I've been to other ranches," Kellen said.

"But you've never been to this one, and Uriah thinks it's the only one that counts. There's a fresh horse waiting for you. If you don't want anything before we go, then we're just wasting time. C'mon."

They set out northwest and rode for miles along the creek. Kellen's horse was a frisky, cinnamon-colored mare that required a firm hand. He was aware of the brothers watching how he handled the animal and suspected they would call an early halt to the tour if he did not manage the mare. Kellen showed them that he could. Eli gave him a quick, approving nod, while Clay, who sat easy on a great gray beast he called Phantom, looked simultaneously disappointed and impressed.

As they rode, Eli pointed out landmarks and talked about grazing and herding and branding the cattle. Clay talked about the history of the place, how his father drove longhorns from Texas to start the spread and eventually mixed the breed with better beef cattle when the advent of the railroad meant long drives were no longer a necessity.

They veered away from the natural boundary of the creek to show him where barbed wire fenced some of the property. When it was all open range, the cattle wandered everywhere. That suited the longhorns, but cultivating good beef cattle meant restricting them in smaller areas in the better grasslands. The best beef for market came from cows that didn't have to walk so far for food that their muscles turned tough and stringy.

Barbed wire also meant they didn't have to hire as many hands to manage the herds.

Kellen asked them about the blizzard from the winter before and how it had affected them.

"Just about killed Uriah," Eli said. "Hard times, for sure."

Clay nodded. "We could only bring in some of the cattle. Two of our best hired hands died trying to get to town for feed for the horses and hens. They lost their way, and they'd been to town and back hundreds of times. That's the kind of storm it was. Over and over. From October to March. The white blinded you when it was falling, and after the snow stopped and the sun came out, well, there's no hat Stetson makes that keeps the glare out of your eyes when it's coming at you from the ground."

"Cattle froze where they stood," said Eli. "Some got buried in drifts. Most of them just starved." Eli extended his arm and waved it in a wide arc that encompassed all the land to the horizon. "It was a graveyard. After the thaw we were working day and night, dragging the dead cattle to bonfires to keep the wolves from picking off the animals we had left."

Clay said, "It will take years to recover, build the herd back."

"What about water?" Kellen asked.

Eli tugged on his woolen scarf so it covered the lower half of his chin. "You saw the creek. That serves the cattle on this parcel of land, but it's been known to dry up in the summer. We need to own the source in the mountains, maybe build a dam and reservoir to keep the flow of all the creeks steady."

"Folks in town would have somethin' to say about that," said Clay. "Same source supplies their wells. The Pennyroyal taps into an underground spring to get its water."

"And a dam would shift the flow?"

"Regulate it, let's say. They'd still have water."

Kellen understood what Clay didn't say: The Burdicks would be the regulators. He decided he would wait until he met Uriah to mention the government survey.

They stayed in the saddle all morning, shared some jerky and biscuits by a grove of cottonwoods and box elders in the afternoon, and headed back before they reached the parcel where new barbed wire fencing was being rolled out. Kellen could see men working in the distance, but when he asked if he could watch, Clay abruptly announced that Uriah was waiting for them. Eli shrugged, agreed with his brother, and that was that. It was the only occasion that Kellen asked if he could make a sketch that his request was declined. Lack of time was the reason offered, and Kellen accepted it without an argument.

It was nearing dusk when they reached the ranch. They gave their horses over to the hands and went into the house through the back. Clay showed Kellen where he could hang his coat and hat, and Kellen transferred his notebook and pencil to his vest. The kitchen was warm and fragrant with loaves of bread fresh from the oven. Beef stew simmered on the stove. Kellen's mouth watered.

The cook, a thin man of indeterminate years with more gristle on his bones than meat, raised the long wooden stirring spoon as a warning to Clay to stay away from the bread. "Your da's waiting in the parlor. Shake the dust off somewhere else unless you want grit in your stew."

"That's O'Malley," Eli said.

Kellen looked back at the man who now worked for the Burdicks in the same capacity Walt once had. O'Malley, tough as old shoe leather and with a face equally creased, looked as if he could take care of himself. The abuses that Walter Mangold suffered at the hands of the Burdicks weren't likely to be visited on this Irish immigrant.

Uriah Burdick was pouring a whiskey for himself when they entered the parlor. He offered a drink to all of them in place of a greeting. When he put the glass in Kellen's hand, he paused.

Kellen stood still for the scrutiny. It was nothing he hadn't experienced upon seeing his own father after a long absence or even a short one. Apparently this met with Uriah's approval because he looked at his sons in a manner that said, "See?"

"So you're Coltrane," Uriah said.

"I am." When Uriah released the whiskey glass, Kellen thanked him for the drink.

"Eli tells me you've wedded and bedded the Widder Berry."

Kellen didn't blink. "She's my wife, yes."

Uriah grunted softly, waved a hand to indicate that they should all sit. He put himself between the wide arms of a plump, gently worn, velveteen-covered chair. "I considered rescinding the invitation once Eli told me about your marriage. I even suggested to my son that in light of this new circumstance, he should have consulted me before he went ahead and offered you our hospitality."

"I understand. You think I have competing interests."

"Competing interests," he repeated. "Don't you?"

"I have a job to do, Mr. Burdick. I will write a fair piece. If you like, I'll let you read it for accuracy and comment before I send it back to New York."

"Then I can make changes?"

"Yes, to the facts if they're wrong. And if you think I've misrepresented something you said, you can comment on it or any other part of the story. I'm interested in your ranch. The cattle market is making a lot of men money, but few people outside of ranchers like yourself and the men who work in the Chicago slaughterhouses understand how it gets from hoof to plate. No one in New York knows how little of the quarter they spend on a Sunday roast ends up in your pocket."

Uriah was silent, thoughtful, as he sipped his whiskey. "Everything you're saying would sound a whole lot better if you hadn't taken up with Lorraine Berry."

"She's the reason I'm here, Mr. Burdick. The idea for the story came after we were married. I got the newspaper to pay for my ticket out here on the strength of the story I promised them. I made some stops along the way, spoke to other ranchers. I have enough notes now to make it a four-part serial. I'd like to have enough for five parts. Something to run all week."

"A week's seven days, son."

"Well, if you give me something to work with, maybe Pulitzer will start it on Sunday and push it through Saturday. I've made some sketches that the artists at the *World* can improve. Would you like to see them?"

Uriah nodded and accepted the notebook that Kellen handed

him. He looked through it, glancing at the sketches but taking his time when he found notes. He closed it, gave it back, and took up his whiskey again. "Seems like you were paying attention."

"The most important part of my job."

Uriah leaned forward. "Then pay attention to this. I'll talk to you, say my piece, and if I like what you've written, there might be more, but if I get a whiff of Lorraine Berry's honeydew all over this story, I'll put you down like a horse with colic. Do you understand what I'm saying?"

Kellen leaned forward, rested his forearms on his knees, and rolled the tumbler of whiskey between his palms. He met Uriah Burdick's stare straight on and never wavered from it. "You're an easy man to understand, Mr. Burdick. You don't mince words. Neither do I. Lorraine Berry is my wife, and while I'd like to tell you that you have to respect her at all times, what I require is that you respect her within my hearing, otherwise you're disrespecting both of us. I see quite a number of books on your shelves and another open on the table at your side. You impress me as someone who is learned, so when I tell you that the pen is mightier than the sword, I expect that you know what I mean."

Except for the crackle of logs in the fireplace, the room was silent. Kellen wasn't sure that Eli and Clay were breathing. In contrast to them, Uriah's nostrils were flared and his chest rose and fell deeply. Kellen did not allow his eyes to stray, and in the end it was Uriah who blinked.

"I appreciate a straight shooter," he said at last. "Even when he's not aiming a gun at me." He knocked back his whiskey and set the glass aside. "I want to hear your questions. Eli. Clay. You boys go see if O'Malley needs some help. Maybe he won't poison us tonight if you set the table."

Kellen expected some small perfunctory protest from the brothers for being summarily dismissed. None came. When they were out of the room, Kellen opened his notebook and pulled out his pencil. "I don't pretend that I can do justice to your profile, but I'd like to make a sketch if you'll permit it."

Uriah gestured his approval. "I hope you can ask a question because I feel like a damn fool right now."

Kellen smiled. "Of course. Clay told me how you drove cattle up from Texas to start your ranch, but I don't know how your influence made Bitter Springs a station for the Union Pacific, or how you managed to build a town around it. It is your town, isn't it?"

"I have heard folks say it is. I don't suppose I've ever said differently."

Kellen continued to sketch while Uriah talked. He warmed to the subject when Kellen finished drawing and began to take notes, and he filled in the blanks left by Eli and Clay during the tour. He talked at length about the movement afoot to fold Wyoming into the Union and shared his doubts that anything good would come of trading territory status for statehood. He made his disdain for politicians clear, but saw the necessity of owning a few.

Kellen wrote furiously. When he pulled out a penknife to shave a sharper tip on his pencil, Uriah called out to Eli to bring some fresh pencils from the desk.

"You can keep them," Uriah said. "Seems a man who scribbles as much as you should carry some extras."

Kellen thanked him and got down to asking him about water rights. Dinner interrupted them, but Kellen was able to broach the subject of the survey over coffee.

"I imagine you are aware that Congress has authorized a comprehensive survey of the arid regions. That will include a good portion of the Wyoming Territory."

"I knew it was a possibility. So it passed?"

"Yes."

Uriah looked at his sons. "You boys knew about this?"

Eli and Clay exchanged glances, shrugged, and shook their heads.

"The Department of the Interior has already sent some surveyors out," said Kellen. "There's one in Bitter Springs now. He doesn't have his men yet, but they'll start arriving once he sends word back to Washington that he's ready to start."

"A surveyor in Bitter Springs," Uriah said quietly. "Well, that's something worth knowing. I ordered some new surveying equipment myself a while back. Eli and Clay took delivery of it almost a month ago."

Kellen recalled the evening that it had been delivered. It was the same night that Jones injured himself during his walk and had to be helped to his room while Rabbit and Finn created a ruckus in his wake.

"Then you're doing your own survey?" Kellen asked.

"Haven't started yet, but that's my intent. I know how the government will want to work this. They'll try to keep out the speculators and take control of the land first so they can run things themselves. It didn't work real well with the railroads, but I suspect they've learned a thing or two since then. I settled this land, fought for it, and I'm not giving it over so the government can parcel out water to all the folks who can't get it for themselves."

"The farmers, you mean."

"Them, too. I've got my eye on some land with a good wellspring. I'm not saying where, mind you, but I won't have any trouble making a claim for it at the land office."

"That's Harry and Charles Sample that work there, is that right?"

"That's right. Cousins. Charles is the dependable one. We don't think as highly of Harry anymore."

Kellen knew that Harry Sample had been on the jury, but he asked the question as a matter of form. "What's Harry done?"

"The man forgot who gave him a leg up," Uriah said. "I don't hold with forgetting the ones who helped you." Uriah finished his coffee and pushed the cup and saucer away. "Are you going to tell me who this surveyor is, or do I find out some other way?"

"His name is Jones," said Kellen. "John Paul Jones from the United States Geological Survey."

"Jones?" Clay asked, getting up to pour himself something stronger than coffee. "That man staying at the Pennyroyal? The one that is hobbling around every time I see him?"

"That's Jones."

Clay curled his lip and shook his head. "I was talking to him last night. He never said a word about being a surveyor."

"May I speak frankly?" asked Kellen. Uriah nodded grudgingly. "I believe Mr. Jones is afraid of you and your sons. He's been warned to tread very carefully where the Burdicks are concerned."

"I guess someone told him about how my boys' mother took off with one of his kind."

"I think that was the gist of it, yes. He would like to meet with you."

Uriah chuckled deeply. "So you're the messenger. I had it figured that your wife put you up to this, but I didn't factor in the government's interest in me."

"I'm here for my story. I don't care whether or not you meet with Mr. Jones, but after what you've told me about water rights and the survey, it occurs to me that the advantages of listening to Mr. Jones are all on your side."

Uriah split his glance between his sons. "He's a clever one. You should have said more about that. You know I don't enjoy surprises."

"Eli spent more time with him than I did," said Clay. "He seemed regular smart to me."

"You want a good story, don't you, Pa?" asked Eli.

"I didn't say I minded clever. I said I like to know about it." He turned back to Kellen. "You tell Mr. Jones I'll consider his request, but if we're meeting, it won't be out here. My boys and I will talk to him in town. Eli. Clay. How about you escort Mr. Coltrane off our property so he doesn't wander and get himself lost? I think he can manage the last five miles on his own if you point his horse in the right direction."

Raine was working in the business ledgers in her office when she heard Kellen's familiar light tread on the stairs. She leaned back in her chair so she could see the door. The key was in the lock, but she knew she had forgotten to turn it. It was certain to be the first thing he mentioned.

Kellen knocked on the door, and when Raine didn't answer,

he tried the knob. It turned under his hand. He saw her sitting at her desk in a pool of lamplight, two ledgers spread out in front of her and scraps of paper in a loose pyramid off to the side.

"You didn't lock the door."

She smiled. Predictability was not entirely boring. "I forgot. I was juggling the ledgers, a couple of newspapers, and some catalogs. Oh, and a cup of hot cocoa."

He took off his coat, hat, and gloves on his way to the bedroom. "That's why you put things down and *then* lock the door."

Lectures, though, were completely boring. She allowed him to reach the bedroom before she said, "You forgot to lock the door."

He glanced at her over his shoulder. "You enjoyed that, didn't you?"

"Enormously." She thought she saw him grinning as he disappeared into the bedroom. She heard the wardrobe open and close when he put away his coat, and then the sound of running water as he washed off the grit that clung to his face and neck. When he returned and brushed her proffered cheek with a kiss, he still smelled like man, horse, and leather but with a hint of peppermint in the fragrant mix.

Kellen retrieved a Windsor chair from the table in the sitting room and placed it near Raine's desk. He slouched against the spindle back and barely made contact with the saddle seat as he stretched his legs toward her.

She gave him a knowing look. "You're not used to so much time on horseback."

"God, no."

"You should soak in the tub. Make the water as hot as you can stand it, and I'll bring you some salts."

"In a little while."

"Did they keep you out most of the day?"

He nodded. "I saw about as much as a man can see in a single day." He flexed his right hand. "My hand's cramped. I wasn't expecting that." He got out his notebook and gave it to her. "I made sketches and took notes. I doubt you can read the latter, but my drawings aren't too badly done."

Raine opened up the book and began fingering through it. Her eyebrows rose as she turned over page after page of notes. She paused over the sketches. "I confess I am surprised at the detail. It didn't occur to me that you would take this part so seriously. I suppose I imagined you would scribble a few things, but this?" She closed the notebook and held it up. "This could become a real story."

Kellen's laugh mocked the idea. "I don't see it appearing in the *New York World*."

"Maybe not, but it would be something, wouldn't it?"

"I told Uriah that if he gave me enough information, Pulitzer might stretch the story for a week. He appeared to like the idea."

"You flattered him."

"He takes to it as well as any other man."

"I didn't realize." She set the notebook on the corner of her desk. "He killed my brother. His sons all had a part in my sister's death. It's difficult for me to think of him as any kind of man at all. He's something more than that, and something less, but he's not a man."

"Does it help you to believe that?" he asked quietly.

"Yes."

"Then I won't try to change your mind." He lifted his boot heels to rest on a rung of her chair. "Was Scott Pennway buried today?"

"Yes. There was a service in Annie's home and then the burial before dusk. The Ransoms didn't attend, but it seemed as if the rest of the town was there. Rabbit and Finn stood with Annie's son. I don't think they've ever been so quiet or so solemn. It was very sad to see them like that."

"I'm sorry, Raine."

She dashed impatiently at a tear. Her brief smile trembled. "It's not your fault. You didn't do anything."

"That's right. I didn't *do* anything."

"I didn't mean it like that."

"I know, but I'm right. I couldn't save Scott Pennway. I couldn't prevent Emily Ransom's death. Nothing connects Emily to the Burdicks except perhaps her friendship with your sister. I can't see how it fits. George Weyman hasn't been found, and Dan Sugar appears to be satisfied that Weyman murdered Emily. The talk I hear is that most people agree. As a guest in the Pennyroyal, Weyman had the opportunity to take one of my cuff links and leave it behind with Emily's body. So instead of being able to assist in finding out who really killed Emily, I've had to enlist your cooperation to create an alibi that helps the deputy point a finger at an innocent man. An innocent dead man."

Kellen let his head fall backward. The muscles in his throat were stretched taut. He closed his eyes. "And I still don't know who gutted Nat Church on the train."

Not wanting to be patronizing, Raine resisted the urge to reach out to put a hand on his knee. "You can't be certain that Mr. Weyman *isn't* Emily's killer any more than Dan Sugar can be certain he *is*. As for Scott Pennway and Nat Church, that's the Burdicks."

Kellen sat up again. "I can't prove it."

"Yet. You can't prove it yet."

He nodded slowly. "I think I'll see about that hot bath."

Raine poked her head in the bathing room half an hour later when she did not hear Kellen stirring. He was slouched in the tub much as he had been earlier in the chair. One foot rested under the hot water tap, positioned so that with a little manipulation he could turn the faucet on and off. Raine couldn't see the other foot, but she suspected it was resting by the drain plug, perhaps with the chain cleverly wrapped around his toe. His neck rested against the curved rim of the tub, and his eyes were closed. His hair was wet, slicked back but already starting to curl at the ends, and there was soapy evidence just below his ear that he had washed it.

He had not shaved. The stubble on his jaw was the same shade of chestnut brown as his hair. She touched her cheek where he had kissed her and could easily recall the texture of that kiss as his face brushed hers.

His chest rose and fell evenly, but there was a moment when

his mouth twitched that made her think that not only wasn't he sleeping but that he knew she was staring at him. Feeling rather foolish, as though she had been caught talking to herself or dancing without a partner, Raine backed out and closed the door.

By the time she was ready for bed, she heard splashing and then more water being added to the tub. This time she knocked on the door to announce her intention to enter. Kellen was sitting up and leaning forward, trying to reach his back with a soapy sponge. Raine thought that his halfhearted attempt was more in the way of an invitation than an example of self-sufficiency.

Smile firmly in check, she asked, "Would you like some assistance?"

He straightened, held out the sponge as though he were offering a gift, and smiled sheepishly. "Please?"

"Pathetic." Raine dropped a couple of towels on the floor beside the tub and knelt. She took the sponge, wrung it out over his back, and then applied it with some vigor between his shoulder blades. "You need a shave."

Kellen rubbed the back of one hand against his jaw. "So I do."

Raine did not hear any enthusiasm for it. Because she considered that ultimately it was in her interest to have him clean shaven, she made the offer to do it for him. His response was a skeptical, sidelong glance. "I used to shave Adam," she told him. "Sometimes he was feeling too poorly to do much for himself. He never complained, and I never cut him. He said I was at least as good as Mr. Stillwell and an improvement over Dave Rogers."

"I suppose if I can't trust you with a razor in your hand, I shouldn't be sleeping in your bed."

Raine's laughter was low and husky and ever so slightly wicked. "I had not considered that, but it's an excellent point. A pillow over your face would work as well."

"Precisely."

"Why *are* you sleeping in my bed?"

"I like it there."

"Convenience?"

He shook his head. "Comfortable."

"You mean the bed."

"No, actually I mean you."

Raine stopped making circles on his back. Her fingers tightened on the sponge and rivulets of water raced down his spine. "I've never thought of myself as a particularly comfortable person to be around."

"Well, you probably shouldn't rush to embrace another opinion. I was only talking about how comfortable you are to be with when you're sleeping."

She slapped him on the back of his head with the sponge.

"See?" he said, unperturbed. "You have a thorny kind of charm when you're awake."

Raine soaked the sponge and thwacked him with it again. "Finish your back," she said, starting to rise. "I'm getting the razor."

Kellen lay in bed on his side with Raine curled to fit the sharper angles of his frame. She *was* comfortable. Awake, she was indeed challenging, and at some point he discovered not only that he had come to admire that quality, but also that she made him better for it. She was stubborn, but then so was he. Faulting her for it left him exposed to the same accusation. She could stand up for herself, and she could also slip sideways out of a confrontation when it served her.

And then there were those qualities of character that kept her in conflict with herself. She understood that her desire for justice was compromised by the insidious nature of revenge. The vulnerability that she would not admit to chipped at her strength. She was humbled that she had to ask for help but not so prideful that she didn't know she needed it. She had concern and consideration for others yet would deny that she was deserving of the same.

He could think of only a few occasions when she had acted with seemingly no regard for the consequences, and he was not merely a witness to them but the beneficiary as well.

She came to him without reserve or expectation. He had suspected the existence of a deep well of passion in her, but he wondered if he had been right or fair to reveal it to her. She had responded to him the first time he kissed her, not tentatively, but fully, ardently, hungrily. Had he tapped her passion or her profound sense of aloneness?

He acknowledged the selfishness of the question that pricked at him so often he expected to find blood: Had circumstance conspired to make him a convenience?

When he stepped off the train, he had been a curious but reluctant visitor to Bitter Springs. It had to be acknowledged that curiosity, while it still existed, no longer exerted the same magnetic pull, and that when he left Bitter Springs, his departure would be infinitely more reluctant than his arrival.

The Widder Berry accounted for the difference. Kellen did not need to look elsewhere for an explanation. *The Widder Berry.* The thought of how unsuited she was to that sobriquet and how convincingly she had embraced it made his wry smile turn a shade rueful. She deserved so much better.

It didn't follow that he was the better that she deserved. Thus far, his contributions had been lying to her and lying with her. It remained to be seen which she regarded as worse, but she would be within her rights to want to see him, in the vernacular of the locals, decorating a cottonwood for it. He preferred the more grisly euphemisms for hanging such as gurgling on a rope and strangulation jig, but they all worked, and Raine had a fine, feminine grace about her, so if she suggested that he look up at the sky through cottonwood leaves, he would be honor bound to fetch the rope.

Under the blankets, Kellen ran his palm from Raine's shoulder to her elbow. His touch was light, tender. He did not want to wake her; he wanted the reassurance that she was there. He could not recall that he had ever known that need before.

He liked her. Liked her a lot. Whether or not he loved her, was in love with her, or wanted her so much that what he had was love's equivalent of fool's gold, Kellen didn't know.

He needed to be sure. He'd never convince her if he had a single doubt of his own.

Raine surprised him by laying her hand over his fingers where they rested on her shoulder. "You should be sleeping," she whispered.

"How do you know I'm not?"

Her chuckle stayed at the back of her throat. "I can hear you thinking."

"My thoughts are that loud?"

"When I'm trying to sleep, they are."

"Do you know what I'm thinking?"

"No. Do you want to tell me?"

"No. Go to sleep."

"All right." She snuggled closer, pulled his arm around her, and threaded her fingers with his. "I fed you when I woke you. Remember that."

Kellen pressed his smile into the soft crown of her hair. In moments she was asleep.

They made slow, sleepy love in the half-light of dawn. Neither one could ever say with certainty who began it, but it was equally true that neither one of them cared.

Sensation was heavy, but not dull. It rested on their skin like honey, made each touch languid, careful. They sought with open hands and closed eyes. The dream was soft and indistinct at the edges, but every touch created a precise center and ripples of clarity.

They spoke, murmured really. The utterances had little structure but communicated everything they should.

"There," she said when his hand cupped her breast. "Mm. Yes. Just there."

"And here?"

"Mm."

Her mouth was damp, her lips faintly swollen. The kisses were drugging, long and slow and deep. Her heart beat with the same resonance in her chest. No frantic fluttering, no stutter. His pounded in precisely the same way.

"God, yes," he whispered when her flat belly moved against him.

Her hand slipped between their bodies, found him, circled his penis with her fingers. She moved her hand along the length of it.

He clenched his jaw and grunted softly.

Small shudders rocked them to the edge of wakefulness but never pushed them over it. They shifted, cradled again, and found a sweet, unhurried rhythm when he entered her from behind.

The pleasure was in the joining, the closeness, and the shared warmth, and when it was over, they were settled by sleep and dreams that floated like liquid through their minds.

Raine knew she had overslept as soon as she heard the steady knock on the apartment door. Kellen was lying on his stomach, a pillow over his head, not under it. She could not tell if he was hiding from the interruption or had just ended up that way. Half-formed memories of making love to him flooded her, and she was uncharacteristically flustered by the time she reached the door.

"What is it?" she called as she fumbled for the key.

"Mrs. Sterling says you better come down," Sue called back. She lowered her voice once Raine opened the door a crack. "There's a problem with the water pressure, and she's trying to fix breakfast for ten and she says she can't fool with it. Walt took some letters and packages down to the station for Mr. Petit, so he's not here to figure it out."

Raine pressed her forehead against the doorjamb and sighed. "Very well. Tell her I'm on my way. Maybe I can get Mr. Coltrane to help."

Sue tugged on her braids as she stood on tiptoe and tried to see over Raine's shoulder into the room.

Raine knew precisely what she was doing. "Is there something you want to ask me, Sue?"

"Is it true what they say? Are you and Mr. Coltrane married?"

"It's true, but how did you hear it?"

"Oh, Mr. Jones told me. I think everyone in the dining room heard him."

Raine sighed again. "Thank you, Sue. I appreciate the warning."

"Warning? I was going to wish you well."

"Consider it done. Go on. Tell Mrs. Sterling I'm on my way." She closed the door and leaned against it.

Kellen sat up in bed and called to her. "I meant to tell you last night that there's something wrong with the water pressure."

"You don't say."

"Give me a few minutes to get dressed, and I'll poke around and see if I can figure out what the problem is."

"You know about plumbing?"

"I know you have a tank on the roof, boilers in the cellar, and pipe in between. The toe bone's connected to the foot bone and so on. I think I can work it out."

"Nothing about dem bones raises my confidence."

But as it turned out, the analogy was close to prophetic. When Kellen climbed up to the roof to measure the water level in the tank, he found Mr. Weyman's swollen body bobbing near the surface and discovered it was one of the two leather satchels strapped to his ankles that was responsible for covering the water release valve.

Chapter Thirteen

The discovery of the whiskey drummer's body was general knowledge in Bitter Springs by the time the Pennyroyal served its midday meal. Folks who did not normally take their luncheon at the hotel crowded the dining room along with the guests and regulars. Only the couple with the young children was absent from the room. The family had decided to end their respite in Bitter Springs when they heard about the tragedy and were now waiting at the station to board the next train out of town.

Sue Hage told Mrs. Sterling that she envied them, and in a rare moment of harmony, the cook did not find fault with her for saying so.

Eventually there were too many people for the dining room, and Raine opened the saloon for eating as well as drinking. Renee and Cecilia arrived to help, and Mrs. Sterling, after wondering aloud if she was expected to feed the multitude with five loaves and two fish, managed to stretch her chicken potpie and spicy chili with cornbread so that everyone was satisfied.

Deputy Dan Sugar was among the diners. He sat with Ted Rush and Mr. Webb from the bank. For once Ted did not have his own story to insert into the conversation, but he hung on every word the deputy exchanged with the bank manager and anyone who stopped by their table to ask what Sugar planned to do next.

Mr. Weyman had suffered a blow to the side of his head, hard enough to crack his skull. Dr. Kent had been able to tell Sugar that much, but whether or not the man had still been alive when he was dropped into the tank was a matter of conjecture. The baggage tied to the drummer's ankles suggested that Weyman may only have been unconscious and left to drown, but it also suggested that the killer merely wanted to get rid of all of the drummer's belongings at once. People wondered aloud how many times the killer climbed the outside stairs to the roof to dispose of George Weyman and his bags.

The question that no one could answer was where had Emily Ransom been while this was happening. Already dead? Unconscious and soon to be dead? Some folks speculated that the murders were not related. Others had no patience with that thinking. Emily and Weyman disappeared on the same evening. To the gamblers among them, the odds seemed incalculable that the murders, while separate and distinct, were done by two different people.

Walt and Kellen arrived in the dining room after the crowd dwindled and only a few stragglers remained. They were as wet, disheveled, and tired as two bird dogs that had spent the morning retrieving dead ducks from a marsh pond. What they had been doing, though, was flushing the waterlines and scrubbing the tank.

Raine pointed them to one of the tables that had been cleared in the dining room. "Just sit down. Mrs. Sterling will make you both a hot meal; she is that glad to have water restored without going to the pump for it." On her way to the kitchen, she passed Renee talking up Dick Faber and one of the Davis boys and gave her a look that said she should show the men the door and get back to work.

She expected the dining room to be cleared of every guest except Kellen and Walt when she returned, but they had been joined at their table by the young masters Cabot Theodore and Carpenter Addison.

Raine set her hands on her hips. "Rabbit. Finn. Does your granny know you're here?"

They wriggled around in their chairs to face her. "Sure she does," said Rabbit. "She heard about what happened from that family leaving town. They could hardly wait for the train to get here. Pap thought they might start walking to Rawlins. Anyway, Granny says we should find out what happened from the horse's mouth. Not that you're a horse, Mrs. Berry, but if you were, you'd be a real pretty filly."

Finn nodded, excitement bringing him to his knees on the chair's saddle seat. He rested his chin on the back rail. "And there's a new guest for you at the desk. Miss Sue is seein' to him. Name's Mr. Mark Irvin of Cincinnati, Ohio. He's an undertaker, so he didn't mind at all when he heard about Mr. Weyman."

"He's thinking about undertaking right here in Bitter Springs," said Rabbit.

Kellen gave Raine a dry look. "There *is* a business opportunity."

"I don't believe this," Raine muttered. Her hands fell to her sides as she swung around and marched off toward the lobby.

Rabbit turned around in his chair and sat and encouraged Finn to do the same. "She don't seem at all pleased about another guest."

Kellen reached under the table and put a hand on Rabbit's knee to still his swinging feet. "She's a little out of sorts right now."

Finn sighed heavily. "So was I until Mr. Irvin told us he was an undertaker. Rabbit and me had it all suspicioned that he was the new headmaster."

"Rabbit and I," said Kellen.

"What?"

"Rabbit and I. Not Rabbit and me. And I don't know what to say about 'suspicioned' except to note that the sooner the school has a headmaster, the better it will be for my ears." He heard himself, grimaced. "And I am not thanking you for causing me to draw upon my father's voice or one of his lectures."

Rabbit frowned. "I never said you should draw on your

father. Didn't even know you could. Seems like the kind of thing that Finn might do."

"Sure would get me in trouble," said Finn.

Kellen surrendered, casting a glance to the heavens.

Enjoying himself, Walt just chuckled. He put out a hand to restrain Finn's legs the same way Kellen had done to discourage Rabbit. "Did you boys bring in all of Mr. Irvin's belongings or is there something for me to do?"

"He only had two leather satchels," said Rabbit. "Nothing that Finn and me . . . Finn and *I* couldn't carry."

Finn nodded. "We told him about the place next to the feed store where Mr. Hood used to have his print shop. It's been empty since Mr. Hood came back to town in a box. Mr. Irvin was interested in that. The place, I mean, not about Mr. Hood. I suppose he figured he missed his chance to be a help there."

Cecilia arrived with hot coffee for Kellen and Walt and glasses of root beer for the boys. "Mrs. Sterling's got the chili back on the stove, and she's warming what's left of the cornbread in the oven. She says I should tell you that it won't be long. Boys, she says she has a big slice of apple ginger cake that she'll split for you if you like."

"They like," said Kellen as the brothers nodded eagerly in unison. When Cecilia was gone, he asked them, "What's this about John Hood owning a print shop?"

Rabbit sipped his root beer and licked the sweetness off his tongue before he answered. "He printed flyers and posters, mostly for the merchants."

"A newspaper?"

"Not like the *Rocky* or the *Prairie Farmer*."

"A newssheet?"

"Sure. Charged two pennies for it. Mr. Hood liked to say folks were always getting their two cents' worth from him."

"I think I misunderstood your grandfather," said Kellen. "I didn't realize Bitter Springs ever had a paper. No one tried to take it over after John Hood?" The answer was obvious to him when the boys looked at him as if he'd grown a third eye. "I guess not."

Walt said, "Someone destroyed the press after Mr. Hood left town."

"Suspects?"

"The usual ones, but no one saw anything, leastways not so they're talking about it."

"Did Mr. Hood report on the trial?"

"He couldn't. Not while it was going on, what with him being a member of the jury, but when it was over, he had some opinions, especially after Isaac Burdick escaped the marshals. Some folks warned he should temper himself, but like the boys said, he had two cents to give."

Kellen understood more clearly why John Hood was one of the first to be killed. Fleeing town couldn't save him, not a man with his talent for writing and stirring opinion. Kellen remembered clearly what he'd told Uriah yesterday about the pen being mightier than the sword. That sentiment rang hollow now. Uriah Burdick had used the sword to better effect.

Finn fiddled with his glass, turning it round and round to keep from drinking all of his root beer before the apple ginger cake arrived. "I miss Mr. Hood. He let Rabbit and me take the newssheets around sometimes."

"He didn't pay us," Rabbit reminded him.

"No, but sometimes people gave us a penny for bringing it to them. It was a fine thing to buy candy at Johnson's Mercantile."

Rabbit agreed. He lifted his bony chin in Kellen's direction. "Granny says I'm supposed to ask if it's true that you and the Widder Berry are hitched."

Kellen managed not to sputter before he swallowed his mouthful of coffee. "Bitter Springs really does not need a newssheet." He returned his cup to its saucer. "Yes, Widder Berry and I are hitched."

"Ain't that somethin'?" said Rabbit. "That means you lost your chance, Finn."

The tips of Finn's ears turned red, but he shrugged his narrow shoulders manfully. "I didn't think it was proper to ask until I was in the sixth grade anyway, and Mr. Coltrane could be dead by then."

Kellen was very glad he had put down the coffee. "You're a deep thinker, Finn, to contemplate the future like that."

"Thank you, sir."

Kellen could only shake his head. Out of the corner of his eye he saw that Walt was doing the same. The boys quieted when Cecilia came to the table bearing steaming bowls of chili, cornbread, and two plates of apple ginger cake. Rabbit and Finn tucked into their dessert as though they were starving, while Kellen and Walt were only marginally more restrained.

After a few bites, the brothers returned to form. Finn wanted to know about the body. "Was it shriveled like my granny's hands after she's had them in the wash all day or swelled up like a cow's belly that's been too long dead in the sun?"

Walt choked, and Kellen had to clap him on the back. "I don't think your granny or your pap asked you to come home with that much detail."

"No," said Rabbit, "but it's something we should know. Finn and me are just about sure that we're going to be detectives someday. That book you gave my pap—*Nat Church and the Chinese Box*—well, that got us thinkin' that it might suit us. I would like to figure out what's in the Chinese box, and Finn, he'd like to have the girl."

Kellen saw Walt's puzzled expression. "I'll explain later, Walt. In fact, I'll give you one of the books."

"I'm not much for reading, but I know all about Nat Church. Adam Berry, then Ellen, used to tell me about him."

"Then I'll read it to you." Kellen intercepted the brightening expressions on the boys and crushed them. "Not to you two. Maybe when Finn's in the sixth grade as long as I'm not dead."

"Won't matter," Finn grumbled. "I'll be able to read it for myself by then."

Two things happened simultaneously that saved Kellen from coming up with a better retort. The first was that Walt lightly smacked Finn on the back of his head, causing the boy to lose the bite of cake teetering on his fork, and the second was Raine's timely return from the lobby.

She waved Kellen and Walt back in their seats as they started to rise and pulled a chair from another table to sit with them. "I just need a moment," she said. "Walt. I told Mr. Irvin that you would take his bags up as soon as you were finished eating. He could have easily carried them himself, but he liked the idea of someone else doing it. I hope he gives you something for your trouble." She glanced at the door to the kitchen. She could hear the occasional rattle of pots and pans, but no raised voices. "Mrs. Sterling's in there with all three of the girls?"

Everyone at the table nodded at once.

Impressed, Raine's eyebrows lifted. "They must be too tired to bicker. It's unfortunate that it takes such a sad series of circumstances to bring it about."

"You mean finding Mr. Weyman's body," Rabbit said.

"Yes. And the questions. And the speculation."

"What's speculation?" asked Finn.

Kellen explained, "That's when people who don't know very much talk as if they do."

"Huh." Finn stabbed another piece of cake. "That happens a powerful lot around here. A powerful lot."

Raine chuckled. "It does, doesn't it?"

"Folks don't know what we know, do they, Rabbit?" Rabbit gave his brother a warning glance, but Finn was undeterred. The boy asked Kellen, "What do you call folks who talk speculation?"

"Speculators."

"Well, then, me and Rabbit aren't—"

Raine interrupted, correcting him. "Rabbit and I." She looked at Kellen and Walt, bewildered when they both laughed under their breath.

Frustrated, Finn blew a puff of air that scattered cake crumbs across his lower lip. He licked them up and went on. "I and Rabbit ain't speculators, and that's a fact. We saw what we saw and we know what we're talking about."

"Only one of us is talking," Rabbit said out of the side of his mouth. "And he's not supposed to. We *agreed*."

Kellen pushed his empty bowl out of the way and leaned forward to rest his forearms on the table. He looked from one boy to the other. "Is there something you want to tell us?"

"No," Rabbit said.

Finn didn't answer.

Raine's approach was gentler. "Boys? Is there something you *should* tell us?"

"Pap wouldn't like it," said Rabbit.

"Do you mean you already told him, and he wouldn't want you to repeat it?" she asked.

Finn shook his head. "He doesn't know. We wouldn't be sitting here so easy if he did."

"He'd have taken a switch to you?" asked Walt.

"Sure," said Finn. "After we went to the graveyard that night a ways back, we had to make a promise."

Rabbit jumped in to explain. "Pap understood, but Granny gave him a stern talkin'-to anyway, especially on account of him having whiskey on his breath, and then she made us all swear we wouldn't do it again. I don't know what Pap promised exactly, but Finn and I crossed our hearts and inside ourselves we were both thinking we wouldn't drink whiskey."

Kellen remained perfectly straight-faced, but it was a test of his endurance. "I see. Then you didn't precisely break the promise you made, did you? Because I'm thinking that you boys might have ventured out again on your own."

"That's speculation," said Finn.

"It is. If you confirm it, it will be a fact."

Rabbit said, "Maybe it's better if you just stay a speculator."

"All right," Kellen said. "I'll speculate, and you boys listen. How will that be?" He watched them exchange glances. Their small, expressive faces telegraphed their thoughts almost as clearly as if they had spoken aloud. It would be years yet before Rabbit and Finn would be able to school their features, and Kellen was prepared to take unashamed advantage of that.

Raine saw that Walt had finished his chili and was putting the last bite of cornbread in his mouth. "Would you take Mr. Irvin his bags now? They're sitting at the foot of the stairs. I gave him the key to the room vacated today. Sue assured me that she had time to clean and freshen it. I would take it as a favor if you would look around and make certain that's so."

"Right away." Walt stood and started to clear the table.

"Leave all that, Walt, but thank you for thinking of it."

When he was gone, Raine said to Kellen, "You may begin to speculate."

"Thank you." He nodded gravely at the boys, but when they bent their heads to scrape the last crumbs from their plates, he winked at Raine. "Rabbit. Finn. I think that you were out of your house again the night after you helped Mr. Jones." Neither boy looked up, but they did look sideways and fiddle with their forks. "I know you boys are brave." Their heads dipped in the briefest of nods. "But sometimes a man needs to prove it to himself . . . or his brother." This time Finn shot a surprised look at Kellen and a more accusing one at Rabbit. "I'm imagining there was a dare, or maybe a small wager, and you waited to leave until your pap and granny were snoring too loudly to hear you."

The boys pressed their lips together to suppress giggles.

"I think you started out for the graveyard by a different route, one that brave and clever young men would use when they do not want to be discovered, one that would not put them on the street but in the alleyways behind the buildings."

Rabbit's eyes widened. Finn's mouth parted a fraction.

"You never made it to the graveyard because you saw someone . . ." He paused because the boys looked at him blankly. He amended his statement. "You saw some*thing* that made you think better about going on because you are not only brave and clever, but you are also wise."

The boys bit their lips again.

"And here you are after the news of finding Mr. Weyman's body is all over town. It's no wonder that I'm speculating. You saw something that night that made you turn around and go home, but it probably didn't seem important then, only a little frightening. It was finding the whiskey drummer's body today that made it seem as if it might have been important."

Finn looked sideways at Raine, partially cupped his hand around his mouth, and whispered, "He's a good speculator."

Raine nodded and whispered back, "Reporters frequently are."

Kellen's mouth twisted to one side as he thought. "You were close to the Pennyroyal when you saw it." He could see Rabbit worrying the inside of his cheek. "Behind the hotel?" The boys offered blank stares again. "Close but not behind." Kellen tried to think where they might have been hiding. "Mr. Stillwell's barbershop is nearby, and there are stairs at the back going up to his second floor. You saw something and hid under the stairs. Very clever."

Two thin chests puffed out a little.

Kellen considered what he had learned thus far and saw no alternative except to take a stab at what the boys might have seen. Not someone. Some*thing*. "Mr. Weyman had two bags," he said, watching Rabbit and Finn closely. "I think you might have seen . . ." He stopped again because while Rabbit was staring straight ahead, Finn was rolling his eyes. It couldn't be one or both of the valises that they had seen behind the hotel. The bags would have been relatively difficult to see sitting on the ground at night, especially since the boys had gotten no closer than the barbershop. If they had witnessed the bags being lowered from or raised to a room or the roof by means of a rope, that would have roused their curiosity, not their fear.

What they saw was not directly connected to Mr. Weyman.

"You saw something that you knew belonged to someone other than Mr. Weyman. You weren't even concerned about the whiskey drummer at the time." Finn began to jiggle in place as he started to swing his feet again. "You were worried about the person this thing belonged to, and it had to be big enough for you to see it clearly at night. It wasn't a gun. Or a knife. No, not a weapon of any kind. Something . . ." He paused to give the boys time to calm themselves. They both had the jitters now. Raine had taken to rubbing Finn's back in slow, soothing circles.

"When I came to town and you boys saw my guns, you asked me if I was here to start trouble or end it. You said it would be a real shame if I had already hired on with the Burdicks." At the mention of the name, the boys went rigid. "Lots of people in this town worry about the Burdicks," Kellen said. "It seems pretty smart of them, if you ask me. The Burdick name comes up a lot when there's some sort of trouble."

Rabbit and Finn remained still as stone.

"You didn't see one of the Burdicks that night, but you saw something you recognized that belonged to them."

A shiver slipped down Rabbit's spine. He didn't have the benefit of Raine's calming hand at his back.

"I think you saw their horses at the back of the Pennyroyal." As soon as he said it, he realized he didn't yet have it quite right. Rabbit and Finn wanted to tell him in the worst way, but they couldn't, and now knowing how close he was to the truth, he understood their need to keep the secret. "You saw *a* horse."

The boys' cheeks puffed and deflated slowly as they released long breaths.

Kellen nodded slowly, looking over their heads to Raine but continuing to speak to them. "I went out to the Burdick ranch yesterday. Did you know that?"

Rabbit and Finn traded looks and shrugged. Rabbit spoke. "We mighta heard something about that."

"You probably saw me leaving the livery again and asked around. It's not a secret that I'm writing a story and that the Burdick ranch is part of it." Kellen folded his hands together on the table. He tapped his thumbs slowly. "Eli and Clay escorted me all over the spread, and I know I still did not see the half of it. They gave me a mare to ride to spare the horse I borrowed from the livery. Eli rode a black stallion that must have been sixteen hands from ground to withers, but Clay rode an even bigger gray, one that I imagine looks silver in a little bit of moonlight. It was a beautiful beast. Long-necked. Lean body. Deep chest. Back East an animal like that would be on the racetrack. Not everyone can handle a horse as bold and spirited as that gray. I bet you boys know that animal's name."

Neither boy spoke up. They kept their lips pressed tightly together.

Raine said, "That's Phantom. Everyone knows him. If I saw him shaking his head or pawing the ground behind the Pennyroyal, I'd look for somewhere to hide. He frightens me in the daylight. At night, he's a ghost."

That brought a quick nod from Finn and a slower one from Rabbit.

Kellen finally sat back in his chair and stretched his legs

under the table. He envied Finn the hand that Raine still had on his back. "I don't imagine you stayed under the stairs for long."

Staring down at their plates, the boys shook their heads hard.

"I wouldn't have either," said Kellen. "You did the right thing to go home."

Raine asked, "Did you hear anything before you left? Something odd that perhaps you didn't understand at the time?"

"No, ma'am," said Rabbit.

"Mostly it was just my own heart," said Finn. "And the snorting."

"Have you told anyone else about this?" asked Kellen.

Rabbit's chin came up. "We didn't tell you."

Kellen smiled appreciatively. "No, you didn't, did you? Well done, men. Is it your intention not to tell anyone else?"

Rabbit gave his brother a narrow look.

"I'm not sayin' anything," said Finn, crossing his heart. "I'm not even goin' to sit still for the speculation."

"Very good," said Kellen.

"Granny would worry," said Rabbit. "Pap would have to turn us over his knee."

"The Burdicks might murder us in our sleep," whispered Finn.

Raine put her arm around Finn's shoulders and squeezed. "That's not going to happen. Don't even think that it can."

"It wouldn't be such a worry," Rabbit said, "if Mr. Coltrane would show folks his guns."

Raine sat on a woolen blanket at the foot of a cottonwood tree watching Kellen reload the .44 Colt. The .45 caliber Peacemaker with the pearl grip lay beside her. It was the first time she had seen the guns since Kellen's arrival. She remembered how he'd set them out on the table in his room as casually as calling cards on a silver plate, and it wasn't until they reappeared that she realized she had no idea where they'd been hidden away.

He reminded her that he'd come to Bitter Springs with two trunks and a bag and that for almost the entire length of his stay, the bag had been squirreled away under the bed in Ellen's old room. She didn't believe him at first, but then she recalled how she'd found him in her apartment one evening. He'd made it seem as if he was there for the express purpose of speaking with her, but he had gone there to hide the valise and everything that followed was improvisation, including the kiss that set her back on her heels.

He did not say as much—in fact, he said very little—but once Raine was prompted to remember something from that night, she remembered *everything.*

Drawing from the holster, Kellen fired off two shots. His target was a smooth stone about the size of his fist resting on top of a stump. The first shot nudged the stone to the left. The second splintered the side of the stump.

"What were you trying to hit?" asked Raine.

"The stone. Both times." He holstered the gun, paused, and drew and fired again. This time he hit the stone twice so that it skipped off the stump's platform. "I'll get it," he told Raine.

"I wasn't moving." She huddled deeper into her coat, lifting the collar and tucking her chin below the frog closure.

Kellen gathered all the stones he had scattered and returned them to the stump. When he turned and saw Raine pulling the corners of the blanket around her shoulders, he just shook his head. "Did I invite you to come with me?"

She scrunched her nose at him.

He chuckled. "I didn't think so." He walked over to the blanket and unfastened his gun belt. He exchanged holsters so he could practice with the smaller .45 caliber. "Do you want to shoot? If you were up and moving around, you wouldn't be so cold."

"Snow's coming. Can't you smell it?"

He arched an eyebrow. "Smell it?"

She sighed. "Never mind. No, I do not want to shoot."

"All right. Let me do a couple more rounds with the .45 and then we'll leave." He stood farther away from the targets this time and picked the stones off one by one. He reloaded, crouched, and fired again. He missed the stones twice but caught the stump on both of those occasions. Kellen backed up another five feet, reloaded, and took aim at the stones he had missed. He got them both this time. "This gun doesn't release as smoothly from the holster as the other." He repeated holstering and drawing the weapon several more times.

"I like this one," Raine said, pointing to the Colt on the blanket. "It's bigger."

"More importantly, I can draw quicker and hit what I'm aiming at."

"I didn't notice a difference between how you did with the two weapons."

"That's because it's not your finger on the trigger. The handling's different, the weight, the pull. I favor the .44." He returned to Raine's side and held out a hand. She took it, and he helped her up. He stooped, picked up the .44, and gave Raine the blanket. "Are you satisfied with what you saw?"

"I never doubted that you could shoot. Nat Church would not have asked you to join him if he couldn't depend on your aim."

"Then I'm glad to know that you have at least as much confidence in my aim as you do in Nat's judgment." He began to exchange holsters again, strapping on the .44. "Why were you so set on coming with me?"

Raine gave herself over to the task of folding and rolling up the blanket.

"Raine?" He tried to catch her eye. "What is it?"

Shrugging almost imperceptibly, she turned in the direction of their tethered mounts. "We should go. We don't want to be out here at night."

Kellen put a hand on her elbow. "Wait. We have time. What is it you don't want to tell me?"

Her laughter was low and ironic. "Now there is a question." She shook off his hand at her elbow and continued walking.

Kellen stayed where he was, watching her go. There was something to be said for maintaining a little distance. He waited until she strapped the blanket to the back of her saddle and was prepared to mount before he approached.

Kellen placed the spare Colt in his saddlebag, took up the reins, and mounted. He asked Raine if she wanted to lead the way through the trees and down the rocky incline to the valley floor. She did not hesitate. Even when the trail widened and could have easily accommodated them riding side by side, Kellen hung back. He did not doubt that she would eventually tell him what was on her mind. What he could not gauge was the span of time between now and eventually.

That was only troubling because he could not gauge how much time he had left.

"How far is Matt Sharp's farm from where we are now?" he asked her.

"Maybe six miles northeast. Why?"

"How does the Sharp farm get its water?"

"I don't know. A well, I suppose."

"Is there a lake? A spring?"

"Hickory Lake. But it's miles from their farm."

"It might supply their water, though."

Raine twisted in her saddle so she could see Kellen. "Why are you asking about this?"

He shrugged. "Something Uriah said to me when we were talking about the government survey. He has his eye on some property that he thinks the survey will take off the market. He wants it for himself. It was just an impression, but I had the sense the property was out this way. I don't know much about the area except what I saw when we were searching for Emily. I'm wondering if Uriah went after the land around the lake whether or not the Sharp farm would be in his way."

"What do you want to do?" she asked, but she knew the answer. She looked at the sky, studied it for a moment.

Watching her, Kellen shook his head. "No. It's too late now. But tomorrow I'll go out."

"I'm going with you."

"You have a business to run."

"I'm going with you."

Kellen said nothing. That argument would be waiting for them in the morning.

Or it should have been. It was only when morning came

around that Kellen realized that he'd left it until too late. Raine was not in the apartment when he woke, and she was not in the kitchen or dining room when he went to steal bacon and biscuits from under Mrs. Sterling's nose. Sue could only tell him that she thought Raine had gone to the rail station. Walt's guess was the same as Sue's.

She was waiting for him at the livery, saddled up and ready to ride. She was wearing a split riding skirt, belted wool jacket, boots, and a white Boss of the Plains short-brimmed Stetson. He recognized the modified stock and butt plate of a Springfield Model 1877 carbine in the scabbard.

He pointed to the carbine. "Do you know how to use that?"

"I'm not Annie Oakley, but I can hold my own."

"You really want to do this?"

"Yes."

Kellen did not have to think about it long. If he said no, she would follow him. He would rather have her at his side than somewhere behind him with a carbine. "All right." If she was surprised that he surrendered so easily, she did not show it.

They spoke very little as they rode toward the lake, but this silence was comfortable and mutually agreed upon, not edgy and one-sided as it had been the previous day. Kellen did not take them close to the Sharp farm; rather, they skirted the property and climbed to a higher elevation once they were well clear of it. They followed Elk Creek to its source, a silver-blue lake nestled in the mountain crag that was a reservoir for the snowmelt every spring.

Kellen dismounted when they reached the edge of the water and let his horse drink. He studied the lake, the land, and tried to imagine how Uriah Burdick might stand on precisely this same spot and see an opportunity.

"What do you expect to find here?" asked Raine.

"I'm not sure, but I want to go around the lake. Do you want to come or wait for me here?" He chuckled when she merely lifted an eyebrow at him. "Very well." He led his horse away from the water and mounted. "Clockwise? Counterclockwise? You choose."

Raine had been looking around much as Kellen had. Her

particular interest, though, as dictated by her hunger, was locating a place where they could spread a blanket and have something to eat on the relative comfort of the ground. At their current elevation, there was not much in the way of cover, but she had noted an outcropping of scraggly pines some three hundred yards away that might offer reasonable shelter from the wind.

"That way," she said, pointing left.

Kellen tugged on the reins, and they were off. "If Uriah could control and divert the natural path of water from this lake, he could irrigate a large portion of his spread that can't support cattle now. He would be able to cut off the smaller ranchers who are just an annoyance to him and buy up their land."

"And farmers like Matt Sharp and his family."

"That's right. Bitter Springs, too. The town will be dependent on him in a way it only imagines that it is now."

"Do you think he knows about Clay?"

Kellen allowed his horse to pick his own way over the rocky ground while he gave his attention to Raine. "Knows *what* about Clay?"

Frustrated, she sighed. "He murdered Mr. Weyman. The boys as good as told us that. I don't know why you want to defend him."

"Rabbit and Finn saw Clay's horse, not Clay. That's the fact we know. It seems likely that Clay is responsible for Weyman's murder. Probably for Emily's as well. 'Likely' and 'probably' are not certain words, Raine, and I have no idea what Uriah suspects or knows about his son. I imagine Uriah would act to protect Clay just as he did Isaac, but I can't even say that with certainty. He pits Eli and Clay against each other, goads them. I observed it several times during my visit. I don't think that it's respect for him that makes them keep their distance; I think it's fear. They don't see Uriah so differently than anyone else in Bitter Springs sees him."

Raine fell silent, thinking. Her eyes followed the curve of the lake to where it disappeared between two crests. "How far do you suppose the lake goes that way?"

"We're going to find out."

"You think the water's important, don't you?"

"What do you mean?"

Kellen's cautious pause before he answered supported Raine's suspicions. "I mean, what if the deaths of John Hood, Hank Thompson, the lawyer from Rawlins, Marshal Sterling, and Scott Pennway have little or nothing to do with Ellen and Isaac and the trial, and have so much more to do with water?"

"It's an interesting idea."

"But is it your idea?"

Kellen turned his head and discovered she was watching him closely. "Let's say that visiting the Burdicks has forced me to consider it."

"Why?"

"Because I've been listening to people since I came to Bitter Springs, and there is information I've had that meant nothing to me in the context of your sister's trial, but when I started to consider another rationale for the murders, there were connections that I would be foolish to ignore."

"Connections? Such as?"

"Raine, I don't think this is solely about one thing or the other. It's about both. I think Uriah Burdick saw an opportunity and seized on it. Two birds, one stone."

"Tell me about these connections," she said flatly.

"John Hood was the mayor of Bitter Springs before he came back to town in a box. Walt told me he was elected months after Ellen's trial, largely because folks saw him as someone willing to stand up to Uriah."

"That's true."

Kellen did not point out that Raine had never mentioned that John Hood had been the mayor. Her narrow view was of him as a member of the jury. He also refrained from reminding her that Rabbit and Finn were the ones who told him that Hood owned the print shop. John Hood had the means to fight back. "I knew that Hank Thompson was the schoolmaster. Ted Rush told me that Thompson regularly explored the Medicine Bow forests to make photographs that he contributed to Eastern periodicals."

"Yes," she said. "Not so different than what Mr. Petit is doing."

"I know. And you've witnessed the Burdick reaction to that."

She had. Raine nodded slowly. "What about Moses T. Parker? What can the Rawlins lawyer possibly have to do with water in Bitter Springs?"

"I had a conversation with Harry Sample and his cousin at the land office. Mr. Parker represented the interests of Carbon County. Had he lived, he would be the person appointed to negotiate water rights with Washington."

"But there's someone new in that position with the same responsibilities. I don't—" She broke off as understanding dawned. "Uriah has influence with this new lawyer, doesn't he?"

"I don't know it for a fact, but I think it's likely. It wouldn't be difficult to discover."

Raine sighed heavily. "Scott Pennway helped people find water. Farmers and ranchers hired him to find and dig new wells. He knew about irrigation. Annie told me he was going to help Matt Sharp open up another ten acres for farming."

"I didn't know that he was set to help Matt. That probably influenced the timing of his death."

"What about Marshal Sterling?"

"He was in the way, Raine. He was killed because he was doing his job. If he hadn't been going out to the ranch to bring Isaac Burdick back, he would have been going out there someday on some other business and come to the same end. It's possible Isaac was merely a lure to draw him out."

"If you're right about all of it, who's next?"

"I'd only be guessing."

"Guess."

"Very well. I think Harry Sample is probably high on Uriah's list. He works at the land office, and Uriah indicated to me that he doesn't have much faith in Harry any longer. He hinted that Harry betrayed him by taking part in your sister's trial. He would rather do business with Charles Sample."

Raine stared straight ahead. "I hate it. I hate all of it." The words settled like stones around her heart. The pressure made her chest ache. "Is there an end to it, Kellen?"

"Yes."

His certainty did not ease her. It filled her with dread. She felt tears sting her eyes, and she blinked them back.

"This way," said Kellen, pointing to the stand of pines that he'd seen Raine eyeing earlier. "There's decent cover. There's probably someplace we can tether the horses where they'll be out of sight." He glanced up at the sky. The wind had picked up since they had reached the lake, and while the sun still shone brightly when it appeared between breaks in the clouds, it brought little warmth. The snow that Raine told him was in the air last night never got to the ground, but he thought she could be right about the advent of an early winter storm.

They dismounted. Raine laid out the blanket and their food while Kellen walked the horses another fifty yards deeper into the stand of trees. Once she looked back and didn't see him. Panic rushed her. The reaction was as swift as it was surprising, and she was aware that she couldn't move, couldn't think. It only lasted a few moments, but the sense of paralysis stayed with her even as she began walking in the direction Kellen had gone.

She stopped when he stepped into view between two stout trunks of mountain pine. He was carrying her carbine. She stared at him, at the Springfield, and she swayed slightly but held her ground.

"Raine?" Kellen was only ten yards away, and he could see she was as pale as salt. "What's wrong?" She was watching him intently, but he looked over his shoulder as if there might be something behind him that would explain her vigilance. There was nothing there, which meant he was the one who had put her on her guard.

Kellen reversed the carbine in his hand and extended it, stock first, to Raine. When she didn't come forward to take it, he went to her. He took her by the wrist, turned her gloved hand over, and slapped the butt of the Springfield against her palm with enough force to make her fingers close around it. He kept on walking.

Raine stayed where she was for several long minutes. When she finally joined Kellen on the blanket, she still had no words to explain herself. He didn't ask, but she thought that might be because he was too angry to speak. Too angry. Too hurt. In his place, she would feel the same.

She took the biscuit he held out to her but did not mistake it for a peace offering. Her hand shook a little as she raised it to her mouth. She pressed the cold biscuit against her lips but did not take a bite. Lowering her hand to her lap, she said, "I'm sorry."

Kellen settled against the scaly, reddish-brown bark of the pine behind him. He opened his canteen and took a deep swallow of water. He did not look at Raine. His eyes tracked as much of the perimeter of the lake as he could see from his vantage point.

"I'm sorry," she repeated. "I didn't think you were *really* going to shoot me."

"Yes, you did. You're still not sure you can trust me."

"That's not true." She hated the lack of inflection in his voice, the dead weight that it lent his words. "The thought that you might turn the carbine on me startled me as much as seeing you with it. I can't account for it."

He cocked an eyebrow at her and then returned to scanning the lakeshore.

Raine bent her head, stared at the biscuit in her lap. She broke off a piece and put it in her mouth. It may as well have been a wet rag for all the taste it had. She eyed her canteen but did not reach for it. "Do you have your flask?"

Kellen reached inside his duster, pulled it out, and gave it to her.

Raine noticed that he was careful to avoid touching her when she took it. She held the flask in both hands. "I'm afraid." The admission came hard to her. Every word that followed came fast. "I looked up earlier and you were gone and I was afraid that something happened to you so I went to find you and you appeared out of nowhere and then I was afraid something was going to happen to me. I'm just afraid." Her fingertips whitened on the silver flask. "My shadow. Yours. I can't distinguish any longer. What I know with absolute certainty is that I was more afraid when I couldn't see you than when I finally did."

Raine fumbled with the lid on the flask until Kellen took it out of her hands and opened it for her.

"Don't drink it all," he said, passing it back.

She pressed the flask to her lips, took a single mouthful, and handed it to him. The whiskey warmed her tongue, her throat, and slid smoothly into her belly. "Thank you."

Kellen drank, capped the flask, and put it away. He tipped the brim of his hat so he was no longer looking at her from a deep shadow. "I don't want you to be afraid."

Raine smiled unevenly. "If only you got everything you wanted."

"I know. If there is a choice to be made, I'd rather have you afraid for me than of me. I will never hurt you, Raine."

She let his words sit on her heart for a moment, long enough to let him know that she wished it were true. "Yes, you will," she said finally. "You won't hurt me the way you mean, not physically. I know that. But you'll hurt me just the same. You won't be able to help yourself, and I won't be able to stop you. It's an unintended consequence of loving someone."

Raine held up a hand, stopping him as his lips parted. "I love you. There's nothing to be done about it. Nothing to be fixed. I don't want you to lecture me about my lack of expectations. Unrequited love is difficult, but no one dies of it except in tragedies and dime novels. I do not think I will be the exception."

She picked up the biscuit in her lap and returned it to his saddlebag. She brushed crumbs off her skirt. "I don't know if intentions matter, but I did not mean to fall in love with you. That it's happened at all mostly rests on my shoulders, but you bear some responsibility, too."

"Are you going to tell me again that I'm decent?"

"Your kisses aren't."

"There's a mercy."

"But you're kind to Walt and patient with Rabbit and Finn, and you don't mind if Sue prattles on because she can't remember what she's supposed to say when she's near you. You allow Mrs. Sterling to order you around as if she's known you all of your life, and you'll fold a winning hand if it means Jessop Davis can win a game against his brothers. I watch you separate yourself from others as though you don't want to be bothered, and yet you come to know the exact things that will put you in the thick of it all. You've never forgotten that Nat Church brought you here or that you want to do right by him. It's hard not to respect that."

Raine studied his face. One corner of his mouth lifted the merest of fractions. It was not amusement that she saw but something more akin to embarrassment. "It's not your fault, I suppose, that you're as handsome on a woman's arm as a ten-dollar bonnet is on her head."

"Ten dollars? I'm not sure that I—"

"Don't fish for compliments. Twelve dollars is the most a sensible woman would spend on a handsome hat."

"Then I'm flattered."

"I don't know why. It's your parents I'm flattering."

"I'll be sure to tell them."

"And that's another thing," she said, lifting her chin. "I believe you will tell them. I don't think you *are* the black sheep in your family. I don't even think there is one. I know you've written letters home to New Haven. Emily told me that she posted them for you. You can't be as estranged from your parents as you would have me believe, and your brother apparently had no qualms about helping you."

Kellen rubbed his knuckles under his chin. He mirrored Raine's thoughtful study. "There's a lot about me that you think you know but don't, and there's even more that you don't suspect."

"You're telling me that you've lied to me."

"Yes. Often by omission, but yes."

"All right. Tell me something I don't know."

"Very well. At the risk of challenging your notion that no one dies of unrequited love except in tragedies and dime novels, I've been thinking lately that it could happen to me."

Chapter Fourteen

Raine's lips parted, closed, then parted again. They remained that way until Kellen gently slipped his gloved hand under her chin and lifted her jaw.

"You were gaping," he said.

She simply nodded.

He leaned forward and took advantage of her silence to kiss her thoroughly. The brims of their hats got in the way. Kellen had to make a grab for his as a gust lifted it off his head. Raine clamped a hand over the crown of hers. Their mouths remained fused, but amusement crept into the kiss and then they were laughing and they had no choice but to draw back.

"That's a hat for Texas," she said as he returned the black Stetson to his head. "Did you buy it there?"

"Bought it and broke it in."

She reached up and tapped the wide brim. "That's for keeping the Texas sun out of your eyes, but Wyoming ranchers favor a narrower brim, one the wind isn't as likely to carry away. You might have noticed that nearly everyone in Bitter Springs wears a white Stetson." She removed her hat, reshaped and creased the crown the way she liked it. "More of a pearl gray,

I suppose." She put it back on her head and tucked her loose coppery braid under it. "Try to keep that one on your head, Mr. Coltrane."

Kellen reached for Raine. He shifted to one side and gave her part of the trunk to lean against and sheltered her with an arm around her shoulders. He plucked her hat off again. She tried to get it from him, but he held it out of her reach until she settled back, and then he dropped it on the blanket and nudged the butt of the carbine onto the brim to keep it in place. He pressed his lips to the crown of her head.

"I do love you, you know," he said.

"I'm warming to the notion."

"Good, but I'm thinking we should have made these mutual declarations when we were closer to a bed and a stove."

"Really?"

"Yes."

"You like your comforts, don't you?"

"I do."

Raine removed herself from the curve of his arm and straddled his legs. "I think I could make you forget certain comforts." Using her teeth to help, she stripped off her gloves and then tucked the gloves under Kellen's thigh. Her fingertips trailed over the beaten, buttery soft brown leather duster. She opened it and set her hands on his belt. Watching him, not what she was doing, she pulled the tongue through the buckle and began to unfasten the buttons of his trousers. She raised her eyebrows in question before she continued. At his faint nod, she reached inside his drawers, found his erection stirring, and freed his penis.

Still watching him, watching his eyes darken and his lids grow heavier, she began to stroke him. "What was it like?" she asked as she leaned closer. "What was it like when you tasted me?"

He didn't answer. His eyes dropped to where she was holding him. Her hand stopped moving. He glanced at her, her eyes, and felt the sweet, hot caress begin again.

Raine smiled, beckoning, beguiling. Her hips lifted, rocked as if they were joined, but it was only her hand that held him captive. She wet her lips, kissed him full on the mouth, engaged his tongue in a languid battle that exactly matched the rhythm she struck with her hand. The pulse and heat of his cock filled her palm.

She drew back slowly. Her breasts felt heavy. She rubbed her hand over them through her jacket. It wasn't enough, not close to enough, but when he reached for her, she shook her head and denied both of them because she wanted something else, something more.

Raine inched down his legs until she could bend forward at the waist and clear his chest. She saw what she planned to do register in his eyes just as she ducked her head. The low growl was back in his throat the moment she took him into her mouth. She thought she felt that vibration against her tongue.

Her hand slipped deeper into his drawers. She manipulated him with her fingers as she suckled.

He might have cursed. She couldn't be certain. Blood was rushing in her ears. If he did curse, it seemed entirely appropriate because she had drawn it out of him. She felt that powerful.

Kellen's fingers slipped into her hair at the top of her braid. She didn't mind his touch there until he applied some leverage and began to pull her back. She resisted at first. He tightened his hold, grew more insistent. Was he saying her name? She released him, but not before she flicked her tongue against the head of his penis.

She heard him curse now as he pushed her out of the way with one hand and yanked at his neckerchief with the other. Her eyes widened at the sight of his milky seed, and she continued to watch when he covered himself with the kerchief and finished spilling into it.

Kellen fell back against the tree while Raine moved to sit up on her knees. She set her palms on her thighs. Fascination warred with embarrassment, but it was an uneven battle and the former was the clear victor. She watched Kellen calmly clean and tuck himself into place and then right his clothes. He stood slowly as though he needed to make certain his legs were going to support him. They did, but it appeared to be a narrow thing. When she thought about it, it was a lovely compliment.

He gave her a slow, thank-you-ma'am smile. There was still heat in his eyes. "I do enjoy explorin' new territory with you, Mrs. Coltrane."

There was no possibility that Raine would not blush. She watched him head toward the lake and eventually disappear behind an outcropping of rocks. She stood, found that her legs were perhaps only a little less wobbly than his, and walked deeper into the stand of trees to stretch them out. When she came around, Kellen was waiting for her. He'd washed out the kerchief. One damp end of it dangled from a pocket in his duster.

It made her think about what he'd said about exploring new territory. She was already warming to the idea that they might . . . She stopped, startled by the direction her mind was taking her. Was what she was thinking even possible? To distract herself, she bent and picked up her hat. "Tell me something else about you that I don't know," she said.

"Later. What there is to tell you isn't about me." Kellen lifted his thumb over his shoulder and pointed behind him to the lake. "We have company."

Raine stepped to the side to see past him. "Company?" She came up on tiptoe, craned her neck, but couldn't see anything through the trees. "Who?"

"Mr. Petit. Mr. Reasoner. And if I'm not mistaken, Mr. Jones is with them."

"All three of them?" She frowned. Her eyes narrowed on Kellen. "When we dismounted, you said we'd have some cover here. You hid the horses. Did you know they were following us?"

"No. I thought Jones might—that's why I wanted the cover. He knows something about this place, wanted to come out here, but I told him I wouldn't be his guide. I suppose Petit and Reasoner were willing."

"Why don't you want them to know we're here?"

"Because I would rather watch than be watched."

Raine was not entirely satisfied with his answer but did not press for more. Kellen was already turning away. She picked up the carbine and followed him, staying behind the tree line and well away from the lakeshore. She had occasional glimpses of Reasoner, Petit, and Jones on the far side of the lake as they picked their way over rocks and around large, spreading juniper shrubs. Raine took Kellen's hand when he offered it. They climbed into a niche made by a pair of boulders and a gnarled, twisted limber pine that shouldn't have been able to grow or thrive in the narrow opening but somehow had managed to do both.

Raine squeezed into a relatively comfortable position on the incline of one of the boulders. Kellen found a place on the other. They had a good view of the lake as seen from between the boulders and a better one when they raised their heads a few degrees above them. The pine offered additional shelter although its boughs were set widely apart and only sparsely covered with needles. When the wind whistled over their heads, the pine tree swayed and small sprays of needles danced in the air.

"They're stopping," said Raine. She watched Mr. Reasoner pull up his horse after Mr. Petit did the same. Jones stayed in the saddle while the other men dismounted and began to take photographic equipment from the packhorse that trailed them. "It doesn't seem that Mr. Jones is interested in helping."

"I think he's directing them," Kellen told her. "Look at how he's pointing around. He's telling them where to set up the equipment and what he wants the camera to see."

"I wish we were closer. I'd enjoy a look at Mr. Reasoner's face. He always strikes me as someone better at giving orders than getting them."

"Why do you think that?"

"He's so very particular. About his room, his tea, the placement of his silverware at the table. He's the only guest I've had that came with more trunks than you."

"Really? How many?"

She held up three fingers. "One is half the size of the other two, but he has so many clothes Emily used to complain that he should have traveled with his valet. He was always sending her out with laundry for the Taylors to take in and usually sending her back at least once, sometimes twice, because he was dissatisfied with the care his clothes received. Apparently Mrs. Taylor frequently asked Emily when Mr. Reasoner was leaving, and even Emily, who once told me Mr. Reasoner's accent was delicious, was beginning to entertain notions of pouring a piping hot cuppa tea in his lap."

Still watching the far side of the lake, Kellen was nevertheless moved to smile. "Emily flirted with him."

"Of course she did. She couldn't help herself."

"That's what Jones said about her."

"What?"

"Just what you said. That she couldn't help herself."

Raine bristled. She watched Jones continue to direct his guides. "Well, I don't know that I like it coming from him. He would not have said it kindly. Government toady. Look at him. He's probably using his sprained ankle as an excuse for not getting down to help them. I don't know that I've ever seen a man so passionate about an injury. The night it happened? I wasn't certain I believed that he hurt himself."

Kellen darted a glance at Raine. "You never told me that."

"I suppose because he changed my mind about it."

"He's been on the receiving end of a lot of attention because of it. Sue. Renee. Cecilia. They all accommodate him. So do you. Bath salts. Dining in his room. Making sure he has a stool for his foot when he visits the saloon."

"I did not suggest that we give the man a stool. That was Renee." When she caught the defensiveness in her tone, she mocked herself with a smile. "I take your point. Frankly, it was easier to accommodate him than have him underfoot. We could give him what he wanted and forget about him for a time."

Kellen nodded. Across the lake, Petit was adjusting the legs on the tripod while Reasoner steadied the camera. Jones was directing them to some point along the northern shoreline.

"What is it that they want to see?" asked Raine. She twisted in place but could not gain the same perspective north as the camera.

"I don't know. I don't have a surveyor's eye. It's probably nothing that would interest us."

Raine sighed, settled back. She saw Jones reach into the scabbard attached to his saddle, but instead of pulling out a rifle, he had a long roll of paper. "A map?" she asked.

"That's my guess." He watched as Jones unrolled the paper, studied it, and gestured at the camera. "I suppose he's making some sort of photographic survey that will help make a new map more accurate."

Raine looked over at him. "You have no idea what he's doing, do you?"

"None."

She laughed, shaking her head.

Kellen put a finger to his lips. "You would be surprised how far your voice will carry over water. We're sitting in a basin anyway."

"I can't hear them," she whispered.

He gave her a wry look.

"Oh. Well, I'll be quiet now."

Raine kept her word. She watched the trio work for the next fifteen minutes without making a sound. She did not speak for another half hour after that, but it was sleep that supported her silence.

Kellen placed one hand over Raine's mouth and nudged her shoulder with the other. She woke abruptly, eyes wide, startled by the leather glove against her lips. He shushed her, and when he knew she understood, he removed his hands.

Raine looked between the rock faces. She had to adjust her position because the men had moved. Her neck supported her head at an awkward angle until she got one hand under her chin. She squinted, uncertain that what she was seeing was not a sleepy double image.

There were four men now. Jones was still on horseback, Reasoner and Petit were resetting the camera on a higher slope, and the mounted newcomer was waving an arm at all three of them.

"Who is that?" asked Raine.

"That's what I wanted you to tell me. Is it Matt Sharp?"

She used a thumb and forefinger to rub her eyes and clear the sandman's grit. "You shouldn't have let me sleep." She peered through the opening again. "Not Matt. He's broader in the shoulders. Sits heavier on his horse. That man sits light and high."

"Tall in the saddle."

"Exactly. He's a cowboy. Charlie Patterson once explained to me how cowboys learn to ride tall so they don't put too much pressure on the horse's back. It spares their mounts on the long rides. Those men love their animals."

"Do you recognize the horse?"

"No," she said dryly. "I know Phantom, same as Rabbit and Finn. He needs to turn more in our direction. The man, I mean, not the horse. I can barely make out his profile under his hat."

"He's wearing a white one."

"Yes. He's a *Wyoming* cowboy."

"One of the Davis brothers? It's odd, but I have the sense that I should know him."

The same sense niggled at Raine, but then she knew everyone. "Jem and his brothers are thicker than that man. It troubles me that I can say who it isn't but can't tell you who it—" Her thoughts froze along with her speech. What did not freeze was her ability to move. She was tugging on the carbine to get it into position when Kellen wrenched it out of her hands.

Kellen swore sharply although his voice never rose above a rough, gravelly whisper. He put the Springfield on the other side of him out of her reach, and when she made a grab for it, he slapped her hand out of the way. "Who the hell do you think you're going to shoot at this distance?"

"Him! I'm going to shoot him!"

The wild fury in her eyes slammed into Kellen like a physical blow. Her knowledge suddenly became his. "Jesus, Raine. I'm sorry. You can't." He grabbed both her wrists when she flailed at him. She began slipping into the crevice between the rocks. "Stop! You're going to trap yourself. Raine! Stop fighting me."

She stopped, let herself go limp. Her breath came raggedly in small bursts. She closed her eyes. Tears burned at the back of them. More clogged her throat. She had always wondered what she would do if she saw him again. And now she knew. Nothing.

"Let me go," she said.

Kellen released her and let her struggle out of the niche on her own. She had to unlace her boot before she could free her wedged foot. He snagged the boot and gave it to her.

"That's Isaac Burdick, isn't it?"

Raine nodded. "I don't understand why I didn't recognize him right away. I was so sure I would always know him." She jammed her foot into her short boot and began lacing it. "Take the carbine. I've seen you shoot. You could hit him."

"Not at this range, and probably not even if we were closer. Not with a weapon I've never fired before. God, Raine. Did you even think before you reached for your weapon? How do you imagine we'd get out of here without being seen?"

She did not try to defend herself. She had neither thought nor imagined, and he knew it. Raine lay back down, turned over on her stomach, and found the position that would give her the best view. A few moments later, Kellen joined her. The carbine was still out of her reach.

"It's been several years since you've seen him," Kellen said.

"Four," said Raine. "Four years since the trial." As she was speaking, Isaac Burdick removed his hat, slapped it once against his thigh as though emphasizing a point, and reset it on his head, covering up the thick, black hair that was the hallmark of every Burdick.

Kellen observed the sharp profile for as long as the hat was gone and studied the seat and gestures of the man once the hat was returned to his head. He understood the sense of familiarity that he'd experienced.

"He looks like his brothers."

Raine nodded. "He favors Eli."

Occasionally Kellen could hear raised voices but none of the words. "He's not happy. Can you tell who is arguing with him?"

"I think they all are."

That was Kellen's observation as well. "The Burdicks I met don't expect an argument."

"The other men are only visitors. Maybe they don't realize he's a Burdick."

"You don't think they've figured it out? They've seen Eli and Clay in the saloon, and Clay has been warning them to stay away from Burdick land."

"This doesn't belong to the Burdicks. It's government land."

"I'm thinking Uriah has a different opinion. When we get back to town, I'm going to visit the land office again and talk to the Sample cousins—separately this time. It's possible one of them will have something to say that the other one won't . . . or can't."

"You think that's what Isaac's doing? Warning them off?"

"Another guess."

"I wonder why Uriah sent Isaac out to meet them."

"Sent? Don't you think this could be accidental?"

Raine thought about it. "I suppose I'm used to believing that Uriah Burdick always has a plan."

"He might have asked Isaac to keep an eye out this way. Still, it would make more sense to send Eli or Clay."

They fell quiet again, watching. Reasoner and Petit made no move to pack up the equipment. Jones rolled up the map but continued to use it like a hammer when he wanted to emphasize a point. Isaac spurred his horse forward. Reasoner jumped away from the camera. Petit held his ground. Jones dropped the map and came up with a gun.

Isaac swung his mount to the side and reached for his weapon at the same time.

It was impossible to tell who fired first. The flashes seemed simultaneous. The sound reached out to Kellen and Raine a moment later just as Mr. Petit fell to the ground.

The story of how Mr. Jones saved Isaac Burdick's life by shooting Mr. Petit at Hickory Lake spread through Bitter Springs like a grease fire on a griddle. Raine and Kellen heard about it from Sue Hage when they arrived in town two hours after Reasoner and Jones returned with Mr. Petit's body. They heard a similar version sometime later from Rabbit and Finn, who were more impressed with Mr. Jones when they learned he had killed someone. Rabbit and Finn aside, most folks talked about the shooting as if it were incidental to the tale. What they really cared about was the sudden appearance of Isaac Burdick. It was one thing to suspect his family had harbored him all these years, quite another to learn that he was testing the boundaries of his confinement.

Kellen and Raine's late return was deliberate. To avoid being suspected of witnessing what happened, they waited while the three men crowded around Petit's body. Petit's fate was made clear to them when Isaac and Reasoner lifted the smaller man and hoisted him over the saddle of his horse. They covered him with a blanket and strapped him down. Jones took the camera and tripod and returned it to the packhorse.

Raine and Kellen did not speak while this was going on. Isaac Burdick left the area first, heading west toward the Burdick spread. Mr. Reasoner and Mr. Jones stood beside Petit's horse and talked for a while. Raine supposed they were agreeing on their story. Kellen supposed exactly the same.

They did not discuss it until they were certain Reasoner and Jones were not going to circle the lake, as it seemed they might at first. When the pair turned their animals in the direction of Bitter Springs and did not reappear over the course of an hour, Kellen declared it was finally safe for them to leave their hiding place.

They accepted the story that Sue told them and listened without argument to the slightly more grisly rendition offered by Rabbit and Finn, although it pained them to do it.

Arrangements had already been made to bury Mr. Petit in the graveyard, although just outside the fence that cordoned off the graves of decent folk. The undertaker, Mr. Irvin, agreed to take care of the body but wanted to know about payment. He was more gracious when Raine returned and offered to pay for his services, which included words appropriate to the burial. Mr. Petit's body was put in the ground with his feet facing west. That way, Mr. Irvin explained, when the sun rose on Judgment Day, Mr. Petit would rise up with his back to the devil and might get a running start.

"Ridiculous man," Raine told Kellen. She was sitting in the tub with her head bowed so Kellen could pour clear, warm water over her hair.

"Who's ridiculous?" He had long since lost track of their conversation. Raine's hair was infinitely more interesting to him. He tipped the pitcher and let the water sluice over her head and rinse away the soap.

"Mr. Irvin. All that business this afternoon about burying Mr. Petit with his feet to the west. It was silly."

"In Texas they often bury people in the opposite direction. Something about their redeemed souls rising to face Judgment. Perhaps Texans put more stock in redemption than Mr. Irvin."

Raine tried to look at him to gauge his truthfulness, but he put his hand over her head and kept her turned away.

"You'll get soap in your eyes," he told her.

She let him have his way because the water felt so good sliding over her hair and shoulders and down her back. She did not want to think about unpleasant things. It was disappointing when those thoughts intruded anyway.

"A lot of people would sleep better tonight if Mr. Jones had shot Isaac Burdick. Poor Mr. Petit. What did he ever do except take pictures?"

Kellen put the pitcher aside and began finger combing Raine's hair. Thoughtful, he asked, "Where are Mr. Petit's things now?"

"I asked Walt to pack everything up and clean out the room. I imagine he stowed it in the back room where he sleeps. It would be like Walt to want to take care of it until we know if there's someone in Mr. Petit's life with a claim to it. I'm thinking of the photographic equipment. I don't know that there was anything else of significant value."

Kellen removed his fingers from Raine's hair and sat up straight.

Raine's head swiveled sideways. "What?"

He swore softly. "The photographs. The goddamn photographs he took when he and Reasoner found Emily's body. I need to see them again." He started to rise from the stool, thought better of it, and bent to drop a swift, hard kiss on Raine's parted lips. "Tempting, but no."

Raine stared at the empty doorway long after he was gone.

Kellen found Walt alone in the saloon, broom in hand as he swept under the tables.

"Everyone's gone, Mr. Coltrane," Walt said as Kellen approached. "Early night for most folks. Had a few stragglers still wantin' to jaw about what happened out at the lake, but I shooed them out. They didn't really know Mr. Petit, so it wasn't right for them to go on as if they did. Mrs. Berry, I mean, Mrs. *Coltrane*, wouldn't have liked it."

"I'm sure you're right," said Kellen. "I'm actually here because Raine asked me to find out about Mr. Petit's things. Are they in the back room?"

"Yes, sir. They're safe there. I figure it's best if I keep an eye on them. I would have done the same for Mr. Weyman, but we both know what became of his belongings."

Kellen nodded. "Did Mr. Reasoner and Mr. Jones return the camera and other equipment?"

"Well, they came back with it, and I was the one that took it off the packhorse, so I suppose I'd have to say they returned it. Leastways, neither of them argued too much about it. They were pretty shaken, trembling like aspens, the pair of them, and Deputy Sugar showed up and asked a lot of questions. Mostly I just minded my business and did what I thought Mrs. Coltrane would want me to do."

"You did well, Walt. Raine is interested in Mr. Petit's photographs. There must have been a lot of those."

"Sure there were. He had a small chest full of them." Walt's forehead creased with worry. "Was I wrong to look inside? I hope I wasn't wrong."

"No, Walt. It's fine. Could you show me the chest?" Walt set the broom aside and led Kellen to the rear of the saloon. Walt's small sleeping area was neatly organized with his belongings hanging on the wall above his cot or in the two wooden crates under it, while cases and kegs, mops, brooms, and buckets occupied most of the space that was left. Kellen had to follow Walt completely into the room before Mr. Petit's equipment and trunks could be revealed in the corner behind the door.

"There you go," said Walt, pointing to the chest. "It's got a satin lining. How about that? Expected to find the crown jewels inside." He chuckled. "Maybe that's why Mr. Reasoner asked after it, too."

"He did?" Kellen lifted the chest by its brass handles. It was not as large as a case of liquor and much lighter. Most of the weight was in the chest itself, not in its contents. "Did he say what he wanted with it?"

"Well, he said seein' how he and Mr. Petit were friends, and what happened out at the lake didn't really change that, and how since he had been helpin' Mr. Petit with the photographs, he thought Mr. Petit would want him to have some of them. Mementos, he said."

"Did you let him take any?"

"No, sir. I would never. Not my place. That's for Mrs. Coltrane to decide, and that's what I told him. He said he would ask her."

"Maybe that's why Raine asked me to get them for her," Kellen said.

"She didn't tell you?"

Kellen sighed. "A consequence of marriage, Walt. I just do her bidding."

Raine rose from the sofa as Kellen unceremoniously dumped the contents of the chest onto the table. She reached the table in time to keep half a dozen photographs from sliding to the floor. She pulled out a chair and rested one knee on it as she glanced over the photographs. "What are we looking for?"

Kellen put the chest on the floor at his feet. He braced his arms on the edge of the table and looked over the bounty. "I'm not certain. I'm hoping we'll know it when we see it."

"There must be two hundred photographs here." Raine

began to finger through those closest to her. "I suppose we should organize them. You realize, don't you, that whatever you're looking for might not be here? Mr. Petit regularly sent photographs back East."

"I know, but Walt said that Reasoner asked about the photographs. It could be nothing. Maybe he really does want a few as a remembrance."

"You don't sound convinced."

"It's hard to be when I know about the photographs that Petit took of Emily. Reasoner was there. I can't help wonder if that's what he's after. Walt wouldn't give him any of the pictures. He told Reasoner to ask you about them. Did he?"

"No, not yet." She continued to sort the photographs by location. "Mr. Petit took a lot of photographs in this waterfall area. It's lovely. I've never seen most of these places. And the views. Look at how he was able to capture the light coming through the trees. Every ray is like the finger of God."

"Uh-huh."

Raine smiled and shook her head. "Perhaps it's not the best time to admire his work." She created a third stack of photographs whose subject was a barren stretch of land along the railroad tracks. In some of them, the station house and platform were evident in the distance. In others she could make out the cluster of businesses and homes that constituted the whole of Bitter Springs. The view from Mr. Petit's eye was a lonely one. "Did you think it was odd that Mr. Reasoner and Mr. Jones shared a table in the dining room this evening?"

"Not particularly." Kellen pushed more photographs toward Raine for sorting. "If Reasoner was finding fault with Jones for shooting and killing his friend, then I would find it odd. That's not the case. *That's* what I find odd."

"Dan Sugar was satisfied with their story."

"He has to be, doesn't he? It would be a problem for him if Isaac Burdick had been gunned down, and even more of a problem if Petit, Reasoner, and Jones had somehow captured Isaac and brought him in." He waved a hand over the table. "I'm not seeing any of the photographs of Emily here."

Raine heard the frustration in his voice. "May I?"

Kellen pushed his hand through his hair and stepped back from the table. "Be my guest."

As Raine moved toward the photographs, her foot bumped hard against the chest. Cursing softly, she stood on one foot while she raised the other to rub it. "Couldn't you find a better place for that?"

Instead of replying, Kellen leaned down to grab the chest. He set it on top of a fan of photographs. Then he opened it, and thrust his hand inside.

Raine realized he was looking for something left behind *under* the lining. She saw his expression change the moment he found it.

Kellen withdrew his hand and pointed to the interior of the chest. "Do you have a pair of scissors? I can feel where the lining's been opened and stitched closed. Remarkably tidy stitches, I might add."

Raine retrieved scissors from her sewing basket. "I'll do it," she said. "I doubt that you have Mr. Petit's fine hand. You can hold the lamp up so I can see what I'm doing."

Kellen obliged and Raine carefully sliced through the neat stitches along the bottom left edge of the chest. When she was done, she took the lamp from him and invited him to take out what was under the lining.

"If they're more photographs of Emily," she said, "I'm not certain I want to see them."

Kellen came away with three photographs. He carefully examined each one in turn, keeping them away from Raine. When he finished, he held them against his chest.

"What is it?" she asked. His expression, a mixture of gravity and resignation, caused her heart to quicken. "Show me." She held out her hand, but he shook his head and held on to them.

"Emily is in all three of them," he said. "Do you remember that I told you Petit took all of the photographs from the same angle?"

Raine nodded. "You realized he moved Emily's body, not the camera."

"Yes, and that was true for the photographs I saw. But these are different. The perspective, the distance. All different from the others." He placed one photograph on the table, using his palm to cover the bottom-right-hand corner so that Emily's body was not visible. "Look at it," he told Raine. "What do you see?"

She studied the area around Kellen's hand first, looking for clues that would have been left close to Emily's body. It was not until she focused her eyes on the broader landscape that she found what he meant her to see. In the deep background, shaded by tall, knobby pines, it was possible to make out the half-hidden figure of a man. The brim of his white hat fairly gleamed in a slanted beam of sunlight. Even that narrow brim would have thrust his face in shadow if he had been wearing the hat. Instead, he was carrying it, holding it against his thigh, his posture frozen by the camera just as it had been at the time. He stood there as rooted to the ground as the tree beside him, afraid to move for fear of being heard. He did not understand the camera's wider lens or the penetration of its unwavering eye. He saw that it was turned toward Emily's abused and battered body so he stayed where he was, watching, waiting, and unwittingly becoming the captive of chemicals and photographic plates.

"It's Clay," she said softly. "My God, it's Clay."

"You're certain? Not Eli? Not Isaac?"

"This is Clay." She looked up. "Show me the others."

Kellen shuffled the photographs. He kept his palm over Emily's body and showed her the second picture. When she nodded, satisfied with what she saw, he showed her the third. He gave her another minute to study it before he turned all the photographs over.

"Do you believe that it's Clay?" Raine asked.

"Yes. I thought I could make out his mustache. I didn't want to influence you. With the Burdicks looking as much alike as they do, we need to be sure."

"Ask Walt," Raine said. "Cover up the bottom half of the picture so he can't possibly understand what he's looking at and ask him."

"First thing tomorrow morning." He sat and stretched his legs. In moments he was slouched, his hands folded in front of him, tapping his thumbs as he thought.

Raine recognized the signs of deep contemplation. She pushed photographs out of the way so she could sit on the table and used the seat of the chair as a stool for her feet. Her own thoughts were tumbling and spinning so fast that she couldn't grasp one to examine. The implications of Clay Burdick being at the site of Emily's murder overwhelmed her. It was beyond comprehension that the town would support another trial with a Burdick standing accused of a crime.

Raine closed her eyes and pressed her thumb and forefinger against the bridge of her nose. "Mr. Petit told someone about these photographs," she said finally. "Is that what you're thinking?"

At the sound of her weary voice, Kellen looked up. "Do you want me to get you a headache powder?"

"No." Smiling a little crookedly, Raine let her hand fall away from her face. "But thank you. What I need is to hear your voice."

Kellen stopped tapping his thumbs and reached for her hand. "Come here." When Raine scooted closer, he turned her ninety degrees so she was facing him. She had to place her feet on his chair on either side of his thighs. He looked up at her. "Mr. Petit definitely told someone about these," he said. "We're of one mind on that. I can't decide if he was foolish enough to tell Clay Burdick or if he merely told someone he thought he could trust."

"Mr. Reasoner, you mean."

"Or Mr. Jones. They had something in common. They were both trying to get onto Burdick land. Petit could have thought that the photographs were his ticket. He might have shared that with Jones. If it was Jones or Reasoner, then I think it's safe to say that Petit was betrayed."

"What about the rest of the photographs that Petit had of Emily?"

"Didn't I hear Walt mention that he delivered some packages to the station for Mr. Petit?"

Raine nodded. "I'd forgotten. Maybe that's why they're not here." She frowned, thinking. "I believe that Clay murdered Emily. I don't imagine anything changing my mind about that, especially with Rabbit and Finn being able to place his horse behind the hotel the night that Emily and Mr. Weyman disappeared, but I don't understand how he was able to place your cuff link near her body. How did he come by it in the first place?"

Kellen's eyes shifted focus briefly, straying to a point past Raine's shoulder before they came back to her. He sighed. "There's no good way to say this," he told her. "There are two explanations that occur to me. The first is one that you and I dismissed, namely that Emily stole the cuff link and had it with her when she was murdered. The second is that someone else put it there, and that, I'm afraid, presents far too many complications and coincidences. The simplest answer is probably the most likely. I'm sorry, Raine, but I think it was Emily who took it."

"Why?"

"Again, the simplest answer. She wanted to make Clay jealous."

Raine had been leaning forward, engaged in the conversation. Now she jerked back, her spine as straight as a flagpole. "No. Emily did not have anything to do with Clay. She wouldn't go near him if she had a choice. She hated him for what he helped his brother do to Ellen."

"Emily the flirt? The girl who couldn't help herself when she was around men? Isn't it possible that she avoided Clay to divert suspicion? She liked you, Raine. She had to know that not only would you be concerned if she admitted that there was something going on between her and Clay, but that you would also be hurt. She might have been afraid you would tell her parents."

"I would have." Raine's eyes grew troubled. A crease appeared between her eyebrows. She spoke softly, more to herself than to Kellen. "I would have had to."

"I understand. So did Emily."

"Oh, God."

"Don't tell yourself that you should have known. You couldn't have. I saw she avoided him in the saloon, and I never suspected another motive for it. The fact that you knew her so well made it more difficult, not easier, to see what was happening." He gave her time to take in what he was telling her before he spoke again. "You said something this morning at the lake that's been niggling at me. About Emily."

Raine frowned, touching her chest. "I said something?"

He nodded. "You said that you knew I'd been writing home because Emily told you she'd posted my letters to the station."

"Oh, that. Yes. I remember telling you."

"It got past me at the time. I suppose that's why it's been sitting at the back of my mind waiting for me to bring it forward. Raine, I never gave Emily letters to take to the station for me. I always gave them to Walt."

"But I'm sure it was Emily who . . . oh, I see. Walt gave them to her."

"He's as susceptible to a pretty woman's wiles as the rest of us. Emily probably made it seem as if she was doing him a favor. You and I both know that Nat Church was killed because someone knew why he was coming to Bitter Springs. I suspected that it was Mr. Collins who was reading all of the correspondence between you and Church and reporting it to the Burdicks, but I was wrong. It was Emily, and she was doing it for Clay."

"I gave all my letters to Walt," she said. "I thought it was as safe as taking them to the station myself. Walt can't read very well."

"I know. He told me when I offered him one of the dime novels. I promised I would read it to him."

Raine could not speak for the sudden swelling in her throat, and when tears hovered against her eyelashes, she did not swipe at them.

"Why are you looking at me like that?" asked Kellen.

She shrugged helplessly as her face crumpled.

Kellen reached for her and drew her off the table and onto his lap. He let her tuck her face in the curve of his neck. Her arms went around his shoulders. "You shouldn't look at me like that. I don't deserve it, Raine. I can't hang the moon for you. It doesn't matter that I want to. I can't. I'm not who you think I am."

She sucked in a breath that made her shudder. "I know who you are," she whispered. "You're the man I love."

Kellen closed his eyes, rubbed his cheek against her hair. "God, but I hope you mean that."

Raine used the sleeve of her robe to dab at her eyes. "Tell me something I don't know about you," she said.

"I read the letters you wrote to Nat Church."

"You did?"

"He gave them to me. They're in my bag."

"Why didn't you say so earlier?" When he simply shrugged, she let it go. "Did Mr. Church use them to convince you to come to Bitter Springs?"

"No. He used them to convince me to stay."

Raine lifted her head and regarded Kellen with suspicion. "*When* did you read them?"

Kellen opened his eyes. He did not avoid her and replied frankly, "Shortly after I arrived. He gave them to me before he died, Raine. I think he wanted me to know you. He had an obligation, and it was important to him that you were not abandoned. He was an honorable man. When I read your letters, I understood why he agreed to come to Bitter Springs. Accepting your terms would have been a mere formality. He was prepared to help you when he boarded the train."

Raine felt the ache of tears again. "I wish we had met." She pressed the crushed handkerchief against her eyes, then her nose when she sniffled. "I haven't forgotten about setting a stone for him."

"Neither have I. We'll do it."

"Do you suppose it was Clay who killed him? I always thought that whoever murdered Emily must have also killed Nat Church because a knife was used against both of them."

"The murders were very different. Whoever used the knife on Nat Church was careful, cold, and deliberate. The murderer struck quickly and disappeared. He had probably moved on before Church even knew he'd been stabbed."

Raine glanced at the overturned photographs. "There was nothing careful or cold about Emily's murder. I'm not sure any longer that it was deliberate. Everything about it was . . ." She bit her lower lip, thinking. "Everything about it was *hot*. What was done to Emily was done in a rage. He lingered afterward, I think, because he didn't know what to do. Perhaps he was even surprised by what he'd done."

Kellen's eyebrows lifted. "I don't disagree with you, but you remember you're talking about Clay Burdick, don't you?"

"I remember. I'm trying to understand what happened. I can't think when I'm in a rage of my own, and it would be so very easy to summon that kind of terrible anger right now."

"All right." He squeezed her shoulders lightly. "Then help me understand how Mr. Weyman figures into all of this. I'm confident he was killed because he was in the wrong place that night. I can imagine that he might have witnessed something going on between Emily and Clay that moved him to interfere. That would have been reason enough for Clay to kill him."

"What is it that you don't understand?"

"It doesn't seem likely that Clay would bother to go to Weyman's room to clean it out. So how did Mr. Weyman's bags end up with him in the water tank?"

"Oh, that. There's a surprisingly simple explanation. I think Mr. Weyman was running out on me."

"Running out? You mean he was trying to avoid paying his bill?"

"That's exactly what I mean."

"Why didn't you say anything?"

"Because it only just occurred to me. I do the books for the saloon regularly, but I only squared the hotel accounts the other day. I thought Sue took his last payment. She thought Walt did. It took some time to get to the bottom of it. I think he might have used the last of his funds to pay back a gambling debt to Jack Clifton. There was some talk about him owing money before he disappeared, but I didn't think much of it. There's always card money owed to someone."

"So Weyman was running out, bags in hand. Bad luck, bad timing, he surprises Clay Burdick in the alley. He sees Clay with Emily, or maybe Emily wasn't even there yet, but seeing Clay is a problem for both men. Clay doesn't want anyone to know he's in town, and Weyman doesn't want anyone to know he's ducking the bill. Clay solves the problem by coercing Weyman up the outside stairs to the roof, killing him, and disposing of the body and bags in the water tank. Rabbit and Finn probably saw Phantom while Clay was on the roof. They said they didn't see anyone else, so it seems more likely that Emily was not around yet."

"Or," said Raine, "she was already trussed and tucked away."

Chapter Fifteen

Raine turned restlessly in her sleep, waking Kellen when she jammed a knee against his groin. Grunting softly, he slipped his hand between what was important to him and her knee and gingerly eased Raine away. She flung an arm sideways, which he deflected with his palm. Before she tried to kick or clobber him again, Kellen turned her over so all of her weapons were pointed in the opposite direction. He slipped his arm around her waist, not to secure her, but to anchor himself.

Before he met Raine, he thought of himself as something of an explorer, an adventurer perhaps, a traveling man, not searching for a particular thing but searching for meaningful things. He never once thought he was adrift. Now he wondered again if he hadn't been exactly that. How else to explain that he felt settled when he was with her?

Raine settled him. The revelation was that he had no intention of fighting it. He *wanted* to be with her. It was his choice, and it felt profoundly right. He loved her. It astonished him that it had ever been a question in his mind. What had once seemed outside his experience was now the whole of it. If he had opened himself to the possibility of love, he might have recognized the first stirrings when he read her letters. He had respected her then, admired her courage and resolve, saw qualities of compassion and thoughtfulness in her writing that made him want to know the woman, but he hadn't been thinking about love.

He had been thinking about what she wanted, and if he could fill those scuffed brown boots with the tarnished silver spurs. Whether Raine understood it or not, whether she could admit it or not, when she went looking for a hired gun, she hadn't really gone looking for the man on the train with the marshal's badge and the shoes that were polished to a military shine. She had gone looking for the renegade hero in the dime novels. Her practical sensibilities had lost some ground to her romantic ones.

The irony, Kellen thought, was that he only had himself to blame.

He brushed his lips against her hair. "I do love you."

She whispered back, "Tell me something about you that I don't know."

He didn't. Couldn't, just then. He made love to her instead. Slowly. Carefully. Taking his time to appreciate all the parts he loved. The faint blue webbing at the backs of her wrists. The soft underside of her jaw. The sweet curve of her bottom. He tasted her, sipping the skin at the base of her neck as though it were a delicacy. He made her moan, made her whimper, and he liked the sounds she made, even the ones that never made it past her throat but stayed there when her breath hitched.

He was gentle until she asked him not to be. The restlessness that accompanied her into sleep now guided her lovemaking. She wanted her hands on him, to feel him under her. She needed to touch and be touched, to know a firm hand. She told him that, bringing his palm to her breast and pressing it hard against her skin. She loved his mouth on her, but she wanted his teeth.

They skimmed the surface of carnal violence. She pressed her nails into his shoulders and left white crescent brands on his skin. The hot suck of his lips on her breast made her think she would come out of her skin. When his teeth closed over her nipple and tugged, she was sure she had. She pushed the heels of her hands against his chest and urged him onto his back. She shed the sheet clinging to her shoulders, hiked up her shift, and straddled him. He rested his hands on her thighs as she rose and then lowered herself onto him. His fingers folded into fists. He sucked in a breath, held it, and waited for her to take all of him inside her. The breath he finally released was as relieved as it was ragged. Inklings of pleasure thickened his blood, sharpened his senses, and fogged his brain.

Raine's shift slipped over one shoulder. Kellen watched it slide away, and his eyes were drawn back to the slope, the defined collarbone, and the smooth expanse of creamy skin it left in its wake. He touched her breast through the soft cotton, traced the damp circle he'd made earlier with the press of his lips and tongue and teeth. She leaned forward, let him glimpse the curve of her naked breast, and then drew back, teasing him with the elegant, nimble grace of a wood nymph.

Raine rose and fell, rose and fell, moved by the pulse of her own blood. She contracted around him, lifting slowly, making him groan. She smiled, liking the sound of it, liking that she could pleasure him. When he palmed her buttocks and squeezed, she rode him harder.

The delicious tension that was always there when he filled her stretched all of her muscles taut. She ran her hands over his chest, felt his hard belly retract under her fingertips. She watched him clench his jaw, arch his neck. He drove his heels into the mattress. The bed shuddered. He lifted himself, lifted her, and she fell forward as he drove himself into her.

He shuddered. A moment later, so did she.

Raine collapsed. She didn't have far to fall, but she felt as if she were falling forever. She pressed her face into the curve of Kellen's neck and shoulder. She breathed deeply. He smelled of leather and sex. Her nostrils flared, and she burrowed deeper. His arms came around her, kept her close, steadied her. She hadn't known she needed a steady hand until she felt his, and then she was glad for it.

He had always been able to seduce her with his calm.

Kellen rubbed her back from shoulder to hip and kept doing it until she stirred, stretched, and finally slid away from him. He turned on his side, propping his head on his arm when she rolled onto her back.

"And I was sure you were sleeping," he said.

"You think too loudly for me to sleep properly."

He smiled crookedly. "Do I?"

"Adam snored. Ellen and I could hear him all the way over in our rooms. You think like that. Lots of rattling."

Kellen chuckled. "I'll try to do it more quietly from now on."

Raine leaned over, kissed him on the lips, and then rolled out of bed. Her shift floated past her knees as she padded to the bathing room. Kellen took her place when she came out, and she was deeply cocooned in the covers when he returned to bed.

"You have to share," he told her.

"I don't, but I will." She tugged and wriggled and gave him at least a third of the blankets. He had to get the remainder of his heat from her, and that suited her just fine. And if she correctly interpreted the laughter that rumbled in his chest, he wasn't much bothered by it either.

Carrying his notebook, spare pencils, and a dozen copies of *Nat Church and the Chinese Box,* Kellen made his rounds the following morning. After having a word with Walt, he stopped by the land office and spoke to Harry Sample away from his cousin about the purchase of government land around Hickory Lake. Kellen scribbled notes, but when he left, he tucked them into one of the dime novels and gave it to Harry. He interviewed Dave Rogers, Mr. Stillwell's apprentice at the barbershop, and left his notes and a novel in Dave's hand along with two bits for the haircut and shave. He found three more members of Ellen Wilson's jury working at the stationhouse restaurant. He spoke to them while they cleaned up after serving a crowd of hungry, weary passengers from the eleven o'clock train out of Denver. When he left, Terrence McCormick, Dick Faber, and Paul Reston were all gripping the latest Nat Church novel bookmarked with the notes he'd made while they were talking. Before he left the station, he dropped in on Mr. Collins and chatted a spell. He didn't leave a second copy of the new Nat Church novel, but he did hand over his notes. Kellen interviewed Richard Allen at the livery, where he was renting a rig from Ed Ransom. Kellen tucked his notes behind the handkerchief in Allen's vest pocket and laid the novel on the seat of the rig. Howard Wheeler and Jack Clifton weren't sure they wanted to talk to Kellen about water or ranching or any town business, not if their words were going to show up in a paper the Burdicks could read, but Kellen was patient and promised them they could read what he wrote first. When he left Howard and Jack in Howard's front parlor, they had his notes in one hand and were thumbing through Nat Church's latest adventure with the other. The checkerboard between them no longer held their interest.

The only member of the jury that Kellen didn't speak to was Matt Sharp. He considered leaving the farmer alone but after thinking about it—loudly, he was sure—he decided that Mr. Sharp had at least as much at stake as any of the others. Taking into consideration the location of his land to the lake, the case could be made that he had more.

He rode out to the Sharp farm after lunch and introduced himself. Matt was repairing a wagon wheel and did not look up. Kellen observed large hands and thick forearms. The farmer's frame was short and sturdy. When he finally glanced in Kellen's direction, he revealed a square chin with a dimple dead center and dark eyes that were more wary than welcoming.

Kellen left his notebook in his pocket this time. Instead, he offered to hold the wheel steady while Matt hammered the steel rim into place. They talked between hammer blows, and when Matt was finished, they moved to the shelter of the porch and talked some more. Mrs. Sharp came to the door and reprimanded her husband for not inviting their visitor inside. Kellen said he wasn't staying long and turned down her offer of coffee and a biscuit.

"I can't promise that it will be tonight or even tomorrow," Kellen told him when Bea Sharp went back inside and closed the door. "It's up to you if you want to be there, but you'd have to make the trip every evening until it was done, and it could be dangerous for you to leave your farm. There's your wife to think of and your children."

"If I come, it will be because of them," he said. "And for Lorraine Berry. That's why I served on the jury." He lifted his hat, mopped his brow with a kerchief from his pocket, and reset his hat. "It's why I want to protect what I have. The town's problem is mine, too. There's no getting around it."

"I don't know who will show," Kellen said. "Or rather, I know they'll show. They always do, but whether they'll come prepared, I can't say."

"No one told you that they would help?"

"No. I didn't ask them to. I left them all an invitation, same as I'm leaving you. They got theirs in writing. Out here, I thought I could do it differently. Come to the Pennyroyal, Mr. Sharp. Shoot for six, or six forty-five."

Matthew Sharp smiled narrowly. "Do you think they'll understand, Mr. Coltrane? Could be you're too clever."

"They'll understand the same as you. My interview with them was the frame. The invitation makes the picture clear."

"I didn't hear you mention Dr. Kent."

"I haven't talked to him. I thought it was better if he came late to the party."

"Help with the cleanup, you figure?"

Kellen nodded faintly and gave him a copy of *Nat Church and the Chinese Box*. "That's what I figure."

Mrs. Sterling served hearty beef stew and dumplings to the diners at the Pennyroyal that evening. So many regulars came for the meal that she had to make an extra batch of dumplings. She was both flattered and annoyed.

"It's a Tuesday," she said to Raine. "Now, Sunday after church I expect a crowd. But Tuesday? Folks need to eat at home."

"Maybe if you'd marry Jack Clifton, he would take his meals at his kitchen table."

Mrs. Sterling stopped stirring the stew and slapped the wooden spoon against the edge of the kettle before she shook it at Raine. "He'd probably want me to keep on working and serve him right here. I'll tell you what would serve him right: cayenne pepper shook all over his stew."

"You wouldn't."

"I sure would." She paused and turned away, making herself busy with the stew once again. "Well, I would if I didn't think his hoppin' mad red face would scare off everyone else."

Raine nodded, relieved that in the end Mrs. Sterling always proved more bark than bite. "I don't suppose I'll mention Howard Wheeler then."

"Better not. He's another one like his friend."

Raine simply shook her head. She picked up the teapot to carry it out to Mr. Reasoner, and then set it down again when Walt stomped into the kitchen from the back. He took off his hat, beat the dusting of snow off the brim and crown, and replaced it on his head. He brushed off the shoulders and sleeves of his coat next. Finally, he took off his gloves and stuffed them into his pockets. He sidled closer to the stove but stayed safely out of reach of Mrs. Sterling's long spoon.

"I knew I smelled stew," he said, grinning widely. He sniffed the air. "That's just about the best smell there ever was."

Mrs. Sterling gave him a flat look. "You've been smelling it for the better part of three hours, Walt, because that's how long I've been cooking it. It didn't just jump in the pot while you were standing outside the door. Where were you anyway? We could have used some help bringing in more chairs and an extra table from the saloon."

Walt whistled softly. "I thought the dining room looked a mite crowded tonight. Saw it from the street when I came back from the livery. Mr. Coltrane asked me to return his horse, and I got to talkin' to Ed Ransom about the weather and such." He shrugged. "Guess I lost some time there with Ed."

"I'm sure Mr. Ransom appreciated talking about the weather and such," said Raine.

Mrs. Sterling agreed. "That's time well spent, Walter, even if I did wonder how you managed to make yourself scarce when I needed you." She picked up a bowl and spooned a generous helping of stew into it. She frowned at the lone dumpling resting on top and added an extra. "Here you go. Eat up. Now you know we need you to put the chairs and table back after dinner. Don't disappear."

Raine cleared a spot at the table for Walt to sit with his bowl. "How long ago did Kellen ask you to take his horse to the livery?"

Walt thought about it while he chewed on a mouthful of stew. "I reckon it's been a couple hours now."

"I was upstairs half an hour ago. He wasn't there."

Walt had another spoonful of stew halfway to his mouth. "Well, I don't think he went into the hotel. I recollect him sayin' something about havin' to see Dr. Kent."

"The doctor? Why? Did Kellen say he was hurt?"

"No, ma'am, and he didn't look hurt either. Leastways, not so's I could see. No blood or broken bones."

"Yet," Raine said under her breath.

"How's that again, ma'am?"

Mrs. Sterling shook her spoon at Walt. "She's thinking about bloodying his nose herself."

"Oh. I see." Walt shoved a dumpling in his mouth to prevent him from saying the wrong thing.

Raine picked up the teapot. "Is it too much to expect that he'll learn to tell me where he's going?"

Mrs. Sterling glanced over her shoulder. "You really want me to answer that?" Raine was already heading for the dining room. Mrs. Sterling gave Walt a knowing smile. "I didn't think so."

Raine wended her way around the tables to reach Mr. Reasoner in the corner by the window. She smiled, raising the teapot to show him that she had it. He returned her greeting and pushed his cup and saucer closer to the edge of the table for the pour.

"Mr. Jones?" she asked. "Would you like some also?"

"Coffee for me, thank you. Miss Renee just went to get a fresh pot."

"Good. Mr. Reasoner? Shall I leave the pot with you?"

"If no one else is drinking it, then yes."

She set the pot on the table. "How are you gentlemen liking Mrs. Sterling's stew?"

"It's very good," Jones said. He made a circling gesture with his hand to indicate the other diners. "Is it what brought the crowd in?"

"I'd have to say it's the dumplings. They're a particular favorite."

Reasoner added sugar to his tea. "I don't see your husband here this evening, Mrs. Coltrane."

"He'll be along directly."

Mr. Jones put down his spoon and dabbed his mouth with his napkin. "I saw him this morning when I was taking my walk. I noticed he was talking to a number of people. He must be working very hard on his story for the *World*."

"He's finishing some of the interviews for something he calls background. Some of the folks were reluctant to talk to Kellen after they saw him on friendly terms with Eli Burdick."

"Yes, well, about the Burdicks," Jones said. "I want to explain about yesterday."

"There's no need. I have the story from Deputy Sugar."

"Still, I feel as if I owe you some sort of explanation myself. I know there's bad blood between you and the Burdicks. I didn't know the particulars until the deputy shared them with me. I've been thinking that perhaps I shot and killed the wrong man."

"There's no perhaps about it, Mr. Jones, but I understand you thought you had your reasons to do as you did. I don't hold it against you. You're not from around here. It wasn't Dan Sugar's place to tell you anything."

The tips of Jones's delicate ears reddened. "I'm sorry, Mrs. Coltrane. I thought you'd want to hear it from me."

Mr. Reasoner turned in his chair to squarely face Raine. "I considered Ben Petit a friend," he said. "But I can tell you that John Paul was right to do what he did. Ben should not have threatened Mr. Burdick. When he did that, he put all of our lives in danger. I do not believe Isaac Burdick would have been satisfied with killing Ben. Neither John Paul nor I would have come back to town yesterday. At least not alive."

Jones nodded gravely. "It's true."

"I don't own a gun," Reasoner said. "I was without defense."

"I did not aim to kill," said Jones. "I couldn't have. Mr. Petit stepped into the shot when he took aim at Isaac Burdick."

Raine said, "I'll tell Mrs. Sterling that you approve of her stew."

Kellen stepped into the dining room in time to see Raine turning sharply away from the table occupied by Jones and Reasoner. It was immediately clear to him that something had put her back up. He raised his hand to get her attention.

Raine greeted him with a forced smile. "You can sit anywhere you like as long you don't mind the company and the company doesn't mind you."

"Good evening to you, too," he said softly, aware that the diners had become his audience. "Am I allowed to kiss you?"

"Only if you want frostbite."

He chuckled. "I'll take my chances." He pecked her on the cheek and then began removing his gloves. "It looks as if Jack and Howard are inviting me to sit with them. I think I'll take them up on it."

"You do that. I'm hearing a lot of talk about *The Chinese Box*. Did you give everyone in town a copy?"

"Gave away some here and there today."

"And I thought you were doing interviews. Do you want me to take your coat? I can put it in the kitchen until you go upstairs."

He shook his head. He pecked her cheek again, but this time he whispered, "I'm wearing a gun belt."

Raine stiffened but made no comment about it. "Go on. Sit down. I'll see that someone brings a bowl of stew." She plucked the hat from his head as he started past her and dusted snow off the crown on her way to the kitchen.

Some folks left for home after dinner; others moved into the saloon. Kellen helped Walt return the table and chairs before he went to the third floor. Raine was already there. He surprised her while she was deep in thought and pacing the area in front of the sofa.

"You forgot to lock the door again," he said, turning the key.

Raine turned on him. She started to rest her hands on her

hips, thought better of it, and let her arms fall loosely to her sides. Without preamble, she asked, "What are you up to?"

He pulled his gloves out of his pocket and set them on the entry table. "I came for my gun."

She stared at him. She could not see a gun belt for his long, leather coat. "Aren't you still wearing it?"

Kellen spread his duster and showed her. "I came for the other Colt." He headed for the bedroom before she blocked his path.

Raine ran to the doorway after him. "Why are you wearing a gun? Why do you need another?"

Kellen knelt beside the bed and reached under it. He found his bag on the first swipe and pulled it out. He opened it, took out the Colt, and checked its load before slipping it under his coat and into his trousers at the small of his back. He stood.

"Did you never think it would come to this?"

"Not today. I didn't think it would be today."

"And maybe it won't. It depends on the Burdicks. The snow might keep them away."

"You think they plan to come into town this evening?"

"After what happened at the lake? Yes, I do. Uriah will have something to say to Jones. I'm guessing he'll send Eli and Clay to do his talking for him. I wouldn't be surprised if Uriah invites the surveyor out to the spread after all. He might think John Paul's earned himself a visit for saving Isaac."

"So what if they do come?" she asked. "You can sit with them, talk to them the same as you usually do. You don't have to confront them. You don't have to start trouble. I know you're thinking about it; otherwise you'd have no use for the guns."

Kellen closed the distance between them and put his hands on her shoulders. "We have an agreement, Raine. Shall I show you your own letters? You thought this all through once before. Don't back away from it now."

"I didn't think *this* through," she said. "I couldn't anticipate falling in love with my hired gun. How could I have imagined that?"

He squeezed her shoulders. "I have to do this, Raine. I wish you weren't afraid. If it helps, I won't be alone."

"What does that mean? Who is going to step up to help you?"

"Not me," he said. "You. That's why they'll do it. For you and for themselves and their families."

She thought about the crowded dining room. "Is that why so many folks showed up for dinner tonight?"

"I think it was Mrs. Sterling's stew. Or maybe her dumplings."

Raine shook off his hands. "I suppose you think you're amusing. You're not."

Kellen did not pretend to be contrite. "Listen to me. I'm not turning away from this, and I'm not telling you that you have to stay here."

"I wouldn't do it anyway."

"Exactly. Allow me to do what I came to do."

She swiped at a fiery copper curl that fell over her forehead when she set her jaw. "I lost my mother, my brother, and my sister in what seemed like the blink of an eye. They were everyone I cared about. Everyone. I don't want to lose you. I *won't* lose you."

"No," he said. "You won't."

Raine closed her eyes a moment. "Oh, God." She wrapped her arms around her chest and stared at him. "I want it to be over."

"I know. So do I. We're not alone in wanting that, Raine. Trust me. Trust the people who stood up for Ellen to stand up for you. They owe it to themselves to see it through."

She nodded slowly, faintly. "All right." Her lips moved to shape the words, but there was hardly a sound to accompany them. "Tell me what you want me to do."

And so he did.

Walt sidled up to Raine behind the bar and took the empty glass out of her hand. "You can't clean it any better than you already have," he said. He set it down out of her reach. "Give me that rag, too, before you scrub the varnish off the bar." He put out his hand, palm up, and Raine gave it to him. "Are you all right? You're about as skittish as an unbroken filly."

"Am I?"

"Yes, ma'am. I never saw you spill more than a couple drops of liquor in an evening, and you've wiped up at least two thimbles' worth since you came back here. Why don't you go sit with Mr. Coltrane for a spell? I'll take care of things here. Charlie's in this evening. Beat the weather. He can help me."

Raine shook her head. Her eyes darted across the saloon to where Kellen was sitting with Richard Allen and the Davis brothers. The five of them were playing a variation of Red Dog that Kellen taught them. Only low stakes were permitted and Jem had to promise at the outset that he wouldn't pick a fight with his brothers or anyone else. Thus far, the occasional burst of laughter aside, none of them had raised more than a murmur and a few chips.

Every man Kellen had spoken to was in her saloon. That made it no different than most evenings at the Pennyroyal, but because Kellen had talked to the men before they came, it made their presence extraordinary in Raine's eyes. Matt Sharp beat the weather, too, arriving ahead of Dave Rogers and Terry McCormick, who only had a short walk to the saloon. Matt was resting an elbow at the end of the bar, drinking a sarsaparilla with no alcohol in the brew and listening to Ted Rush discuss the blizzard of '86, just as if Matt had not lived through it along with everyone else in Bitter Springs.

"I'll stay right here, Walt," she said. "I think it's the snow rolling in that's making me feel as if there are ants crawling under my skin. I like the snow just fine until I'm hip deep in it."

"Now it ain't that kind of storm coming this way. We'll have a few inches by morning and that'll be it."

"How do you know?"

Walt shrugged. "Just do. And it'll relax you some if you believe me."

Smiling, Raine laid a hand on his forearm. "You're right. Sometimes it's simply better if you believe it is. Thank you." She turned to Charlie Patterson as he bellied up to the bar. "A beer, Charlie?"

"Sure. I was wondering if you'd let Sue have a turn at the piano. You have Renee and Cecilia taking drinks to the tables. I thought it would cheer the place a bit and give Sue something to set her mind on. She's a little tetchy tonight and won't say a word about it. The only one with something to talk about is Ted Rush. I reckon he's the only one that doesn't mind that snow's comin'."

Raine cast her glance around again and realized Charlie was right. The conversation in the saloon was at a low hum. Everyone had a drink, but not everyone was drinking. "An excellent idea. Why don't you escort Sue to the piano and help her out? I know for a fact she likes that. Here, don't rush off without your beer." She crooked a finger at him and got him to lean toward her across the bar. "You might want to think about asking her to marry you before winter comes and goes."

Blushing deeply, Charlie grabbed his beer and hurried away.

"Now, you shouldn't have gone and embarrassed the boy," Walt said.

"Someone's got to put a burr under his saddle. Sue's not going to be satisfied with him turning pages for her for the rest of her life."

Walt chortled. He took a swipe at the beer stain left on the bar when Charlie hightailed it and then poked one corner of the rag under his belt so his hands were free. "What can I get you, Mr. Reasoner?" he asked as the Englishman stepped up to the bar. "A dram of whiskey for your tea?" Walt's attempt to mimic the man's accent fell flat with the man himself, but out of the corner of his eye, he saw Raine smile, and that had been his purpose all along.

"Just a whiskey, Walter," Reasoner said. "And another for my friend, Mr. Jones."

"Coming right up."

Reasoner addressed Raine while Walter was pouring the drinks. "I was wondering what is to become of Ben Petit's photographs, Mrs. Coltrane. I understand you felt a need to pack and store his belongings, but most particular care should be taken with the photographs. I would be grateful for the opportunity to look through them and choose a few from among the dozens that we took together. I also know which ones he still wanted to send to the Eastern periodicals. It would be a privilege to do that on his behalf."

"You'll allow me some time to consider your request, won't you? You don't really have any tie to Mr. Petit beyond knowing him as a fellow guest and companion these last few months. I'm sure you appreciate that I want to make certain there is no family claim to his belongings."

"I do not believe I ever heard him speak of family beyond being a widower. There were some children, all dead young. Very sad. I always thought that having no one in the East was what brought him here."

"We know Mr. Petit was from Appomattox, Virginia, and we delivered enough packages for him to know where to send inquiries in New York City. I want to know that I've done everything I can to be sure his belongings, especially his photographs, go to his relatives, however few or distant they might be."

"Admirable, Mrs. Coltrane. Admirable." He picked up both whiskey glasses. "I would still like to have a few photographs for myself. I do not imagine any family he might have would begrudge me that."

"Perhaps not, Mr. Reasoner. Let me think on it, please. I'll give you my answer tomorrow."

"Very well." He looked Walt over. "You are keeping them safe?"

"Yes, sir. Got them put away. Ain't no one going to bother them."

Mr. Reasoner nodded. "Thank you."

As soon as he was out of earshot, Walt whispered to Raine, "Did I do right letting him think I still have them? Seemed to me that I should."

"Yes, Walt. You did right."

Walt and Raine set more drinks on the bar when Renee returned with a request from Dick Faber and the men he had enjoined to play poker with him. Sue was at the piano playing Stephen Foster favorites. Charlie no longer needed her cues to know when to turn the pages. The customers sitting close to the piano had turned their chairs to face it. Some of them tapped their heels; others hummed along. Conversation in the saloon began to rise to its normal pitch, and the good-natured ribbing and laughter that most times accompanied it finally returned this evening.

Walt said, "You suppose they're worried about the weather or expectin' someone?"

Raine blinked. "What?"

Walt lifted his chin to indicate the crowd while he continued to clean out a glass with his rag. "I'm makin' an observation. Seems to me a lot of folks got their minds in two places tonight. Thought it could be the weather since that always stirs people to sit indoors and look out. Also thought maybe someone's expected. I didn't hear a noise about Uriah Burdick coming this way." He winked at her. "But there's always people that know something I don't."

Walt's wink did not calm her nerves. She turned away from the bar to straighten liquor bottles and looked over the saloon from this new perspective. Walt was right. She watched long enough to be aware that certain men—the same men Kellen had invited to join him tonight—were taking a moment now and again to glance at the doorway. On any other evening, it might have been the falling snow that drew their eyes toward the street, but Raine knew that was not the case now.

She watched Kellen longer than she watched any of the others. He sat with his back to the doors and never once showed an interest in who came through them. He happened to look up once while she was watching him in the mirror. Their eyes met briefly. His smile lingered longer.

She wanted to throw something at him.

Raine let Walt stay at the bar while she went into the storeroom to retrieve a few bottles of ginger beer and another sarsaparilla. She came out holding two bottles in each hand and found herself squeezing the necks more tightly when the Burdicks brought the weather in.

A gust of wind carried a flurry of snowflakes to the tables on either side of the doors. Someone started to call out to shut the doors but stopped when he saw who was coming through them. Most of the men caught by the gust and flurry simply turned up the collars on their coats.

Eli and Clay did not arrive alone. Four of their ranch hands followed them inside. Wind and snow eddied around them until the last one in pulled the doors shut.

Eli took off his hat, shook it, and used it to flag Raine. "Hey, Lorrainey. We brought some thirsty tanks to fill. Why don't you set them up with beers and whiskey all around? Fellas, you take that table over there." He pointed to the one occupied by Jones and Reasoner. "You gentlemen don't mind, do you? No, stay where you are. These boys will share. Drinks for the gentlemen, too, Lorrainey. Whatever they're havin'."

Clay brushed past his brother and waved Dick Faber and his fellow poker players out of their chairs. The men got up, although not as quickly as Clay wanted. He scowled at them.

Eli lifted his dark brows. "Apparently Clay's found a table for him and me." He gestured to his hands. "You go on over there. You gentlemen make these men feel welcome. Lorrainey, I think you might need to get a few more chairs. You've got some of your town folk standing around. That's no way to treat your regulars like Mr. Faber here." He nodded and smiled crookedly at Dick Faber.

Raine set the bottles on the bar and looked over at Walt. He did not require a word from her but immediately began walking in the direction of the dining room.

"You've been drinking, Eli," said Raine. She began setting up drinks on a tray for the hands and motioned to Cecilia to come forward to get them. "I don't suppose this is your first stop of the evening."

"You'd be wrong on the second count. Right on the first."

Clay gestured to Eli to come over to the table and sit.

"In a moment, little brother." Eli slapped his hat back on his head. He looked around. "No reason for it to be so quiet in here. I ain't exactly a stranger to you. Go on about your business." His eyes fell on Sue at the piano. "I swear I heard music when I was outside. Go on. Play something. I like that 'Old Virginny' song. Play that one."

Sue turned back to the piano, and after an encouraging look from Charlie, she placed her trembling fingers on the keys. She started softly and increased the volume gradually.

"That's good," said Eli. "Nothin' wrong in the world that music don't soothe."

"Over here, Eli," said Clay. He pushed out a chair for his brother. "Put yourself in it."

"Don't seem right. These other men are still standing. Oh, here's Walt with some chairs. You fellas just put them wherever you like." Eli braced his arms on the back of the chair Clay gave him. "Lorrainey, where's your husband tonight? I don't see—"

Kellen's chair scraped the floor as he turned it around without rising from the seat. He lifted a hand to acknowledge Eli.

"There you are. I'll be damned. You're playin' cards. What's your game?"

"Red Dog."

Eli laughed. "On account of you bein' lousy at poker."

"On account of that," Kellen said.

"Why don't you join Clay and me?"

Clay growled softly. "Let him be."

Eli ignored him and waved Kellen over. "The sooner you leave that table, the sooner those men can get to playin' a real game of cards."

Kellen chuckled. "You're right." Excusing himself, he stood, picked up his drink, and offered his chair to one of the men Clay had dismissed from the other table. He crossed the saloon and took up a chair opposite Clay, shrugging apologetically as he sat.

Eli spun his chair around and straddled it. He elbowed Clay to move a few inches sideways so he wasn't crowded. Once Clay was out of his way, he ignored his brother and spoke to Kellen. "Do you know if there are any rooms to let tonight? Could be we don't get back so easy on account of the snow."

"We're not staying here," said Clay. He jerked his chin at the bar, where Raine was standing. "She wouldn't give us a room if all of them were empty, and I wouldn't take one from her."

"Then you can stay at Sedgwick's boardinghouse. If I have to stay in town, it's going to be here." He looked at Kellen. "Seems like the photographer's room can't be gone already. It's only been a day."

"It's still vacant," said Kellen. "But I have to agree with your brother. Raine won't give you a room."

"Now that's downright inhopspitable . . . inhostipable . . . unfriendly."

"She has her reasons."

Renee carried drinks to the table. She placed one glass of whiskey in front of Clay, and a glass and a bottle in front of Eli. "Mrs. Coltrane says to mind that you go easy, Mr. Burdick."

Eli's pale blue eyes narrowed as he looked Renee over. "She sent *you* with that message. You're just a bit of a thing. Tell her I said if she has another message for me, I would take it more kindly if she delivered it herself. Go on." He waved her away, almost knocking over his bottle in the process. Kellen reached across the table and grabbed it before it fell. Eli thanked him and elbowed his brother for having a laugh at his expense.

"Do you know Rabbit and Finn?" asked Kellen.

Eli poured himself a drink. "Jeff Collins's grandsons? Sure, we do. Why?"

"Oddly enough, you and Clay remind me of them." Eli grinned, but Clay gave him a sour look. Kellen sipped his drink. There was only enough whiskey in his glass to give it color. The rest was water. It was hard not to pull a face. "I have to admit I'm surprised to see you tonight. I thought the snow would keep you away."

"It's not so bad," said Eli.

Clay shrugged. "Uriah always sends some of the hands away at the first snow. Money's tight. There isn't enough work for everyone and too many mouths to feed. We have to look to the cattle first."

"Those are the men he dismissed?"

Eli nodded. "Six others went straight to the livery. Ransom will give them a fair price for their horses, then they'll go south to New Mexico or Arizona and pick up work. Maybe they'll come back, and maybe they won't. Doesn't matter. There's always men looking for work come spring."

"Ten men. That's about half of your hands."

"That's right," said Clay.

"They required an escort?" asked Kellen.

Clay knocked back half of his whiskey. "Uriah likes to make sure they leave the spread, and he's not in favor of them takin' up with any of the other ranchers."

"Surely that's for them to decide."

Eli laughed. "Funny, but Uriah thinks it's for *him* to decide."

"They know what's expected," Clay said. "They sign an agreement straight off."

"What about those four?" Kellen put a hand over his glass when Eli offered to top it off. "Why didn't they go with the others?"

Eli glanced over at them. He raised his glass in their direction but did not have the salute returned. "They intend to ride out, not take the train. Probably should have left a few weeks ago, but Uriah's been hemmin' and hawin' about how many he could keep. I suppose they thought they were safe from eviction. They've been around longer than some of the others."

"They seem like they might be a little out of sorts with you, Eli."

Clay answered for his brother. "Eli might have promised a couple of them that they'd be stayin' on." His eyes found Renee, and he waved her over. Before she arrived, he said to Eli, "You shouldn't have done that. I don't care that you got Uriah spittin' and pissin' at you, but I couldn't get clear of it. He expects me to keep you from makin' a fool of yourself. Ain't no one I know who can do that."

For the first time since the brothers entered the saloon, Kellen recognized that Eli was not the only one who had been drinking. While Eli Burdick became expansive, almost warm in his expression, Clay just became meaner.

Kellen took another sip of his whiskey. "So you're not here to thank Mr. Jones."

"Thank him?" asked Clay. "For what?"

"It's all over town. He shot Mr. Petit to keep the man from killing your brother." He watched the brothers exchange glances but no words. "I know you know something about what happened yesterday. Eli asked about Petit's room earlier. You expected it to be vacant." Now he saw Clay cast a disagreeable, sideways look at Eli.

"Eli and I were together all day," said Clay. "Neither of us saw Mr. Petit."

"I'm talking about your *other* brother. Isaac."

"Then you don't know what you're talking about. Apparently neither does Jones, if he mentioned Isaac's name. My baby brother hasn't been around for years, thanks to your wife."

Eli blew out a long, weary breath. "Don't pitch your venom at Lorrainey, Clay. She's this man's wife and my old sweetheart."

"She's one of those things," Clay said. He held out his glass while Renee poured whiskey into it. "Be careful. You're spilling as much outside of the glass as in it." Neither Renee nor anyone at the table pointed out that his hand was shaking. Renee finished pouring, tipped the bottle back, and fled. Clay's eyes followed her. "She's jumpy for a whore. Seems like she should be broken in by now."

Kellen had given a great deal of thought to how the evening should unfold, and it seemed to him that there was no better opening than the one Clay had just presented him.

"You mean like Ellen," he said.

Clay's head snapped around. "What did you say?"

"I'm sorry. Did I have it wrong? I meant Emily. I thought you'd want to break Renee in the same as you did Emily. Break. Broken. They're both apt."

Clay pushed his chair back so hard that it tipped over. In a single motion, he was on his feet and drawing his gun from its holster.

The advantage was still Kellen's. He did not trouble himself to get to his feet. He stalled Clay's motion by pointing his long-barreled Colt just below the man's heart. "Put it down, Clay. Easy. On the table. Eli, don't go for your gun. Keep your hands where I can see them. The men right behind you want to see them, too. They'll shoot you in the back and not lose any sleep over it if that's what they have to do. Keep your eyes this way. You don't need to see who they are. I can see them just fine. Trust me. Clay, I'm giving you to three to put the gun down. Sometimes I don't count that high. Take your chances. One."

Clay set his gun on the table.

"Push it over here. Real gentle. Walt? You want to take this away for me?"

"Yes, sir." With no hesitation, Walt moved quickly around the bar and over to the table. He picked up Lightning, the .38 caliber double-action revolver that Clay prized almost as much as his horse. "He'll have a derringer in his boot, Mr. Coltrane."

"Well, I guess we should have that, too. Stay where you are, Clay. Let Walt dig out that derringer. I'll shoot you if you move. Don't test me."

Clay's posture half in and out of the chair was awkward, but he maintained it while Walt fiddled inside his boot until he got his fingers around the derringer and pulled it out.

"Renee, come over here and take Mr. Burdick's derringer from Walt. Have you ever held a pistol like that before?"

"No, Mr. Coltrane. I do all right with my pa's Henry rifle, though."

"Good girl. Step back. Walt, you need to take Eli's gun. Eli, it would be a shame if Walt has to shoot you with your brother's Colt, but I believe he will do it. If he won't, I will."

"What the hell, Coltrane?" Eli said. "I mean, what the *hell*?"

Walt carefully removed the gun from Eli's holster and got out of elbow range.

Kellen nodded toward the bar. "Take them over there, Walt. Wait. Is Eli carrying anything else?"

"Doesn't usually."

"Perhaps we should be sure. Looks like we need more hands here. Raine? How about taking these guns from Walt while he makes sure Eli doesn't have any surprises for us."

Raine came over and took the revolvers. When Walt was finished with Eli, she only gave one of them back.

Kellen kept his eyes on Clay but spoke to Raine. "Why don't you pour Eli another drink? I didn't think it was possible, but he looks as if he needs one."

Keeping the Colt out of Eli's reach, Raine poured from the bottle in front of him and then moved out of the way.

"Thank you," said Kellen. "Sit down, Clay. Someone will put your chair under you."

Behind him, Clay heard his chair being picked up and

pushed forward. When he felt the edge of the seat at the back of his knees, he sat down.

Kellen nodded, satisfied. "All right. Is there anyone who wants to leave? Besides the Burdicks, I mean? This is a good time to speak up." Kellen stood. He kept his gun out but lowered it to his side. He regarded the four ranch hands who accompanied Eli and Clay into the Pennyroyal. "You're free to go if you like. You'll have to leave your guns."

"I'm kinda curious," one of them said. "I'd like to stay."

"Fine, but you still have to hand over your guns."

"We don't work for the Burdicks anymore," another one said. "Didn't they tell you?"

"They told me. Humor me. Turn over your guns. Put them on the floor and kick them this way. Cecilia will collect them." Kellen watched the four men look to one another as though agreement rested with all or none of them. When they shrugged collectively, he knew he had them. They placed their revolvers on the floor and booted them sideways. Cecelia rushed in and scooped them up. At Raine's nod, she put them behind the bar.

"Better," said Kellen. "Charlie? Are you carrying?"

"No, sir." He opened his jacket carefully to show that it was true.

"Jem? What about you and your brothers?"

Jem shook his head. "One of us would have shot the other by now. We don't bring guns to the card table."

Kellen's narrow smile appeared. "And folks say you three boys don't have enough sense to pay attention."

The brothers frowned deeply. Jessop's face was the first to clear, but Jake was the first to chuckle. A moment later Jem joined him. "Sense. Cents," Jessop said. "Good one, Mr. Coltrane."

Mr. Reasoner slowly raised his hand. "A very good one," he said in dry accents. "This foreigner begs to be excused."

Mr. Jones put up his hand. "The government also."

Kellen regarded them and their raised hands a long moment before he shook his head. "No, gentlemen. I like you right there. I'm going to tell everyone a story, and I want you to hear it."

Chapter Sixteen

Kellen backed up to the table behind him and hitched his hip on it. He rested the Peacemaker on his thigh in plain view of Eli and Clay and looked around the room. His gaze stopped on John Paul Jones.

"Mr. Jones. You represent the government's interests. I believe that makes you the best choice for judging these proceedings."

Clay started to come out of his seat, and Kellen put him back in it by lifting the Colt just a hair.

"What do you say, Mr. Jones?"

"This isn't a court. I'm not a judge. You can't—"

"Mr. Jones accepts." Kellen's attention went to Mr. Reasoner. "These men will need some sort of defense. That will be your job."

"It is a ridiculous notion. I am hardly qualified to give these men counsel. I know nothing at all about American jurisprudence."

"And you're already talking like a lawyer." He smiled thinly. "Mr. Reasoner accepts." Kellen's eyes settled on Raine. "Would you please introduce the jury?"

Raine nodded. She wound her way between the tables and touched each man lightly on the shoulder as she said his name. "Dick Faber. Richard Allen. Howard Wheeler. Jack Clifton. Dave Rogers. Harry Sample. Terry McCormick. Paul Reston." She stopped at the end of the bar. "And Matthew Sharp."

"Nine. We really should have twelve. Remind everyone why we don't have twelve."

"John Hood and Scott Pennway are dead. Hank Thompson is missing and presumed to be dead."

"Judge Jones. We need a ruling. Will nine good men suffice?"

"You cannot seriously expect me to sanction this."

Kellen simply shook his head. "Raine, explain to Mr. Jones why he needs to make a decision."

Raine moved away from Matt Sharp's side and put herself in Jones's line of sight. "Some of us think you belong at the table with Eli and Clay. By your own admission, you killed a man yesterday in order to stop him from shooting Isaac Burdick. We heard your explanation, but it doesn't go down well."

"Your deputy was satisfied," said Jones.

"That may be, but he isn't here, is he? What I'm telling you is that you better judge, lest you be judged."

"I believe the correct verse in Matthew is judge not, that ye be not judged."

"It is, but I was quoting Matthew Sharp, not the gospel of."

Kellen chuckled. "Well, Jones?"

"Nine men will be sufficient."

"Good. Are there any other positions to fill?" Kellen put the question to the room at large and waited for an answer.

Jefferson Collins put up his hand to be recognized. "Should have a prosecutor. Last trial we had in Bitter Springs had a prosecutor." There was a general murmur of agreement. A few men nodded. "Moses T. Parker. From Rawlins."

"It would be difficult to get Mr. Parker on such short notice and in this weather."

"Short notice and bad weather have nothing to do with it."

"Why is that, Mr. Collins?"

"Moses T. Parker is dead."

"Is that right?"

Clay slapped the table with the palm of his hand. "That man hanged himself. It's got nothing to do with us one way or the other."

Kellen raised his eyebrows a fraction. "The man's dead, isn't he?"

Clay nodded abruptly.

"I believe that's all Mr. Collins is saying."

"I *know* what he's sayin'." Clay set his narrowed, pale blue eyes on the station agent. "Don't think I don't."

Kellen would not have found fault with Collins for flinching under Clay Burdick's threatening stare, but the older man held his ground and did not blink. "Judge Jones? Do you have something you want to say about Mr. Burdick's behavior?"

Jones stopped stroking his neatly trimmed mustache. He cast a sideways glance at Reasoner. "It would behoove your client to control himself."

Reasoner's cheeks puffed out as he blew out a long breath. "Mr. Burdick. Mr. *Clay* Burdick. It appears that not only are your comments unwelcome, you are not permitted to act in a threatening manner."

"Well done," said Kellen, nodding in turn to Jones and Reasoner. "I believe now that we have established the whereabouts of Parker, Pennway, Thompson, and Hood, we can begin."

Raine cleared her throat loudly enough to draw everyone's attention.

"What is it, Raine?"

"Well, I believe Marshal Sterling should be mentioned here."

"And why is that?"

"Because he was important to the last trial we had in Bitter Springs."

"I never met the marshal."

"He was shot and killed riding out to the Burdick ranch."

Eli pointed a finger at Reasoner. "Say something."

Reasoner bristled. "I am quite certain I do not know what you expect me to say."

"Tell Coltrane it was an accident."

"It was an accident," said Reasoner.

Eli set his jaw. "Sterling was mistaken for a rustler."

"Oh, I see." Reasoner addressed Jones. "Apparently this Sterling fellow was mistaken for a cattle thief. His demise has nothing at all to do with why we are assembled this evening."

Jones swiveled in his chair to speak directly to Raine. "Mrs. Coltrane, you will please refrain from speaking out of turn. Comments from the gallery must naturally be limited."

Raine accepted the rebuke graciously, holding her sardonic smile in check.

Kellen asked the judge, "You agree we can begin?"

Jones nodded.

"I believe I am allowed to say my piece first," said Kellen.

"You have the gun," Jones said.

"So I do." Kellen tapped the Colt once against his thigh. "I am Kellen Coltrane, representing the interests of Bitter Springs in the matter of the recent deaths of Emily Ransom, George Weyman, and Nat Church." Kellen observed the stirring in the saloon in response to this last name. "Let me be clear that this Nat Church is not the man you might have read about in the dime novels. He was a former U.S. marshal, a widower, and most recently, a hired gun. Mr. Collins, everyone here might not know what happened to Nat Church while he was a passenger on the U.P. line. It would be a help if you would tell us what you know about Mr. Nat Church, you being an employee of the Union Pacific and privy to official information."

Jefferson Collins got to his feet. He straightened his shoulders and cleared his throat. His Adam's apple bobbed when he swallowed hard. "Nat Church was traveling to Bitter Springs when he met a bad end in the number six coach. He was stabbed when he boarded after a stop at Rocky Hill. He didn't make it to Westerville before he died of his wounds. The company wired me about the incident because Mr. Kellen Coltrane was with Nat Church when he died, and Mr. Coltrane had announced his intention to the conductor that he was getting off the train in Bitter Springs. As a company man, it was my duty to keep an eye out, report anything suspicious to the U.P. detectives."

"And did you make a report?"

"No, sir. There wasn't anything to tell them." Collins made eye contact with his audience. "You all know my grandsons, and you all know they favor their granny when it comes to sniffing out what's suspicious. There's no better recommendation than having those boys vouch for your character, and they vouched for Mr. Coltrane. They told me right off that he was sweet on the Widder Berry, and ain't that turned out to be the truth?"

Laughter, some elbow nudging, and murmurs of agreement greeted this last statement.

"Well, thank you, Mr. Collins."

Collins nodded, started to sit, but popped up again. "And they just told me the other day that Mr. Coltrane is real good at speculating. Seemed like something the nine good men should know." With that, he dropped into his chair.

Kellen tapped his gun again. "I was indeed sitting with Nat Church when he died. He could not name the person who gutted him, but he did give me some things before he passed to help me learn the answer for myself." He motioned to Raine to step forward. "You all know Lorraine Berry Coltrane, the owner of the Pennyroyal Saloon and Hotel. Raine, you had special knowledge of Mr. Church's purpose in coming to Bitter Springs. Explain that, please."

As though she were taking the witness stand, Raine moved from the bar to Mr. Jones's side. She did not try to hide the revolver she was carrying. It was clearly visible in her right hand resting against her green-and-white-striped sateen gown. The Colt's four-and-one-half-inch barrel pointed at the floor. Raine's finger remained on the trigger.

"I answered an advertisement placed by Mr. Church in the Chicago *Times-Herald*. He presented himself as a gun for hire, a reputable former lawman with experience in settling disputes and the organization of responsible town committees."

Clay Burdick snorted. "That's just fancy vigilante talk. Tell them, Reasoner. Do your job. You see what's goin' on here, don't you?"

"I do indeed, and I find it as disturbing as it is distasteful."

"Then do something about it." Clay pointed his lawyer to the judge. "Tell *him*."

Reasoner looked sideways at Jones. "These proceedings are naught but a farce. I believe this is what is called vigilante justice, which is to say that justice cannot be served."

"Your point is noted," said Jones. "But they have the guns."

Kellen nodded. "Excellent ruling, Judge. Go on, Raine."

"I expressed interest in Mr. Church's services. There had been a number of deaths associated with my sister's trial that I believed deserved investigating. I was particularly interested in how the Burdicks might be involved."

Clay swore and jabbed his brother. "*You* say something."

Eli shook his head slowly, leaned back, and rested his folded arms on his chest.

"She was never your woman, Eli. She despises you. She always has."

"Shut up," Eli said. "Let her talk."

Raine seized her opportunity when Clay was surprised into silence. "Mr. Church accepted my offer and was on his way here to finalize our agreement. His trip would have been without incident except someone else read at least some of our correspondence. Mr. Church's arrival was anticipated by someone other than me, and he was murdered to keep him out of Bitter Springs."

Kellen raised his free hand to quiet the saloon. "Thank you. Stay where you are because we will need to hear more from you in a moment, but for now, I would like everyone to hear from Walter Mangold. Walt?"

Walt set the revolver he had taken from Eli on the table between Howard Wheeler and Jack Clifton. Visibly nervous, he wiped his damp palms on his trousers. "Yes, sir. Do I tell folks about the letters now?"

"Yes. Tell them just what you told me this morning."

"Well, Mrs. Coltrane—she was the Widder Berry then—trusted me to take her letters to Mr. Collins at the station. I was happy to do it for her, but Emily Ransom took it in her head that it would be a help if *she* took the letters. I didn't see the harm, so I let her deliver letters and packages and such. It

wasn't only the things the widder gave me, but also the things guests asked me to post for them."

Mr. Reasoner put up his hand. "I see where this is going, and poor Miss Ransom is not able to defend herself. How do we know Mr. Mangold is not blaming her for something he did?"

Kellen pointed to Mr. Collins. "We need to hear from you again."

Mr. Collins stood. "Most everything that came for posting from the Pennyroyal was delivered by Miss Ransom. Sometimes a guest would bring his own letters to post. Mr. Petit was particular about his photographs, for example. Most of the time he liked to put them in my hands himself."

Reasoner spoke up after the station agent sat. "Mrs. Coltrane indicated that someone read her correspondence. If we can believe what is being said, we now know that at least three people had the letters in their hands: Mr. Mangold, Miss Ransom, and Mr. Collins."

Frowning deeply, Walter rocked forward on the balls of his feet. "Mr. Coltrane won't say it. I don't suppose other folks want to say it either, but everyone knows I don't read so well. Mr. Clay used to make fun of me regular about it. Mr. Eli, too, if he was in a mood to kick someone."

Reasoner threw up both hands and sat back in his chair. He stared hard at the men he was charged with defending and shook his head slowly.

"Mr. Collins can read just fine," said Clay. "Say something about *him*."

Mr. Reasoner rolled his eyes.

Kellen said, "Even more important than who read the letters is what that person did with the information. No one is saying that Emily Ransom or Mr. Collins murdered Nat Church."

Jefferson Collins jumped to his feet. "And I do *not* read anyone's mail."

Kellen said, "Judge. A ruling please."

Jones sighed heavily. "Mr. Collins does not read anyone's mail."

The station agent eased himself back into his chair, and

Kellen continued. "Raine, you recently learned that Emily Ransom had a secret admirer. Will you tell us about that?"

"Emily was keeping company with Clay Burdick."

"That's a goddamn lie," said Clay. "Where the hell is Dan Sugar? Why isn't the real law here tonight?"

"Deputy Sugar was not invited," Kellen said. "What would his contribution be? People have always told me that you and Eli are the real law in Bitter Springs."

"Us? If someone said it was us, they meant it was Uriah."

Eli said, "You probably want to stop talkin', Clay."

"Why? No one else is speakin' up. You're not." He jerked his chin at Reasoner. "He's not. You know Emily never spoke to me if she could help it. You've said as much yourself."

Eli shrugged.

"Where's your proof?" Clay asked Raine.

"In good time, Clay." She spoke to her audience. "You should take into account how naïve our Emily was. She was a harmless flirt, encouraged by most of you because she made you feel important. Some of you might think she had the good sense to stay away from Clay and Eli because my sister was her friend and, well, because they are the Burdicks. To Emily's way of thinking, though, she was showing good sense by keeping it from everyone, including her family. Keeping it a secret and hiding it are really two different things, and while Emily didn't say a word, there was at least one person who noticed her attachment to Clay Burdick. Sue?"

A harsh, discordant sound rose from the piano when Sue stood and used the keyboard to brace herself. As startled by the noise as anyone else in the saloon, she jumped away from the piano and quickly tucked her trembling hands in the folds of her skirt. Her eyes darted nervously around the room until they rested on Raine.

"DoIsaymypiecenow?"

Raine nodded. "Just like you told me earlier. But slowly, so everyone can understand you. Charlie, maybe you could stand a little closer to Sue."

Charlie stepped up to Sue's side and placed a hand at the

small of her back. "Ain't no one goin' to bother you. Say what you have to say."

Sue took a deep breath and released it in a single gust. "Most evenings Emily and I left the Pennyroyal together. I'd walk her home and then go to my own because that was the easiest. Sometimes Walt came along. If Charlie was around, he would escort both of us." She looked at him. "Isn't that right?"

"Yes, it is."

"I got to noticing that some nights Emily would take longer doing her chores. She'd tell me to go on by myself and most times I did because she would just dawdle if I waited around. I figured she was probably wanting time alone with someone special same as I was wanting time with Charlie." Sue's hand flew to her mouth. Her face flushed pink.

"It's all right, Sue," said Raine. "It's no secret to us how you feel about Charlie. Go on."

"Itjustcametomeoneeveningthat—" She stopped, took another deep breath, and began again. "It just came to me one evening that Emily took her time on the same nights Mr. Clay Burdick was in town. I thought that was plenty peculiar, and I did think I could be making something out of nothing, so I teased her about it. She called me flat-out crazy, and that was the end of it between her and me. I don't think I ever brought it up again, but I noticed it just the same, and when Emily disappeared with the whiskey drummer—Mr. Weyman, I mean—I figured I was flat-out crazy to think she was ever sweet on Mr. Clay Burdick."

Clay snorted. "Flat-out crazy is right. I never met up with Emily Ransom. I don't wait around for women."

Kellen ignored Clay's outburst. "Did you ever see Clay and Emily alone?"

"No, sir. I didn't see them, but I did overhear them once. Way back in September it was. Right here, behind the Pennyroyal. I went looking for Emily, and when I couldn't find her inside, I opened the back door. That's when I heard them talking. I didn't hear the words exactly. I didn't want to. I waited in the kitchen until she came back in, and I pretended I didn't know that she had been talking to Mr. Burdick. I could tell she was angry, so I thought she'd given him a piece of her mind."

"If you didn't see Clay, how can you be certain he was with Emily? Why couldn't it have been Eli?"

"I saw Phantom. There's no mistaking Mr. Clay's horse."

"Thank you, Sue," said Kellen. "You can sit down now." His attention shifted from his witness to the judge. "Since there already has been mention of Clay Burdick's horse, I want to add that on the night George Weyman and Emily Ransom disappeared, two people saw Phantom behind the Pennyroyal."

Clay gave the table a shove. "That's a lie!"

Jones pointed to Clay. "Enough."

Clay huffed loudly, but he did not challenge Jones.

Kellen went on. "No one but Clay Burdick rides Phantom." He waited for the wave of agreement to roll through the saloon. "In summary, we have testimony that Emily and Clay were meeting secretly, that Emily delivered correspondence between Raine and Nat Church to the station, and that on the evening the whiskey drummer and Emily went missing, Clay Burdick was in town."

Mr. Collins stood again. "I'd like to say something else." When he got a nod from Kellen and Jones, he went on. "Emily came by regular to check for the hotel's mail. It used to be Walt I could set my clock by, but about six months ago, it was Emily who dropped in. She wasn't steady in her time the way Walt was, but I could depend on seeing her."

Kellen said, "Now we know that Emily also picked up correspondence from Nat Church. That circles the wagons. It is my contention, Judge, that Emily read the letters between the parties and reported what was written to Clay Burdick. This gave Mr. Burdick all the information he needed to stop Mr. Church from reaching Bitter Springs."

"It's all lies," said Clay. He jabbed a finger at Reasoner again. "Seems like you should be telling them it's all lies."

Reasoner rubbed the underside of his chin. "It does seem as though you are arriving at unwarranted conclusions, Mr. Coltrane. This wagon circle of yours is not as tight as you would have us believe."

"That's right," Clay said. "The Sioux Nation could ride through all the holes it's got."

Kellen sighed. "There is some evidence that places Mr. Burdick with Emily Ransom around the time of her death. I have hesitated to produce it out of respect for Miss Ransom."

Clay turned his accusing finger on Kellen. "You haven't shown it because it doesn't exist. Just like those two witnesses who say they saw my horse behind the Pennyroyal. You didn't produce either one of them. And why is this all about me anyway? Wouldn't be the first time someone mistook me for Eli. I don't hear his name being brought up."

Kellen raised an eyebrow at Eli. "Are you dissatisfied that your brother is receiving all of the attention?"

"Suits me fine."

"Do you want to say anything in his defense?"

"Nothing comes to mind."

"Do you want to say anything that supports the case being made against him?"

Eli showed his thoughtful side, scratching just behind his ear. "That would make things real difficult for me, wouldn't it?" he said at last. "Seems like the Burdicks are always getting tarred with the same brush. A man in this family can't have a reputation of his own for the one that swallows him up."

"Oh, I think you might be overstating it, Eli. I'm fairly certain you have a reputation separate from your family."

Eli nodded slowly. He pointed to his empty glass and the bottle in front of him. "May I?"

"Of course."

Eli poured a drink and threw it back. He set down the glass. "I figure the best thing for me to do is hang my hat on the fifth."

Clay glared at him. He had to raise his voice above the sudden burst of chatter. "What the hell's that mean? You going to help me or not?"

John Paul Jones used the empty tumbler in front of him as a gavel and brought silence back to the saloon. "Mr. Eli Burdick is saying he will not speak against you because he has the right not to incriminate himself."

"Is that what you're sayin', Eli?"

"It is."

Clay drew back his fist. The gun Kellen leveled at his head stayed his arm. His fist remained raised and full of promise for a few seconds before he finally lowered it.

Raine waited for Kellen to rest his gun before she prompted him. "You were telling us about some evidence."

"So I was. Will you get it, please?"

Raine nodded and left Jones's side to go behind the bar. Everyone followed her progress, and when she stood in front of the large mirror with her back to her audience, she saw mostly curiosity in the eyes turned on her. Raine set down the revolver long enough to lift the bottom edge of the mirror away from the wall. She caught the photographs as they began to fall. Holding them close to her chest, she picked up the Colt, and returned to her place beside the judge.

"What's that she's carrying?" asked Clay. "I want to see what she's got." He started to come out of his chair, but it was Eli who pushed him back this time, not Kellen's gun. "Damn it! If it's about me, I have a right to see what she's holding."

Raine leveled her gaze on Clay, but she spoke to everyone. "I believe all of you know that Mr. Petit and Mr. Reasoner were the ones who found Emily's body. You might not know that Mr. Petit took photographs. He gave several to Deputy Sugar. None of the photographs would have been a comfort to the family, so he kept the rest. After a promising start, the photographs that he gave Dan Sugar ultimately proved to be unhelpful."

She glanced at the Davis brothers. "Would any of you like to say anything about those photographs?"

Jem spoke up. "Sugar showed us the pictures. Turned out there was nothin' about them that could help us find Emily's killer."

Raine continued, her attention on Clay once again. "There were other photographs, though, far more interesting in composition and perspective, that Mr. Petit did not show to Deputy Sugar. I can only guess at his reasons. Since Mr. Petit cannot answer for himself, our nine good men will have to draw their own conclusions. I am holding three photographs for them to review."

Clay shot out of his chair. This time he ignored the gun Kellen pointed at him. In a single motion, he braced his arms on the table and vaulted it. Kellen had to lean away to avoid having the Colt kicked out of his hand. He recovered quickly, took aim, but didn't fire.

No one else did either, even when Clay stumbled over his own feet as he was brought short by all the weapons drawn in his direction. He caught himself, straightened, and threw up his hands. Every member of the jury had a gun pointed at his chest. Even Raine had her Colt raised, and her hand was as steady as the others. Glancing over his shoulder, he saw Kellen's revolver aimed at his back. He kept his hands in the air. After facing forward again, he didn't move.

"Well, Clay," said Kellen, "I hope you appreciate your jury's restraint."

"And mine," said Raine.

"And my wife's."

Clay gritted his teeth. "I want to see them."

"Why?" asked Kellen. "Haven't you seen at least one like them before? I have to believe Mr. Petit shared one with you. You would have demanded proof when he tried to blackmail you. Eli? I swear you look as if you could use another drink, and you might want to pour one for Clay. He'd probably appreciate it."

There was nothing left in the bottle after Eli poured two drinks. He pushed Clay's glass across the table. "I suppose they'll let you put your hands down to get it."

"I don't want a goddamn drink."

Kellen motioned to the jury and Raine. "Put your guns down. Clay, take your seat."

Clay lowered his hands, but he didn't retreat. He jerked his square chin at the table where Jones and Reasoner were sitting. "Say something! You better goddamn say something. Uriah will take you out himself for this. Didn't I say he would? You're supposed to be watching out for our interests. Everyone's got it in their mind it's about that whore Emily Ransom and the whiskey drummer. Seems like folks are forgetting Sterling and Pennway and all the others. You don't hear them talkin' about the water, do you? Well, I might have something to say about that. Something to say about John Hood and Hank Thompson, too, and the money you got sitting in the Cattlemen's Trust. Have you been thinking about that while you've been sitting there? We have an agreement. You said you'd take care of Petit. Well, he ain't cared for if she's got photographs like she says she does."

Frowning in unison, Jones and Reasoner each turned his head to regard the other.

Eli tossed back his drink.

Kellen stood.

Raine pressed the photographs more tightly against her breast.

Nine good men did not flinch.

Clay Burdick's pale blue eyes cut between Jones and Reasoner.

No one breathed. No one stirred.

And no one who saw what happened next doubted that it was the silence that moved Clay Burdick past the edge of reason.

Head down, shoulders bunched around his neck, he attacked Jones and Reasoner. Some folks said he pawed the floor before he charged at them like a mad bull.

Pushing the table forward, Jones leapt to his feet. He snapped his wrist. His hand closed over the hilt of a four-inch blade. His throw was fluid, the trajectory of the knife a blur.

The flight of the lead ball from Reasoner's palm pistol could also be seen, but no one was looking for it. Reasoner never left his chair. The ball shattered the empty bottle on the table in front of Eli. Eli staggered to his feet and fell sideways against Walt.

Momentum kept Clay upright and headed in the direction of Jones and Reasoner. For five full steps he was oblivious to the blade plunged deeply into his chest or the hilt sticking out of it. He overturned the table and spread his arms high and wide as he began to fall.

Walter braced himself to take Eli's weight but never bore the full brunt of it. Eli tore the gun from his hand and took aim at Reasoner. Raine moved out of the way until she was backed up against the bar. Men who were on the periphery of Eli's line of sight pushed themselves outside of it.

Reasoner dove for the floor. His shoulder collided with Clay, who was on his way down. He was knocked off course. Instead of dodging the bullet, he met it head on.

Kellen turned his gun on Eli. "Put your weapon on the table, Eli. Mr. Jones. Just because I'm occupied doesn't mean you should move. There are nine other men here who will feel obliged to shoot you if you do."

"And one woman," said Raine.

"And one woman."

Eli stared rather blankly at the gun in his hand while he wavered on his feet. He frowned slightly, shaking his head, and placed the gun on the table. Walt quickly seized it.

"Take a seat, Eli," said Kellen. "Walt, you give Eli plenty of room. I can't believe he's still standing. Aren't you about ready to drop, Eli?"

Eli did just that, barely catching the chair that Cecilia shoved under him. Walt pushed the table close enough so that when Eli's head dropped, there was something almost as hard in place to catch it.

Kellen looked around the saloon. His shrug was meant as an apology to the room at large. "Sometimes there's no accounting for the way a story ends." He waved Raine over to his side. She came carrying the revolver and the photographs, and when she stood next to him, he placed a hand lightly on her shoulder. "You talk to them."

Raine looked over the members of the jury. "In the matter of the death of Emily Ransom, what do you have to say for Clay Burdick?"

Nine men spoke with a single voice. "Guilty."

"And in the murder attempt against Eli Burdick by Mr. Alexander Reasoner, what do you say?"

"Guilty."

"And in the murder of Mr. Reasoner, what do you have to say for Eli Burdick?"

"Not guilty by reason of self-defense."

"And in the death of Clay Burdick, what do you have to say for Mr. John Paul Jones?"

"Guilty."

Jones drew himself up stiffly. "It was self-defense. He was coming after me. You all saw him. None of you tried to stop him. He wanted to kill me."

"He had no weapon," said Raine.

"I'm telling you, he was coming after me."

"Was he?" Kellen asked. "It wasn't entirely clear to me, nor I suspect to anyone else, who he was charging. I speak for all of us when I say I appreciate your clarification. I thought Reasoner's shot might have been meant for Clay, not Eli, but it wasn't like that at all." He smiled, but there was no humor in it. "You each needed to get rid of a brother. You couldn't have Eli start talking once Clay stopped. You and Reasoner were partners, working together from the beginning."

The saloon fell quiet as John Paul Jones took a moment to look every man with a gun pointed in his direction in the eye. What he saw made him sink slowly into his chair.

Raine looked up at Kellen, her voice gentle but clear. "I think Nat Church would agree with what you said earlier. Sometimes there's no accounting for the way a story ends." She rose on tiptoe and whispered in his ear. "Even when you're the one writing it."

Epilogue

When Judge Abel Darlington returned to Rawlins after presiding over the trials in Bitter Springs, he showed everyone in the courthouse his signed copy of *Nat Church and the Chinese Box.* In the event that someone construed the novel as a ten-cent bribe, he was careful to explain that he had accepted the gift when the trials were over, not before they began. Regardless, he told his clerk, as satisfied as he was to finally pass sentence on John Paul Jones and Uriah and Eli Burdick and oversee the apprehension and incarceration of Isaac Burdick, and as pleasing as it was to take possession of *Nat Church and the Chinese Box* with the author's bold signature and personal inscription on the cover, the most gratifying aspect of his visit to Bitter Springs was quietly changing the status of a certain marriage from fiction to fact.

The judge slid his copy of the Nat Church adventure across the desk for his admiring clerk to study. "The author told me afterward that my signature on that marriage record was infinitely more valuable to him than his would ever be to me. You should have seen the way he looked at his wife when he said it. I can't help but think well of a man like that."

The clerk nodded, mildly distracted as he picked up the dime novel and examined the cover. "I'm sure, Judge, but tell me, what is Nat Church really like?"

Many of the passengers on No. 38 of the Union Pacific line found it a pleasant diversion to wonder aloud about the couple in the private Pullman coach. As the couple rarely left their luxury accommodations when the train stopped on route to New York, there was little opportunity to observe them. The assistant conductors and porters were polite in taking inquiries but remained maddeningly mum. Someone who had boarded the train in Rawlins remembered a crowd of people at the station in Bitter Springs and the crowd still being there when the train pulled away. He thought that was where the couple had gotten on because folks on the platform waved hats and handkerchiefs, and two little fellas ran alongside the train until they just plum tuckered out.

The man from Rawlins couldn't tell anyone much about Bitter Springs except that he heard the town had a decent hotel and might be the first in the territory to get a government dam and reservoir. A couple of farmers were interested in what he had to say about the water, but it wasn't information that appealed to the gossips and speculators.

Some passengers remembered there was an unusually long stop when the train reached Westerville. It went well past the twenty minutes generally allowed for filling the water tanks, and the passengers who got off to eat at the station restaurant were afforded the unexpected treat of ordering, eating, and digesting their food before the call to board forced them to leave their tables. The stop became worth noting when no one remembered seeing the couple in the restaurant, although many people recalled seeing them leave their coach. Some folks said they walked arm in arm toward the town. Others said it was merely shoulder to shoulder on account of the cold. One passenger repeated an exchange she overheard between two porters: The couple went straightaway to the graveyard.

The No. 38 train rolled on with all of the questions that followed unanswered.

Kellen put down his pen, leaned back in his chair, and stretched his arms wide. It was indeed a luxury to spread his arms and unfold his legs and not have to consider the comfort of his fellow passengers. "I could swing a cat in here and not hit anyone."

Raine did not look up from her reading. "Hmm."

He grinned, watching her. She was curled in the corner of a thickly padded upholstered bench, close enough to the stove to feel its pleasant heat but not so close that she did not need a shawl over her nightgown. It lay loosely across her shoulders; she absently stroked the fringe where it clustered just below the knot between her breasts. A small vertical crease appeared between her eyebrows as she slipped the page she had been reading under the stack of papers in her lap and concentrated on the one on top.

"Maybe two cats," he said. "Different directions."

"Hmm."

"You haven't heard a word I've said."

"I'm pretending not to hear. Let me read."

Kellen supposed he should be gratified she was engrossed, but then he was struck by the thought that perhaps she was pretending that as well. He observed her for several long minutes before he finally surrendered to niggling doubt.

"I need to hear it from you, Raine. Is it good enough?"

His question brought her head up sharply. "Good enough? Don't you know?"

He shook his head, gave her a slightly sheepish smile. "I never know."

"It's better than good enough, Kellen. It might be your finest story yet. I can say that—"

Kellen put out a hand to stop her. " 'Better than good enough' was good enough. I have modest expectations. I don't need to hear more than that."

"You interrupted me, and now you have to listen. This is going to sell as fast as Mrs. Sterling's cherry pie on Washington's birthday."

"Fast is good. More would be better."

"Naturally it will be more. Mrs. Sterling only makes a dozen pies."

He laughed. "All right. That is an excellent distinction. Thank you."

Raine lifted the pages briefly. "Will your father read this?"

"Once it's published."

"You won't show it to him before that?"

"We'll reach New York before we get to New Haven. I'd like to put it in my publisher's hands first."

"You could show it to your father and then send it to New York. You usually send your work by post, don't you?"

"Usually, yes."

"Then . . ."

Kellen shook his head. "You haven't met my father, Raine, so you can't know, but you will meet him, and then I believe you'll understand. He has always wanted something for me that I've never wanted for myself. I couldn't possibly disappoint him as frequently or as deeply as I do if that were not the case."

"But to call yourself the black sheep . . . you've never been that."

"An overstatement, but not as large as you might think. I write as Max McCartney for a reason, Raine. My father teaches Homer, and he frequently reminds me that Nat Church can never be mistaken for Ulysses."

"Nat Church is heroic. So are you."

He grinned again. "You're going to say that to my father, aren't you?"

"Yes, and more besides."

"Then I can honestly tell you that I have never looked more forward to Sunday dinner with all my family present."

Raine pressed her lips together. Humor edged out censure. "You shouldn't expect that I will be disagreeable. I merely intend to hold firm to my opinions."

"Well, that will certainly win the admiration of my mother and sisters."

"Your father?"

"Grudging respect."

"And your brothers?"

"Rob will want to marry someone just like you, and Michael will wish he had."

Laughing, she waved him and his comments away. Her eyes returned to the page.

Kellen clasped his hands behind his head as he slid lower into his chair. "Did you know that some passengers believe we're European royalty?"

She sighed. "You're not going to allow me to read anymore this evening, are you?" When he shook his head, Raine set the pages aside. "European royalty? Who told you that?"

"One of the porters. Hayes, I think. The soft-spoken one."

"Hmm. Do we have a particular country to call our own?"

"Holland is popular. Denmark also."

"I'm sure they're both lovely, but I fancied the rumor that we were Annie Oakley and Frank Butler."

"It would be unusual for them to travel without the rest of the show."

Raine's eyes narrowed. "You've *met* them?"

"I have. I traveled with Buffalo Bill's Wild West Show for a spell." He dropped his folded hands to his lap. "Let's see, that was about a dozen stories ago. *Nat Church and the*—"

"Shooting Contest," said Raine. "I know. I read it. Honestly, Kellen, you might have told me before now. What was she like?"

"Tiny."

"And Mr. Butler?"

"Taller."

She rolled her eyes. "I'll read the book again."

"That would be more instructive than relying on my memory."

Raine snorted. "You don't forget anything." She cocked her head and regarded him for so long and with such intensity that he actually squirmed.

"What is it?"

"Did Miss Oakley and Mr. Butler teach you to shoot?"

Kellen relaxed. "Well, I could shoot a gun before I met them, but they showed me the fast draw and how to hit what I was aiming at more often than I missed."

"And what about picking the locks at the Pennyroyal? It seemed to me that you were in and out of the rooms at will."

"*Nat Church and the Best Gang.* Tutoring compliments of a Chicago hotel thief."

"I know you're a better card player than you let on. I watched you lose when you could have won, and that isn't easy to do."

"Hmm. *Nat Church and the Frisco Fancy.*"

"You sent a telegraph message to your brother without Mr. Collins's help."

"Morse Code. I learned that writing *Nat Church and the Sleeping Detective.*"

Raine nodded slowly. "I also thought you were unusually confident when it came to orchestrating the trial at the Pennyroyal."

"My brother is a lawyer."

"Somehow I don't think that accounts for it. I'm torn between *Nat Church and the Committee of Vigilance* and *Nat Church and the Hanging at Harrisonville.*"

Humor tugged at Kellen's narrow smile. "I might have learned a thing or two while I was researching those stories."

Raine fell quiet, thinking. "Researching them? I think you lived them. When you stepped off the train in Bitter Springs, did you know that you would have to call on every one of those experiences?"

"When I stepped off the train, I didn't know there were two guns in my bag. I didn't know there was a redheaded woman waiting for me or that a killer was sleeping down the hall from my room and that another hired gun would take up the room next door. What I did know was that a man who called himself Nat Church died sitting beside me. It seemed to me that I should find out why."

"I don't think anyone else could have done what you did for Bitter Springs, but if you'd told me at the outset that you wrote dime novels, that you were Nat Church's creator, I would have sent you away."

"It's my recollection that you tried."

"You wouldn't go."

"Couldn't."

Raine drew her knees toward her chest and hugged them. "You made them all turn on one another. I never thought I would see a Burdick give up another Burdick."

"It was the interview with Uriah that made me think it was possible. I watched him set his sons against each other."

"I saw that same thing over the years," she said. "But I never realized there was a way to take advantage of it. That was your doing."

He shrugged. "I had a lot of help. Ellen's jury. Walt. Sue Hage. Mr. Collins. Everyone came forward. And then there was Mr. Jones's testimony at Uriah's trial. Judge Darlington could not get him to *stop* talking."

Raine remembered. Jones had hoped to save himself by implicating Uriah in every one of the murders that he or Reasoner had committed. They had all been ordered, and Jones offered his bank deposits as proof that he had been paid. As it happened, Mr. Webb at the Cattlemen's Trust kept very good records.

Uriah hanged, but then so did Jones. Eli, with his knowledge of the murder contracts, was found guilty as a conspirator and followed Isaac to prison escorted by a half-dozen U.S. marshals. There was no one left to come to his rescue. The vast Burdick holdings were scheduled to be sold at auction. The interested parties were mostly local ranchers and Eastern speculators. First, though, there had to be a new appraisal by a legitimate government surveyor. Ted Rush made sure everyone heard him say that Uriah Burdick was spinning in his unmarked grave.

Raine smoothed her nightgown over her knees and tucked her bare toes under the hem. "Nat Church made a good choice when he found you on that train."

"I don't know that he could have gone any farther. Or maybe he stopped when he did because he saw what I was reading and liked the irony of it."

"Or maybe he just liked the looks of you. I did."

Kellen's narrow, secretive smile played about his mouth. "You thought I was a shootist."

"You made certain I thought that, and I can own that it was a comfort in the beginning, but I also came to realize you were a good man, and that was infinitely more reassuring. I trusted you would do what was right even if it wasn't what I wanted."

"I am certainly glad that you kept that last part to yourself. I would have folded as quickly as Jem Davis with a pair of sevens."

Chuckling, Raine left the bench in favor of Kellen's lap. She nestled, content in the cradle he made for her. "You would have bluffed. You *did* bluff. I gave you any number of opportunities to tell me something about you that I didn't know, and you never once offered that you were Nat Church."

He regarded her with an arched eyebrow.

"You know what I mean," she said. "I had to arrive at the truth on my own. That's when you finally folded. I think everyone else in Bitter Springs had already seen your hand."

"I gave away a lot of copies of *Nat Church and the Chinese Box* to make certain they did."

"It was an inspired move. Masterly, really. You packed the saloon."

He shook his head. "*You* brought the men in, Raine. I only needed to give them a reason to trust that I could end it."

"You know that some of them will never be convinced that you're not Nat Church."

"Just as long as there's no confusion in your mind."

She nodded, smiling softly. Her eyes took him in. "Oh, there's none. I know the fundamental difference."

"And that is?"

"Nat Church might save the day, but he never wins the woman." She leaned in, whispered against his ear. "Or wins her over. Take me to bed, Mr. Coltrane."

Their narrow berth wasn't far, but his writing desk was closer. They pushed the working manuscript aside. Pages fell, scattered. Some slid under the upholstered bench. Others fluttered to the floor under the chair. Several more slipped under the stove, where the heat toasted the edges and curled the corners. One page, the first page, traveled farther than any of the others, resting for a time on the lid of one of Kellen's trunks before finally falling into the sliver of space behind it.

While all the other pages were later collected and reordered, much of that accomplished between laughter and lovemaking, neither Kellen nor Raine could put their hands on the first one. Their search for it, which occupied them now and again between Chicago and New York, came to nothing, and although Kellen regretted the loss of the page, especially as he was forced to rewrite it, he did not regret how he had come to lose it.

An ending with Raine cradled in his arms would always be more satisfying than any beginning without her.

Turn the page for a preview of

Jo Goodman's next novel

TRUE TO THE LAW

October 1889
Bitter Springs, Wyoming

Finn Collins decided he would stare at Priscilla Taylor's braid until his eyes crossed. The braid, perfectly plaited with every hair still in place at the end of the day, rested along the line of Priscilla's ramrod straight backbone. Priscilla never slumped on her bench. She never fidgeted. The braid never moved except when Priscilla raised her hand to answer a question; then it slid ever so slightly to one side and the tip curled like an apostrophe. Or maybe a comma. Those punctuation marks were suspiciously similar, except one was high and one was low. It was no wonder he got them confused.

"Finn?"

Finn did not stir. In point of fact, he did not hear his name being called. He sat with his elbows on the desk, his head cupped in his hands. His chin and cheeks rested warmly between his palms. His eyes had begun to relax. Priscilla had two braids today. Two ramrods. And when she raised her hand to show everyone that she knew the answer to something no one cared about—like the name of the fifth president—the tail of one braid curled in a comma, the other in an apostrophe.

"Carpenter Addison Collins."

Finn came to attention with the jerkiness of someone suddenly roused from a deep sleep. His elbows slid off the edge of the desk, his head snapped up, and his feet, which had been swinging in a lazy rhythm under the bench, kicked spasmodically before slamming hard to the floor. He blinked widely. There was only one person who called him by all three of his proper names.

"Gran?"

Thirteen of Finn's classmates were moved to laughter. Finn's brother, Rabbit, was an exception. He glanced over his shoulder at Finn and rolled his eyes. Somehow he managed to convey disapproval *and* embarrassment. Just like Granny.

Finn felt color rush into his face and knew his cheeks were glowing like hot coals. If someone poked at him, he was sure he would burst into flames. For himself, he didn't mind so much. In some ways it would be a relief. More concerning was that no one would be safe from the conflagration. Priscilla's braids would take to the fire like a candlewick. She'd whip her head around then, he was certain of it, and shoot tongues of fire at anyone who tried to save her. Stupid girl. She would burn down the school. Probably the town. It would be his fault because no one ever blamed girls. To save the school, the town, to save everyone, really, he had to act. The solution was clear.

He yanked hard on Priscilla's offending braid.

She squealed. It was a sound no one had ever heard her make before, but everyone knew how a piglet sounded when it was in want of its mother's teat. Priscilla squealed like that, and all eyes shifted to her. A moment later, so did the laughter.

Priscilla swiveled on her bench seat, slate in hand, and swung it at Finn's head. Finn ducked instinctively, but he was never in any danger. Miss Morrow stepped in and stayed Priscilla's arm. Out of the corner of his eye, Finn saw her calmly remove the slate from Priscilla's hand and set it gently on the desk. She had a small, quiet smile for Priscilla, one that was more understanding than quelling. For the class, she effectively used a single raised eyebrow to stopper the laughter. It was

Finn for whom she had words. He held his breath, waiting for the pronouncement.

"Finn, you will stay after the others leave today."

Finn kept his head down, his eyes averted. He knew better than to look pleased. He kept his voice small, penitent. "Yes, ma'am."

"Is there something you want to say to Priscilla?"

Now Finn looked up and stared squarely at Priscilla's back. "Sure is. Prissy, that pigtail is nuthin' but a temptation. And now that I heard you squeal, well, giving it a yank now and again is a thing that can't be resisted." He risked a glance at Miss Morrow. For reasons he did not entirely understand, she looked as if she was going to choke on her spit. "That's all I got to say, ma'am."

Tru Morrow covered her mouth with the back of her hand and politely cleared her throat. "We will speak later, and you can write your apology."

Finn's narrow shoulders slumped. Staying after school with Miss Morrow was nothing but a pleasure. Writing, whether it was an apology to Priscilla or "I will raise my hand before I speak" twenty times, well, that cast a long shadow on the pleasure of Miss Morrow's company. His pap would tell him that a man has to pay for his pleasure, and it seemed to Finn that his pap was proved right again. He tucked that thought away so he could use it when Pap asked him to account for his behavior today. There was nothing like flattering a man with the rightness of his thinking to stay another lecture on the same subject. Granny would be a little trickier. She wasn't impressed by flattery, and it seemed that a man paying for his pleasure had a different meaning to her because when Pap said it she snorted and set his plate down hard. If she didn't have a plate in her hand, she just cuffed him.

Finn sighed. He would consider the problem of his granny later. Miss Morrow was walking to the front of the classroom. His eyes followed her. The carefully tied bow at the small of her back perched as daintily above her bustle as a bird hovering on the edge of its nest. It was as severe a temptation as Priscilla Taylor's braid. Even if he could keep himself from tugging on it, he still might blurt out the question he was asking himself: How did she tie it?

Finn sat on his hands. For the moment, it was the best way to stay out of trouble.

Tru Morrow stood to one side of the door as she ushered her students out. She made certain they left with their coats, hats, and scarves. Most of the girls wore mittens or carried a muff. The boys, if they had gloves, wore them. Those with mittens simply jammed their hands into their pockets. Mittens were for girls and babies, she'd learned. Finn had explained it to her.

She closed the door as soon as the last student filed out. The bitter in Bitter Springs didn't refer to the quality of the water, but the quality of the wind. Born and raised in Chicago, she had been confident that she understood cold. She was familiar with the wind blowing over the water of Lake Michigan, funneling ice into the collective breath of the city. That was frigid. It was only October, and she was coming to learn that there was a qualitative difference between frigid and bitter. Here in the high plains country, wind seared her lungs. It was so cold, it was hot, and even when she sipped the air carefully, she seemed to taste it at the very back of her tongue. Bitter.

Tru lifted her poppy red shawl and drew it more closely around her shoulders. The wool felt substantial and warm and smelled faintly of smoke from the stove.

"Finn, would you add some coals to the stove? Half a scoop. That will keep us warm long enough for you to write your apology."

Finn stood. Tru sensed his uncertainty as she passed him.

"What is it?" she asked without pausing.

"Well, it's just that you're awful confident that I know what I'm apologizin' for."

Careful not to smile, Tru took her seat behind her desk. She folded her hands and placed them in front of her where Finn could see them. Her posture was correct, spine perfectly aligned, shoulders back, chin lifted. She envisioned herself as a model of rectitude, and she was impressed with herself even if she could see that Finn wasn't. It was probably her eyes that gave her away, she thought. She had been told they were a merry shade of green, a color, according to her father, that could not be easily captured by an artist's palette because the substance of it was a quality of character as much as a quality of light. It was a fanciful notion, but one she brought to mind when she was in danger of taking herself too seriously.

Now was such a time. She relaxed her spine and leaned forward, unclasping her hands as Finn moved to the stove to add coals. She smoothed back a wayward coil of hair that had been pushed out of place by her brief encounter with the wind. She could not help but notice that Finn's eyes followed this small movement, and when her hand fell away from her hair, he remained exactly as he was a moment longer, transfixed. She could only guess at what he was thinking.

"Are you tempted to give my hair a tug?" she asked.

Finn blinked. "How's that again, ma'am?"

"I wondered if you were tempted to yank on my hair."

He ducked his head, cheeks flushing, and hurried to the stove. "Uh, no. No, ma'am." Finn used the sleeve of his shirt like a mitt to open the stove door and toss half a scoop of coals inside. "Wasn't tempted at all."

Tru watched Finn poke at the fire and warm himself in front of the stove long enough to provide an explanation for his rosy cheeks. "I just wondered," she said. "After all, my hair is the same color as Priscilla's."

Finn turned his backside to the stove and stared at her. "I sure hope you'll pardon me for setting you straight, Miss Morrow, but you ever hear tell of a man named Rumple Sticks?"

"Rumplestiltskin?"

"That's the fellow. You know of him?"

"I believe I've heard of him."

"That's good because I couldn't explain it all. Rabbit's better with stories than I am. Well, anyway, I can see you want me to get on with it. It's like this: Priscilla's got hair that puts me in mind of the straw that Mr. Stiltskin wanted for his spinning wheel, and your hair is what Mr. Stiltskin spun it into. So you see, one color's not at all like the other. Yellow. Gold. I got some idea there's a big difference." Finn rocked back on his heels. "Besides, you got your hair lassoed so tight to your head that it would be hard to know what thread to pull."

Now it was Tru who blinked and blushed. "How old are you again, Finn?"

"Ten. Or I will be soon enough."

"So you're nine. Maybe you shouldn't be in such a hurry to grow up."

Finn moved away from the stove and shut the door. "That's what everyone says. Even Rabbit. He's eleven and thinks he can say things like that now. Sort of like he's wise. He's not."

Tru knew better than to make any judgment on Rabbit's wisdom. Finn was certain to carry the tale, and it did not take much provocation to start a war of words between the brothers. She'd seen them use elbows and fists like periods and exclamation points to punctuate their threats.

"Sit down, Finn, and clean your slate. I trust that given sufficient contemplation you'll arrive at what you need to write."

His shoulders slumped, and he jammed his hands in his pockets. "Suppose I will."

"You'll read it to the class tomorrow morning, first thing after prayers."

He grimaced but slid into his seat without a word.

"And perhaps at the end of the day, you will be so kind as to help me clean all the slates." She reasoned that if she found small tasks for him to do, he might not choose getting into trouble in order to remain in her company. He would probably tire of that soon enough. This was her first encounter with a boy's infatuation, and she had been slow to recognize it for what it was. Her sense was that it would pass quickly. She thought she might be a little sorry when it did.

Tru left the schoolhouse ten minutes after Finn shuffled out. He had done everything he could think of to draw out his time. She admired his creativity, was even a tad flattered by his motives, but was careful not to encourage either. She listened with half an ear when he prattled on about the most recent visitor to Bitter Springs and nodded at what she hoped were the proper intervals when he gave a full account of the birth of a foal in Mr. Ransom's livery just that morning. He also added a rapid, if somewhat incoherent, story about the milliner's daughter accepting Mr. Irvin's proposal of marriage. Finn wasn't clear if it was Millicent Garvin who was marrying the undertaker, or her younger sister Marianna, but there was definitely a wedding being planned because Mrs. Garvin was ordering catalogues and silk from Paris.

Tru thought that even if she hadn't been apprised of some of the town's more interesting citizens when she interviewed for the teaching position, it would not have taken her long to identify Heather Collins, grandmother of Rabbit and Finn, as the one who invariably had her ear to the ground and her tongue positioned for wagging. While her husband was the station agent for Bitter Springs, and privy to all the comings and goings of the trains and travelers, he was still merely the human hub. Mrs. Collins, on the other hand, was the human hubbub.

Tru had a suspicion that Finn's ear was similarly pressed and his mouth similarly positioned as his grandmother's.

Pulling her scarf up so that it covered her mouth and the bottom half of her nose, Tru stepped out of the schoolhouse. Wind whipped at her skirts. She ignored the flare of her petticoats but surrendered to the shiver that rattled her teeth. She tucked her chin against her chest and watched her step on the uneven ground as she bucked the wind.

She would have been knocked to the ground if the same force that stopped her forward progress had not also stopped her downward plunge. In that first moment, she lost her breath. In the next, she recovered it.

And promptly lost a little of it again when she met the direct, crystalline blue gaze of the man who was at once an obstruction and her protection.

"I beg your pardon," he said.

Feeling rather foolish, Tru sought purchase on the ground with the toes of her boots. He immediately set her down.

"Better?"

"Yes." Tru could feel her bonnet slipping backward. She made a grab for it, exposing her tightly coiled hair to the wind's icy teeth, and set it properly on her head before it could blow away.

Still watching her, he frowned. "Are you all right?"

Tru realized that her scarf had muffled her answer. Rather than expose her face to the cold, she nodded.

"I'm afraid I wasn't watching where I was going," he said.

She nodded again and pointed to herself, hoping he understood she was offering the same explanation.

"Are you certain you can walk? You didn't twist an ankle?"

The answer to the first required another nod. The answer to the second required a shake. It would be too confusing if she did both. Tru pulled the scarf just below her bottom lip. "Really, I'm fine." Her moist breath was made visible by the cold air. She burrowed her mouth and nose into the warm wool again. When he continued to stare at her as though gauging the truth of her words, Tru took a step sideways. The wind slipped under her petticoats and her skirt fluttered wildly against his legs as she made to pass.

"You're Miss Morrow. The schoolteacher."

Tru stopped. She supposed that if he had any doubt about her identity, the simple act of pausing was sufficient to confirm it.

"My name's Bridger," he said, touching the brim of his pearl gray Stetson with a gloved hand. "Cobb Bridger."

She sighed and tugged on her scarf again. "I know who you are, Mr. Bridger."

"You do?"

She felt strangely pleased that she had surprised him. "I eliminated all the faces I know. Since I don't know yours that makes you new to town and therefore the gambler who has taken up lodgings at the Pennyroyal."

"I'm staying at the Pennyroyal."

"I don't pass any judgment about gambling, Mr. Bridger. Or drinking for that matter." The Pennyroyal was a hotel *and* saloon. "Your affairs are your own." She thought she sounded a bit priggish for someone who professed to pass no judgment, but it was too late to make amends for it. "Excuse me, please."

He retreated a step and let her move out of his reach before he said, "I thought you'd be more curious."

If he'd put out a hand to block her path, he could not have stopped her with more ease. Tru turned her head and arched a single spun-gold eyebrow.

"Don't you wonder how I recognized you, Miss Morrow?"

Tru yanked on her scarf. "I imagine you learned something about everyone in Bitter Springs in the same manner I did. You cannot get from the train station to the hotel without the assistance of Rabbit and Finn Collins, and no personal detail is too small for them to miss about you or relate about others. As the young masters are both my pupils, I can suppose one or both pointed me out to you as you rode by or told you all of the six ways I've made their lives miserable by accepting the position to teach in Bitter Springs. You probably noticed my horns and cloven feet."

Almost immediately, Tru regretted calling attention to herself in that manner. Cobb Bridger's scrutiny was thorough, though not particularly personal. He regarded her with a certain remoteness that was almost clinical, more akin to the dispassionate observation of a scientist. She was most definitely not flattered, but then neither, she realized, was she embarrassed.

"What I noticed," he said, returning his gaze to hers, "is that the color of your hair is as fine as Rumplestiltskin could spin it."

Tru felt her jaw go slack. Gaping like a fish was unattractive, and she recovered quickly. Quite against her will, though, the dimple on the left side of her mouth appeared as a short laugh changed the shape of her lips. "Pardon me, Mr. Bridger, but this is the second time today that someone has made that rather odd comparison. I do have to ask myself whether you heard it first from Finn or whether he came by it from you."

"No doubt about it, Miss Morrow. That's a puzzler."

Tru smiled again, this time appreciatively. Mr. Bridger had obviously decided to give nothing away. "So you and Finn have become fast friends."

"I don't remember that he gave me a choice."

"No, I don't suppose he did." Her smile faltered, became earnest. "You'll have a care with him, won't you? He doesn't know a stranger, and I understand from his grandmother that he's drawn most particularly to gamblers."

"He asked me right off if I knew his father."

She nodded. "He believes his father is riding the rails playing high-stakes poker from one end of the country to the other. He might be. No one knows, but no one but Finn holds out any hope that one day he'll turn up in Bitter Springs with his winnings in a wheelbarrow."

"I see."

Tru wasn't sure what he saw. When he tilted his head, the brim of his hat cast a shadow over his eyes. She couldn't tell whether he was being reflective or dismissive. "So you'll have a care," she repeated. "It would be a kindness if you did."

"You are certain of that?"

His question seemed to suggest that she could be wrong. She felt herself bristling and responded with rather more sharpness than she intended. "It's no burden to show kindness."

"What if kindness is merely a deceit? There's a burden there, I think, and usually unfortunate consequences."

Tru shivered inside her coat. She tried to form a response, but her teeth chattered so violently that she would have bitten her tongue.

"Perhaps we should agree to disagree," he said. "Before you are chilled to the bone."

"T-too l-l-late."

"May I escort you home?"

She shook her head.

"As you wish." He tapped his brim again. "Good day, Miss Morrow."

Tru thought she might have seen something like humor play about his mouth, but she couldn't be sure. He did not strike her as a man who smiled as a matter of course but as one who offered it more judiciously and to far more devastating effect.

Tru covered the lower half of her face again and turned away. She fought the temptation to glance over her shoulder to see if he was watching her. She had the sensation that he was. The most disturbing thing about that particular fancy was that she was warmed by it.

About the Author

Jo Goodman is a licensed professional counselor working with children and families in West Virginia's Northern Panhandle. Always a fan of the happily ever after, Jo turned to writing romances early in her career as a child-care worker when she realized the only life script she could control was the one she wrote herself. She is inspired by the resiliency and courage of the children she meets, and feels privileged to be trusted with their stories, the ones that they alone have the right to tell.

Once upon a time, Jo believed she was going to be a marine biologist. She feels lucky that seasickness made her change course. She lives with her family in landlocked Colliers, West Virginia. Please visit her website at www.jogoodman.com.